THE GOLDEN CODEX

The Golden Codex

Christian E Bannard

For more information, or to book an event, contact :

christian@bannard.com.au
www.bannard.com.au

Book design by C. E. Bannard
Cover design by C. E. Bannard

ISBN – Electronic: 978-1-7645130-4-3
ISBN - Paperback: 978-1-7645130-3-6

First Edition: February, 2026

DEDICATION

Thank you to my amazing wife, Ginky, for her support and love, to my mother, Bev, for teaching me to cook and showing me that persistence in life is the key to success, especially with the 40+ years she's been making quilts and to my sister, Claire, for pushing me harder to succeed.

To Jason Wright, a long-ago work colleague who, through his own trials and tribulations with illness, beat me to the punchline of becoming an author, and inspiring me on reconnecting with him to give writing a shot for myself.

To Drs Paul Verrills and David Vivian, thank you for your friendship and belief in me throughout some very difficult years and helping me get back on my feet after my world fell apart and I had to climb back out of the black hole of despair my life had become.

Finally, thank you to all the people that doubted me; your belief that I would never do it only drove me harder to prove you wrong.

PROLOGUE

Maní, Yucatán - 12th July 1562

The books burned like souls departing for the underworld. Fray Diego de Landa stood in the courtyard of the Franciscan monastery, watching the flames consume five centuries of Maya knowledge. The bonfire had been burning since dawn, fed by an endless procession of codices carried from the surrounding villages by soldiers and converts. Thousands of books, painted on bark paper in colours that had remained vibrant for generations, folded like accordions in the manner the Maya had used since before the time of Christ, now curled and blackened in the heat, their wisdom rising as smoke toward an indifferent sky.

Around the courtyard, the Maya watched in silence. Some wept openly, tears cutting tracks through the dust on their weathered faces. Others stood rigid, their expressions carved from stone, revealing nothing of what they felt. A few, the converts, the collaborators, those who had traded their heritage for survival, helped the soldiers feed the flames, their movements mechanical, their eyes empty.

De Landa felt no remorse. These books were instruments of the Devil, filled with lies and superstitions that kept the native people trapped in darkness. By destroying them, he was freeing their souls, opening the path to salvation. It was an act of mercy, though the heathens were too ignorant to understand it.

"How many more?" he asked Father Gaspar, his assistant, who stood nearby with a ledger recording the day's holy work.

"We have collected five thousand and seventy-three volumes from this district alone, Your Excellency. Plus, twenty-seven stone idols, thirteen altars, and one hundred and ninety-seven vessels used in their pagan ceremonies." Father Gaspar's quill scratched across the parchment. "The soldiers report that several villages are still holding back. They claim their books were lost or destroyed years ago, but the informants say otherwise."

"Then we shall have to be more... persuasive." De Landa's eyes swept the crowd of Maya, searching for signs of resistance, of hidden defiance. "The Governor has given me authority to use whatever means necessary. These people must understand that their old ways are finished. There is no room in New Spain for divided loyalties."

"Yes, Your Excellency."

The flames crackled and roared, sending sparks spiralling upward like fireflies. A gust of wind carried the smell of burning paper across the courtyard, an acrid, bitter scent that would linger in de Landa's nostrils for years afterward, though he would never admit it troubled him.

In the crowd, an old man watched with eyes that had seen the fall of empires.

His name was Ik'anil, and he was eighty-three years old, ancient by the standards of his people, who rarely lived past fifty in these times of plague and conquest. He had been born in the reign of the great Ah Xupan, had witnessed the arrival of the Spanish as a young man, had survived the wars and the diseases and the systematic destruction of everything his ancestors had built. He had outlived his children and most of his grandchildren. He had seen the temples torn down and the cities abandoned and the sacred groves cut for Spanish timber.

And now he watched the last of the books burn.

Ik'anil carried a secret that had been passed down through his family for more generations than anyone could count. He was a Guardian, one of a scattered network of men and women who had preserved the most sacred knowledge of the Maya through centuries of war and upheaval. There had been many Guardians once, in every city and village across the Yucatán and the highlands beyond. Now there were fewer than a dozen left, and their numbers dwindled with each passing year.

The knowledge they protected was older than the Maya themselves. It had come from a time before the Long Count calendar began, before the first cities rose from the jungle, before the Hero Twins descended to Xibalba and defeated the Lords of Death. It was knowledge that the Maya had inherited from an even more ancient people, a people whose name had been forgotten, whose cities had crumbled to dust, but whose secrets had been preserved in a single codex that was never meant to be found.

The Codex of Seven Serpents.

Ik'anil had never seen the codex himself. No Guardian had, for over a thousand years. It was hidden somewhere in the highlands, in a place known only to the Guardian who had hidden it, and that Guardian had died in the first wave of Spanish conquest, taking the location to his grave. For three decades, Ik'anil had searched for clues, following threads of legend and rumour, piecing together fragments of a puzzle that seemed designed to remain unsolved.

And then, six months ago, he had found it.

The discovery had come by accident, a chance conversation with a dying priest in a village near Chichicastenango, a man who had converted to Christianity but who remembered the old stories his grandmother had told him as a child. The priest had spoken of a cave in the mountains, a place where the ancestors had hidden their greatest treasures before the Spanish came. He had given Ik'anil directions, crude but sufficient, before breathing his last.

Ik'anil had found the cave. He had found the codex, wrapped in oilcloth and preserved in a stone chest that had kept out the moisture for untold centuries. He had opened it with trembling hands, knowing that he was the first human being to look upon these pages in over a thousand years.

And what he had found had terrified him.

The Codex of Seven Serpents was not a religious text, not a history, not a calendar or a prophecy. It was a formula. A set of instructions, written in a language so old that even Ik'anil could barely decipher it, describing a process that should have been impossible.

The transmutation of base metals into gold.

Ik'anil had spent three months studying the codex, cross-referencing it with other texts, testing his understanding against the fragments of ancient knowledge that had survived in oral traditions. The more he learned, the more certain he became this was real. This was not myth or metaphor or priestly deception. The ancients had discovered a way to transform the fundamental nature of matter itself, and they had hidden that knowledge because they understood what it would mean if it fell into the wrong hands.

Gold was power. Gold was conquest. Gold was the reason the Spanish had crossed the ocean, the reason they had destroyed the Maya cities, the reason they were burning the books in this very courtyard. If they learned that such a formula existed, if they found a way to make unlimited gold from common lead or copper, there would be no end to their hunger. They would tear apart the entire continent searching for the secret. They would torture and kill anyone who might know where it was hidden.

The codex had to be protected. It had to be hidden again, somewhere the Spanish would never find it and divided, so that no single person could ever possess the complete formula.

Ik'anil had made his decision three days ago. He had spent those days preparing, copying certain sections of the codex, writing instructions in a code that only another Guardian could decipher, arranging for trusted messengers to carry fragments to the far corners of the Maya world. One piece would go to the highlands of Guatemala, where a small community of K'iche' priests still preserved the old ways in secret. One piece would go south, to the lands of the Muisca, where a different Guardian network maintained similar secrets. One piece would go further still, to the mountains of Peru, where the Inca had their own traditions of hidden knowledge.

And one piece, the most important piece, the key that would allow the others to be understood, would stay here. Hidden in plain sight, where the Spanish would never think to look.

That was why Ik'anil had come to Maní today. Not to witness the burning, though his heart broke with every book that turned to ash. He had come to find someone he could trust. Someone who could protect the final fragment for generations to come.

He had come to find a Spanish priest.

***

Fray Tomás de Ávila was twenty-six years old, and he was beginning to suspect that he had made a terrible mistake.

He had come to the New World three years ago, filled with the fervent conviction that he was doing God's work. The Maya were heathens, trapped in ignorance and superstition, and it was his sacred duty to bring them the light of Christ. He had studied their language with dedication, learned their customs with academic interest, and preached the Gospel with the passion of a man who believed absolutely in the righteousness of his cause.

But the longer he stayed, the more his certainty eroded.

The Maya were not the ignorant savages he had been taught to expect. Their cities, the ruins he had seen in the jungle, the remnants of a civilisation that had flourished while his own ancestors were still living in mud huts, spoke of a sophistication that rivalled anything in Europe. Their mathematics was more advanced than what was taught in Spanish universities. Their astronomy was precise enough to predict eclipses centuries in advance. Their medicine, their architecture, their art, all of it suggested a people who had achieved greatness through their own efforts, without any help from the Christian God.

And now Fray Diego de Landa was burning their books.

Tomás stood at the edge of the courtyard, watching the flames with growing horror. He had been ordered to attend, to bear witness to this holy work, but he could not bring himself to participate. Each book that burned was a piece of knowledge lost forever, histories and sciences and philosophies that would never be recovered, never be understood. It was not salvation. It was annihilation.

"You do not approve."

The voice came from beside him, quiet and calm. Tomás turned to find an old Maya man standing at his elbow, ancient, weathered, with eyes that seemed to look through him rather than at him. The man wore the simple clothes of a farmer, but there was something in his bearing that suggested otherwise. A dignity. A presence.

"I did not say that" Tomás replied carefully, aware that spies were everywhere, that a careless word could end his career, or his life.

"You did not need to say it. Your face speaks clearly enough." The old man's Spanish was fluent, educated, not the broken pidgin most converts used. "You are troubled by what you see."

"I am troubled by many things." Tomás glanced around, ensuring no one was close enough to overhear. "But I am a servant of the Church. It is not my place to question the decisions of my superiors."

"Even when those decisions are wrong?"

The question hung in the air between them. Tomás felt sweat prickling on his forehead, though the morning was cool.

"Who are you?" he asked.

"My name is Ik'anil. I am... a keeper of stories." The old man's eyes never left Tomás's face. "I have been watching you for many months, Fray Tomás. I have seen how you treat my people, with respect, with curiosity, with genuine desire to understand rather than simply to conquer. You are not like the others."

"I am exactly like the others. I came here to convert your people to the true faith."

"And have you succeeded?"

Tomás thought of the converts he had baptised, the confessions he had heard, the masses he had celebrated in villages where the old altars still stood, barely hidden, behind the new churches. He thought of the way the Maya accepted Christian names while keeping their calendar names secret, attended Christian services while still performing their ancient rituals in caves and clearings far from Spanish eyes.

"I have... tried," he said finally.

"Then perhaps you are ready to understand something that few of your countrymen could accept." Ik'anil's voice dropped even lower. "There is something I must show you. Something that must be protected from men like de Landa. Will you come with me?"

Every instinct Tomás possessed screamed warnings. This was a trap, a test, a trick designed to expose his doubts and destroy him. He should refuse. He should report this conversation to his superiors immediately.

But he looked at the burning books, at the weeping Maya, at the smug satisfaction on de Landa's face, and something shifted inside him.

"Yes," he said. "I will come."

***

They left Maní that night, slipping away under cover of darkness while the bonfire still smouldered in the courtyard. Ik'anil led Tomás through jungle paths that no Spaniard had ever walked, guided by starlight and knowledge passed down through generations. They travelled for three days, sleeping in caves and abandoned temples, eating food that Ik'anil produced from hidden caches along the route.

On the fourth day, they reached a cenote, a natural sinkhole filled with water so blue it seemed to glow from within. The Maya considered such places sacred, doorways to the underworld, and Tomás felt the weight of that belief pressing down on him as they descended a crude stairway carved into the limestone.

At the bottom, hidden behind a curtain of vines, was a chamber.

The chamber was small, perhaps twenty feet across, but every inch of the walls was covered in paintings so vivid they seemed to move in the flickering torchlight. Jaguars and serpents, gods and heroes, scenes of creation and destruction that told stories Tomás could not begin to understand.

In the centre of the chamber, on a stone pedestal worn smooth by centuries of reverent touch, lay a book. Not a European book, bound in leather with pages of vellum. It was a Maya book, a codex, folded like an accordion, its bark-paper pages covered in glyphs painted in colours that had somehow remained bright despite the passage of countless years.

"This is the Codex of Seven Serpents," Ik'anil said. "It is the most dangerous object in the world."

Tomás approached the pedestal slowly, his heart pounding. He had seen Maya codices before, had helped de Landa burn them, to his eternal shame, but he had never seen anything like this. The glyphs were different from the standard Maya script, older and more complex, and interspersed among them were symbols he did not recognise at all.

"What does it contain?"

"Instructions. A formula." Ik'anil's voice was heavy with the weight of ages. "The ancients, the people who came before my people, whose names have been forgotten, they discovered a way to transform base metals into gold. Not through magic or divine intervention, but through a process. A science, if you will, though it is a science your people have never imagined."

Tomás felt his blood run cold. "That's impossible. Transmutation is a fantasy. Alchemists have been searching for centuries,"

"And they have failed because they do not have this." Ik'anil touched the codex with reverent fingers. "The ancients succeeded. They created gold from lead, silver from copper, transformed the very nature of matter itself and then they realised what they had done."

"What do you mean?"

"They realised that they had created a weapon more terrible than any sword or spear. Gold drives men mad, Fray Tomás. It makes them capable of horrors beyond imagination. Your own people crossed an ocean and destroyed civilisations for the promise of gold. What would they do if they could *make* gold? If there was no limit to their wealth, no end to their power?"

Tomás stared at the codex, his mind reeling. "They would never stop. They would conquer the entire world."

"Yes. The ancients understood this. So, they hid the formula. They divided the knowledge among trusted guardians, scattered the pieces across continents, and prayed that it would never be reassembled." Ik'anil met Tomás's eyes. "But now de Landa is burning everything. The hiding places are being destroyed. The guardians are dying. Soon there will be no one left who knows how to protect this secret."

"Why are you telling me this? I am Spanish. I am a priest. I am everything you should hate."

"Because I have watched you. Because I have seen your heart." Ik'anil's ancient face was calm, certain. "You are not a conquistador, Fray Tomás. You are a seeker of truth and the truth is that this knowledge must be protected, not destroyed, but hidden, until humanity is wise enough to use it without destroying itself."

"And you want me to be its guardian?"

"I want you to help me ensure it survives. I am old. I will be dead within a year, perhaps sooner. But you are young. You have access to places and resources that no Maya can reach. You can hide the codex where even de Landa would never think to look."

Tomás looked at the book, at the paintings on the walls, at the old man who had placed so much faith in him. He thought of everything he had been taught, everything he had believed, and he felt those certainties crumbling like ancient stone.

"What do you need me to do?"

***

They worked through the night, Ik'anil translating the critical sections while Tomás copied them onto fresh paper using ink and quills he had brought from Maní. The original codex would be divided, physically cut into four sections, each containing part of the formula but meaningless without the others. The fragments would be hidden in different locations, entrusted to different guardians, protected by different methods.

As dawn approached, Ik'anil explained the plan.

"One fragment will go to the highlands of Guatemala, to a community of K'iche' priests who still preserve the old ways. They will hide it beneath a sacred site, a place the Spanish will eventually claim as their own, never knowing what lies beneath."

"The church at Chichicastenango," Tomás said, remembering the reports he had read about a new mission being established in the highlands.

"Precisely. The second fragment will go south, to the Muisca people of what your people call New Granada. They have their own traditions of guardianship, their own secrets to protect. The third will go further still, to the descendants of the Inca, who are even now resisting Spanish rule in the mountains of Peru."

"And the fourth?"

Ik'anil smiled, a sad, weary expression that spoke of long years and heavy burdens. "The fourth is the key. Without it, the other three fragments are merely curiosities, interesting but incomplete. This piece must be hidden most carefully of all and that is where you come in."

He handed Tomás a sheaf of papers, the copies he had made during the night, plus a small journal bound in leather.

"Take these. The papers contain what you need to understand the formula, though it will take you years of study to fully comprehend it. The journal is my gift to you, a record of everything I know about the codex, the guardians, the hiding places. Use it wisely."

"But where should I hide the fourth fragment?"

"That is for you to decide. You know your own world better than I do. Find a place where it will be safe for centuries, where it will wait for someone worthy to find it." Ik'anil placed his weathered hand on Tomás's shoulder. "You are a Guardian now, Fray Tomás. The last Guardian of the Old World. May the gods of your people and mine watch over you."

Tomás left the cenote as the sun rose over the jungle. He carried the fourth fragment of the codex hidden beneath his robes, along with Ik'anil's journal and the copies he had made. He never saw the old man again.

It would take him fifteen years to find the perfect hiding place.

***

Chichicastenango, Guatemala - 1703

Fray Tomás de Ávila was sixty-seven years old, and he was dying.

He sat in his small cell in the monastery attached to the church of Santo Tomás, listening to the sounds of the Maya market drifting through the narrow window. He had spent the last four decades here, in this highland town where the old ways persisted despite every effort to suppress them. He had learned the K'iche' language, had studied their histories and their beliefs, had come to understand them in ways that few Europeans ever had.

Then had found the Popol Vuh. The discovery had come twenty years ago, when a K'iche' elder had shown him a manuscript written in the Latin alphabet but in the K'iche' language, a transcription of the Maya creation myth, made by a native scholar in the years after the conquest. The manuscript was extraordinary, a window into a worldview that the Spanish had tried so hard to destroy. Tomás had spent years copying it, annotating it, preparing it for posterity.

Hidden within his copy, invisible to anyone who did not know to look for it, was the fourth fragment of the Codex of Seven Serpents.

He had embedded it in the text using a cipher of his own devising, a code that used the structure of the Popol Vuh itself as a key, hiding the formula in plain sight among the stories of the Hero Twins and the Lords of Xibalba. Only someone who understood both the Maya creation myth and the secret of the codex would be able to extract the hidden message. It was, he believed, the perfect hiding place.

Now, with death approaching, he had one final task to complete.

The journal lay open on his desk, its pages filled with his small, precise handwriting. He had been working on it for months, recording everything he knew about the codex, the formula, the guardians who protected the other fragments. It was his legacy, the sum of everything he had learned in forty years of secret study.

He picked up his quill and wrote the final entry:

> *July 12, 1703*
>
> *I have seen the formula. I have tested it, in small ways, and I know that it is real. The ancients discovered a process that transforms the very nature of matter, a process requiring seven elements, seven procedures, seven days. Lead becomes gold. Copper becomes silver. The base is made precious through application of knowledge that our science cannot yet explain.*
>
> *I could have used this knowledge. I could have made myself wealthy beyond imagination, could have funded missions and churches and hospitals across the New World. But I chose not to. The formula is too dangerous. Humanity is not ready for it. Perhaps humanity will never be ready.*
>
> *I have hidden the final fragment where only a worthy seeker will find it. The Popol Vuh will preserve it, carrying the secret forward through generations until the time is right. The other fragments wait in their own hiding places, Guatemala, Colombia, Peru, each one protected by guardians who have sworn to keep them safe.*

El Dorado was never a city of gold. It was a city that MADE gold. It must remain hidden until we have learned to be better than we are.

I am the last Guardian of the old order. When I die, the secret will sleep. But it will not be lost. Someday, someone will come who is worthy of this knowledge. Someday, the Seven Serpents will wake.

Until then, I commend my soul to God, and my secret to the ages.

Fray Tomás de Ávila

He set down the quill and closed the journal. Outside, the market continued its ancient rhythms, unchanged by the centuries of conquest and conversion. The Maya endured, as they always had and the secret with them.

Tomás closed his eyes and began to pray.

1

Discovery

Chicago, Illinois, USA

The Newberry Library closed at five o'clock, but Martin Thorne had a key.

He had been coming here for thirty years, ever since he had first arrived in Chicago as a young professor with a head full of theories and a heart full of passion for the lost civilisations of Mesoamerica. The library's collection of colonial manuscripts was one of the finest in the world, and Martin had built his career on the treasures hidden in its climate-controlled vaults. He had published twelve books, supervised forty-seven doctoral students, and become one of the most respected Mesoamericanists of his generation, all because of what he had found in these quiet rooms.

Now, at seventy-three, he was about to make the discovery that would define his legacy.

Or destroy it.

The reading room was silent except for the soft hum of the climate control system and the occasional creak of the old building settling into the January cold. Martin sat alone at his usual table, surrounded by the tools of his trade: cotton gloves, magnifying glasses, digital cameras, and a laptop running specialised imaging software. Before him, protected by a foam cradle and illuminated by carefully calibrated lights, lay the Ximénez manuscript of the Popol Vuh.

The manuscript was not supposed to be here. It belonged in Guatemala, where it had been created three centuries ago by a Dominican friar who had recognised the importance of preserving Maya knowledge even as his colleagues were destroying it. But history had scattered Guatemala's treasures across the world, and the Ximénez manuscript had ended up here, in this American library, where scholars like Martin could study it without the complications of Central American politics.

Martin had examined this manuscript hundreds of times over the years. He knew every page, every glyph, every annotation that Ximénez had added in his cramped colonial handwriting. He had written three papers on it, had used it as the foundation for his most influential book, had spent countless hours trying to understand why Ximénez had transcribed certain passages differently from other versions of the Maya creation myth.

But he had never looked at it like this before.

The infrared camera was a recent acquisition, purchased with the last of a research grant that his university had been trying to cancel. Infrared imaging could reveal text that was invisible to the naked eye, words that had been erased, overwritten, or hidden beneath layers of later additions. It was a technique more commonly used on medieval European manuscripts, but Martin had a theory that it might reveal secrets in colonial-era documents as well.

He had been right.

The screen of his laptop showed the familiar opening pages of the Popol Vuh but transformed. The visible text, the K'iche' creation myth that generations of scholars had studied, was still there, rendered in ghostly blue. But beneath it, in faint lines of red that had been invisible for three hundred years, was something else.

A map.

Martin leaned closer, his heart pounding so hard he could feel it in his temples. The map was crude, sketched in hurried strokes as if the artist had been working in secret, afraid of being discovered. It showed a coastline he did not recognise; mountain ranges marked with symbols he had never seen, and a path leading from what might be Guatemala to somewhere in the south, Colombia, perhaps, or Ecuador.

But it was the glyphs that made his hands tremble.

Some of them were Maya, standard glyphs that he could read as easily as English, marking locations and directions in the manner of any ancient map. But others were different. They were similar to Maya script but older, more angular, with a precision that suggested a mathematical notation rather than a written language and interspersed among them were symbols that were definitely not Maya at all.

They were Muisca.

Martin had spent enough time studying the gold-working cultures of Colombia to recognise the distinctive style of Muisca iconography. The symbols were unmistakable: the spiral patterns, the stylised human figures, the geometric abstractions that had decorated Muisca goldwork for centuries before the Spanish arrived.

But that was impossible. The Maya and the Muisca had been separated by thousands of miles of jungle and ocean. There was no evidence that they had ever had contact with each other, no artefacts suggesting trade or communication, no linguistic links between their languages. The academic consensus was clear: these two civilisations had developed independently, in isolation, with no knowledge of each other's existence.

So why were Muisca symbols hidden in a Maya manuscript?

Martin's hands were shaking so badly that he had to set down his magnifying glass. He took several deep breaths, trying to calm himself, trying to think through the implications of what he was seeing.

There were only two possibilities.

The first was that the map was a forgery, a hoax created by Ximénez or someone else, for reasons that were impossible to guess. But that didn't make sense. Why would anyone create a fake map and then hide it so carefully that it remained invisible for three hundred years? What would be the point of a hoax that no one could see?

The second possibility was that the map was real. That somehow, impossibly, there had been contact between the Maya and the Muisca, contact that had been kept secret, hidden from the Spanish and from subsequent generations of scholars. Contact that had involved knowledge so valuable, so dangerous, that men had gone to extraordinary lengths to protect it.

Martin thought of the legends he had spent his career studying. The stories of El Dorado, the city of gold that had obsessed the Spanish conquistadors. The tales of secret knowledge possessed by the Maya priests, knowledge that had been lost when de Landa burned the codices. The whispered rumours, dismissed by serious academics, of a formula that could transform base metals into precious ones.

He had always assumed those stories were myths. Fantasies invented by desperate men, amplified by centuries of retelling.

But what if they were true?

What if El Dorado was not a city of gold, but something else entirely? What if the Maya and the Muisca had shared a secret so powerful that it had to be hidden from the world?

Martin reached for his phone and took several photographs of the laptop screen, making sure to capture every detail of the hidden map. Then, with trembling fingers, he began to type an email to the one person he trusted enough to share this discovery.

His protégé. His intellectual heir. The best student he had ever had.

Elena Vasquez.

***

He was still typing when the door to the reading room opened.

Martin looked up, startled. The library had been empty when he arrived; he had checked carefully, wanting privacy for this final session with the manuscript. But now a figure stood in the doorway, silhouetted against the dim light of the corridor beyond.

"Dr. Thorne." The voice was accented, German, Martin thought, though softened by years of living elsewhere. "Working late, I see."

Martin's blood went cold.

He knew that voice. He had heard it before, years ago, at a conference in Vienna where he had presented a paper on Maya astronomy. A man had approached him afterward, asking questions about the Popol Vuh, about Ximénez, about hidden texts and secret knowledge. Martin had dismissed him as a crank, one of the many amateur treasure hunters who plagued academic conferences, convinced that they were on the verge of discovering Atlantis or the Ark of the Covenant.

But there had been something in the man's eyes that had stayed with Martin. A coldness. A patience. The look of a predator who was willing to wait years, decades, for the right moment to strike.

"Who are you?" Martin asked, though he already knew the answer.

The figure stepped into the reading room, and the overhead lights revealed a face that had aged considerably since that conference in Vienna. The man was old now, eighty at least, perhaps older, with white hair cropped close to his skull and a scar that ran from his left temple to his jaw. But his eyes were unchanged: pale blue, empty of warmth, filled with an intelligence that bordered on madness.

"My name is Werner Kroeger," the man said. "I believe you have found something that belongs to me."

Martin's hand moved instinctively toward his phone, but Kroeger was faster. He crossed the room in three quick strides, impossibly quick for a man his age, and snatched the phone from the table before Martin could reach it.

"Ah," Kroeger said, examining the screen. "You've been taking photographs. How thorough of you." He scrolled through the images, his thin lips curving into a smile that contained no warmth. "And you were about to share them with someone. Elena Vasquez. Your former student."

"How do you know about Elena?"

"I know everything about you, Dr. Thorne. I have been watching you for a very long time. Waiting for this moment." Kroeger slipped the phone into his pocket. "You have found the hidden text in the Ximénez manuscript. The map that points to the second fragment of the Codex of Seven Serpents."

Martin felt the world tilt beneath him. "How do you know about that?"

"Because I have been searching for it for sixty years. Because I have dedicated my entire life to finding what you have just discovered." Kroeger's voice was calm, almost gentle, but his eyes burned with an intensity that was terrifying to behold. "You have no idea what you have found, do you? You think it is an academic curiosity, a footnote to be published in some obscure journal. But it is so much more than that."

"What do you want?"

"I want the codex. All of it, every fragment, every piece of the puzzle. I want the formula that will change the world." Kroeger leaned closer, and Martin could smell something on his breath, something medicinal, chemical, wrong. "You can help me find it, Dr. Thorne. You can share what you have discovered, and together we can complete the work that has consumed both our lives."

"And if I refuse?"

Kroeger's smile widened. "That would be... unfortunate."

Martin looked at the old man, at the madness burning behind those pale eyes, and he made his decision. He would not help this creature. He would not hand over knowledge that could be used for God only knew what purposes. He would die before he betrayed everything he had spent his life protecting.

His hand shot out toward the laptop, intending to delete the photographs, to destroy the evidence of what he had found. But Kroeger was ready. His hand closed around Martin's wrist with a grip that was shockingly strong, and with his other hand he produced something from beneath his coat.

A rosary. The beads were dark wood, polished smooth by years of use, and they clicked softly as Kroeger wound them around Martin's throat.

"I had hoped it would not come to this," Kroeger said softly. "I truly did. But some secrets are worth killing for."

The beads tightened. Martin struggled, but Kroeger's grip was iron, and the life was leaving him quickly. As darkness closed in at the edges of his vision, he had one final, desperate thought.

Elena. I sent Elena the photographs before he arrived. She has the key. She will understand.

Then the darkness took him, and Martin Thorne knew no more.

***

Kroeger held the garrotte tight for a full minute after the old man stopped struggling. He had learned long ago that it was always better to be certain. The human body had a remarkable capacity for survival, and more than one target had surprised him by recovering from what should have been a fatal injury.

When he was satisfied that Thorne was truly dead, he loosened the rosary and let the body slump across the manuscript. A regrettable necessity. He had hoped to extract more information from the professor, but the old man's defiance had made that impossible. No matter. The photographs on the phone would provide what he needed.

He reached for the phone and scrolled through the recent activity. Thorne had been typing an email when Kroeger arrived, but he had not finished sending it. Good. The photographs remained contained, their secret still,

Kroeger froze.

The email had been addressed to Elena Vasquez. But above it, in the sent folder, was another message. Sent five minutes before Kroeger's arrival.

A message containing the same photographs.

Kroeger stared at the screen, his jaw tightening. Thorne had been more clever than he appeared. He had already shared his discovery, already passed the secret to someone else. The trail was no longer cold.

He considered his options. He could go after Vasquez directly, eliminate her before she understood what she had received. But that would be risky. She was not an isolated old man working alone in a library. She had colleagues, connections, people who would notice if she disappeared and if she had already shared the photographs with others...

No. Better to wait. Better to watch. Better to let her do the work of finding the fragments and then take everything from her at once.

Kroeger pocketed the phone and took one last look around the reading room. The manuscript lay on the table, stained now with Thorne's blood. A pity, it was a valuable artefact. But the photographs would suffice.

He left the same way he had entered, through a side door that the library's security cameras did not cover. Outside, the January night was bitter, the streets of Chicago empty and cold. Kroeger pulled his coat tighter and walked toward the rental car waiting on the next block.

The hunt was on.

2

Inheritance

Chicago, Illinois - The Next Day

Elena Vasquez had always been good at compartmentalising. It was a skill she had learned early, growing up between two worlds, her mother's K'iche' Maya heritage and her father's Spanish colonial legacy, the academic rigour of American universities and the mystical traditions of the Guatemalan highlands. She had learned to hold contradictions in her mind without trying to resolve them, to function in one reality while never forgetting that others existed.

But standing in the reading room of the Newberry Library, looking at the chalk outline where Martin Thorne's body had been found, she felt her carefully constructed walls beginning to crack.

He was my mentor, she thought. *He was the closest thing I had to a father after my own father died.. Now he's gone, and I wasn't there, and I didn't even know he was in danger.*

"Dr. Vasquez?"

The voice belonged to Detective Sarah Chen, a compact woman with tired eyes and a notebook that she had been filling with careful observations since Elena arrived. The Chicago Police Department had contacted Elena that morning, informing her that Martin Thorne was dead and requesting her presence at the crime scene. They had questions, they said. About Martin's work. About his enemies. About why someone would murder a seventy-three-year-old academic in a library.

Elena had questions too. But she wasn't sure the police would be able to answer them.

"I'm sorry," she said, pulling her attention back to the present. "What did you ask?"

"I asked if Professor Thorne had mentioned anything unusual in your recent conversations. Any concerns about his safety, any new research projects that might have attracted unwanted attention?"

Elena thought about the email she had received last night. The photographs Martin had sent, along with a brief message: *Elena, I've found something extraordinary. Hidden text in the Ximénez manuscript. I need your help understanding it. Call me as soon as you can.*

She had tried calling. The phone had gone straight to voicemail. She had assumed Martin was working late, lost in his research as he so often was. She had planned to try again in the morning.

But by morning, Martin was dead.

"He was working on the Popol Vuh," Elena said carefully. "The Maya creation myth. He'd been studying a particular manuscript for years, the Ximénez copy, which the library holds in its collection."

"The manuscript that was found on the table. The one his body was lying across."

"Yes."

Detective Chen made a note. "And this research, was it controversial? Could it have made him enemies?"

Enemies, Elena thought. *What an inadequate word.*

She thought about the photographs on her phone. The hidden map, the impossible combination of Maya and Muisca glyphs, the implications that would shake the foundations of Mesoamerican archaeology if they were true. She thought about the stories Martin had told her over the years, stories of secret knowledge, of ancient guardians, of treasures that powerful men would kill to possess.

She thought about the rosary that had been found wrapped around his throat.

"Professor Thorne studied Maya history," she said. "It's not a field that usually attracts violent attention. But..." She hesitated. "He did receive some strange inquiries over the years. From people outside academia. Treasure hunters, conspiracy theorists, that sort of thing. He usually ignored them."

"Anyone specific?"

Elena shook her head. "I don't know names. He mentioned them occasionally, but he treated them as jokes. Nuisances, not threats."

Detective Chen studied her for a long moment, her expression unreadable. "Dr. Vasquez, we found the professor's phone in his pocket. It had been wiped, factory reset, no data recoverable. Someone took the time to erase everything on it before they left."

Elena's heart skipped. "What does that mean?"

"It means someone wanted to make sure we couldn't see what he was working on. Or who he was communicating with." The detective's eyes narrowed slightly. "You wouldn't happen to know anything about that, would you?"

He sent me the photographs, Elena thought. *Whoever killed him doesn't know that. They think they erased the evidence, but I have copies. I have the key to whatever he discovered.*

"No," she said. "I'm sorry. I don't."

It was the first lie she had told a police officer. She suspected it would not be the last.

***

She left the library an hour later, her mind churning with questions that had no answers.

The detective had told her the basics: Martin had been strangled, probably with the rosary that had been left around his neck. There were no signs of forced entry, no witnesses, no fingerprints or DNA that didn't belong to library staff or regular researchers. The killer had been professional, methodical, leaving almost nothing behind.

Almost nothing.

Elena walked through the winter streets of Chicago, barely noticing the cold that bit at her exposed skin. Her phone felt heavy in her pocket, weighted with the photographs that Martin had sent. She had not looked at them closely yet, there had been no time, and she had not wanted to examine them in front of the police. But she knew, with a certainty that went beyond logic, that those photographs were the reason Martin was dead.

Someone had killed him for what he found and now she was the only person who knew what that was.

She should go to the police. She should show them the photographs, tell them about Martin's research, let the professionals handle whatever dangerous secret he had uncovered. That was the sensible thing to do. The safe thing.

But Elena had never been particularly good at safe.

She had grown up in the highlands of Guatemala, in a village where the old ways persisted beneath the surface of Catholic conformity. Her grandmother had been a *daykeeper*, a keeper of the Maya calendar, a woman who spoke to the ancestors and interpreted their messages for the living. Elena had spent her childhood hearing stories of hidden knowledge, of secrets passed down through generations, of truths that the conquistadors had tried to destroy but that endured in the blood and bones of her people.

Martin had recognised something in her, that same hunger for truth, that same willingness to look beyond the accepted narratives. He had taken her under his wing, guided her through graduate school, helped her build a career that straddled the line between academic rigour and indigenous wisdom. He had trusted her with his most precious theories, his most dangerous speculations.

And now he had trusted her with this.

She found a coffee shop on a quiet side street and took a table in the back, away from the windows and the other customers. Then she pulled out her phone and, for the first time, looked carefully at what Martin had sent her.

The photographs were remarkable.

Even on the small screen, she could see the significance of what Martin had discovered. The hidden map, invisible for three centuries, now revealed in ghostly lines of infrared red. The Maya glyphs she recognised immediately, cardinal directions, distance markers, the names of places she had read about in colonial documents. But the other symbols...

Elena zoomed in, her breath catching in her throat.

She had studied the Muisca during her graduate work, had spent a semester in Colombia examining their goldwork and trying to understand the complex mythology that surrounded it. She knew their iconography as well as Maya script, with these symbols being unmistakably Muisca.

That was impossible, though.

She scrolled through the photographs, looking for more details, more clues. The map showed a route, that much was clear. It started somewhere in Guatemala, near what might be the highlands around Chichicastenango, and wound south through terrain that could be Central America or northern South America. The final destination was marked with a symbol she did not recognise: a serpent swallowing its own tail, surrounded by seven smaller serpents arranged in a circle.

The ouroboros. The ancient symbol of eternity, of cycles, of transformation.

Elena stared at the image, her mind racing. She thought about the stories Martin had told her over the years. The legends of El Dorado, the city of gold. The tales of the Maya priests who had possessed knowledge beyond anything the Spanish understood. The whispered rumours of a formula, a process that could transform base metals into precious ones.

El Dorado was never a city of gold, Martin had written in one of his private journals, which he had shared with Elena years ago. *It was a city that MADE gold and the knowledge of how it was done has been hidden for five centuries.*

She had thought it was speculation. Fantasy. The kind of wild theory that serious academics entertained in private but never published.

But what if it was true?

What if Martin had found proof?

Her phone buzzed with an incoming text message. The number was not one she recognised, a long international string that suggested it had been routed through multiple servers.

Dr. Vasquez. I know what Martin found. I know who killed him. I also know you have the photographs. We should talk.

Elena stared at the message, her heart pounding. She should ignore it. She should delete it and go straight to the police and let them handle whatever was happening.

But her fingers were already typing a response: *Who are you?*

The reply came instantly: *A friend, or at least, someone who wants the same thing you do; justice for Martin, plus the truth he discovered. My name is Octavio Méndez-Castellón. I believe we have much to discuss.*

Elena's blood went cold.

She knew that name. Everyone in Mesoamerican archaeology knew that name. Octavio Méndez-Castellón was a Venezuelan oil billionaire with a legendary collection of pre-Columbian art, some of it acquired legitimately, some of it through channels that didn't bear close examination. He had funded archaeological expeditions across Latin America, endowed chairs at universities, published lavish coffee-table books about indigenous cultures.

He was also rumoured to be obsessed with El Dorado.

For thirty years, according to the gossip that circulated at academic conferences, Méndez-Castellón had been searching for the legendary city. He had spent millions on expeditions, hired archaeologists and adventurers and treasure hunters, explored every corner of the Amazon and the Andes looking for evidence that the Spanish conquistadors had missed. He had never found it, no one had, but his obsession had never wavered.

And now he was contacting her. Hours after Martin's murder. Claiming to know who was responsible.

How do I know I can trust you? she typed.

You don't. But consider this: if I wanted to harm you, I could have done so already. I know where you are. I have resources you cannot imagine. Instead, I am offering you information and assistance. Does that not suggest my intentions are benign?

It suggests you want something from me.

Of course I do. I want the same thing Martin wanted: to find the truth about El Dorado. To understand the secrets that have been hidden for five centuries. I also want to stop the man who killed your mentor before he finds those secrets first.

Elena hesitated, her fingers hovering over the screen. Every instinct told her this was dangerous. Méndez-Castellón was a billionaire with a shadowy reputation, contacting her through anonymous channels, making promises that sounded too good to be true.

But he knew about Martin. He knew about the photographs. He claimed to know who the killer was.

And she had no other leads.

Tell me about the killer, she typed.

His name is Werner Kroeger. He is eighty-seven years old. He was born in Berlin in 1939, the son of Heinrich Kroeger, a senior researcher for the Ahnenerbe, the Nazi organisation that searched for proof of Aryan racial superiority through archaeology. His father spent the war years hunting evidence of lost civilisations across three continents. When the Reich collapsed, Heinrich passed everything to his son — his files, his research, his obsessions. Werner inherited a lifetime of work that was never his father's to finish. After the war, he worked for various intelligence agencies, various criminal or-

ganisations, various wealthy patrons who shared his obsession with ancient secrets. For the past sixty years, he has been searching for El Dorado.

Why?

Because he believes it will prove his theories about human history. He believes that the civilisations of the Americas were founded by travellers from elsewhere, Europe, Asia, Atlantis, take your pick, and that the indigenous peoples were merely inheritors of knowledge they did not create. El Dorado, he believes, will provide the evidence he needs to validate a lifetime of racist pseudoscience.

Elena felt sick. She thought of Martin, strangled with a rosary in a quiet library, murdered by a man who wanted to use ancient knowledge to justify hatred and oppression.

Why are you telling me this?

Because Kroeger is dangerous; you are in danger. He knows Martin sent you those photographs and he will be coming for you! I am the only one who can help you survive what is coming.

The message was followed by an address: a hotel in downtown Chicago, a suite number, a time. *Come alone*, the final line read. *I will explain everything.*

Elena sat in the coffee shop for a long time, staring at the screen, weighing her options. She could go to the police. She could run. She could try to forget everything she had learned and return to her quiet life at the Smithsonian, cataloguing artefacts and writing papers that a few hundred people would read.

Or she could walk into the unknown and find out what Martin had died for.

In the end, it wasn't really a choice at all.

***

The Drake Hotel was old Chicago money, marble lobbies, crystal chandeliers, the kind of understated elegance that whispered of wealth rather than shouting it. Elena walked through the entrance feeling conspicuously underdressed in her jeans and winter coat, but the staff barely glanced at her as she crossed to the elevators.

The suite was on the top floor, at the end of a corridor lined with oil paintings of Lake Michigan sunsets. She knocked twice and waited, her hand resting on the small of her back where she had tucked the Glock that Diego had given her years ago, a gift when she had first started doing fieldwork in dangerous parts of Central America.

The door opened to reveal a man in his sixties, or perhaps seventies; it was hard to tell. He was handsome in the way that wealthy men often were, with silver hair swept back from a high forehead and dark eyes that held both intelligence and something harder to define. He wore a tailored suit that probably cost more than her monthly rent, and he held a glass of amber liquid in one hand.

"Dr. Vasquez," he said. "Thank you for coming."

"Mr. Méndez-Castellón."

"Please, call me Octavio." He stepped back, gesturing for her to enter. "We have much to discuss, and I suspect neither of us wants to waste time on formalities."

The suite was vast, with floor-to-ceiling windows that offered a panoramic view of the Chicago skyline. Elena noted the security details automatically: multiple exits, no obvious guards, expensive art on the walls that suggested this was a permanent residence rather than a temporary booking. Méndez-Castellón moved to a sideboard and poured her a drink without asking.

"Rum," he said, handing her the glass. "Venezuelan, from a distillery my family has owned for generations. I find it helps with difficult conversations."

Elena accepted the drink but didn't taste it. "You said you know who killed Martin."

"Yes, I did. I know who did it." Méndez-Castellón settled into a leather armchair and gestured for her to take the one opposite. "His name is Werner Kroeger and he has been my enemy for almost thirty years. We were allies once, both searching for the same thing, pooling our resources and our knowledge. Then I learned what he truly believed and what he intended to do with El Dorado if he found it, so I severed our partnership."

"What does he intend to do?"

"He intends to prove that the indigenous peoples of the Americas were merely custodians of knowledge that originated elsewhere. That the Maya, the Inca, the Aztec, all of them inherited their achievements from a superior civilisation, a civilisation that Kroeger believes was Aryan in origin." Méndez-Castellón's lip curled with disgust. "It is racist Nazi-doctrine nonsense, of course. Pseudoscience dressed up in archaeological jargon, though Kroeger is a true believer. He has dedicated his entire life to proving a theory that any competent scholar would dismiss as fantasy fiction."

"And you? What do you believe?"

"I believe that the civilisations of the Americas achieved what they achieved through their own genius, their own labour, their own creativity. I believe that El Dorado, if it exists, represents indigenous knowledge, indigenous discovery, indigenous science." His eyes met hers. "I believe that if we find it, we must ensure that it is understood on its own terms, not twisted to serve the agendas of men like Kroeger."

Elena studied him, searching for signs of deception. Méndez-Castellón was smooth, polished, clearly accustomed to getting what he wanted. But there was something in his voice when he spoke of indigenous achievement, a passion that seemed genuine.

"Why contact me?" she asked. "You have resources, connections, experts of your own. Why do you need a Smithsonian archaeologist?"

"Because you have what I need." Méndez-Castellón leaned forward. "You have the photographs Martin sent. The hidden map, the glyphs, the clues that point to the next fragment of the Codex of Seven Serpents. I have been searching for those clues for thirty years. Martin found them in a single night and now you are the only person alive who possesses them."

"Except for Kroeger."

"Kroeger has Martin's phone. But Martin sent the photographs before Kroeger arrived, I know this because my people intercepted the transmission. Kroeger knows the photographs exist, but he doesn't have them. He will be searching for you, Dr. Vasquez. He will find you eventually. When he does, he will kill you just as he killed Martin."

Elena felt a chill run down her spine. "So, you're offering to protect me," she asked.

"I'm offering you a partnership. You have knowledge and skills I need. I have resources and protection you need. Together, we can find what Martin was searching for before Kroeger does." Méndez-Castellón raised his glass. "It is not an entirely selfless offer. I will not pretend otherwise. I have been obsessed with El Dorado for most of my adult life and I believe our interests may align. I am not a good person, though I believe that whatever Martin discovered, it should not fall into the hands of a man who will use it to simply justify hatred."

Elena thought about the photographs on her phone. The hidden map, the impossible combination of symbols, the serpent swallowing its own tail. She thought about Martin, dead in a library, his life's work stolen by a man who wanted to twist it into propaganda.

She thought about her grandmother, telling stories of secret knowledge passed down through generations.

"What exactly are you proposing?"

Méndez-Castellón smiled. "I propose we follow this map and find the codex fragments before Kroeger does. We uncover the truth about El Dorado, whatever that may be."

He set down his glass. "I have a jet waiting at O'Hare. It can take us to Guatemala tonight. The hidden text in Martin's photographs points to Chichicastenango, a church of Santo Tomás, which is where we start."

"How do you know that?"

"Because I have been studying the same clues Martin was studying, for much longer than he was. I know the legends. I know the hiding places. I know that Ximénez transcribed the Popol Vuh in Chichicastenango, and I know that the church there was built on the foundations of a Maya temple." His eyes burned with intensity. "Something is hidden beneath that altar, Dr. Vasquez. Something that has been waiting for five hundred years to be found."

Elena looked at the billionaire, at his expensive suit and his burning eyes and his confident smile. She should refuse. She should walk away, go to the police, let someone else handle this.

But Martin was dead and the only way to understand why was to follow the trail he had uncovered.

"I'll need to make some arrangements," she said. "And I'll need to see those legends you mentioned. Everything you know about the codex and the fragments."

"Of course. My people can have anything you need delivered to the airport." Méndez-Castellón stood and extended his hand. "Do we have a deal, Dr. Vasquez?"

Elena hesitated for only a moment. Then she clasped his hand.

"We have a deal."

***

That night, Elena checked into the Drake under a false name, using cash and a fake ID that Diego Ixchel had created for her years ago — a precaution arranged through Martin, who had trusted Diego with the kind of quiet logistics that academic fieldwork sometimes required and that no one ever put in writing.

She ate dinner alone in her room, studying the photographs Martin had sent, making notes, trying to understand what she was seeing.

By midnight, she had the beginnings of a plan. By two in the morning, she had fallen into a restless sleep, haunted by dreams of burning books and serpents made of gold.

She did not know that she was being watched.

She did not know that Werner Kroeger sat in a darkened room across Michigan Avenue, observing her window through a scope that had seen service on three continents.

She did not know that, in the morning, her life would change forever.

But when the dawn came, she was ready.

3

Watcher

Chicago, Illinois - That Night

The old man sat in darkness, watching the hotel through a scope that had seen service in conflicts Elena Vasquez had never heard of.

Werner Kroeger had learned patience in places where impatience meant death, in the frozen passes of Tibet, where he had spent three weeks motionless in a snow cave waiting for a Chinese patrol to pass; in the burning jungles of Paraguay, where he had tracked Josef Mengele for six months before losing the trail at the Brazilian border; in a dozen forgotten corners of the world where he had searched for proof of truths that lesser minds refused to accept.

Eighty-seven years had not dimmed his eyes or his purpose. If anything, the proximity of death had sharpened both. When you knew the end was coming, when you could feel it in the ache of your bones and the faltering rhythm of your heart, every moment became precious. Every decision carried weight. There was no time left for half-measures or hesitation.

He watched the light in the woman's window. Third floor, corner room, the Drake Hotel. She had not closed the curtains fully, an amateur's mistake, though perhaps forgivable given the circumstances. Her mentor had been dead less than twelve hours. Grief made people careless.

Kroeger adjusted the scope's focus, a Zeiss Victory that had cost more than most people earned in a month. Through the gap in the curtains, he could see her hunched over a laptop, the screen's blue glow painting her face in spectral light. Dark hair pulled back in a practical ponytail. Strong features, more handsome than beautiful. The determined set of her jaw suggested a woman who did not give up easily.

Good, he thought. *She will need that determination for what lies ahead.*

She was working. Researching. Following the trail that Martin Thorne had left behind. Kroeger could imagine what she was finding, the same breadcrumbs he had followed for sixty years, the same tantalising hints that always seemed to lead nowhere. But Thorne had found something new. Something that had cost him his life.

Kroeger had ordered that death. He had wanted Thorne alive, but only until the photographs were sent — and Thorne, ever the meticulous academic, had sent them the moment he understood what he had found. The old professor had not even realised he was doing it. He had simply reached for the person he trusted most, the way scholars always did.

Once the photographs left Thorne's phone, the man had become a liability. A frightened seventy-three-year-old who would run to the police, the university, the press — anyone who would listen. Kroeger had made the decision with the same dispassion he brought to every operational necessity. Brecker had been ready. The rosary had been his own small flourish, a message to anyone who found the body and understood the symbolism.

A waste, perhaps. But a necessary one.

And perhaps not a total loss.

The woman had Thorne's phone, his people had confirmed that much. Whatever Thorne had found, whatever revelation had signed his death warrant, she now possessed it. Unlike Thorne though, she could be followed. Tracked. Allowed to do the dangerous work of discovery while Kroeger's team watched from the shadows.

He shifted in his chair, feeling the familiar protest of joints that had endured too many years of abuse. The safe house was a rented apartment on the fourteenth floor of a building across Michigan Avenue from the Drake, chosen for its sight lines and its anonymity. The furniture was sparse, a chair, a table, a cot in the corner for the rare moments when he allowed himself to sleep. Kroeger had lived in places like this for most of his adult life. Hotels and safe houses, temporary shelters that left no trace. A nomad's existence, driven by a quest that had consumed everything else.

His phone buzzed once. A text from a number that existed nowhere in any database, routed through a series of encrypted servers that would take even the NSA months to unravel: *Status?*

Kroeger set down the scope and picked up the phone. The screen's glow illuminated his face, gaunt, weathered, marked by a scar that ran from his left temple to his jaw. A souvenir from a knife fight in Buenos Aires, 1962. The man who had given it to him had not survived the encounter.

He typed his reply with fingers that remained steady despite his age: *Target acquired. She has Thorne's phone. Appears to be researching. Likely proceeding to Guatemala.*

The response came immediately: *Intercept?*

Kroeger considered the question, turning it over in his mind the way he had turned over a thousand similar questions across six decades of hunting. It would be easy enough to take her now, a woman alone in a hotel room, distracted by grief and discovery. His people could be there in minutes. Brecker was reliable, professional, utterly without conscience. They could extract whatever she knew and dispose of her before dawn. The Chicago police would find nothing. They never did.

But that would be inefficient. Wasteful. Kroeger had not survived this long by being wasteful.

Negative, he typed. *Let her run. She will lead us to the second fragment.*

A pause. The encrypted connection hummed with digital silence. Then: *The principal is impatient. He wants results.*

Kroeger felt a flicker of irritation, the closest thing to genuine emotion he had experienced in years. Méndez-Castellón. The Venezuelan billionaire who had funded this operation, who believed his money entitled him to control every aspect of the search. The man understood nothing about hunting, nothing about patience, nothing about the delicate art of allowing your quarry to lead you to the prize.

Tell the principal, Kroeger typed, *that I have been searching for El Dorado since before he was born. I will not fail now because he lacks the discipline to wait.*

Another pause. Longer this time. Kroeger could imagine the conversation happening somewhere far away, his handler relaying the message, Méndez-Castellón's face darkening with anger, the careful diplomatic dance that kept the operation funded without giving the billionaire actual control.

Finally: *Acknowledged. Do not lose her.*

Kroeger smiled thinly and set down the phone. Lose her? He had been tracking quarry across continents since before this woman's parents were born. He had hunted Nazis for the Mossad in the years after the war, young and hungry and burning with a righteousness that he had long since abandoned. Then he had hunted the hunters when the price was right, selling his skills to whoever could afford them. He had found cities that cartographers swore did not exist and tombs that archaeologists had searched for across generations.

He would not lose Dr. Elena Vasquez.

***

The night stretched on, and Kroeger watched, and remembered.

He had first heard of El Dorado in 1958, in a cramped office in the basement of the Reichssicherheitshauptamt building in Berlin. The war had been over for thirteen years, but the building still stood, repurposed by the new German government for more mundane bureaucratic functions. Kroeger had been there to collect a file, one of thousands that the Allies had failed to seize in the chaos of 1945, hidden away by men who knew their value.

The file had belonged to the Ahnenerbe, the SS organisation dedicated to proving the racial superiority of the Aryan people through archaeological research. Most of their work had been pseudoscientific nonsense, expeditions to Tibet searching for evidence of a lost Aryan homeland, excavations in the Middle East looking for proof that ancient civilisations had been founded by Nordic peoples. His father had known that. Heinrich Kroeger had been too good a scientist to believe the ideology — but he had believed the evidence, the one thread running through the Ahnenerbe's work that the ideologues had stumbled onto by accident. The Americas. The anomalies that didn't fit any known model of pre-Columbian civilisation. That was the inheritance Werner had carried out of Berlin in 1945, six years old, his father's leather satchel strapped across his small chest because Heinrich had known he would not make it out himself. Kroeger had dismissed most of it as the ravings of madmen drunk on ideology.

But the El Dorado file had been different.

It contained reports from German agents in South America during the 1930s and 1940s, men who had been searching for the legendary city of gold while the rest of the world focused on the coming war. Most of them had died in the jungle, victims of disease or hostile natives or their own incompetence. But one had survived long enough to send back a report that had changed Kroeger's life.

The agent had written:

The city exists! I have seen evidence of it, artefacts, inscriptions, maps drawn by people who knew its location. But

El Dorado is not what the Spanish believed. It is not a city OF gold. It is a city that MAKES gold. The ancients discovered a process, a formula, a method of transmuting base metals into precious ones. This is what the legends truly describe. This is what the conquistadors failed to understand.

I am close now. Another week, perhaps two. I will find it, and when I do, the Reich will possess wealth beyond imagination. We will be able to fund our operations forever. The war will never end, because we will never run out of resources.

Heil Hitler.

The agent had never sent another report. His body had been found three months later, floating in a tributary of the Amazon, riddled with arrows. The natives who had killed him had taken everything, his equipment, his notes, his maps. Whatever he had discovered had died with him.

But Kroeger had never forgotten. The file had planted a seed in his mind, a seed that had grown into an obsession that consumed six decades of his life. He had followed every lead, tracked down every rumour, interrogated every scholar who might possess a fragment of the truth. He had found pieces of the puzzle scattered across the Americas, Maya codices that hinted at ancient knowledge, Muisca goldwork that depicted impossible processes, Inca legends that spoke of a time before time when men had learned to reshape the very nature of matter.

And always, always, the trail had gone cold before he could find the final answers.

Until Martin Thorne.

* * *

Kroeger had been watching Thorne for five years, ever since the professor had published a paper suggesting that the Ximénez manuscript of the Popol Vuh contained hidden layers of text that had never been properly examined. Most scholars had dismissed the paper as speculation. Kroeger had recognised it for what it was: the work of a man who was close to a breakthrough.

He had considered approaching Thorne directly. Offering funding, resources, protection. But Thorne was idealistic, principled, the kind of academic who believed that knowledge should be shared freely with the world. He would never have agreed to work with a man like Kroeger, a man whose methods were as ruthless as his goals.

So, Kroeger watched and waited. When Thorne had finally found what he was looking for, his infrared scanners revealing the hidden text beneath the Popol Vuh, Kroeger's people moved to acquire the discovery.

They had moved too quickly, too violently and Thorne was now dead, so now the only person who understood what he had found was the woman in the hotel room across the street: Elena Vasquez.

Kroeger studied her through the scope, watching as she typed something on her laptop, paused, typed again. She was making travel arrangements, probably. Booking flights to Guatemala, where Ximénez had found the Popol Vuh, where the next piece of the puzzle surely waited.

She was smart, this one. Trained. She would not be easy to follow without being detected. But Kroeger had resources she could not imagine, satellite surveillance, hacked airline databases, a network of informants that spanned three continents. He would know where she was going before she arrived. He would be waiting for her when she got there.

And when she had found what he needed, when she had assembled the fragments that would lead him to El Dorado, he would take it from her.

It was nothing personal. It never was.

Kroeger had killed many people in his long career. Men and women, young and old, innocent and guilty. He did not enjoy it, but he did not shy away from it either. Death was simply a tool, like any other. You used it when it was necessary, and you did not waste time on regret.

Elena Vasquez would die when she had served her purpose. Not before, and not after. Efficiency in all things.

He reached for his phone and dialled a number from memory. It rang twice before a voice answered, young, German, professional.

"Brecker."

"The woman will be travelling to Guatemala within the next forty-eight hours. I want a team in place before she arrives. Three men, full surveillance kit. No contact unless I authorise it."

"Understood. Rules of engagement?"

"Observe only. She is not to be harmed or approached. Not yet." Kroeger paused. "But be prepared to move quickly if the situation changes. She may lead us to others who are searching for the same thing. If she does, those others are fair game."

"If she finds what she's looking for?"

"We take it from her, then eliminate anyone who knows what she found."

"Understood."

The line went dead. Kroeger set down the phone and returned his attention to the scope.

The light in Elena Vasquez's window had gone out. She was sleeping now or trying to. Tomorrow she would fly to Guatemala, following clues that Martin Thorne had died to discover. She thought she was hunting for the truth.

She did not realise that she was being hunted in return.

Kroeger settled back in his chair and allowed himself a thin smile. The end game was approaching. After sixty years, after countless dead ends and false leads and bitter disappointments, he was finally close to the prize that had eluded him for so long.

El Dorado.

The city that made gold.

The secret that would change the world.

He would find it and anyone who stood in his way would be swept aside like chaff before the wind.

That was not a threat, it was a simple truth.

4

Benefactor

Chicago, Illinois - The Next Morning

Elena had not slept.

She had tried, lying in the hotel bed with the lights off and the curtains drawn, forcing herself to breathe slowly, to quiet the chaos of her thoughts. But every time she closed her eyes, she saw Martin's face. The way his hand had fallen across the manuscript, protective even in death. The rosary wound tight around his throat, the beads cutting into flesh that had already begun to cool.

By four in the morning, she had given up on sleep entirely. She had spent the remaining hours before dawn going through everything she could find about Octavio Méndez-Castellón, cross-referencing his public biography with court records, academic publications, and the kind of deep-web databases that most people didn't know existed.

What she found was a man of contradictions.

On the surface, Méndez-Castellón was exactly what he appeared to be: a Venezuelan oil billionaire with a passion for pre-Columbian antiquities. His collection was legendary, rivalling those of major museums. He had funded archaeological expeditions across Latin America, endowing chairs at universities from Bogotá to Mexico City. Scholars praised his generosity. Governments awarded him medals for his contributions to cultural preservation.

But beneath the surface, the picture grew murkier.

There were lawsuits, quietly settled, records sealed, alleging that some of his acquisitions had been obtained through less than legal means. Competitors who had crossed him had a tendency to suffer misfortunes: bankruptcies, scandals, accidents that were ruled accidental but seemed suspiciously convenient. Three of his former employees had disappeared over the years, their fates unknown. The Venezuelan government, before its collapse into chaos, had opened an investigation into his business practices. That investigation had been closed without explanation six months later.

None of it was proof of anything. Rich men accumulated enemies and rumours the way ships accumulated barnacles. But Elena had learned to trust her instincts, and her instincts told her that Octavio Méndez-Castellón was not a man to be trusted lightly.

And yet here she was, preparing to fly to Guatemala on his private jet, to search for a secret that men had killed and died for across five centuries.

Martin trusted him, she reminded herself. *They corresponded for years.*

But Martin was dead and the people who had killed him were still out there, watching, waiting.

She showered, dressed in practical clothes, jeans, hiking boots, a light jacket with plenty of pockets, and packed her single bag with the efficiency of someone who had spent years on archaeological digs in remote locations. Laptop. Satellite phone. The Glock that Diego had given her, broken down and hidden in a compartment that would not show up on standard security scans. Martin's phone, with its precious photograph of the hidden text.

And the jade pendant that Santiago Ajpop would give her in Guatemala, though she did not know that yet.

At precisely eleven-thirty, a black sedan pulled up to the hotel's side entrance. Elena watched it arrive from her window, noting the diplomatic plates, the tinted windows, the way the driver scanned the street before opening the rear door.

Time to decide.

She could still walk away. Take her evidence to the FBI, let them handle it. Go back to her quiet life at the Smithsonian, cataloguing artefacts and writing papers that a few hundred people would read. Safe. Comfortable. Alive.

But Martin would still be dead and the secret he had died for would remain buried, or worse, would fall into the hands of people like Kroeger, people who would use it for purposes she could not even imagine.

Elena picked up her bag and walked out the door.

***

The sedan took her to a private terminal at O'Hare, bypassing the chaos of commercial aviation entirely. Méndez-Castellón was waiting beside the Gulfstream, dressed casually in linen trousers and a white shirt that probably cost more than her monthly rent. He smiled as she approached, but the smile did not reach his eyes.

"Dr. Vasquez. I was not entirely certain you would come."

"Neither was I."

"And yet here you are." He gestured toward the aircraft's open door. "Shall we?"

The interior of the jet was as luxurious as she had expected, leather seats, polished wood, a bar stocked with bottles whose labels she did not recognise. A steward in a crisp uniform offered her coffee, orange juice, champagne. She took the coffee and settled into a seat by the window, watching as Méndez-Castellón took the seat across from her.

"You've been researching me," he said. It was not a question.

"Wouldn't you?"

"Of course. I would be disappointed if you hadn't." He accepted a glass of something amber from the steward, rum, she guessed, the same drink he had ordered at the Drake. "What did you find?"

"A man who collects beautiful things. A man who funds legitimate research while acquiring artefacts through channels that don't bear close examination. A man whose enemies have a tendency to suffer unfortunate accidents." Elena met his gaze. "A man who has been searching for El Dorado for thirty years and has left a trail of unanswered questions behind him."

"All true." Méndez-Castellón swirled his rum. "Though I would quibble with your characterisation of my acquisition methods. Everything in my collection was obtained legally, or at least through processes that were legal in the jurisdictions where they occurred. The antiquities trade is... complicated. What is theft in one country is legitimate salvage in another."

"And your enemies? The ones who suffered accidents?"

"I have enemies because I am successful. Successful men always have enemies." He shrugged. "Some of those enemies made poor decisions. Some suffered consequences. I cannot be held responsible for every misfortune that befalls people who have wronged me."

"That's not exactly a denial."

"It's not meant to be." He leaned forward, and for a moment Elena saw something beneath the polished facade, something harder, colder, more dangerous than the cultured billionaire he presented to the world. "Let me be clear, Dr. Vasquez. I am not a good man. I have done things in my life that I am not proud of, things that would shock you if you knew the details. I have pursued my goals with a single-mindedness that some would call obsession and others would call madness. I have sacrificed relationships, principles, and occasionally people to get what I want."

"And what do you want?"

"The same thing Martin Thorne wanted. The same thing you want." His eyes locked onto hers. "The truth. The answer to a mystery that has haunted humanity for five hundred years. The secret of El Dorado."

"Most people think El Dorado is just a legend. A fantasy invented by conquistadors to justify their greed."

"Most people are wrong." Méndez-Castellón sat back, and the hardness faded from his expression, replaced by something that looked almost like weariness. "I have spent three decades and more money than I can count proving that they are wrong. I have found fragments of evidence scattered across two continents, codices, inscriptions, artefacts that should not exist. I have pieced together a picture that no one else has seen, a picture that suggests El Dorado was real. Not a city of gold, perhaps, but something. Something that the ancients considered so valuable, so dangerous, that they went to extraordinary lengths to hide it."

"And you think Martin found the key to that something."

"I think Martin found a piece of the key. One piece among several." He reached into his jacket and produced a photograph, old, faded, showing a carved stone tablet covered in glyphs. "This was taken in 1943, by a German agent working in the Amazon basin. The tablet was found in a cave system near the border between Colombia and Brazil. The agent photographed it, made notes, and then disappeared. His body was never recovered. The tablet has never been found."

Elena studied the photograph. The glyphs were similar to those in Martin's infrared image, Maya symbols mixed with something else, something that didn't belong in any known writing system.

"Where did you get this?"

"From the archives of the Ahnenerbe. The Nazi organisation that searched for proof of Aryan superiority in the ancient world." Méndez-Castellón's lip curled with distaste. "Madmen, most of them. Ideologues who twisted evidence to fit their theories. But they had resources, and they were thorough. They found things that legitimate archaeologists missed, things that were dismissed or ignored because they didn't fit the accepted narrative."

"And this fits your narrative?"

"It fits the evidence." He tapped the photograph. "This tablet describes a process. A transformation. The Germans didn't understand it, they thought it was religious ritual, mystical nonsense. But I've had it analysed by chemists, metallurgists, people who understand what the symbols actually mean. It's not mysticism, Dr. Vasquez. It's science. A science so advanced that it looks like magic to people who don't understand it."

Elena felt a chill run down her spine. "What kind of science?"

"The kind that changes everything we think we know about the ancient world. The kind that explains why civilisations from the Maya to the Muisca to the Inca all possessed quantities of gold that should have been impossible given their technological capabilities." He leaned forward again. "The kind that turns lead into gold."

The words hung in the air between them.

"Transmutation," Elena said slowly. "You're talking about alchemy. The philosopher's stone."

"I'm talking about chemistry. About a process that our ancestors discovered thousands of years ago and then deliberately hid because they understood how dangerous it would be in the wrong hands." Méndez-Castellón's voice was intense now, passionate. "Think about it. If you could make gold from base metals, what would happen? The entire economic system would collapse. Gold would become worthless. Wars would be fought, are being fought, over resources that could be created from nothing. The people who discovered this process understood the implications. They saw what greed did to men, what it made them capable of, so decided that some knowledge was too dangerous to share."

"So, they hid it."

"They hid it. In a city so remote, so well-protected, that five centuries of searching have failed to find it. They scattered the clues across continents, entrusted them to guardians who would protect them with their lives. They created a puzzle that could only be solved by someone who understood what they were looking for, and who could be trusted not to misuse what they found."

Elena thought about Martin, hunched over his manuscripts in the quiet of his office, searching for secrets that others had dismissed as fantasy. She thought about the rosary around his throat, the message it was meant to send.

"And you think you're that person? The one who can be trusted?"

Méndez-Castellón was silent for a long moment. When he spoke again, his voice was quieter, more reflective.

"I don't know. I've asked myself that question many times over the years. I've done terrible things in pursuit of this secret. I've justified them by telling myself that the end would vindicate the means, that when I finally found El Dorado, I would use its knowledge for good. But..." He shook his head. "The truth is, I don't know what I'll do when I find it. I don't know if anyone can be trusted with that kind of power."

"Then why keep searching?"

"Because someone will find it eventually. The technology exists now to scan the jungle from space, to find hidden structures beneath the canopy. Lidar, ground-penetrating radar, satellite imaging, every year the hiding places grow fewer. Sooner or later, someone will stumble across El Dorado and when they do, I want to be there. I want to have a voice in what happens next."

"What if that voice says the secret should stay buried?"

He met her eyes. "Then I will bury it so deep no one will ever find it again."

Elena wanted to believe him. She wanted to believe that beneath the ruthlessness and the obsession, there was a man who understood the weight of what he was seeking. But she had seen too much, learned too much about the corrupting influence of power and wealth.

She would work with Méndez-Castellón because she had no choice. She would use his resources, his connections, his knowledge. But she would not trust him.

Not yet.

Maybe not ever.

***

The jet reached cruising altitude, and the steward brought lunch, grilled fish, fresh vegetables, a bottle of wine that Elena declined. She ate mechanically, her mind churning through everything she had learned in the past twenty-four hours.

Martin was dead. Someone had killed him for what he found.

The Popol Vuh manuscript contained a hidden text, a fragment of a larger document called the Codex of Seven Serpents.

That codex, if it existed, contained directions to El Dorado.

And El Dorado, according to Méndez-Castellón, was not a city of gold but something far more valuable: a repository of knowledge that could transform base metals into precious ones.

It sounded insane. It sounded like the fever dreams of conquistadors who had spent too long in the jungle, like the fantasies of alchemists who had wasted their lives chasing an impossible dream.

But Martin had believed it. Martin, who was one of the most rigorous scholars she had ever known, who never published anything he couldn't support with evidence, who had spent his career separating fact from fiction in the murky waters of pre-Columbian history.

Martin had found something. Something real. Something that had cost him his life.

Elena pulled out her laptop and opened the photograph from Martin's phone. The hidden text glowed on the screen, its glyphs strange and haunting in the cabin's dim light.

The second key sleeps beneath the altar of the Converted. Wake it only when the seven align.

The altar of the Converted. Santo Tomás Chichicastenango, where Ximénez had found the Popol Vuh. Where the Spanish had built their church on top of a Maya temple, converting the sacred space to their own purposes.

Something was hidden there. Another fragment of the codex, another piece of the puzzle. *Martin had been killed before he could find it,* she thought.

"You're thinking about him."

Elena looked up to find Méndez-Castellón watching her from across the aisle. She hadn't heard him approach.

"Martin. You're thinking about what happened to him."

"Yes, I'm thinking about what it cost him."

"He knew the risks." Méndez-Castellón settled into the seat beside her. "We all know the risks. The search for El Dorado has claimed thousands of lives over the centuries. Conquistadors, explorers, treasure hunters, archaeologists, they all went into the jungle, and most of them never came out. Martin understood that. He chose to continue anyway."

"Did he know about Kroeger?"

The name produced a visible reaction, a tightening of Méndez-Castellón's jaw, a darkening of his expression. "What do you know about Kroeger?"

"Only what you told me yesterday. That he's dangerous. That he worked for the Nazis. That he's been searching for El Dorado as long as you have." Elena closed her laptop. "And that you employed him for fifteen years before you severed ties."

"That was a mistake. One of many I've made in this search." Méndez-Castellón's voice was heavy with something that might have been regret. "When I first met Kroeger, he seemed... useful. He had knowledge, connections, resources that I lacked. He had spent decades following leads that I had only just discovered. I thought we could work together, pool our information, find El Dorado faster than either of us could alone."

"What changed?"

"I learned what he really believed. What he intended to do with the knowledge if he found it." Méndez-Castellón shook his head. "Kroeger is not interested in El Dorado for its historical significance, or even for its wealth. He's interested in it because he thinks it will prove his theories about human history. He believes that the civilisation that built El Dorado was not indigenous to the Americas, that it was founded by travellers from elsewhere, from Europe or Asia or some lost homeland that sank beneath the waves thousands of years ago. He believes that the Maya, the Muisca, the Inca, all of them learned what they knew from these outsiders. That their achievements were not their own."

"That's... insane."

"It's worse than insane. It's dangerous." Méndez-Castellón's eyes were hard. "If Kroeger finds El Dorado, he will use it to justify centuries of colonialism and exploitation. He will claim that the indigenous peoples of the Americas were merely caretakers of knowledge that rightfully belonged to others. He will give ammunition to every racist, every supremacist, every person who believes that some races are inherently superior to others."

"And you think he killed Martin?"

"I think it's likely. The rosary around his throat, that's Kroeger's signature. He fancies himself a crusader, purifying history of lies. He's killed before, always with some symbolic flourish that announces his presence." Méndez-Castellón's hands clenched into fists. "I should have stopped him years ago. I had opportunities. But I thought... I thought he might still be useful. That his knowledge was worth the risk of keeping him alive."

"And now Martin is dead because of that calculation."

"Yes." The word was barely a whisper. "Now Martin is dead and I have to live with that."

They sat in silence for a long moment. Outside the window, clouds stretched to the horizon, white and endless.

"Tell me about Diego Ixchel," Elena said finally. "Martin trusted him. I want to know why."

"Diego is local. K'iche' Maya, educated in the United States, returned to Guatemala fifteen years ago to excavate his people's heritage. He's one of the best field archaeologists in Central America, maybe in the world. He's also honest, which is rare in a region where corruption is endemic."

"Can he be trusted?"

"I trust him more than I trust most people. Which, I admit, is not saying much." Méndez-Castellón managed a thin smile. "Diego doesn't like me. He thinks I'm a grave robber with a chequebook. But he respects the work, and he understands what's at stake. He'll help us find what we're looking for."

"And after we find it? What then?"

"Then we move to the next fragment. Colombia, Peru, Mexico, wherever the trail leads." He paused. "Assuming we survive that long."

"You think Kroeger will try to stop us?"

"I think Kroeger will do whatever it takes to get what he wants. If that means killing us, he won't hesitate." Méndez-Castellón reached into his jacket and produced a satellite phone, which he handed to her. "This is encrypted, untraceable. If anything happens to me, if we get separated, use it to contact Diego. He'll know what to do."

Elena took the phone, feeling its weight in her hand. A lifeline. Or possibly a leash.

"One more question," she said.

"Yes?"

"The Guardians. The people who have been protecting the codex fragments for five centuries. What do you know about them?"

Something flickered across Méndez-Castellón's face, surprise, perhaps, or wariness. "Where did you hear about the Guardians?"

"Martin's notes. He mentioned them several times. A secret society, dedicated to keeping El Dorado hidden. He thought they were still active."

"They are." Méndez-Castellón's voice was careful now, measured. "I've encountered them before. They're... formidable. Dedicated. They've been passing down their mission from generation to generation since the Spanish conquest. Some of them would rather die than let the secret fall into the wrong hands."

"And how do they feel about us? About what we're trying to do?"

"That," Méndez-Castellón said slowly, "is an excellent question. One that I suspect we're about to find out the answer to."

The jet began its descent toward Guatemala City.

5

Followers

Thirty Thousand Feet Below - The Same Morning

The commercial flight from Miami to Guatemala City was fully booked, but the three men in business class drew no particular attention. They looked like what their passports claimed they were: German businessmen on a routine trip to assess manufacturing opportunities in Central America. They wore expensive but understated suits. They carried leather briefcases containing laptops loaded with convincing spreadsheets and market analyses. They spoke quietly among themselves in German, discussing supply chains and labour costs with the easy fluency of men who had made such trips many times before.

The passports, like so much else about them, were lies.

Hans Brecker sat in the window seat, watching the same clouds that Elena Vasquez was watching from her private jet somewhere above. He was thirty-four years old, built like a middleweight boxer, with close-cropped blond hair and pale blue eyes that revealed nothing of what lay behind them. His hands rested loosely on his thighs, hands that had killed eleven people in the past six years, though the official count would never be established. The police in four countries had files on unsolved murders that bore his signature: clean, professional, untraceable. But police files were just paper, and paper proved nothing.

Brecker had not always been a killer.

He had grown up in Stuttgart, the son of a factory worker and a schoolteacher, in a small apartment that always smelled of his mother's cooking and his father's cigarettes. His childhood had been unremarkable, decent grades, a few close friends, weekend football matches in the park behind the housing blocks. He had dreamed of becoming a professional footballer, had even been scouted by VfB Stuttgart's youth academy when he was sixteen. The coach had said he had potential. Quick feet, good instincts, a willingness to play through pain that set him apart from boys who had grown up softer.

Those dreams had ended at nineteen.

The robbery had been Stefan's idea, Stefan Müller, his best friend since primary school, who had dropped out of university and fallen in with a crew that dealt drugs in the clubs around Königstraße. Brecker had known it was stupid even as he agreed to it. A convenience store on the edge of town, late at night, the owner an old Turkish man who kept the day's receipts in a lockbox under the counter. Easy money, Stefan had said. In and out in two minutes. No one gets hurt.

But the old man had not cooperated. He had reached for something under the counter, a phone, Brecker had thought later, though in the moment he had been certain it was a gun, and Brecker had reacted with the instincts that the football coach had praised. Quick feet. Good instincts. He had grabbed the cricket bat Stefan was carrying and swung it before his conscious mind could catch up with his body.

The old man's skull had made a sound that Brecker still heard sometimes in his dreams. A wet crack, like a melon dropped on concrete. He had been dead before he hit the floor.

Brecker had fled that night, taking nothing from the store, leaving Stefan behind to face the consequences alone. He had crossed into

France on a stolen passport, then made his way to Spain, then to the shadowy world of private military contractors where his capacity for violence was an asset rather than a liability. The French Foreign Legion had been his first stop, five years of brutal training and deployment that had burned away whatever softness remained from his Stuttgart childhood. After that, the private sector: Syria, Libya, Yemen, places that had no names on any map. He had learned to kill quickly and efficiently, without hesitation or remorse. The old Turkish shopkeeper had been an accident, a moment of panic that had destroyed his old life. The eleven who came after were something else entirely.

Professional. Clean. Necessary.

When Werner Kroeger had recruited him three years ago, offering triple his usual rate for work that required discretion and absolute loyalty, Brecker had not hesitated. The old man was strange, obsessed with ancient history, with theories about lost civilisations that sounded like the ravings of a lunatic, but his money was real, and his jobs were interesting. Not the usual bodyguard work or corporate espionage that filled most of Brecker's calendar. Kroeger's assignments took him to remote corners of the world, searching for artefacts and documents that most people didn't know existed. It was almost like treasure hunting, if treasure hunters regularly had to eliminate competitors who got too close.

He did not know what Kroeger was searching for. Not exactly. He had picked up fragments over the years, references to El Dorado, to ancient formulas, to knowledge that could change the world, but he had learned not to ask too many questions. His job was surveillance and, when necessary, elimination. The reasons were above his pay grade.

His phone buzzed with an encrypted message, routed through a series of servers that would take even the most determined intelligence agency months to trace: *Target airborne. Private jet, tail number*

VP-CGR. ETA Guatemala City 0900 local. Proceed to Chichicastenango. Observe and report.

Brecker acknowledged the message with a single character, *K,* for *verstanden,* and deleted it. The phone would wipe itself automatically in twelve hours, destroying any evidence that the message had ever existed.

He glanced at the man beside him. Kurt Weller was reviewing building schematics on a tablet; his brow furrowed in concentration. The tablet's screen showed floor plans of the church at Chichicastenango, obtained from the Guatemalan heritage ministry through channels that didn't bear close examination. Weller was the technical specialist of their three-man team: locks, alarms, extraction. If there was a door that needed opening or a security system that needed bypassing, Weller was the man for the job.

He had spent eight years with Germany's GSG 9, the elite counter-terrorism unit that had made its reputation during the Lufthansa Flight 181 hijacking in 1977. Weller had joined too late for that legendary operation, but he had seen action in a dozen hostage rescues and counter-terrorism raids across Europe and the Middle East. He had been good at his job, one of the best, according to the commendations in his file, until an operation in Hamburg had gone wrong.

The details were classified, buried in files that even Kroeger's contacts couldn't access. But Brecker had pieced together enough from Weller's occasional drunken remarks to understand the broad outlines. A suspected terrorist cell. A pre-dawn raid. Intelligence that turned out to be wrong. By the time the shooting stopped, three civilians were dead, including a twelve-year-old girl who had been sleeping in the wrong bedroom.

The inquiry had cleared Weller of wrongdoing. The intelligence failure had come from higher up the chain, and Weller had followed his orders exactly as trained. But something had broken in him that night. He had resigned from GSG 9 six months later, and within a year he was working for the same private contractors who had employed Brecker.

They had met in Libya, during the chaos that followed Gaddafi's fall. Weller had been running security for an oil company; Brecker had been eliminating rivals for a different oil company. They had nearly killed each other before realising they were both professionals who could be more useful as allies than enemies. When Kroeger had asked Brecker to assemble a team for the El Dorado operation, Weller had been his first call.

"The church," Weller said quietly, tilting the tablet so Brecker could see. "Colonial era, built 1540 on the foundations of a pre-Columbian temple. Stone construction, walls approximately one metre thick. Multiple entry points, main doors, side chapel, sacristy entrance, but only the main doors are regularly used. No modern security to speak of. A few cameras covering the exterior, easily avoided. Motion sensors in the sacristy, but they're fifteen years old and poorly maintained."

"Complications?"

"Several." Weller scrolled through his notes. "The target will have local support, Méndez-Castellón has people in Guatemala. At least one fixer, probably armed. There may be others at the church itself and the indigenous population is... protective of their sacred sites. The church isn't just a tourist attraction to them. They still practice traditional ceremonies there, right alongside the Catholic services. If they suspect we're there to steal something, things could get ugly fast."

"How ugly?"

"1982 ugly." Weller's voice was flat. "The Ixil Maya in this region fought a guerrilla war against the government for decades. Most of them are farmers now, but they haven't forgotten how to fight. They have long memories for outsiders who disrespect their sacred places."

Brecker filed the information away. He had worked in environments like this before, places where the locals viewed outsiders with suspicion, where a wrong move could turn a simple surveillance operation into a firefight. The key was patience. Blend in. Watch. Wait for the moment when the target was isolated and vulnerable.

"Rules of engagement?" Weller asked.

"Observe only, for now. The old man wants her alive until she finds what she's looking for."

"And after?"

Brecker's expression did not change. "After, we take what she found and eliminate anyone who can connect it to us."

Behind them, in the aisle seat of the next row, Stefan Holtz pretended to sleep. His eyes were closed, his breathing slow and regular, but his ears missed nothing of the conversation in front of him. Holtz was the driver, the planner, the one who made sure they had exit routes and contingencies for every operation. He was also the oldest of the three, forty-seven, with grey threading through his dark hair and a face that had seen too many years of hard living.

Unlike Brecker and Weller, Holtz had never served in any military or police force. His education had come from the streets of East Berlin, where he had grown up in the shadow of the Wall, learning to navigate a world where the wrong word to the wrong person could mean a prison cell or worse. He had been a smuggler before the Wall fell, people, goods, information, whatever paid. After reunification, when the old networks collapsed and new opportunities emerged, he had transitioned into the private security industry. Not as a shooter, his skills lay elsewhere, but as a fixer, a planner, a man who could make arrangements in places where arrangements were difficult to make.

It was Holtz who had sourced their weapons from a contact in Guatemala City, a former Kaibil, one of the Guatemalan special forces soldiers who had earned a reputation for brutality during the civil war. Three Glock 19s with suppressors, two MP5 submachine guns, enough ammunition to fight a small war. The weapons were waiting in a storage locker near the airport, along with a vehicle, forged credentials, and a selection of identity documents that would allow them to move freely through the country.

Holtz had also prepared their exit strategy. A charter flight from a private airstrip near Antigua, ready to leave on two hours' notice. A boat waiting in Puerto Barrios, in case air travel became impossible. Safe houses in three different cities, stocked with supplies and clean passports. Whatever happened in Chichicastenango, they would have options.

Three men. Three specialists. More than enough for one archaeologist and whatever local help she might have.

But Brecker had learned long ago not to be overconfident. The jobs that went wrong were always the ones that looked easy. The targets who seemed soft turned out to have hidden resources. The simple surveillance operations turned into bloodbaths that left bodies scattered across multiple countries.

He would watch and wait, then when the moment came, he would act with the speed and precision that had kept him alive through a decade of violence.

The plane began its descent toward Guatemala City.

***

They cleared customs without incident.

The passports were excellent forgeries, Holtz had contacts in the German underworld who could produce documents that would fool anyone short of a dedicated forensic examiner, and the customs officials were easily distracted by a combination of boredom and a small bribe tucked inside a German business card. The officials barely glanced at their luggage, waving them through with the mechanical indifference of men who processed thousands of travellers every day.

Within forty minutes of landing, they had collected their weapons from the storage locker, loaded their vehicle, a white Toyota Land

Cruiser, the most common vehicle in Guatemala, virtually invisible, and were heading northwest toward the highlands.

The road out of Guatemala City climbed quickly, leaving behind the sprawl of the capital and entering a landscape that seemed to belong to a different world. Mountains rose on either side, their slopes carpeted with dense forest that had barely changed since the Maya had ruled these highlands a thousand years ago. Small villages clung to the hillsides, their tin roofs glinting in the afternoon sun. Farmers worked terraced fields that had been carved into the steep terrain by generations of their ancestors, growing maize and beans and coffee using methods that predated the Spanish conquest.

Brecker drove while Weller monitored communications on a laptop connected to a satellite uplink. Holtz sat in the back seat, studying satellite imagery of their target area on a tablet.

"The church is here," Holtz said, pointing to a cluster of buildings on the screen. "Main plaza, east side. The target's jet landed forty minutes ago, she should be arriving within the hour, depending on traffic."

"Security?"

"Méndez-Castellón has a vehicle waiting at the airport. Black SUV, diplomatic plates. One driver probably armed. There may be others waiting at the church, he has a network of informants and fixers throughout Guatemala." Holtz scrolled through additional images. "The plaza will be crowded. Today is market day, which means thousands of locals and tourists. Good for blending in. Bad for maintaining clear sight lines."

Brecker considered the situation. The old man had been clear: observe only, do not engage unless necessary. But the target was moving faster than expected. If she found what she was looking for in the church before they could position themselves properly...

"We need eyes inside," he said. "Weller, you're the least conspicuous. Buy a camera, play tourist. Get close enough to see what she's doing without being noticed."

"And if she finds something?"

"Then we follow her. See where she goes next." Brecker's hands tightened on the steering wheel. "The old man wants the complete picture, not just one piece. We let her do the work, then we take everything at once."

"And the local support? Méndez-Castellón's people?"

"Expendable. If they get in the way, we remove them."

The vehicle climbed higher into the mountains, and the temperature dropped noticeably. They had left the tropical heat of the lowlands behind and entered a different climate zone, cool, misty, with clouds that seemed to brush the tops of the trees. The road narrowed, winding through villages where women in traditional dress walked along the shoulder carrying impossible loads on their heads.

"There," Holtz said, pointing ahead.

The town of Chichicastenango appeared through the mist like something from a dream. Whitewashed buildings clustered around a central plaza, their red-tiled roofs bright against the grey sky. Cobblestone streets radiated outward like the spokes of a wheel. And dominating the eastern side of the plaza, the twin towers of Santo Tomás church rose above everything else, white and imposing, a monument to five centuries of colonial power.

Brecker pulled into a small hotel on the outskirts of town, chosen in advance by Holtz for its anonymity and its clear sight lines to the main road. The building was unremarkable, three stories, crumbling stucco, a faded sign advertising rooms by the night or the week. The kind of place where no one asked questions and no one remembered faces.

"Weller, you're on point," Brecker said as he killed the engine. "Get into position in the plaza. I want to know the moment she arrives."

"And if she goes straight to the church?"

"Then you follow her in. Play the tourist. Take pictures. Don't let her out of your sight."

Weller nodded and slipped out of the vehicle, transforming himself as he walked. His posture changed, becoming looser, more casual. He pulled a camera from his bag and slung it around his neck. By the time he reached the end of the block, he looked exactly like what he was pretending to be: a middle-aged German tourist, slightly overweight, eager to capture memories of his exotic vacation.

"Holtz, find us a position with sight lines on the church," Brecker continued. "Somewhere we can watch without being seen. And make sure our exit routes are clear."

"Already done." Holtz pulled out a map he had marked during the drive. "There's a restaurant on the second floor of this building", he tapped a location overlooking the plaza, "with a balcony that has direct line of sight to the church entrance. I've reserved a table for the afternoon. And I've identified three different routes out of town, depending on which direction we need to go."

"Good. I'll coordinate with the old man, let him know we're in position."

Holtz hesitated. "Hans... what are we actually looking for here? The old man has been searching for this El Dorado for decades. What makes him think this woman can find it when he couldn't?"

Brecker considered the question. It was unusual for Holtz to express curiosity about their missions, he was usually content to plan the logistics and leave the strategy to others.

"She has something he doesn't," Brecker said finally. "Information. Her mentor found something in an old manuscript, something that points to the next piece of the puzzle. The old man had the mentor killed before he could share what he knew. But this woman, she has his notes. His research. She knows things that the old man doesn't."

"So, we follow her until she finds what she's looking for, and then we take it from her."

"That's the plan."

"And if she doesn't find anything? If the whole thing is a dead end?"

Brecker opened the car door. "Then we eliminate her and move on to the next lead. Either way, our job stays the same."

He stepped out into the cool mountain air, leaving Holtz to gather their equipment. Somewhere in the town below, Elena Vasquez was approaching the church that might hold the answers she was seeking.

She didn't know it yet, but she was being watched by wolves.

And wolves, Brecker knew from long experience, always got their prey in the end.

6

Church of Conversions

Chichicastenango, Guatemala - That Afternoon

The church of Santo Tomás rose from the eastern side of the plaza like a white fist raised against the sky.

Elena stood at the base of the eighteen steps that led to its entrance, feeling the weight of centuries pressing down upon her. The steps themselves were significant, eighteen, one for each month of the Maya calendar, a subtle incorporation of indigenous symbolism into what the Spanish had intended as a monument to Christian conquest. She had read about this detail in Martin's notes, had seen photographs in academic papers, but standing here in person was something else entirely. The stones beneath her feet had been worn smooth by millions of footsteps over five hundred years, each one a small act of devotion, or defiance, against the forces that had tried to erase an entire civilisation.

Around her, the plaza exploded with colour and noise and life.

It was market day, the famous *mercado* that had drawn traders to Chichicastenango for centuries before the Spanish arrived and would continue long after the last tourist had gone home. Vendors had set up stalls in seemingly random patterns across the cobblestones, creating a labyrinth of narrow passages that wound between mountains of merchandise. Hand-woven textiles in colours so vivid they hurt the eyes; crimson, cobalt and yellows that seemed to glow with their own inner light. Wooden masks carved in the shapes of jaguars and eagles and demons, their painted eyes following passersby with unsettling intensity. Pottery, leather goods, bootleg electronics, medicinal herbs, chunks of copal incense wrapped in corn husks, live chickens in wire cages, vegetables Elena didn't recognise, fruits she had never seen.

The smell was overwhelming, cooking meat from the food stalls, wood smoke from the incense burners, diesel exhaust from the buses that had carried traders from villages throughout the highlands, the earthy musk of too many bodies pressed too close together. And beneath it all, something else. Something older. The faint sweetness of copal, the same incense the Maya had burned for their gods a thousand years before Christ was born.

K'iche' women in traditional *huipiles,* hand-woven blouses embroidered with geometric patterns that encoded information about their villages, their families, their place in the social order, haggled with tourists over the price of blankets. The tourists, mostly American and European, clutched their guidebooks and their cameras and their money belts, clearly out of their depth in this ancient marketplace. They wanted souvenirs, authentic experiences, stories to tell when they returned to their comfortable lives. They did not understand that they were walking through a world that had survived conquest and genocide and five centuries of systematic oppression, a world that had learned to hide its true self behind a mask of colourful folklore.

Children darted between the stalls, laughing and shouting in a mixture of Spanish and K'iche'. Some of them were selling, gum, small toys, postcards of the church, while others were simply playing, oblivious to the commerce and chaos around them. An old woman sat cross-legged beside a pile of tomatoes, her face as weathered as the mountains that surrounded the town, her eyes tracking Elena with an intensity that made her uncomfortable.

And on the steps of the church, the old religion persisted.

Elena watched as a *chuchkajau,* a Maya spiritual guide, sometimes called a *daykeeper* in the anthropological literature, performed a ceremony on the broad stone landing halfway up the steps. He was an old man, dressed in the traditional clothing of the highlands, his face hidden behind a cloud of copal smoke. Before him, a small fire burned in a clay brazier, fed with chips of the sacred resin. Candles of different colours surrounded the fire, red, black, white, yellow, each colour representing a different direction, a different aspect of the divine. Flower petals and pine needles had been scattered in careful patterns around the brazier, forming symbols that Elena recognised from her studies: the four directions, the world tree, the double-headed serpent that connected earth and sky.

The *chuchkajau* chanted in K'iche', his voice rising and falling in patterns that had been passed down through generations of spiritual practitioners. Elena caught fragments she could understand, names of days from the Maya calendar, invocations to the ancestors, prayers for health and prosperity and protection. But woven through the Maya words were Catholic elements: Hail Marys and Our Fathers, names of saints, references to Jesus and the Virgin. It was not syncretism in the academic sense, not two religions blended together into something new, but rather two religions existing simultaneously in the same space, like two rivers flowing parallel without ever quite merging.

Nearby, women in traditional dress scattered rose petals and poured libations of *aguardiente* onto the stone steps, their lips moving in silent prayers. A group of men in ceremonial clothing, embroidered jackets, knee-length pants, leather sandals, waited their turn to approach the fire, carrying bundles wrapped in cloth. Offerings, Elena guessed. Gifts for the spirits that still inhabited this place, despite five centuries of Christian overlay.

"They call it *costumbre*," said a voice beside her, quiet and assured. "The custom. The way things have always been done."

Elena turned to find a man watching her with dark, intelligent eyes. He was short and compact, with the broad features and copper skin of the highland Maya, his black hair cut short in a practical style that suggested someone who spent more time in the field than in lecture halls. He wore practical clothes, khaki trousers, a light jacket with many pockets, sturdy boots that had seen hard use, and carried himself with the easy confidence of someone who knew exactly who he was and where he belonged.

He was perhaps forty years old, though the lines around his eyes suggested he had lived those years hard. There was a stillness to him that Elena recognised from her years working with indigenous communities, the patience of people who had learned to wait, to watch, to survive.

"Diego Ixchel," he said, extending his hand. "Méndez-Castellón sent me."

"Elena Vasquez." She shook his hand, noting the calluses on his palm, the strength in his grip. Not a man who spent his days behind a desk. "You're the archaeologist."

"Among other things." Diego's gaze swept the plaza, casual but thorough, the way a soldier might scan terrain for threats. His eyes lingered for a moment on something behind Elena, a blond man with a camera, photographing the market stalls near the church steps, before moving on. "I'm also K'iche', which means I grew up hearing stories about this church that you won't find in any textbook. And I'm someone who owes Martin Thorne a debt I can never repay."

Elena felt a sharp pang at the mention of Martin's name. "You knew him?"

"He was my doctoral advisor, twenty years ago. Believed in me when no one else did. Helped me understand that studying my own people's history wasn't a betrayal of academic objectivity, it was the only way to get at the truth." Diego's expression softened momentarily, then hardened again. "When I heard what happened to him, I..." He shook his head. "We should move. This isn't the place for that conversation."

"Why not?"

"Because you're being watched." Diego began walking toward the church steps, and Elena fell into step beside him, forcing herself not to look around for whoever was observing them. "Don't turn around. The man with the camera, near the textile stall, he's been photographing you since you arrived. And there are at least two others I've spotted. One in the restaurant overlooking the plaza, one in a white Land Cruiser parked near the municipal building."

Elena's hand moved instinctively toward the small of her back, where the Glock rested in a concealed holster beneath her jacket. Diego noticed the movement and shook his head slightly.

"Not here. Too many civilians. And if these are Kroeger's people, they won't move against us in public, too many witnesses, too much chance of things going wrong." He began climbing the church steps, weaving between the devotees and the tourists. "They're waiting to see what we find. Which means, for now, our interests align. We both want to get inside that church."

"Méndez-Castellón warned me about Kroeger," Elena said quietly. "He said the man is dangerous. Obsessed."

"Octavio has a talent for understatement." Diego paused on the landing where the *chuchkajau* was still performing his ceremony, and for a moment he stood with his head bowed, as if paying respects to the old ways. When he spoke again, his voice was barely above a whisper. "Kroeger has been searching for El Dorado since before I was born. He's left bodies on three continents. And he believes, truly believes, that whatever he finds will prove his theories about the superiority of certain races over others. He's not a treasure hunter, Dr. Vasquez. He's a zealot."

"And Méndez-Castellón? What is he?"

Diego was silent for a long moment. The copal smoke swirled around them, thick and sweet, carrying prayers to gods whose names had almost been forgotten.

"Octavio is... complicated," he said finally. "He's done things I can't forgive. Used his money to acquire artefacts that should have stayed with the communities that created them. Funded expeditions that damaged sites before they could be properly documented. Made deals with governments and collectors who treated Maya heritage as a commodity to be bought and sold." He paused. "But he also saved my sister's life, ten years ago. Paid for treatments that I could never have afforded. Never asked for anything in return. Never even mentioned it again."

"So, you trust him?"

"I trust that he wants to find El Dorado more than he wants anything else in the world. And I trust that, unlike Kroeger, he's capable of changing his mind about what to do with it once he finds it." Diego resumed climbing the steps. "Whether that's enough... I suppose we'll find out."

They reached the top of the steps and paused before the massive wooden doors of the church. The doors were old, colonial era, Elena guessed, though they had been repaired and restored many times over the centuries. Carved panels depicted scenes from the Passion of Christ, but here and there, almost hidden among the thorns and nails and weeping figures, she spotted other symbols. A serpent. A jaguar. A face that might have been Christ or might have been Tohil, the K'iche' god of fire and sacrifice.

"The Spanish thought they were converting the Maya to Christianity," Diego said, following her gaze. "They didn't understand that the Maya were simply adding Christ to their pantheon, the way they had added other gods over thousands of years. The old beliefs didn't disappear. They just... adapted. Went underground. Hid in plain sight."

"Like whatever is hidden beneath the altar."

Diego's expression flickered, surprise, then quickly suppressed. "Méndez-Castellón told you about that?"

"Martin's notes mentioned it. The hidden text we found in the Popol Vuh manuscript, it refers to something sleeping beneath 'the altar of the Converted.' This is the church where Ximénez found the Popol Vuh. Where he transcribed it in the early 1700s." Elena met Diego's eyes. "If there's another fragment of the Codex of Seven Serpents, this is where it would be."

For a long moment, Diego simply looked at her. Then he laughed, a short, surprised sound that seemed to escape against his will.

"Martin always said you were the best student he ever had. That you saw connections others missed." He shook his head. "It took me five years to figure out what you worked out in two days."

"I had Martin's notes. And a head start." Elena's throat tightened. "He did most of the work. I'm just... following the trail he left behind."

"Then let's make sure his work wasn't wasted." Diego pushed open the church doors. "Come. I have someone I want you to meet."

***

The interior of Santo Tomás was cool and dim, a refuge from the chaos of the market outside.

Elena paused just inside the entrance, letting her eyes adjust to the darkness. The nave stretched before her, longer than she had expected, its vaulted ceiling disappearing into shadows above. Massive stone columns lined the sides of the church, supporting arches that seemed to grow organically from the floor like ancient trees. Candles flickered everywhere, hundreds of them, thousands perhaps, their tiny flames creating constellations of light in the darkness.

The air was thick with smoke and incense, heavy with the accumulated prayers of generations. Elena felt it pressing against her skin, filling her lungs, as if the church itself were alive and breathing around her.

This was not a museum.

The pews had been pushed to the sides of the nave, leaving the central floor open for the indigenous worshippers who preferred to pray the way their ancestors had prayed, on their knees, on the bare stone, surrounded by candles and flowers and offerings. Families knelt in clusters across the floor, their voices a soft murmur that blended with the echo of footsteps and the crackle of flames. Some were praying in Spanish, reciting the familiar words of Catholic devotion. Others prayed in K'iche', their words older and stranger, directed at powers that had no names in any Christian liturgy.

Elena saw offerings scattered across the floor among the candles, bottles of Coca-Cola, plates of food, bundles of herbs, small figurines made of clay or wood. A woman near the front of the church was performing what looked like a divination ritual, casting seeds onto a cloth and studying the patterns they made. A man knelt before a side altar dedicated to a saint Elena didn't recognise, his lips moving in silent prayer while tears streamed down his face.

And everywhere, everywhere, the flowers. Marigolds and roses and flowers Elena had no names for, scattered in patterns across the floor, draped over altars and statues, woven into garlands that hung from the columns. The smell was intoxicating, sweet and heavy and alive, cutting through the smoke and incense like a message from another world.

"The Spanish built this church on top of a Maya temple," Diego said quietly, guiding her along the side aisle. "They thought they were conquering the old gods, replacing them with the new. But the Maya understood something the Spanish didn't. Sacred space is sacred space, regardless of what you build on top of it. The temple is still here, beneath the floor. The spirits are still here, accepting offerings. The priests may wear different robes and speak different words, but the essential nature of this place hasn't changed in a thousand years."

"Does the Church know?" Elena asked. "About the temple beneath?"

"The Vatican knows everything and acknowledges nothing." Diego's smile was thin, bitter. "There have been archaeological surveys, ground-penetrating radar, seismic analysis. Everyone knows there are structures beneath the church. But the local archbishop has forbidden any excavation. He says it would be disrespectful to disturb the sacred space. What he means is that it would be embarrassing to admit that Christianity in Guatemala has been built on foundations it doesn't fully understand."

They passed a side chapel dedicated to Santo Tomás himself, Thomas the Apostle, the doubting one, who would not believe until he had touched the wounds of Christ. The chapel was empty except for an old woman lighting candles before the painted statue of the saint. She glanced at Elena as they passed, her eyes dark and knowing, and Elena felt a shiver run down her spine.

Near the front of the church, a side door led to a narrow corridor that smelled of dust and old paper. Diego knocked on a door at the end of the corridor, three quick raps, a pause, two more, and waited.

The door opened to reveal a young man in clerical garb. He was in his early twenties, round-faced and nervous, his eyes darting from Diego to Elena and back again with obvious anxiety.

"Father Tomás Ixchel," Diego said. "My cousin. He's the assistant to the parish priest, which means he has access to parts of the church that are normally off-limits."

"You're the woman," Tomás said, his voice barely above a whisper. "The one Martin Thorne wrote about in his letters."

Elena blinked. "Martin wrote to you?"

"For years. Asking questions about the church, about Ximénez, about..." He glanced up and down the corridor, then stepped back to let them enter. "We shouldn't talk here. Come. Quickly."

The room beyond was small and cluttered, a sacristy, Elena realised, where the priests prepared for services. Vestments hung on hooks along one wall. A cabinet held chalices and patens and other liturgical objects. A small desk was buried under stacks of papers and books, and the air smelled of candle wax and old incense.

Tomás closed the door behind them and leaned against it, as if afraid someone might try to force their way in.

"I told Diego this was dangerous," he said, his words tumbling out in a rush. "I told him we should wait, that the archbishop would never approve, that if anyone found out what we were doing, "

"Tomás." Diego's voice was calm but firm. "Breathe."

The young priest took a deep breath, visibly forcing himself to calm down. "I'm sorry. It's just... I've been keeping this secret for so long. Ever since Martin first contacted me, years ago. He believed there was something hidden beneath the altar, something important, and he asked me to watch for anyone else who might come looking for it. And now you're here, and Martin is dead, and there are men outside who look like they want to kill someone, and I don't, "

"Wait." Elena held up her hand. "Martin contacted you years ago. How many years?"

"Seven. Almost eight." Tomás's eyes met hers. "He said he'd found references to a hidden chamber beneath the church, in documents from the colonial period. He asked me to let him know if anyone came asking questions about Ximénez, or about the Popol Vuh, or about anything to do with the church's foundations."

"And did anyone come?"

"Three times." Tomás's voice dropped even lower. "Three years ago, a German man came. Old, very old, with a scar on his face. He asked to see the church records, anything related to Ximénez or the early colonial period. He was polite, but there was something... wrong about him. Something cold. I showed him the public archives and nothing else, and he left after two days. But I saw him in the plaza several times after that, watching the church. Watching me."

Kroeger. It had to be.

"Who else?"

"Two men, last year. They claimed to be archaeologists from a Mexican university, but their credentials didn't check out. They tried to bribe one of the groundskeepers to let them into the crypt. When that didn't work, they tried to break in at night. The police caught them before they got very far."

"And the third?"

Tomás was silent for a moment. When he spoke again, his voice was barely audible.

"He came three weeks ago. He didn't ask questions or try to break in. He just stood in the plaza for hours, looking at the church. An old man, indigenous, K'iche' by his clothes. I thought he was just another worshipper, but there was something about the way he looked at the building. Like he was waiting for something. Or someone."

"Where is he now?"

"I don't know. He disappeared after a few days. But before he left..." Tomás reached into his cassock and pulled out a folded piece of paper. "He gave me this. Told me to give it to the woman who would come looking for the truth about Ximénez."

Elena took the paper with trembling fingers. It was old, yellowed, the creases worn soft from repeated folding. When she opened it, she found a single line of text, handwritten in faded ink:

The Serpent waits for the Serpent's daughter. Find me where the blood remembers.

"What does it mean?" Tomás asked.

Elena didn't answer. She was staring at the words, her mind racing. The Serpent's daughter. The Codex of Seven Serpents. And *the blood remembers,* a phrase that appeared in several Maya texts, referring to the ancestral memories carried in the blood of descendants.

Someone knew she was coming. Someone had been waiting for her.

Before she could speak, a sound from outside made all three of them freeze.

Footsteps in the corridor. Heavy. Deliberate. Coming closer.

Diego's hand moved to the small of his back, where Elena knew he carried a weapon. Tomás pressed himself against the door, his face pale with terror.

The footsteps stopped outside the sacristy.

A knock. Three slow beats, then silence.

"Father Tomás." The voice was old, cracked with age, but there was steel beneath the frailty. "I know you have visitors. It's time we all had a conversation."

Diego looked at Elena. She nodded.

Tomás opened the door.

The man who stood in the corridor was ancient, eighty at least, perhaps older, his face a landscape of wrinkles carved by decades of sun and wind. He wore the simple clothes of a highland farmer: hand-woven trousers, a cotton shirt, leather sandals worn thin by years of walking mountain paths. His hair was white, cut short, and his eyes were the colour of obsidian, black and deep and holding secrets that stretched back generations.

Around his neck, on a leather cord, hung a pendant of carved jade. A serpent, swallowing its own tail.

"I am Santiago Ajpop," he said. "And I have been waiting for you, Elena Vasquez, for a very long time." Santiago's voice carried the cadence of the K'iche' highlands beneath his Spanish.

7

The Guardian

Chichicastenango, Guatemala - That Afternoon

The old man stood in the shadows of the sacristy like something that had grown there—rooted, ancient, as much a part of the church as the stones beneath their feet. His face was a landscape of time, carved by eight decades of highland sun and mountain wind into something that resembled the weathered bark of a ceiba tree. His eyes, dark as obsidian and twice as sharp, moved from Elena to Diego to Father Tomás with the unhurried patience of someone who had spent a lifetime watching and waiting.

Elena's hand moved instinctively toward the small of her back, where her Glock rested in its concealed holster. Diego caught the movement and shook his head slightly—a warning. Whatever this old man was, he was not an immediate threat.

"How do you know my name?" Elena asked.

"I know many things." Santiago stepped further into the light, and Elena saw that despite his age, he moved with a fluid grace that belied his years. "I know that Martin Thorne spent thirty years searching for the secret hidden in the Ximénez manuscript. I know that he found it three nights ago, and that he died for what he discovered. I know that you carry his photographs on your phone and that you have come here seeking the second fragment of the Codex of Seven Serpents."

Father Tomás crossed himself, his face pale. "Santiago, how—"

"Peace, young one." The old man's smile was gentle but sad. "I have known your family for three generations. I knew your grandfather when he was a boy, running through these very streets. Did you think I would not know what happens in my own church?"

"Your church?" Diego's voice was sharp. "The Church belongs to—"

"The Church belongs to Rome, yes. But this place—this sacred ground—belonged to my people long before the Spanish came. Long before the Christians built their altar over our temple." Santiago's eyes swept the sacristy, taking in the vestments and chalices and all the trappings of Catholic worship. "The friars thought they were conquering our gods when they raised these walls. They did not understand that gods cannot be conquered. They can only be hidden."

Elena forced herself to think clearly, to push past the strangeness of the moment and focus on what mattered. "You said you've been waiting for me. Why? How did you know I would come?"

"Because it was written." Santiago reached into his simple cotton shirt and produced a folded piece of paper—old, yellowed, covered in handwriting that Elena recognised even from across the room. "Martin Thorne and I corresponded for seven years. He never knew my true name, never knew my role, but he understood that I possessed knowledge he needed. I guided him toward the hidden text in the Ximénez manuscript. I told him where to look, what tools to use. And I told him that when the time came, he should send what he found to you."

"Martin never mentioned—"

"Martin understood the importance of secrecy. He knew that if he spoke openly about our correspondence, if he revealed the existence of the Guardians to anyone, he would put both himself and me in danger." Santiago's expression darkened. "I warned him that others were searching for the same knowledge. I told him to be careful. But Martin was a scholar, not a warrior. He did not truly understand what men like Kroeger are capable of."

The name hung in the air like a curse.

"You know about Kroeger," Elena said.

"I know that he has been hunting the codex for sixty years. I know that he murdered your mentor and that he has sent men to follow you here." Santiago's obsidian eyes locked onto hers. "I know that three of them are in the plaza right now, watching this church, waiting to see what you find. And I know that if they take the fragment, everything my family has protected for twenty generations will fall into the hands of a man who wishes to use it for evil."

Diego moved to the small window that overlooked the plaza, peering through the grimy glass. "He's right. The German tourist is still there, near the textile stalls. And I can see two more—one in the restaurant balcony, one in a white Land Cruiser near the municipal building."

"They will not enter the church," Santiago said. "Not yet. They are watchers, not warriors. Their orders are to observe, to follow, to report. The killing comes later, when they have what they need."

"Then we should leave," Father Tomás said, his voice tight with fear. "We should go to the police, tell them—"

"The police cannot help us." Santiago's voice was flat, final. "The men outside have money, connections, resources that the local authorities cannot match. If we involve the police, we will only delay the inevitable—and we will reveal to Kroeger exactly how much we know." He turned to Elena. "There is only one path forward. We must retrieve the fragment before they understand what we are doing. And then we must disappear."

"Retrieve it how?" Elena asked. "Diego said the entrance is beneath the altar, but we don't know how to open it."

Santiago's weathered hand rose to touch the jade pendant at his throat. "This is the key. It has been passed down through my family since the time of Ximénez himself. My ancestor, Ik'anil, entrusted it to the first Guardian of this church—a K'iche' priest who converted to Christianity but never abandoned the old ways. For five hundred years, we have kept it safe, waiting for the one who would be worthy to use it."

"And you think I'm worthy?"

"I think Martin Thorne believed you were worthy. And I trust his judgment more than I trust my own." Santiago lifted the pendant over his head and held it out to Elena. "Take it. The entrance is behind the main altar, hidden in the floor. The pendant fits into a depression shaped like the serpent. Turn it three times to the left, once to the right, and the way will open."

Elena hesitated. The jade felt cool against her palm when she finally accepted it, but there was something else—a faint vibration, like the echo of a distant heartbeat that seemed to pulse through the stone.

"What will I find down there?"

"The second fragment of the codex, and something else. Something that Ximénez left behind when he divided the formula." Santiago's voice dropped to barely a whisper. "His journal. It's everything he learned about the codex, the Guardians, the hiding places. Martin searched for that journal his entire life. Now you will find it."

"And what about you? What will you do while we're down there?"

Santiago smiled—a sad, knowing expression that made Elena's heart clench with sudden foreboding. "I will do what Guardians have always done. I will protect the secret with my life."

"Santiago—"

"I am eighty-three years old, Elena Vasquez. I have been waiting for this moment since I was a young man, since my father placed this pendant around my neck and told me the stories of our ancestors. I have lived a good life. I have seen my children grow and my grandchildren flourish. I have kept the faith that was entrusted to me." His obsidian eyes were calm, accepting. "If today is the day I join my ancestors, then I will go gladly, knowing that the secret passes to worthy hands."

"I won't let you sacrifice yourself for—"

"You will do what must be done." Santiago's voice hardened, and for a moment Elena glimpsed the steel beneath the gentle exterior. "The fragment is more important than any single life—mine, yours, anyone's. If Kroeger's men take it, they will have the key to finding the other pieces. They will reassemble the formula. And they will use it to reshape the world in their own image." He gripped her shoulders with surprising strength. "This is not a request, Dr. Vasquez. This is the duty that Martin passed to you when he sent those photographs. You are a Guardian now, whether you wished for it or not. Act like one."

Elena stared at the old man, seeing in his weathered face the echoes of all the Guardians who had come before—the priests and farmers and warriors who had kept this secret through five centuries of conquest and oppression, who had passed it from generation to generation like a sacred flame. She thought of Martin, dying alone in a library, trusting her to continue his work. She thought of her grandmother, whispering stories of hidden knowledge in the firelight of a highland village.

"How long will it take?" she asked quietly. "To retrieve the fragment?"

"Ten minutes. Perhaps fifteen. The chamber is small, and the path is straightforward." Santiago released her shoulders and stepped back. "But you must move quickly. The men outside will notice if you are gone too long. And once they realise what you have found..."

He didn't need to finish the sentence.

"Diego," Elena said. "You're with me. Father Tomás, stay here and watch the door. If anyone comes—"

"I will delay them as long as I can." The young priest's voice was steadier now, though his hands still trembled. "Go. Find what Martin died for."

Santiago led them through a door at the back of the sacristy, into a narrow corridor that smelled of dust and centuries. They emerged behind the main altar, hidden from the congregation by a heavy curtain of embroidered velvet. The altar itself loomed above them—a baroque masterpiece of gilt and paint, covered with images of saints and angels that seemed to watch their every move.

"There." Santiago pointed to a stone in the floor, worn smooth by generations of priests' feet. At its centre, barely visible in the dim light, was a depression shaped like a serpent swallowing its own tail. "The entrance. Once you are below, follow the passage until you reach the chamber. The fragment and the journal will be on a pedestal at the centre. Take them both and return the same way you came."

Elena knelt and fitted the jade pendant into the depression. It slid into place with a soft click, as if it had been waiting for this moment.

"Three times left," Santiago said. "Once right."

She turned the pendant, feeling ancient mechanisms grinding to life beneath the stone. One turn. Two. Three. Then right.

For a moment, nothing happened.

Then the stone beneath her began to sink, revealing a narrow stairway descending into darkness.

"Go," Santiago said. "I will watch the entrance. When you return, we will—"

He was interrupted by a sound from the front of the church—raised voices, a crash, the unmistakable report of a gunshot.

Santiago's expression didn't change. "They're moving faster than I expected. Go. Now."

"Santiago—"

"GO!"

Elena grabbed Diego's arm and pulled him toward the stairway. Behind her, she heard Santiago's footsteps moving toward the curtain, toward the sounds of chaos erupting in the nave.

Then she was descending into darkness, and the stone was sliding closed above her head, and the last thing she heard was the old man's voice raised in prayer—not to the Christian God, but to older powers, in a language that had been spoken in these highlands for three thousand years.

8

The Chamber

Beneath Santo Tomás Church — Moments Later

The stairway descended into absolute darkness.

Elena pulled a small flashlight from her jacket pocket—she had learned long ago never to enter an archaeological site without one—and clicked it on. The beam revealed ancient stonework, walls carved from the living rock of the mountain, covered in glyphs that seemed to writhe and shift in the uncertain light.

"Maya," Diego breathed from behind her. "Classic period, maybe earlier. This temple must predate the Spanish conquest by centuries."

"Keep moving." Elena's voice was tight, her mind still echoing with the sound of that gunshot from above. Santiago was up there, facing God knew what, and she was descending into the earth like a coward. But he was right. The fragment was more important than any single life. She had to believe that, or everything Martin had died for would be meaningless.

The stairway was steep and narrow, carved for people smaller than modern humans, and Elena had to duck her head to avoid scraping it on the low ceiling. The air grew cooler as they descended, taking on the damp, mineral smell of deep caves. Water trickled somewhere in the darkness, a sound that might have been soothing under other circumstances but now seemed ominous, threatening.

She counted fifty-three steps before the stairway finally levelled out into a horizontal passage. The walls here were smoother, the glyphs more elaborate, scenes of gods and heroes, creation and destruction, knowledge being passed from divine beings to mortal hands. Elena recognised imagery from her studies: the Hero Twins, the Lords of Xibalba, the great world tree that connected earth and sky.

But there were other images too. Images that didn't belong to any Maya tradition she knew.

"Diego, look at this." She stopped before a section of wall where the carving style changed abruptly. The figures here were different—taller, more angular, dressed in garments that suggested a different culture entirely. They stood before what appeared to be a furnace or crucible, performing operations on materials that flowed like liquid fire.

"That's not Maya," Diego said slowly. "I've never seen anything like it."

"I have. In Colombia. In the goldwork of the Muisca." Elena's flashlight trembled slightly in her hand. "This temple... it's a meeting place. A site where different cultures came together to share knowledge."

"That's impossible. The Maya and the Muisca never—"

"Never officially, no. Never in any record that survived the conquest." Elena moved her light across the wall, revealing more hybrid imagery—Maya gods standing alongside figures that could only be Muisca, South American vegetation growing alongside Central American flora, symbols from both cultures intertwined in ways that suggested not mere contact but deep collaboration. "But what if there were connections we don't know about? Secret connections, maintained by people who understood that some knowledge was too valuable, too dangerous, to be shared openly?"

"The Guardians."

"Yes." Elena resumed walking, faster now, driven by a hunger to understand that temporarily overshadowed her fear. "Santiago said his family has been protecting this secret for twenty generations. That's five hundred years, minimum. But the traditions could go back much further. The Guardian network could predate the Spanish by centuries—maybe millennia."

The passage widened ahead, opening into a chamber that made Elena stop in her tracks.

It was perhaps thirty feet across, circular, with a domed ceiling that rose into darkness beyond the reach of her flashlight. The walls were covered floor to ceiling with murals—paintings so vivid, so perfectly preserved, that they seemed to glow with their own inner light. And at the center of the chamber, on a pedestal of carved stone, sat two objects that made Elena's breath catch in her throat.

A book, bound in leather that had somehow survived centuries of underground storage.

And a crystal case containing what appeared to be pages of bark paper, covered in glyphs that mixed Maya and Muisca symbols in impossible combinations.

The second fragment of the Codex of Seven Serpents.

"Mother of God," Diego whispered.

Elena approached the pedestal slowly, reverently, as if she were entering the presence of something holy. The murals surrounding her told a story she was only beginning to understand—a story of ancient peoples discovering secrets that defied the laws of nature, of civilisations rising and falling while the knowledge was passed from guardian to guardian, of men and women dedicating their lives to protecting a truth that could transform or destroy the world.

She reached for the leather-bound book first. It was heavy in her hands, its pages yellowed but intact, filled with handwriting she recognised from her studies of colonial documents. The language was Spanish, the script the careful, educated hand of a Franciscan friar.

The journal of Fray Tomás de Ávila. The man who had divided the codex and hidden its fragments across the Americas.

She opened to a random page and began to read:

March 15, 1698

I have been studying the formula for nearly forty years now, and I believe I finally understand what the ancients discovered. It is not magic, as I once feared. It is not demonic power, as the Inquisition would certainly claim. It is science, seemingly so advanced that it appears supernatural to those who do not comprehend its principles.

The process requires seven elements, combined in seven specific procedures, over the course of seven days. The elements are common enough; lead, mercury, sulphur, salt and three others that I have not yet been able to identify with certainty. But the procedures are extraordinarily precise, requiring temperatures and pressures that can only be achieved through methods the ancients developed over generations of experimentation.

I have evaluated the process in small ways, using fragments of the formula I was able to piece together from Ik'anil's teachings. The results are... remarkable. A nugget of lead, no larger than my thumbnail, transformed into gold of the purest quality. It took six days, though I must admit I nearly died twice from toxic fumes, though it worked. The formula is real, and that is precisely why it must remain hidden.

Elena's hands were shaking so badly she could barely turn the pages. She flipped forward, scanning entries that chronicled decades of study, of moral wrestling, of decisions that would shape the fate of the world.

June 3, 1702

I have made my final decision. The formula will not be destroyed. I simply cannot bring myself to erase this amazing knowledge that took millennia to develop, but it will be hidden so thoroughly that only the most determined and worthy scholars seeking it may ever find it.

I am dividing the codex into multiple fragments, each containing part of the formula but useless without the others.

One fragment will remain here, in Guatemala, hidden beneath the church where I have spent the happiest years of my life. One will go to Colombia, to the descendants of the Muisca who first shared this knowledge with my Maya brothers. One will travel to Peru, to the guardians who maintain similar secrets in the mountains of the Inca. And one—the key that makes the others comprehensible—will be hidden in the Popol Vuh itself, encoded in a cipher that only a true scholar will be able to decipher.

I have entrusted each fragment to a Guardian, bound by oaths older than Christianity; they will protect it with their lives and pass the duty on to their descendants. If the world ever becomes ready for this knowledge, if humanity ever develops the wisdom to use it without destroying itself, the Guardians will recognize the worthy seeker and reveal what they protect.

Until then, the secret will sleep.

El Dorado was never a city of gold. It was a city that made gold. It must remain hidden until we have learned to be better than we presently are.

Elena closed the journal and pressed it against her chest, feeling the weight of centuries pressing down upon her. This was what Martin had been searching for. This was what he had died for. The proof that El Dorado was real, where an ancient people discovered the secrets of transmutation and then ultimately decided to deliberately hide it from the world.

"Elena." Diego's voice was urgent, cutting through her reverie. "We need to move. Those sounds from above—"

As if in response, a distant rumble reached them through the stone—the unmistakable report of gunfire, muffled by tons of rock but audible, nonetheless.

Santiago.

Elena grabbed the crystal case containing the codex fragment, tucking it carefully into her jacket alongside the journal. The objects felt impossibly heavy, weighted with the burden of knowledge they contained.

"Let's go."

They ran back through the passage, their flashlights bobbing wildly as they navigated the ancient corridor. The glyphs on the walls seemed to watch them pass, the carved figures of gods and guardians bearing witness to this moment in an endless chain of moments stretching back through millennia.

The stairway was harder going up than coming down. Elena's lungs burned and her legs ached as she climbed, but she didn't slow. The sounds from above were growing louder—shouts, crashes, the sharp crack of pistol fire interspersed with the deeper boom of something larger.

She reached the top of the stairs and found the stone still closed above her. For a terrible moment, she feared they were trapped—that Kroeger's men had found the entrance and sealed them in. But then she saw the jade pendant, still fitted into its depression on the underside of the stone, and remembered Santiago's instructions.

Three turns left. One turn right.

The stone ground upward, revealing the dim light of the church above.

Elena emerged into chaos.

The curtain behind the altar had been torn down, revealing the hidden entrance to anyone who cared to look. Candles had been knocked over, their flames spreading across the wooden pews in a dozen small fires that filled the nave with smoke. Somewhere in the haze, she could hear screaming—the terrified cries of worshippers who had been caught in the crossfire of a battle they didn't understand.

And near the main entrance, she saw Santiago.

The old man stood with his back against the massive wooden doors, facing three figures who advanced through the smoke with weapons raised. He held something in his hands—a staff, it looked like, carved from ancient wood and tipped with a blade of obsidian—and even as Elena watched, he moved.

For a man of eighty-three, it was impossible. He flowed like water, like shadow, dodging a gunshot that should have taken him in the chest and striking back with the obsidian blade in a single fluid motion. One of the attackers—the blond man Elena had seen photographing the market—stumbled backward, clutching a wound in his shoulder that sprayed blood across the flagstones.

But there were three of them, and Santiago was old, and even the greatest warrior cannot fight forever.

"SANTIAGO!" Elena screamed.

The old man's head turned toward her voice, and in that moment of distraction, one of the other attackers fired.

The bullet took Santiago in the chest. He staggered, his obsidian staff clattering to the floor, but he did not fall. Instead, he turned back to face his killers, and Elena saw him smile—a peaceful, accepting expression that made her heart shatter.

"Run," he said. His voice was quiet, but somehow it carried across the chaos of the burning church. "Run, and do not look back. The Guardians will find you when you need them."

"I can't—"

"You MUST." Blood bubbled at the corner of his mouth, but his eyes were clear, burning with a fierce light that seemed to come from somewhere beyond the mortal world. "This is my purpose, Elena Vasquez. This is what I was born for. Let me fulfill it."

He turned back to face the attackers, spreading his arms wide as if to embrace them—or to block their path with his own body.

Diego grabbed Elena's arm. "We have to go. Now. The back entrance—"

"I can't leave him—"

"He's giving us a chance. Don't waste it."

Another gunshot. Santiago jerked but still did not fall. The attackers were advancing, their weapons raised, their faces masks of cold determination.

Elena let Diego pull her away.

They ran through the sacristy, past Father Tomás who was huddled behind the desk with blood streaming from a cut on his forehead, through a door that led to a narrow alley behind the church. The smoke followed them, carrying the smell of burning wood and incense and something else—the copper tang of blood, the bitter reek of gunpowder.

Behind them, a single shot echoed through the church.

Then silence.

9

The Pursuit

Mountain Roads, Chichicastenango — Late Afternoon

The road out of Chichicastenango wound through the highlands like a serpent, coiling back on itself as it descended toward the valleys below. Diego drove with the focused intensity of a man who knew these mountains intimately—who had spent years navigating roads that were little more than suggestions carved into the steep terrain. The Land Cruiser's engine roared as they climbed a ridge, then dropped into a lower gear as the road plunged downward again.

Elena sat in the passenger seat, the journal open in her lap, the crystal case containing the codex fragment wedged securely between her feet. Her hands were still trembling, aftershocks of adrenaline and grief that she couldn't quite suppress. Every time she closed her eyes, she saw Santiago's face in that final moment. The peace in his expression. The acceptance.

This is my purpose, he had said. *This is what I was born for.*

She wondered if she would ever find that kind of certainty. That kind of faith.

"We're being followed," Diego said quietly.

Elena's head snapped up. She twisted in her seat, peering through the rear window at the road behind them. For a moment, she saw nothing but dust and distant mountains. Then, perhaps half a mile back, a glint of sunlight on metal.

A white Land Cruiser. The same vehicle she had seen parked near the municipal building in Chichicastenango.

"How long?"

"Since we left town. They're keeping their distance, but they're not trying to hide." Diego's jaw tightened. "They know we can't outrun them on these roads. They're waiting for the right moment."

"What moment?"

"Somewhere isolated. Somewhere without witnesses." He glanced at her, his dark eyes hard. "These men are professionals, Elena. They won't make a move until they're certain of success."

Elena looked down at the journal in her lap, at the crystal case between her feet. Everything Santiago had died for. Everything Martin had died for. If Kroeger's men took these artifacts, all of that sacrifice would be meaningless.

"Can we lose them?"

"Maybe. There's a turnoff about three kilometres ahead—a back road that leads through the coffee plantations toward Antigua. It's rough, barely maintained, but I've driven it before. If we can get enough distance, we might be able to disappear before they realize where we've gone."

"Do it."

Diego nodded and pressed the accelerator. The Land Cruiser surged forward, its engine growling as they climbed another ridge. The road here was narrow, barely wide enough for two vehicles to pass, with a sheer drop on one side that plunged hundreds of feet to the valley floor below. Elena gripped the door handle and tried not to look down.

Behind them, the white vehicle accelerated to match their speed.

"They're closing," Elena said.

"I see them." Diego's hands were steady on the wheel, his movements precise and controlled. "The turnoff is just ahead. When I make the turn, hold on—it's going to be rough."

The road curved sharply to the left, following the contour of the mountain. As they rounded the bend, Elena saw a break in the vegetation on the right side—a gap barely wide enough for the Land Cruiser, overgrown with vines and marked by a weathered wooden sign that had long since become illegible.

Diego didn't slow down. He wrenched the wheel to the right, and suddenly they were airborne, the Land Cruiser launching off the main road and crashing through the undergrowth onto a track that was more suggestion than surface. Branches scraped against the windows like clawing fingers. The suspension groaned as they bounced over rocks and ruts that threatened to tear the wheels from the axles.

"Jesus Christ," Elena gasped, bracing herself against the dashboard.

"Welcome to Guatemalan back roads." Diego's voice was tight but controlled. "Keep your eyes on the mirror. Tell me if they follow."

Elena twisted again, peering through the dust cloud that billowed behind them. For a long moment, she saw nothing—just the swirling brown haze and the dark shapes of trees flashing past.

Then a white shape emerged from the dust.

"They're coming."

"Damn." Diego pushed the accelerator harder, coaxing every ounce of power from the straining engine. "There's a fork about a kilometre ahead. Left goes deeper into the plantations—it's a dead end, but they won't know that. Right continues toward Antigua. I'm going to slow down just before the fork, make it look like I'm going left, then cut right at the last second. With luck, they'll take the bait."

"And if they don't?"

Diego reached beneath his seat and pulled out a Glock identical to the one Elena carried. "Then we do this the hard way."

The plantation road was a nightmare of mud and rocks and vegetation that seemed determined to reclaim every inch of cleared ground. The Land Cruiser bucked and lurched, its tires spinning for traction on surfaces that alternated between slick clay and loose gravel. Behind them, the white vehicle was gaining—its driver clearly as skilled as Diego, pushing through conditions that would have stopped a lesser operator.

The fork appeared ahead, marked by a massive ceiba tree whose branches spread across the road like a canopy. Diego eased off the accelerator, letting the Land Cruiser slow just enough to suggest hesitation. He turned the wheel left, pointing the nose toward the plantation road—

Then wrenched it right, cutting across the intersection in a spray of mud and gravel that sent them skidding toward the edge of a drainage ditch.

For a terrible moment, Elena was certain they were going over. The Land Cruiser tilted, its right wheels lifting off the ground, the world outside the windows rotating sickeningly. She heard Diego curse in K'iche', felt the vehicle hanging in the balance between salvation and disaster.

Then the tires caught. The Land Cruiser slammed back onto all four wheels and surged forward, leaving the intersection behind.

Elena looked back. The white vehicle had taken the bait—its driver, unable to match Diego's last-second manoeuvre, had committed to the left fork and was now disappearing into the plantation, following a road that would be dead-end in a coffee processing facility three kilometres ahead.

"It worked," she breathed.

"Don't celebrate yet." Diego's knuckles were white on the steering wheel. "They'll figure out the mistake soon enough. We need to reach the safe house before they can pick up our trail again."

They drove in tense silence for the next hour, following roads that grew progressively better as they descended from the highlands toward the colonial city of Antigua. The landscape changed around them—from pine forests and mountain villages to coffee plantations and sugarcane fields, from the cool air of the altiplano to the humid warmth of the lower elevations. Elena watched the passing scenery without really seeing it, her mind churning through everything that had happened.

Santiago was dead. The old Guardian who had waited eighty-three years for this moment, who had sacrificed himself so that she could escape with the fragment. She thought of his obsidian eyes, his weathered face, the way he had moved with impossible grace when he faced his killers. He had been a warrior to the end, fighting for something he believed in with every fibre of his being.

And now she carried his burden.

She opened the journal again, turning to a section she had not yet read:

> *August 22, 1695*
>
> *The Guardian network is more extensive than I had imagined. Ik'anil spoke of it only in general terms, but in the years since his death, I have made contact with others who share the sacred duty. There are Guardians among the K'iche' of Guatemala, the Muisca of Colombia, the Quechua of Peru. There are Guardians in places I had not expected—among the Aztec descendants of Mexico, the Maya of the Yucatán, even scattered communities in the Caribbean where the old knowledge somehow survived the genocide of the conquest.*
>
> *They do not all know each other. The network was designed to be decentralized, compartmentalized, so that the capture or betrayal of one Guardian could not compromise the others. Each cell knows only its own piece of the puzzle, its own fragment of the secret. Only a few—the Keepers, they call themselves—understand the full scope of what we protect.*

I have become one of those Keepers. Not by choice, but by circumstance. Ik'anil's death left a void that someone had to fill, and the other Guardians recognized in me the same qualities that he had seen.

I am the only European in the network, the only outsider, but they have accepted me as a brother. We are bound not by blood or culture, but by purpose.

The purpose of protecting a secret that could change the world.

Elena closed the journal, her mind racing. A network of Guardians, spanning continents, preserving knowledge for centuries. It seemed impossible—the kind of conspiracy theory that serious academics dismissed with contempt. But she held the proof in her hands. The journal, the codex fragment, the hidden chamber beneath Santo Tomás church.

It was all real. All of it.

"You're very quiet," Diego said.

"I'm trying to understand what we've gotten into." Elena looked at him. "You knew about the Guardians, didn't you? Before today."

Diego was silent for a moment. Then: "My grandmother was one of them. She never told me directly—the secret is not shared with those who are not ready—but I understood enough. The stories she told, the rituals she performed, the way she spoke of the ancestors and their wisdom. It was not just folklore to her. It was a living tradition, a sacred duty."

"Why didn't you tell me?"

"Because I wasn't sure you would believe me. And because..." He hesitated. "Because knowing the truth makes you a target. The fewer people who know, the safer everyone is."

Elena thought about Martin, strangled in a library. Santiago, shot in a church. The centuries of Guardians who had died protecting this secret, passing it on to the next generation with their final breaths.

"I think I'm already a target," she said.

"Yes." Diego's voice was heavy. "You are. We all are now."

They drove on in silence as the sun began to set behind the mountains, painting the sky in shades of orange and crimson that reminded Elena, uncomfortably, of fire.

* * *

The safe house was not what Elena had expected.

She had imagined something modest—a farmhouse, perhaps, or a secluded cabin in the hills outside Antigua. Instead, Diego turned off the main road onto a private drive that wound through manicured grounds for nearly a kilometre before arriving at a compound that could only be described as a fortress.

High walls topped with security cameras surrounded a sprawling estate that blended colonial architecture with modern defensive features. Guards patrolled the perimeter, their weapons visible, their movements professional. The main house was a two-story structure of whitewashed adobe and red tile, beautiful in the traditional Guatemalan style, but Elena noticed the reinforced windows, the steel doors, the subtle bulges in the walls that suggested armour plating.

"Méndez-Castellón doesn't do anything halfway," she murmured.

"He's spent thirty years making enemies," Diego replied. "He's learned to be careful."

They were met at the entrance by a security team that checked their credentials, searched the vehicle, and escorted them through multiple checkpoints before finally admitting them to the main house. The interior was as lavish as the exterior suggested—antique furniture, pre-Columbian artifacts in climate-controlled cases, paintings that Elena recognized from museum catalogues as pieces that had disappeared from public collections years ago.

Méndez-Castellón was waiting for them in a study that overlooked a courtyard garden filled with orchids and hummingbirds. He rose as they entered, his expression shifting from concern to relief when he saw what Elena carried.

"You found it," he said. "Thank God."

"Santiago found it." Elena's voice was harder than she intended. "Santiago died for it."

Something flickered across Méndez-Castellón's face—grief, perhaps, or guilt. "I know. My people in Chichicastenango reported what happened. The church is badly damaged. The police are investigating. And Kroeger's men have disappeared."

"They followed us out of town. We lost them in the plantations, but they'll find their way here eventually."

"Let them come." Méndez-Castellón's jaw tightened. "This compound can withstand a small army. They won't get within a hundred meters of the house."

Elena wanted to believe him. But she had seen what Kroeger's men were capable of—the cold efficiency with which they had attacked the church, the professional coordination of their pursuit. These were not common criminals or hired thugs. These were operators, trained in the arts of violence and infiltration.

"We need to keep moving," she said. "The longer we stay in one place, the more time they have to plan their next move."

"I agree. But first, we need to understand what you've found." Méndez-Castellón gestured to a table where a laptop, magnifying glasses, and other research tools had been arranged. "The fragment, the journal—they may contain information that will help us find the remaining pieces. We need to study them before we proceed."

Elena hesitated, then nodded. He was right. They had the key and the second fragment now, but there were still two more pieces scattered across South America. Without understanding what they were looking for, they would be searching blindly.

She placed the crystal case on the table and carefully removed the codex fragment. The bark paper was incredibly well-preserved; its surface covered in glyphs that seemed to shift and change as the light caught them at different angles. Maya symbols intertwined with Muisca iconography, and beneath both, she glimpsed traces of something older—a notation system that predated either culture.

"It's beautiful," Méndez-Castellón breathed. "In thirty years of searching, I've never seen anything like it."

"It's a piece of the formula," Elena said. "According to the journal, each fragment contains part of the transmutation process. This one probably describes some of the elements or procedures required. But without the other pieces, it's incomplete—a recipe with missing ingredients."

Diego had moved to the laptop and was photographing the fragment from multiple angles. "I can run these glyphs through translation software, see if anything matches our databases. But the older symbols—the ones that aren't Maya or Muisca—those are going to be harder."

"The journal might help." Elena opened the leather-bound book to the section where Fray Tomás had recorded his analysis of the codex. "He spent forty years studying the formula. He must have made notes about the symbols, the procedures, the scientific principles involved."

They worked through the night, cross-referencing the journal entries with the glyphs on the fragment, building a picture of what the ancients had discovered. It was slow, painstaking work—the kind of detailed analysis that Elena had spent her career performing—but gradually, a pattern began to emerge.

The formula required seven elements, seven procedures, and seven days. The elements were mostly identifiable—lead, mercury, sulphur, salt, and three others that Fray Tomás had not been able to name but which modern chemistry might recognize. The procedures were more complex, involving precise temperatures, specific durations, and combinations that suggested an understanding of molecular transformation that should have been impossible for pre-industrial civilizations.

And woven through everything was a philosophy—a worldview that saw matter not as fixed and immutable, but as fluid, changeable, responsive to the will of those who understood its true nature.

"They weren't just making gold," Elena said slowly, as dawn began to lighten the sky outside the windows. "They were proving something about the nature of reality itself. That transformation is possible. That what seems permanent can be changed."

"That's a dangerous idea," Méndez-Castellón said. "Dangerous to the powerful, anyway. If anyone can make gold, then gold loses its value. If matter can be transformed, then the hierarchies built on controlling resources become meaningless."

"That's why they hid it." Elena looked at the fragment, at the centuries of accumulated wisdom encoded in its glyphs. "They understood that this knowledge would be used as a weapon if it fell into the wrong hands. So they scattered it, protected it, waited for a time when humanity might be ready."

"And are we ready now?"

Elena thought about Kroeger, hunting for the codex to prove his theories of racial superiority. She thought about the billionaires and governments who would weaponize transmutation if they controlled it. She thought about a world already tearing itself apart over oil and minerals and the concentrated wealth that flowed from them.

"No," she said. "I don't think we are."

"Then what do we do?"

Elena was quiet for a long moment. Then she closed the journal and looked at Méndez-Castellón with eyes that had hardened with resolve.

"We find the remaining fragments before Kroeger does. We assemble the complete formula. And then we make a decision about what to do with it—a decision that should be made by the Guardians, not by treasure hunters or billionaires or anyone else who might use it for their own purposes."

"And if the Guardians decide to destroy it?"

"Then we destroy it. Some knowledge might be better lost."

Méndez-Castellón studied her for a long moment, his expression unreadable. Then, slowly, he nodded.

"Colombia," he said. "The third fragment. Do you know where to look?"

Elena turned to a page in the journal she had marked earlier:

> *The Muisca fragment is hidden near the sacred lake of Guatavita, where the ceremony that inspired the legend of El Dorado was once performed.*
>
> *The Guardian there is a descendant of the priests who witnessed the last golden raft, the last offering to the gods of the water. He will know the true location, but he will not reveal it to anyone who has not proven themselves worthy.*

"Guatavita," she said. "That's where we start."

10

Road to Colombia

Méndez-Castellón's Estate, Antigua — The Next Morning

The sun rose over the mountains of Guatemala in a blaze of gold and crimson, but Elena had not slept.

She stood on the balcony of her guest room, watching the light transform the landscape below—the coffee plantations, the distant volcanoes, the colonial spires of Antigua gleaming in the early morning haze. In her hands, she held the jade pendant that Santiago had given her, turning it over and over, feeling the weight of the responsibility it represented.

You are a Guardian now, the old man had said. *Whether you wished for it or not.*

She had never asked for this. She had spent her career in the quiet world of academic archaeology, studying the past from the safe distance of libraries and museums. She had written papers and taught classes and attended conferences where the most dangerous thing was a cutting peer review. She had believed, in her naive way, that knowledge was its own reward—that understanding the past was valuable for its own sake, without practical consequences.

Now she understood how wrong she had been.

Knowledge was power. It had always been power. The people who controlled what was known controlled what was possible. And some knowledge was so powerful that men would kill for it—had killed for it, were killing for it still.

A knock at the door pulled her from her thoughts. She tucked the pendant inside her shirt and crossed to answer it.

Diego stood in the hallway, holding two cups of coffee. He looked as tired as she felt—dark circles under his eyes, a day's worth of stubble on his jaw—but there was an alertness to his expression that suggested the exhaustion was purely physical.

"Méndez-Castellón wants to see us," he said, handing her one of the cups. "He's arranged transportation to Colombia. We leave in two hours."

Elena took the coffee gratefully, letting its warmth seep into her hands. "What kind of transportation?"

"Private jet to Bogotá, then a helicopter to a staging area near Guatavita. He has contacts in the Colombian government who can smooth our way past customs and security." Diego paused. "He also has news about Kroeger's men."

Elena's stomach tightened. "What news?"

"They've regrouped. Three of them flew out of Guatemala City last night on a charter flight—destination unknown, but the flight plan filed was for Cartagena. They're heading to Colombia too."

"Then they know about the Muisca fragment."

"It seems likely. Either they found information we missed, or..." Diego's expression darkened. "Or they have other sources. Other ways of learning what we know."

Elena thought about the journal, about the detailed descriptions of the Guardian network and the hiding places of the fragments. If Kroeger had access to similar information—if the Ahnenerbe archives contained records she didn't know about—then they might be walking into a trap.

"We need to be careful," she said. "We can't assume we're the only ones who know where to look."

"Agreed. Méndez-Castellón is arranging security—a team of his best people will accompany us. But in the end, it may come down to who gets there first."

They found Méndez-Castellón in the main dining room, presiding over a breakfast spread that seemed absurdly lavish given the circumstances. Fresh fruit, eggs prepared three different ways, breads and pastries still warm from the oven—the kind of meal that Elena associated with resort vacations, not desperate races to find ancient artifacts before murderous Nazi treasure hunters.

"Please, sit," Méndez-Castellón said, gesturing to the empty chairs across from him. "Eat. We have a long journey ahead, and you'll need your strength."

Elena sat, but she didn't touch the food. "Diego said you have news about Kroeger's men."

"I do. My intelligence network has been tracking their movements since the incident in Chichicastenango." Méndez-Castellón set down his coffee cup. "Three men flew to Cartagena last night—Hans Brecker, Kurt Weller, and Stefan Holtz. They are all former military, with experience in... unconventional operations. They were met at the airport by a fourth man; someone my people haven't been able to identify yet."

"Kroeger himself?"

"Possibly, or another operative we don't know about." Méndez-Castellón's expression was troubled.

"Kroeger has been building his organization for sixty years. We don't know how many people work for him, or what resources he has access to. We must assume he has capabilities that will surprise us."

Elena absorbed this information, trying to calculate the odds. Four men, maybe far more, against whatever security team Méndez-Castellón could provide. Professional killers against archaeologists and bodyguards. It wasn't a comforting equation.

"Tell me about Guatavita," she said. "What do we know about the hiding place?"

Méndez-Castellón reached into his jacket and produced a folder thick with photographs and documents.

"Lake Guatavita is about fifty kilometres northeast of Bogotá, in the Eastern Ranges of the Colombian Andes. It's a volcanic crater lake, almost perfectly circular, roughly two kilometres in diameter. The Muisca considered it sacred, the dwelling place of a goddess who demanded offerings of gold and precious objects."

Elena nodded. She knew the basic myth. "The El Dorado ceremony. The Muisca chief covered himself in gold dust and rowed to the centre of the lake on a raft, then dove in as an offering to the goddess. The Spanish heard about it and assumed there must be a city of gold somewhere nearby."

"Exactly. The Spanish tried to drain the lake multiple times, hoping to recover the gold that had been thrown in over centuries. They partially succeeded—the notch you can still see in the crater rim was cut by a colonial engineer in 1580, trying to lower the water level. But they never found the real treasure."

"Because there was no treasure. Not in the way they understood it."

"Precisely." Méndez-Castellón spread the photographs across the table. "According to the journal though, the Muisca did hide something near Guatavita—the third fragment of the Codex of Seven Serpents. The question is: where?"

Elena studied the photographs. Aerial shots of the lake, its dark waters reflecting the clouds above. Ground-level images of the surrounding terrain—steep hills covered in cloud forest, rocky outcroppings, ancient paths worn into the mountainside. Archaeological surveys showing the locations of pre-Columbian structures, most of them unexcavated.

"The journal says the Guardian is a descendant of the priests who performed the El Dorado ceremony," she said slowly. "If the tradition has been maintained, there should be a family somewhere near the lake who still knows the old ways. We need to find them."

"Easier said than done. The area around Guatavita has changed dramatically since colonial times. The original Muisca population was decimated by disease and forced labour. Their descendants scattered across the region, intermarrying with Spanish colonists and other indigenous groups. Identifying a continuous lineage of Guardians won't be simple."

"Then we start with what we know." Elena pulled a notebook from her bag and began making notes. "The journal mentions a sacred cave system near the lake—a place where the Muisca priests performed private rituals away from the public ceremonies. If the fragment is hidden anywhere, it's probably there."

"There are several cave systems in the area," Diego said, leaning over the photographs. "But most of them have been explored by archaeologists and tourists. If something was hidden there, it would have been found by now."

"Unless the entrance is concealed. Hidden the same way the entrance in Chichicastenango was hidden." Elena thought about the stone in the floor of Santo Tomás, the jade pendant that served as the key. "We need to look for places that don't appear on the surveys. Places that the Guardians have kept secret."

Méndez-Castellón nodded slowly. "I have a contact in Bogotá—an anthropologist who has spent decades studying Muisca culture. She might be able to point us in the right direction. I'll arrange a meeting for when we arrive."

"What about the Museo del Oro?" Elena asked. "The Gold Museum in Bogotá has the largest collection of Muisca artifacts in the world. There might be clues there—objects or inscriptions that point to the hiding place."

"An excellent thought. We can visit the museum after meeting with my contact." Méndez-Castellón began gathering the photographs. "But we should be cautious. If Kroeger's people are in

Colombia, they may be watching the obvious locations. We don't want to lead them directly to what we're looking for."

"Then we need a cover story. A reason to be in the area that doesn't involve treasure hunting." Elena thought for a moment. "I'm a legitimate archaeologist with credentials from the Smithsonian. I can claim to be researching Muisca gold-working techniques for an upcoming exhibition. It's plausible, and it gives me access to places that might otherwise be restricted."

"And if Kroeger's men recognize you?"

"Then we deal with that problem when it arises." Elena's voice was harder than she had expected. Something had changed in her since Chichicastenango—since watching Santiago die to protect her, since reading Fray Tomás's journal and understanding the weight of what she now carried. She was still afraid, but the fear had transformed into something else. Determination. Resolve.

She would find the remaining fragments. She would honour the sacrifice of those who had died to protect them. And she would make sure that Kroeger never got his hands on the complete formula.

Whatever it took.

***

The jet was a Gulfstream G650, the same aircraft that had brought Elena from Chicago to Guatemala two days ago. It felt like a lifetime had passed since then—since she had been a Smithsonian archaeologist with a quiet life and a murdered mentor, since the biggest danger she faced was academic politics and grant applications.

Now she was a Guardian, flying toward a confrontation with enemies who had already proved their willingness to kill.

Elena settled into her seat and opened the journal, returning to the sections about the Muisca fragment. Fray Tomás had been less detailed here than in his descriptions of the Guatemala hiding place—understandable, since he had entrusted the fragment to others rather than hiding it himself. But there were clues scattered through the entries, hints about what to look for.

The Muisca Guardian told me that the fragment is hidden in a place of transformation, she read. *Not the lake itself—that is too obvious, too vulnerable to those who seek to drain it and claim its treasures. Rather, a cave system nearby, where the priests performed the sacred rituals of metallurgy that gave rise to the legend of El Dorado.*

The Muisca were master goldsmiths, perhaps the finest in all the Americas. Their techniques—the lost-wax casting, the alloys of gold and copper they called tumbaga, the intricate filigree that decorated their sacred objects—all of this required knowledge passed down through generations of specialist priests. And some of that knowledge, my contact hints, came from the same source as the Codex of Seven Serpents.

The fragment is hidden where gold is born. That is all he would tell me. The Guardian in that place will recognize the worthy seeker and reveal the location when the time is right.

Where gold is born. Elena turned the phrase over in her mind. It could mean a mine, a smelting site, a workshop where raw metal was transformed into sacred objects. Or it could be something more metaphorical—a place associated with the mythology of gold's origins, the stories the Muisca told, about where the precious metal came from and why it was sacred.

She pulled out her phone and began searching through her files for information about Muisca mythology. The Muisca, like many cultures, had multiple creation stories, but one theme appeared consistently: the goddess Bachué, who emerged from the sacred lake with a child in her arms and populated the earth with her descendants. She was associated with water, fertility, and the gifts that came from beneath the earth—including gold.

But there was another figure in Muisca mythology who was more directly connected to metallurgy: Chibchacum, the god who supported the world on his shoulders and was punished by the supreme deity for trying to flood the earth. Some accounts described him as a patron of miners and metalworkers, a figure who understood the secrets of transformation that lay beneath the surface of things.

Where gold is born.

Elena felt a spark of intuition—the same instinct that had guided her through countless hours of research, helping her see connections that others missed.

"Diego," she said, leaning across the aisle. "Do you know anything about the Muisca god Chibchacum?"

Diego looked up from the satellite phone he had been using to coordinate with Méndez-Castellón's people on the ground. "A little. He's associated with earthquakes—the Muisca believed that when he shifted the world on his shoulders, the earth shook. Why?"

"The journal says the fragment is hidden 'where gold is born.' I've been assuming that means a metallurgical site—a forge or a workshop. But what if it's more specific than that? What if it refers to a place sacred to Chibchacum, a cave or temple associated with the god who understood the secrets of transformation?"

Diego's eyes widened slightly. "There are sites like that. Caves in the mountains around Guatavita that were used for rituals, some of them associated with Chibchacum. Most of them have been looted or excavated over the centuries, but..."

"But not all of them. Not the ones the Guardians kept secret."

"It's possible." Diego pulled out his own phone and began searching through his contacts. "I know an archaeologist at the Universidad Nacional in Bogotá—she's spent years mapping cave systems in the region. If anyone knows about undocumented sites, it's her."

"Is she trustworthy?"

"She's my sister."

Elena blinked. "You have a sister in Bogotá?"

"I have family all over Latin America. We K'iche' have been migrants for centuries—long before the borders were drawn." Diego smiled slightly. "Ana is a good person. She'll help us if she can."

"Then call her. Find out if there are any caves near Guatavita associated with Chibchacum that aren't on the official surveys." Elena looked out the window at the clouds below, the endless white expanse that separated them from the green mountains of Colombia. "If I'm right, that's where we'll find the third fragment."

The jet flew on, carrying them toward whatever awaited in the land of the Muisca.

Behind them, somewhere over the Caribbean, another aircraft followed the same route.

And in a hotel room in Cartagena, Werner Kroeger studied a map of the Colombian Andes, planning the next move in a game that had consumed his entire life.

The hunt continued.

11

City of Gold

Bogotá, Colombia — Two Days Later

Bogotá sprawled across a high plateau in the Andes like a living organism, eight million souls pressed against the mountains that rose on every side. From the air, Elena watched the city unfold beneath them—the gleaming towers of the financial district, the red-brick barrios that climbed the hillsides, the green ribbon of parks that wound through the urban density. It was a city of contradictions, she knew. Immense wealth alongside desperate poverty. Ancient traditions coexisting with cutting-edge modernity. A capital that had survived centuries of colonialism, civil war, and drug violence to become one of the most vibrant metropolises in South America.

And somewhere in the mountains beyond, hidden for five hundred years, lay the third fragment of the Codex of Seven Serpents.

The jet touched down at El Dorado International Airport—a name that made Elena smile grimly at the irony—and taxied to a private terminal where Méndez-Castellón's people were waiting. Three black SUVs with tinted windows, a security team of six men who looked like they had walked off the set of an action movie, and a woman in her forties with sharp eyes and silver-streaked hair who Diego embraced warmly.

"Ana," he said. "Thank you for coming."

"You said it was urgent. You said it was important." Ana Ixchel—Diego's sister, Elena realized—pulled back from the embrace and studied her brother with an expression that mixed affection with concern. "You also said it was dangerous. What have you gotten yourself into, hermano?"

"Something that started long before either of us was born." Diego gestured to Elena. "This is Dr. Elena Vasquez, from the Smithsonian. Elena, my sister Ana—Professor of Archaeology at the Universidad Nacional."

Ana shook Elena's hand with a firm grip. "Diego mentioned you on the phone. He said you're looking for caves near Guatavita that aren't on the official surveys."

"That's right. Caves that might be associated with Muisca metallurgical rituals. Specifically, sites connected to the god Chibchacum."

Ana's expression flickered surprise, then was quickly controlled. "That's a very specific request. Most archaeologists don't know enough about Muisca mythology to ask questions like that."

"I'm not most archaeologists."

"Clearly." Ana looked at Diego, then back at Elena, her eyes sharp with intelligence. "We should talk somewhere more private. There are things I can tell you that I wouldn't say in front of..." She glanced at Méndez-Castellón, who was directing his security team with quiet authority. "...others."

They drove into the city in a convoy, the SUVs weaving through traffic that seemed to operate on principles of chaos theory rather than traffic law. Elena sat in the back seat with Ana, while Diego rode up front with the driver. Through the tinted windows, she watched Bogotá scroll past—street vendors selling arepas and fresh juice, businessmen in suits talking on cell phones, students from the nearby universities laughing and arguing on the sidewalks.

"You're looking for something that most people don't believe exists," Ana said quietly, her voice pitched below the noise of the traffic. "Something my grandmother told me about when I was a little girl, something I spent years trying to prove was real before I finally gave up and focused on more... acceptable research."

Elena felt her pulse quicken. "Your grandmother was a Guardian."

Ana's eyes widened. "How do you know that word?"

"Because I've become one. Whether I wanted to or not." Elena reached into her bag and produced the jade pendant that Santiago had given her. "This belonged to Santiago Ajpop, the Guardian of Chichicastenango. He died three days ago, protecting me while I retrieved the second fragment of the Codex of Seven Serpents."

Ana stared at the pendant, her face pale. "The serpent that swallows itself. My grandmother had one just like it. She said it was a symbol of the eternal cycle—of knowledge that destroys and creates itself across the ages." She reached out, her fingers trembling slightly, and touched the jade. "She said that someday, someone would come who was worthy of what she protected. Someone who would understand."

"Did she tell you where the fragment is hidden?"

"No. She died before she could pass on the full knowledge. The location died with her—or so I thought." Ana's expression hardened with old grief, old frustration. "I spent a decade searching. I explored every cave system in the region, followed every lead in the historical records. But I never found it. Eventually, I convinced myself that the stories were just that—stories. Legends that had no basis in reality."

"They're real." Elena opened the journal of Fray Tomás and showed Ana the relevant pages. "This was written by the man who divided the codex and hid its fragments across the Americas. He describes the Muisca hiding place as a cave system near Guatavita, a place sacred to Chibchacum, where gold is born."

Ana read the pages slowly, her lips moving silently. When she finished, her eyes were bright with tears.

"All those years," she whispered. "I was so close. If I had just known where to look..."

"You couldn't have known. The Guardians kept their secrets for a reason." Elena touched Ana's hand gently. "But now we have the journal. We have clues that weren't available before. Will you help us?"

Ana was silent for a long moment. Then she nodded.

"There's a cave system about five kilometres from the lake," she said. "It's not on any of the official surveys—the entrance is hidden, accessible only through a narrow fissure in the rock that most people would walk right past. I found it years ago, during my initial surveys, but I couldn't explore it properly. The passages were too narrow, too deep. I always meant to go back with better equipment, but..." She shrugged. "Life happened. I moved on to other projects. I told myself the cave wasn't important."

"But you never forgot about it."

"No. I never forgot." Ana's jaw tightened with determination. "If the fragment is anywhere, it's there. I'll take you to it."

***

They stopped first at Ana's apartment—a comfortable space in a colonial building near the university, filled with books and artifacts and the detritus of an academic life devoted to understanding the past. While Diego and Méndez-Castellón coordinated logistics with the security team, Ana spread maps across her dining table and began briefing Elena on the terrain they would face.

"Guatavita is about an hour northeast of here, in the mountains above the Bogotá plateau," she explained, tracing the route with her finger. "The lake itself is a tourist attraction now—there's a paved road, a visitors' centre, guided tours that explain the El Dorado legend. But the surrounding area is still largely wild. Cloud forest, steep ravines, terrain that's difficult to navigate even with modern equipment."

"And the cave?"

"Here." Ana pointed to a spot on the map, perhaps five kilometres from the lake's shore. "The entrance is in a ravine that doesn't appear on most topographical maps. I only found it because I was surveying the area on foot, looking for rock art sites that might indicate Muisca ritual activity."

Elena studied the map, noting the contours, the elevation changes, the distance from the nearest roads. It would be a difficult hike—several hours through challenging terrain, with no guarantee of what they would find at the end.

"What about Kroeger's men?" she asked. "They're somewhere in Colombia. If they're watching the obvious approaches to Guatavita, they might spot us."

"We won't go through the tourist areas," Méndez-Castellón said, joining them at the table. "I have contacts in the local communities—farmers and guides who know paths through the mountains that outsiders would never find. We'll approach from the north, through the forest, and reach the cave without ever coming near the main roads."

"How long?"

"Six hours if we move quickly. Longer if the terrain is difficult." He paused. "We should leave at dawn tomorrow. That will give us the full day to reach the cave and explore it before we have to make camp."

Elena nodded, already calculating supplies and equipment. "We'll need lights, climbing gear, maybe rappelling equipment if the passages go deep. And weapons—if Kroeger's people find us, I want to be able to fight back."

"My team is already assembling everything we need." Méndez-Castellón's expression was grim. "But Elena... I should warn you. The mountains around Guatavita are not entirely safe. The FARC may have demobilized, but there are still armed groups operating in the region—drug traffickers, dissident guerrillas, criminal organizations that control the coca trade. If we encounter them..."

"Then we deal with that when it happens." Elena's voice was harder than she felt. "We've come too far to turn back now."

They spent the rest of the day preparing. Ana gathered her caving equipment—helmets, lights, ropes, carabiners—from a storage unit near the university. Diego coordinated with his contacts in Guatemala, checking for any sign that Kroeger's men had picked up their trail. Méndez-Castellón made phone calls in rapid Spanish, arranging transport, securing weapons, calling in favours from a network of connections that spanned the continent.

And Elena studied the journal, searching for any additional clues about what they would find in the cave.

She found one entry, buried among descriptions of Muisca ritual practices, that made her blood run cold:

> *October 3, 1697*
>
> *The Muisca Guardian has told me something that changes everything I thought I knew about the codex. The four fragments I have hidden are not the complete formula. They are only the first layer—the foundation upon which the true knowledge is built.*
>
> *According to his tradition, the ancients divided their discovery into seven parts, not four. The four fragments I possess contain the basic principles of transmutation—the elements, the procedures, the timing. But there are three additional components, hidden separately, that contain the keys to applying those principles safely.*
>
> *Without these keys, he says, any attempt to use the formula will fail. Or worse—it will succeed in ways that bring destruction rather than creation. The ancients learned this through bitter experience. Early experiments with the incomplete formula produced not gold, but poisonous compounds that killed those who created them. Only when all*

seven components are assembled can the process be performed without danger.

I asked him where the other three components are hidden. He said he did not know—that each Guardian cell protects only its own piece of the puzzle, and the complete picture is known only to the Keepers who maintain the entire network. But he gave me names. Places where I might find answers, if I had the courage to seek them.

The Amazon. The mountains of the Inca. The pyramids of the Aztec homeland.

Three more pieces. Three more journeys. Three more chances to fail—or to succeed in protecting knowledge that could transform the world.

Elena closed the journal, her mind reeling.

Seven components. Not four.

Everything she had assumed about the quest was wrong.

***

She found Méndez-Castellón on the balcony of Ana's apartment, staring out at the lights of Bogotá as night fell over the city. He turned when he heard her approach, his expression guarded.

"You've found something," he said. It wasn't a question.

"The journal mentions seven components, not four." Elena handed him the book, open to the relevant page. "The four fragments we've been chasing are only part of the formula. There are three additional pieces—keys, the Guardian called them—hidden in other locations. The Amazon. Peru. Mexico."

Méndez-Castellón read the entry slowly, his face unreadable. When he finished, he closed the journal and stared out at the city for a long moment.

"I suspected something like this," he said finally. "The formula was too important, too dangerous, to be protected by only four safeguards. The ancients would have built redundancies into the system—multiple layers of security, multiple opportunities for the unworthy to fail." He turned to face her. "This doesn't change our immediate goal. We still need the Muisca fragment. But it does change the scope of what we're undertaking."

"It changes everything." Elena's voice was tight with frustration. "We're not just racing Kroeger to four locations. We're racing him to seven. And we don't even know where three of them are."

"The journal gives us clues. The Amazon, Peru, Mexico. Those are starting points."

"Starting points for expeditions that could take months. We don't have months. Kroeger is right behind us—maybe ahead of us, if he has information we don't." Elena ran her hands through her hair, fighting the urge to scream. "This is impossible. We can't do this alone."

"We're not alone." Méndez-Castellón's voice was calm, steady. "The Guardian network has survived for five centuries. It didn't survive by accident. There are others out there—people like Santiago, like Ana's grandmother, who have dedicated their lives to protecting this secret. We need to find them. We need to convince them that we're worthy of their trust."

"And if they don't trust us?"

"Then we convince them." His dark eyes met hers. "You are a Guardian now, Elena. Santiago chose you. The network will recognize that choice—if you present yourself correctly, if you demonstrate that you understand the weight of what you carry."

Elena thought about the jade pendant against her chest, the journal in her hands, the fragments of ancient knowledge she had gathered over the past week. She thought about Martin, about Santiago, about all the people who had died to protect this secret.

She thought about Kroeger, hunting her across continents, willing to kill anyone who stood between him and his twisted vision of history.

"We start with the Muisca fragment," she said. "We find it, we secure it, and then we figure out how to find the others. One step at a time."

"One step at a time," Méndez-Castellón agreed.

They stood in silence, watching the lights of Bogotá twinkle in the darkness below. Somewhere out there, Kroeger's men were planning their next move. Somewhere out there, the other fragments waited to be found.

And somewhere, in hidden places scattered across the Americas, the Guardians watched and waited, judging whether the seekers who approached them were worthy of the secrets they protected.

Tomorrow, Elena would begin the next leg of her journey, though tonight she needed to rest.

12

Hidden Entrance

Mountains Above Guatavita, Colombia — The Next Morning

The trail wound upward through cloud forest so dense that Elena could barely see ten meters in any direction.

Mist hung between the trees like gauze, diffusing the morning light into a ghostly luminescence that made everything seem dreamlike, unreal. The vegetation pressed in on all sides—ferns taller than she was, orchids clinging to every branch, moss covering the rocks and tree trunks in carpets of green so vivid they almost hurt to look at. The air was thick with moisture, rich with the smell of decay and growth, the eternal cycle of the forest consuming and creating itself.

They had been walking for four hours.

Elena's legs burned with the effort of climbing, and her lungs ached from the thin air at this altitude—nearly three thousand meters above sea level. The trail—if it could be called that—was little more than a suggestion, a slightly less impenetrable path through the undergrowth that Ana navigated with the confidence of someone who had walked it before.

Behind Elena, Diego moved with the sure-footedness of a man accustomed to mountain terrain. Behind him came Méndez-Castellón's security team—four men in tactical gear, carrying weapons that looked incongruous in this primeval landscape. And at the rear, Méndez-Castellón himself, keeping pace despite his age, his expression focused and determined.

"How much further?" Elena asked during a brief rest stop, accepting a water bottle from one of the security men.

"Another kilometre, maybe less." Ana consulted her GPS, frowning at the screen. "The signal is weak here—too much vegetation, too much terrain interference. But we should be close to the ravine."

"Any sign of pursuit?"

"None that my people have detected," Méndez-Castellón said. "But that doesn't mean Kroeger's men aren't out there. They could be approaching from a different direction, using a different route."

"Or they could already be at the cave, waiting for us."

"That's possible too." Méndez-Castellón's voice was calm, matter of fact. "We proceed with caution. If there's any sign of hostiles, we fall back and reassess."

They moved on, pushing deeper into the forest. The terrain grew steeper, the vegetation thicker, the mist more oppressive. Elena felt as if she were descending into another world—a world that existed outside of time, where the rules of the modern age did not apply. This was ancient land, she realized. Land that had been sacred to the Muisca long before the Spanish arrived, long before the concept of Colombia or Bogotá or anything else that defined the modern nation.

The land remembered. She could feel it in her bones.

An hour later, they reached the ravine.

It appeared suddenly, the ground dropping away into a narrow cleft in the rock that plunged perhaps fifty meters into shadow. The walls were sheer, covered with vegetation that hung down like curtains, and at the bottom, Elena could just make out the glint of water—a stream that had carved this passage through the mountain over millions of years.

"The entrance is down there," Ana said, pointing to a spot on the far wall of the ravine where the rock face was slightly different in colour—darker, smoother, as if something had worn away the surface over centuries of use. "There's a ledge about twenty meters down, and behind it, a fissure that leads into the cave system."

"How do we get down?"

"We climb." Ana began unpacking her equipment—ropes, harnesses, carabiners. "The rock is solid, and there are good handholds. I've done this descent before, though never with this many people."

They rigged the ropes carefully, testing each anchor point multiple times before trusting it with their weight. Elena went first, rappelling down the sheer face with her heart pounding and her hands slick with sweat. The rock was cold and wet, covered with a thin layer of moss that made every foothold treacherous. Below her, the stream churned through the narrow passage, its sound amplified by the ravine walls into a constant roar that drowned out all other noise.

She reached the ledge without incident—a narrow shelf of rock, perhaps two meters wide, that jutted out from the cliff face above the churning water. Behind her, the entrance to the cave was exactly as Ana had described: a fissure in the rock, barely wide enough for a person to squeeze through, invisible from above and unremarkable from below.

If you didn't know it was there, you would never find it.

One by one, the others descended. Diego came next, then Ana, then the security team, and finally Méndez-Castellón. They gathered on the ledge, checking their equipment, preparing for the next phase of the journey.

"The passage is tight for the first twenty meters," Ana said, clicking on her headlamp. "After that, it opens into a larger chamber. I explored that far on my previous visit, but I didn't go deeper. The passages branch, and without proper mapping equipment, I didn't want to risk getting lost."

"We go together," Elena said. "No one separates from the group. And we mark our path as we go—I don't want to be stuck in there if something goes wrong."

They entered the fissure in single file, squeezing through the narrow opening into darkness. The rock pressed against Elena's shoulders on both sides, and for a terrifying moment, she felt a surge of claustrophobia—the primitive fear of being trapped, crushed, buried alive. She forced herself to breathe slowly, to focus on the light ahead, to keep moving.

The passage twisted and turned, descending gradually into the mountain. The air grew cooler, damper, thick with the mineral smell of deep caves. Elena's headlamp cast dancing shadows on the walls, revealing glimpses of formations that had taken millennia to create—stalactites dripping from the ceiling, flowstone cascading down the walls like frozen waterfalls, crystals glinting in the light like scattered diamonds.

And then, suddenly, the passage opened up.

Elena emerged into a chamber that took her breath away.

It was perhaps forty meters across and nearly as high, a natural cathedral carved from the living rock by forces older than humanity. The ceiling was covered with stalactites that hung down like the pipes of a vast organ, and the floor was a jumble of boulders and formations that created a landscape of surreal beauty. Water dripped from somewhere above, creating a constant rhythm that echoed through the chamber like a heartbeat.

But it was the walls that made Elena's knees go weak.

They were covered with carvings.

Not the simple geometric patterns she might have expected from a pre-Columbian site, but elaborate, detailed reliefs that depicted scenes of incredible complexity. Figures in ceremonial regalia, performing rituals around structures that might have been forges or furnaces. Animals—jaguars, serpents, eagles—intertwined with human forms in ways that suggested transformation, metamorphosis. And scattered throughout, the spiral patterns and stylized figures that Elena recognized from her studies of Muisca goldwork.

"Mother of God," Ana whispered beside her. "I never... I never imagined..."

"This is it." Elena's voice was barely audible, choked with emotion. "This is where gold is born."

She moved forward slowly, reverently, her headlamp sweeping across the carvings. The more she looked, the more she saw—layers of meaning encoded in every image, stories that would take years to fully decipher. But certain themes emerged clearly: the transformation of base materials into precious ones, the rituals required to effect that transformation, the knowledge that had been passed down through generations of priests and guardians.

And at the far end of the chamber, set into an alcove that had been carved from the rock with obvious care, she saw what they had come for.

A stone pedestal, similar to the one in Chichicastenango.

And on it, a crystal case containing pages of bark paper covered in glyphs.

The third fragment of the Codex of Seven Serpents.

***

Elena approached the pedestal slowly, her heart pounding so loud she was sure the others could hear it. The fragment was smaller than the one from Guatemala—perhaps a dozen pages, folded accordion-style in the traditional Maya manner. But the glyphs were similar: a mixture of Muisca and Maya symbols, interspersed with the older notation system that predated both cultures.

"Is it trapped?" Diego asked from behind her. "Some kind of protective mechanism?"

"I don't think so." Elena studied the pedestal, looking for any sign of the hidden mechanisms that had protected the Guatemala fragment. "This site was designed differently. The entrance was the protection—hidden, difficult to find, impossible to reach without significant effort. Anyone who made it this far was already presumed worthy."

She reached out and lifted the crystal case from the pedestal. It came away easily, no resistance, no grinding of ancient machinery. Just a case, and the pages within it, and the weight of five centuries of protection.

"We have it," she said, turning to face the others. "We have the third fragment."

Before anyone could respond, a sound reached them from the passage they had entered through.

Voices. Getting closer.

"Kill your lights," Diego hissed, reaching for his weapon. "Everyone, move to cover."

They scattered across the chamber, pressing themselves against boulders and formations that would provide concealment. Elena clutched the crystal case against her chest, her free hand finding the grip of her Glock. The chamber plunged into darkness as headlamps clicked off, and for a long moment, there was only the drip of water and the pounding of Elena's heart.

Then lights appeared at the entrance to the chamber.

Three beams, sweeping across the space, illuminating the carvings on the walls. And behind the lights, three figures in tactical gear, their weapons raised, their movements professional and coordinated.

Kroeger's men. They had found the cave.

"Spread out," a voice commanded—German accent, cold and precise. "They're in here somewhere. Find them. Weller — check the eastern passage."

Elena pressed herself deeper into the shadow of a massive stalagmite, barely breathing. Beside her, she could sense Diego doing the same. The lights swept closer, probing the darkness, searching for any sign of movement.

One of the men passed within three meters of Elena's position. She could see his face in the reflected glow of his headlamp—young, hard, focused. He moved with the casual confidence of someone who had done this many times before, someone who was accustomed to hunting human prey in difficult terrain.

He didn't see her. He moved on, his light sweeping past her hiding spot without pausing.

Elena let out a silent breath.

Then one of Méndez-Castellón's security team made a mistake.

She didn't see what happened—a loose rock, perhaps, or a moment of impatience. But she heard it: the scrape of boots on stone, the clatter of dislodged pebbles. And then the shout:

"Contact! Northwest corner!"

The chamber erupted into chaos.

Gunfire exploded through the darkness, muzzle flashes strobe-lighting the ancient carvings in a hellish display. Elena threw herself flat, clutching the crystal case, as bullets ricocheted off the rocks around her. She heard screaming—someone hit, impossible to tell who—and the deeper boom of Méndez-Castellón's security team returning fire.

"Elena! Move!" Diego's voice, somewhere to her left.

She scrambled to her feet and ran, keeping low, using the formations for cover. A bullet whined past her ear, close enough that she felt the wind of its passage. She fired back blindly, two shots toward the muzzle flash she had seen, not expecting to hit anything but hoping to buy herself a few seconds.

The passage they had entered through was blocked; Kroeger's men had come that way and more might be coming behind them.

From somewhere deep in the eastern passage, a sound reached her — not gunfire, but a sharp mechanical crack, ancient stone against stone, and then a single truncated cry that echoed once through the cave system and went silent. Whatever the Guardians had left behind in the tunnels they did not want explored, Weller had found it.

But Ana had said the cave system branched.

There had to be another way out.

"Ana!" Elena shouted. "Is there another exit?"

"This way!" Ana's voice came from somewhere ahead, barely audible over the gunfire. "There's a passage on the far side—it goes deeper, but it might connect to another entrance!"

Elena ran toward the voice, her headlamp clicking on automatically as she moved. Behind her, the firefight continued—Méndez-Castellón's men engaging Kroeger's team, buying time for the others to escape. She heard someone cry out in pain, heard the sharp crack of a grenade detonating somewhere in the chamber.

She didn't look back.

The passage Ana had found was narrow but passable, sloping downward into the mountain at a steep angle. Elena plunged into it without hesitation, trusting that the others were behind her. The rock walls pressed close, scraping her shoulders, tearing at her clothes. But she kept moving, kept running, kept clutching the crystal case that contained everything they had come for.

Behind her, the sounds of battle faded into echoes, and then into silence.

She didn't know how long she ran. Minutes, maybe longer. The passage twisted and turned, descended and climbed, until she had no idea which direction she was facing or how deep into the mountain she had gone. But finally—finally—she saw light ahead.

Not the artificial light of headlamps, but the grey, diffuse light of day.

She emerged from the cave onto a ledge overlooking a valley she had never seen. Cloud forest stretched below her in an unbroken carpet of green, and in the distance, mountains rose toward a sky heavy with approaching rain. There was no sign of the ravine they had descended, no sign of the route they had taken to reach the cave. She had emerged on the opposite side of the mountain, kilometers from where they had started.

Diego appeared behind her, breathing hard, blood streaming from a cut on his forehead. Then Ana, her face pale with shock. Then two of Méndez-Castellón's security men, one of them supporting the other, who had taken a round in the leg.

"The others?" Elena asked, already knowing the answer.

"They didn't make it." Diego's voice was flat, empty. "Méndez-Castellón ordered them to hold the chamber while we escaped. They bought us time."

"And Méndez-Castellón himself?"

Silence. Diego shook his head.

Elena closed her eyes, feeling the weight of the crystal case in her hands. More death. More sacrifice. More blood spilled in the name of a secret that had consumed lives for five centuries.

When she opened her eyes, her expression had hardened into something that frightened even her.

"We keep moving," she said. "We find a way out of these mountains, and we get to safety. And then we find the remaining fragments before Kroeger does."

"He has us outgunned, outmanned—"

"He has nothing." Elena's voice was ice. "He has money and mercenaries. We have knowledge. We have the fragments. And we have something he will never have."

"What's that?"

Elena thought of Santiago, dying in a burning church. Of Martin, strangled in a library. Of the security men who had just sacrificed their lives so that she could escape.

"We have people willing to die for this," she said. "And I'm willing to be one of them."

She started down the slope toward the valley below, and after a moment, the others followed.

The hunt continued.

13

Breathing Space

Medellín, Colombia — Three Days Later

The city of eternal spring stretched across the valley below, a tapestry of red-brick buildings and green mountainsides that seemed impossibly peaceful after everything Elena had endured.

Medellín had reinvented itself in the decades since the dark days of Pablo Escobar, transforming from one of the most dangerous city on the planet into a vibrant metropolis that attracted tourists, entrepreneurs, and digital nomads from around the world.

The hotel they took refuge in was perched on a hillside in El Poblado, an upscale district where modern towers rose alongside colonial architecture and the streets were lined with restaurants, cafes and boutiques that would have been just as at home in Barcelona or Madrid.

It felt surreal. Three days ago, Elena had been running for her life through a cave system in the mountains, bullets whining past her head, the screams of dying men echoing in her ears. Now she sat by a rooftop pool in relative tranquillity, watching the sunset paint the sky in shades of orange and pink, a glass of aguardiente sweating in her hand.

The stark contrast was almost too much to process.

They had made it out of the mountains through a combination of luck, skill, and the help of local farmers who asked no questions about the blood-soaked strangers who emerged from the cloud forest. Ana had contacts in the region—archaeologists and anthropologists who had worked with indigenous communities for years—and those contacts had provided transport, medical care for the wounded security man, and a safe route to Medellín that avoided the main roads where Kroeger's people might be watching.

The journey had taken two days. Two days of hiking through terrain that tested the limits of Elena's endurance, of sleeping in farmhouses that smelled of wood smoke and coffee, of jumping at every sound and scanning every horizon for signs of pursuit. By the time they reached the outskirts of Medellín, Elena was running on nothing but adrenaline and willpower.

Méndez-Castellón's people had been waiting for them. The billionaire maintained a network of safe houses throughout Colombia—a legacy of decades of operating in a country where security could never be taken for granted—and his staff had prepared everything they needed. Clean clothes, hot food, medical supplies, secure communications. And most importantly, time to rest and recover before the next phase of their journey.

They still didn't know what had happened to Méndez-Castellón himself. The security men who had stayed behind to cover their escape had not been heard from since the firefight in the cave. Diego's contacts in the region were making inquiries, but so far, there was only silence. Elena tried not to think about what that silence meant.

She had the fragment. That was what mattered. The third piece of the Codex of Seven Serpents, safely stored in the hotel's secure room along with the other artifacts they had gathered. Three down, four to go.

Four more pieces. Four more journeys into danger. Four more opportunities for people to die.

Elena took a long drink of her aguardiente and tried to silence the voice in her head that kept asking whether it was worth it.

***

The hotel pool was an oasis of calm in the chaos of Elena's life.

It occupied the rooftop of the building, surrounded by tropical plants and comfortable loungers, with a view of the city that stretched to the mountains on every side. During the day, it attracted a mix of tourists and business travellers—young couples on romantic getaways, families with children splashing in the shallow end, executives taking conference calls from poolside cabanas. In the late afternoon, as the heat of the day began to fade, the atmosphere shifted to something more relaxed, more intimate.

Elena had taken to spending her evenings here, after the work of analysing the fragments and planning their next moves was done for the day. It was the closest thing to peace she had found since Chicago—a few hours when she could pretend to be a normal person, a tourist enjoying the amenities of a beautiful hotel in a beautiful city.

She was working on her third aguardiente when she noticed the couple.

They were young—late twenties, Elena guessed—and obviously in love. The woman was striking, with dark hair and olive skin that spoke of Latin heritage, her smile bright and frequent as she laughed at something her companion said. The man was tall and athletic, with the kind of easy confidence that suggested success without arrogance. They wore matching gold bands on their left hands, and the woman's finger also bore a diamond engagement ring that caught the fading sunlight.

Newlyweds. Elena felt a pang of something that might have been envy, watching them. They looked so happy, so unburdened by the weight of ancient secrets and murderous enemies. They looked like people whose biggest concern was choosing between the hotel restaurant and the trendy fusion place down the street.

She was about to look away, to return to her drink and her dark thoughts, when the woman caught her eye and smiled.

"Beautiful evening, isn't it?" The woman's English was accented but fluent, her voice warm and friendly. "We've been coming to this pool every day since we arrived, and I don't think I'll ever get tired of this view."

Elena returned the smile, grateful for the distraction. "It's stunning. I've been in Colombia for almost a week now, and I still can't believe how green everything is."

"First time in Medellín?"

"First time in Colombia, actually. I'm usually based in Washington, D.C."

"Oh, you're American!" The woman's smile widened. "I'm Katia. And this is my husband, Jay." She said the word *husband* with a slight emphasis, as if she was still getting used to it. "We just got married three days ago."

"Congratulations." Elena raised her glass in a toast. "That's wonderful news."

"Thank you! It was beautiful—we had the ceremony at my family's *finca* in the mountains outside the city. My whole family was there, all my cousins and aunts and uncles. It was..." Katia's eyes glistened slightly. "It was everything I ever dreamed of."

Jay leaned forward, extending his hand to Elena. "Howdie! I'm Jay. Pleasure to meet you." His accent was unmistakably Australian—broad vowels and casual inflection that reminded Elena of the surfing documentaries and outback adventure shows she'd seen on late-night television. "We're from Melbourne. We flew in a few weeks ago so Katia's family could be part of our wedding before we head back to Australia."

"That's lovely," Elena said, shaking his hand. "It must mean so much to have everyone together."

"It does." Katia reached over to squeeze Jay's arm affectionately. "My grandmother is ninety-three years old. She's never been on an airplane, never left Colombia. If we'd gotten married in Australia, she would never have seen it. This way, she got to dance at my wedding." Her voice caught slightly. "She told me it was the happiest day of her life."

Elena felt something loosen in her chest—the constant tension she had been carrying for days easing slightly in the presence of these two strangers and their uncomplicated joy. "That's beautiful. Really."

"What about you?" Katia asked, settling into the lounger next to Elena's with the easy familiarity of someone who made friends wherever she went. "What brings you to Colombia? Business or pleasure?"

Elena hesitated. The cover story she had prepared—research on Muisca gold-working techniques—felt hollow in the face of Katia's genuine warmth. And besides, what harm could it do to share a little of the truth? These were tourists, newlyweds, people who would be on a plane back to Australia in a few days. They had no connection to Kroeger or the Guardians or any of the dangerous forces that had consumed Elena's life.

"I'm an archaeologist," she said. "I work for the Smithsonian Institution in Washington. I'm here researching... well, it's going to sound a bit crazy, but I'm researching the legend of El Dorado."

Katia's eyes widened. "El Dorado? The lost city of gold?"

"That's the one. Although..." Elena took another sip of her drink. "It's not quite what most people think. The legend has been distorted over the centuries, twisted by treasure hunters and Conquistadors looking for something they could steal. The real story is more complicated. Actually, far more interesting."

Jay leaned forward, his expression curious. "What do you mean? I thought El Dorado was just a myth."

"That's what most people believe, but there's evidence, fragmented and scattered, but real, that the legend was based on something true. Not a city made of gold, but a place where the original peoples that inhabited South America developed knowledge that the Spanish couldn't understand. It was so valuable and dangerous that they hid it rather than let it fall into the hands of the Conquistadors."

"What kind of knowledge?" Katia asked, her voice hushed with fascination.

Elena considered how much to reveal. The full truth was too dangerous, too unbelievable but a simplified version...

"The Muisca people of Colombia were master goldsmiths," she said. "They created some of the most beautiful metalwork in the ancient Americas. According to some traditions though, their skill went beyond simple craftsmanship. They understood things about the nature of metal, the nature of matter itself, that we're only beginning to rediscover today."

"Like what, alchemy? Turning lead into gold?" Jay laughed at the absurdity.

Elena smiled. "Something like that, although the reality is probably more nuanced than the medieval European version. The Muisca weren't trying to get rich; they had plenty of gold already. They were trying to understand the fundamental nature of transformation. How things change from one state to another. How the base can become precious."

"That's fascinating." Katia's eyes were bright with interest. "Growing up here in South America, I was raised on stories about El Dorado, but I always thought they were just... you know, fairy tales. Something to entertain children."

"Often fairy tales are based on truth," Elena said. "They just get distorted over time, exaggerated, simplified. At their core though, there's usually something real that people once knew, then forgot and is remember only as a legend or old tale handed down generationally."

They talked for another hour as the sun set and the city lights began to twinkle across the valley. Elena learned that Jay had built a successful technology company in Melbourne, that he and Katia had met at a conference in Miami three years ago and that they planned to divide their time between Australia and Colombia so Katia could stay connected to her family.

They were warm, funny, genuinely interested in Elena's work, the kind of people she might have been friends with in another life, a life where she wasn't carrying the weight of ancient secrets and running from killers.

When they finally said goodnight, Katia insisting that Elena join them for dinner the following evening, Jay pressing his business card into her hand with instructions to look them up if she ever visited Melbourne. Elena felt more normal and something she hadn't felt in days, hope.

Not hope for herself, necessarily, but for the world and the idea that ordinary people could still find happiness and build lives of meaning and connection, even in a world that contained men like Kroeger and secrets people would kill for.

Maybe that was worth protecting and was what these Guardians had been fighting for all along.

She tucked Jay's card into her pocket and headed back to her room, her mind already turning to the challenges that lay ahead.

***

The war room, as Diego had taken to calling it, occupied the hotel's largest suite, its windows covered with blackout curtains, its surfaces buried under maps, documents and the artifacts they had gathered.

Elena found Diego and Ana hunched over the table when she arrived the next morning, their faces illuminated by the glow of laptop screens. The two wounded security men were there as well, Carlos and Miguel, brothers from Bogotá who had worked for Méndez-Castellón for nearly a decade.

Carlos's leg was healing well, the bullet having passed through muscle without hitting bone, but he still moved with a pronounced limp.

"Anything new?" Elena asked, pouring herself a cup of coffee from the carafe on the sideboard.

"We've finished the preliminary translation of the Muisca fragment," Ana said, looking up from her laptop. "It's... remarkable. The level of detail is extraordinary. This isn't just mythology or ritual—it's genuine technical knowledge, encoded in symbolic form."

"What does it describe?"

"Procedures. Specific steps in a process that involves heating, cooling, and combining materials in precise sequences." Ana pulled up an image on her screen—a photograph of the bark paper pages, annotated with her translations. "The Muisca fragment focuses on the middle stages of the transformation. The Guatemala fragment described the initial preparation—the elements required, the equipment needed. This one describes what to do once you have everything assembled."

"And the fragment from the Popol Vuh?"

"That one's different. It's more... philosophical. It describes the principles underlying the transformation. It is basically a theory if you will, rather than the practice. Without it, the other fragments would just be a series of steps without context. You could follow them mechanically, but you wouldn't understand why they worked."

Elena nodded slowly, fitting the pieces together in her mind. "So, we have the theory, the preparation and the middle stages, so what are we missing?"

"The beginning and the end." Diego pulled up a map on his laptop, a satellite image of South America, marked with pins at various locations.

"According to the journal, there are four more components. Three of them are the 'keys' that Fray Tomás mentioned—additional safeguards that prevent the formula from being used incorrectly. And one of them is the final piece of the formula itself—the completion of the process, the steps that actually produce the transformation."

"Where?"

Diego pointed to the pins on his map. "The journal gives us hints, but not precise locations. One key is hidden somewhere in the Amazon, probably Colombia or Brazil, in territory that was controlled by indigenous groups who had contact with both the Muisca and the Maya. Another is in Peru, in the mountains of the Inca. The third is in Mexico, in what was once Aztec territory."

"And the final piece of the formula?"

"That's the question." Diego's expression was troubled. "The journal suggests it's hidden with one of the keys, but it doesn't say which one. We won't know until we find all of them I'd guess."

Elena studied the map, calculating distances, considering logistics. The Amazon. Peru. Mexico. Three more expeditions into dangerous territory, all of which were opportunities for Kroeger's men to intercept and try to take them out.

"We need to prioritize," she said. "We can't just chase all three leads at once, so which one is most likely to yield results?"

"Peru." Ana's voice was confident. "The Inca maintained extensive records of their sacred sites and many of those records survived the conquest. If there's a Guardian network in Peru, we have the best chance of finding them through academic channels. I have colleagues at the *Universidad Nacional Mayor de San Marcos* in Lima who specialize in Inca archaeology. They might be able to point us in the right direction."

"What about the Amazon?"

Diego shook his head. "That's a real wild card. The Amazon basin is huge, literally millions of square kilometres of jungle, hundreds of different indigenous groups and countless potential hiding places, all overgrown and about as wild a place as anywhere in the world. Without more specific information, we'd be searching for a needle in a field of haystacks the size of Western Europe."

"Mexico?"

"Mexico is a bit... complicated." Diego pulled up another map, this one showing the Yucatan Peninsula and the surrounding regions.

"The Aztec and Maya were rivals, but they also traded, communicated, exchanged ideas. If there's a connection between the Maya guardians and the Aztec territory, it might be through sites that both cultures considered sacred. The problem is, most of those sites are major tourist attractions now. Chichen Itza, Tulum and the temples around Cancun; they're crawling with visitors and archaeologists. Hiding something there would be incredibly difficult."

"Unless it's hidden in plain sight," Elena murmured, thinking out loud of the fragment concealed in the Popol Vuh manuscript. "The best hiding places are often the ones where no one thinks to look."

They debated for another hour, weighing options and considering risks. In the end, they decided on a two-pronged approach: Elena and Ana would travel to Peru, following the academic contacts that offered the clearest path forward, while Diego would begin gathering intelligence on the Amazon lead, reaching out to indigenous communities who might have preserved knowledge of the Guardian network.

It wasn't a perfect plan, yet for now, that would have to be enough.

***

The evening before they were scheduled to leave for Lima, Elena returned to the rooftop pool.

She found Jay and Katia in their usual spot, lounging on adjacent chairs with tropical drinks in their hands. They waved when they saw her, and Katia immediately began making room on the lounger beside her.

"Elena! We were hoping we'd see you again. Come and sit with us! We ordered too much food and need help finishing it."

Elena smiled and joined them, accepting a plate of *empanadas* and a glass of wine. For a few hours, she let herself forget about fragments and Guardians and Nazi treasure hunters and recent trauma. She listened to Jay's stories about building his import business, the challenges of entrepreneurship in a competitive market, about how he had first met Katia and known that despite resisting her charms, he joked, that somehow that his life was going to change.

She listened to Katia talk about her childhood in Colombia, the culture shock of moving to Melbourne and the slow process of building a life in a new country while staying connected to the one she had left behind.

They were good people. Kind. The sort of people who made the world worth saving.

When they finally said goodbye, Katia pressed Elena into a long hug, Jay giving her a hug also and reminding her about his standing invitation to come and visit Melbourne one day.

Elena felt a strange mix of emotions. Sadness, because she would probably never see them again. Gratitude, because they had reminded her what normal life looked like and determination, because people like Jay and Katia deserved to live in a world where ancient secrets didn't fall into the hands of men who would use them for evil.

She returned to her room and began packing for Peru.

The next leg of the journey awaited and it appeared that it was only going to get harder. She just hoped she made it home alive.

14

The Sacred Valley

Lima, Peru — Five Days Later

The plane descended through a layer of clouds that seemed to stretch forever, a grey blanket that obscured everything below. Elena pressed her face to the window, straining for a glimpse of the land she had studied for years but never visited—the ancient homeland of the Inca, the empire that had once stretched from Colombia to Chile, the civilization that had built Machu Picchu and the road system that connected a continent.

Then, suddenly, the clouds parted.

Lima sprawled across the coastal desert like a fever dream; ten million people crammed into a narrow strip between the Pacific Ocean and the Andes Mountains. The city was a study in contrasts—gleaming skyscrapers rising beside colonial cathedrals, wealthy neighbourhoods pressed against sprawling shanty towns, the grey Pacific crashing against beaches where surfers rode waves within sight of one of the largest cities in South America.

Elena had never seen anything quite like it.

"First time in Peru?" Ana asked from the seat beside her.

"First time. I've studied Inca civilization for years, but I've never had the chance to visit." Elena felt a flutter of excitement beneath the anxiety that had become her constant companion. "It feels strange, finally being here. Like meeting someone you've only known through letters."

"Peru will surprise you. It's not what the textbooks describe. It's messier, more complicated, more alive." Ana smiled slightly. "The Inca didn't disappear when the Spanish came. They adapted, survived, preserved what they could. Their descendants are still here—millions of them, speaking Quechua, maintaining traditions that go back centuries. If there's a Guardian network in Peru, they're the ones who kept it alive."

They cleared customs without incident—Elena traveling on her legitimate Smithsonian credentials, Ana on her Colombian academic passport—and emerged into the chaos of Jorge Chávez International Airport. The heat hit Elena like a physical force, heavy and humid despite the coastal location, and she was grateful when their contact appeared with an air-conditioned SUV.

Dr. Fernando Quispe was a professor of archaeology at the Universidad Nacional Mayor de San Marcos, Peru's oldest and most prestigious university. He was a small man, perhaps sixty years old, with silver hair cropped close to his skull and dark eyes that seemed to see more than they revealed. He greeted Ana with the warmth of an old colleague and Elena with the careful courtesy of someone reserving judgment.

"Dr. Vasquez," he said, shaking her hand. "Ana has told me about your research. She says you're looking for something that most of my colleagues would dismiss as fantasy."

"I'm looking for the truth," Elena replied. "Whatever form that takes."

Quispe studied her for a long moment, his expression unreadable. Then he nodded slowly.

"Truth is a dangerous thing in Peru. It has a way of unsettling comfortable assumptions." He gestured toward the waiting vehicle. "Come. We have much to discuss, and I prefer to do it somewhere more private than an airport."

They drove through Lima's chaotic streets, past colonial churches and modern shopping malls, through neighbourhoods that ranged from desperate poverty to ostentatious wealth. Quispe narrated as they went, pointing out landmarks, explaining the city's history, painting a picture of a place where the past was never quite past.

"Lima was the capital of Spanish South America," he said. "The centre of colonial power, the seat of the Viceroy. The Spanish built their churches on top of Inca temples, just as they did in Guatemala and Mexico. They thought they were erasing the old ways. They didn't understand that some things cannot be erased."

"The Guardian network," Elena said quietly.

Quispe's eyes met hers in the rearview mirror. "Ana mentioned you know about the Guardians. May I ask how?"

"I've become one. Whether I wanted to or not."

She told him the story—abbreviated, edited, but essentially true. Martin's discovery and death. The fragments in Chicago and Guatemala. The cave in Colombia. The journal of Fray Tomás de Ávila and the revelation that there were seven components to the formula, not four. When she finished, Quispe was silent for a long moment.

"I have heard rumours of such things," he said finally. "Stories passed down through certain families, certain communities. I always assumed they were legends—the kind of tales that comfort people who have lost so much, who need to believe that something of value survived the conquest." He paused. "But you have proof. Physical evidence."

"I have fragments of a codex that describes a process for transmuting base metals into gold. I have a journal written by a Spanish friar who witnessed the formula work. And I have enemies who have already killed multiple people to prevent this knowledge from being revealed."

"Kroeger."

"You know the name?"

"I know of him. He came to Peru fifteen years ago, asking questions about Inca metallurgy, about sacred sites in the mountains, about traditions that had been preserved despite the conquest. I refused to help him." Quispe's jaw tightened. "There was something wrong about him. Something cold. I could see in his eyes that he didn't want to understand our history—he wanted to use it."

"He's still looking. He's closer than ever. And if he finds the remaining fragments before we do..."

"Then everything my ancestors died to protect will fall into the hands of a man who would use it to justify centuries of oppression." Quispe nodded slowly. "I understand. And I will help you, Dr. Vasquez. Not because I believe the formula should be recovered—I'm not sure I believe that—but because I trust that you will make the right decision about what to do with it when you find it."

"What makes you think that?"

"Because you asked the right question." His eyes met hers again. "You asked about truth. Not gold, not power, not proof of theories you already believe. Truth. That tells me something about the kind of person you are."

They drove on through the fading afternoon light, leaving the chaos of Lima behind and climbing into the foothills of the Andes. Ahead, invisible behind layers of cloud and distance, the mountains waited.

And somewhere in those mountains, hidden for five centuries, lay the next piece of the puzzle.

***

The next morning, they flew to Cusco.

The ancient capital of the Inca Empire sat at an altitude of nearly 3,400 meters, in a valley surrounded by peaks that rose even higher. Elena felt the thin air immediately—a lightness in her head, a shortness of breath that made every movement feel slightly wrong. Quispe had warned her about altitude sickness, had given her coca tea to chew and instructions to move slowly until her body adjusted.

But even the altitude couldn't diminish the impact of Cusco itself.

The city was a palimpsest of history—Inca walls supporting Spanish churches, colonial mansions built on foundations that had been laid a thousand years before Columbus was born. The Plaza de Armas, the main square, was surrounded by arcaded buildings that could have been transplanted from any Spanish colonial city, but the stones beneath them were fitted with the precision that had made Inca masonry legendary. No mortar, no gaps—just blocks carved so perfectly that a knife blade couldn't fit between them.

"The Spanish tried to destroy everything," Quispe said as they walked through the narrow streets. "They tore down temples, melted sacred objects, burned the *quipus* that recorded Inca history. But they couldn't destroy the stones. The walls were too strong, too well-built. So, they built on top of them instead, and the Inca foundations remained."

"Like the knowledge," Elena murmured. "Hidden beneath layers of conquest, waiting to be rediscovered."

"Exactly."

They spent two days in Cusco, meeting with scholars and community leaders, following threads of inquiry that led through academic offices and indigenous ceremonies. Quispe had contacts everywhere—archaeologists who had spent decades excavating Inca sites, *curanderos* who practiced traditional medicine, elders who remembered stories their grandparents had told them about the old ways.

And gradually, a picture began to emerge.

The Inca had been aware of the codex—or at least, of the knowledge it contained. Their own traditions spoke of a secret passed down from the time before time, a process that could transform the nature of matter itself. They called it *quri ruway*—the making of gold—and they had hidden it in a place so sacred, so inaccessible, that even the Spanish with all their greed and determination had never found it.

Machu Picchu.

"Not the ruins themselves," Quispe explained on their third evening in Cusco, as they sat in his hotel room poring over maps and documents. "The site that tourists visit is impressive, but it's not the whole picture. There are chambers beneath the main complex, passages that have never been fully explored, sections of the mountain that were deliberately sealed off by the Inca before they abandoned the city."

"How do you know this?"

"Because I've seen them." Quispe's voice was quiet, almost reverent. "Twenty years ago, I was part of an excavation that discovered a sealed entrance beneath the Temple of the Sun. We opened it, expecting to find a tomb or a storage chamber. Instead, we found a passage that descended deep into the mountain—deeper than we could safely explore with the equipment we had."

"What was down there?"

"We don't know. The Peruvian government ordered the passage sealed before we could investigate further. They said it was too dangerous, that the structural integrity of the main site might be compromised. But I've always suspected there was another reason." He met Elena's eyes. "Someone didn't want us to find what was hidden there."

"The Guardians?"

"Perhaps. Or perhaps just bureaucrats protecting a tourist attraction. It's hard to say." Quispe spread a map of Machu Picchu across the table. "But if the fragment is anywhere, it's there. The Temple of the Sun was the most sacred building in the complex—dedicated to Inti, the sun god, the source of all gold. If the Inca were hiding something related to the transformation of metals, that's where they would have put it."

Elena studied the map, noting the layout of the ruins, the locations of the major structures, the topography of the mountain that surrounded them.

Machu Picchu was one of the most famous archaeological sites in the world—visited by thousands of tourists every day, photographed millions of times, studied by generations of scholars.

The idea that something could still be hidden there seemed almost absurd, but then again, she had found fragments hidden in a Chicago library, a Guatemalan church and Colombian cave, so if the Guardians had proven anything, it was that secrets could survive in the most unlikely places.

"How do we get access?" she asked. "The site is heavily protected. We can't just walk in and start exploring sealed passages."

"Leave that to me." Quispe's expression was unreadable. "I have friends in the Ministry of Culture. And I have favours to call in—favours I've been saving for something important."

He folded the map carefully. "We leave for Machu Picchu tomorrow. And if we're lucky, we'll find what we're looking for before Kroeger's people realize we're there."

"And if we're not lucky?"

Quispe smiled grimly. "Then we improvise. It's what archaeologists do best."

***

They took the train from Cusco the next morning, winding through the Sacred Valley along tracks that followed the Urubamba River toward the cloud-shrouded peak of Machu Picchu.

Elena sat by the window, watching the landscape unfold—terraced hillsides that had been cultivated for millennia, Inca ruins perched on seemingly inaccessible ridges, villages where women in traditional dress herded llamas along paths that had been walked for countless generations.

Ana sat beside her, working on translations of the fragments they had gathered. Carlos and Miguel, the two surviving members of Méndez-Castellón's security team, occupied seats across the aisle, their eyes constantly scanning for threats.

Fernando Quispe sat in the seat behind them, reading through documents that his contacts at the Ministry of Culture had provided, his brow furrowed in concentration.

The train climbed higher into the mountains, and the vegetation changed—from dry scrubland to lush cloud forest, the trees draped with moss and bromeliads that seemed to drink moisture directly from the mist.

The air grew cooler, thinner, and Elena felt again the strange lightness of altitude, the sense that she was leaving the normal world behind and entering somewhere older, stranger, more powerful.

And then, suddenly, she saw it.

Machu Picchu appeared through a gap in the clouds, impossibly beautiful, impossibly remote—a city of stone perched on a ridge between two peaks, surrounded by sheer cliffs that dropped thousands of feet to the river below.

Even from a distance, Elena could see the precision of its construction, the way the buildings seemed to grow from the mountain itself, as if they had been there since the beginning of time.

"The Inca called it the *llaqta*—the city," Quispe said quietly, leaning forward to look through her window. "They never gave it the name we use today. *Machu Picchu* means 'old peak' in Quechua—a name given by the farmers who lived in the valley below.

The Spanish never found the city and it remained hidden until 1911, when an American historian stumbled across it while searching for a different lost city entirely."

"It's incredible," Elena breathed.

"It's sacred." Quispe's voice was reverent. "More than five hundred years after the fall of the Inca Empire, my people still come here to pray. The spirits of the ancestors are strong in this place. Whatever we find beneath those stones, we must approach it with respect."

The train reached the station at Aguas Calientes, the small town at the base of the mountain that served as the gateway to Machu Picchu.

They spent the night in a modest hotel, going over their plans, checking their equipment, preparing for what the next day would bring.

Elena slept poorly, her dreams filled with images of stone passages and hidden chambers, of serpents made of gold and flames that consumed everything they touched.

In the morning, they began the final ascent.

15

Temple of the Sun

Machu Picchu, Peru — The Next Morning

The bus wound up the mountainside in a series of switchbacks so tight that Elena could look out her window and see the road they had just travelled directly below, separated by nothing but a sheer drop into the valley.

The driver navigated the curves with the casual confidence of someone who had made this journey thousands of times, his attention divided between the road and a conversation he was having with another passenger in rapid Quechua.

Elena gripped the armrest and tried not to think about the absence of guardrails.

They had left Aguas Calientes before dawn, joining a small group of tourists and researchers who had special permits to enter the site before the main gates opened.

Quispe's connections had proven invaluable—a phone call to the right person at the Ministry of Culture, a few documents signed and stamped, and suddenly they had access that would normally require months of bureaucratic negotiation.

The bus crested the final ridge, and Machu Picchu spread out before them in the pale morning light.

Elena had seen photographs, of course. Everyone had seen photographs. But nothing could prepare her for the reality of the place—the sheer scale of it, the impossible precision of its construction, the way it seemed to emerge from the mountain itself as if grown rather than built.

Terraces cascaded down the hillsides like giant steps, their retaining walls still holding back the soil after five centuries. Stone buildings rose in orderly rows; their walls fitted together with the mathematical perfection that had made Inca masonry legendary. Above it all, the peak of Huayna Picchu thrust into the sky like a stone finger pointing toward the heavens.

"The Inca believed this was a sacred landscape," Quispe said quietly, standing beside her at the entrance to the site. "The mountains were *apus*—spirits, deities, sources of power. Machu Picchu was built to honour them, to channel their energy, to connect the human world with the divine."

"It feels like it," Elena murmured. "There's something here. Something I can't explain."

"The altitude affects people differently. Some feel euphoria, others anxiety. But most people feel *something*." Quispe began walking toward the main complex, gesturing for the others to follow. "The Spanish never found this place. It was abandoned before they arrived, hidden by the jungle for four centuries. When Hiram Bingham stumbled across it in 1911, it was still largely intact—one of the few Inca sites that hadn't been looted or destroyed."

"Why was it abandoned?"

"No one knows for certain. Disease, perhaps—the plagues that the Spanish brought killed millions, even in places the conquistadors never reached. Or maybe the Inca simply left, taking their most sacred objects with them to hide them from the invaders." Quispe paused at a junction in the path, looking up at the structures that surrounded them. "Whatever the reason, they left something behind. Something hidden so well that five hundred years of exploration hasn't found it."

They made their way through the site, past the agricultural terraces and the guardhouse, past the Temple of the Three Windows and the Principal Temple, past groups of early tourists who snapped photographs and consulted guidebooks. Elena tried to look like just another visitor, but her eyes were constantly searching, analysing, looking for clues that might point toward hidden passages or concealed chambers.

The Temple of the Sun was located near the centre of the complex, built around a natural rock formation that jutted up from the ground like the prow of a ship. The structure itself was a marvel of engineering—curved walls that followed the contours of the stone, windows precisely aligned to catch the first rays of sunlight on the winter and summer solstices, surfaces polished to a shine that had survived centuries of exposure to the elements.

"This was the most sacred building in Machu Picchu," Quispe said, his voice dropping to barely above a whisper. "Dedicated to Inti, the sun god, the divine ancestor of the Inca emperors. Only the highest priests were allowed to enter. The rituals performed here were the most important in the entire empire."

Elena studied the structure, noting the way it wrapped around the central rock, the precision of the joints where the stones met, the subtle asymmetries that suggested the builders had adapted their design to accommodate natural features rather than imposing a rigid plan. Beneath the main chamber, she could see the entrance to a cave—a natural grotto that had been incorporated into the temple's design.

"The Royal Tomb," Quispe said, following her gaze. "That's what Bingham called it, though no burial has ever been found there. It's possible the Inca used it for mummification rituals, or for storing sacred objects. But the cave itself goes deeper than anyone has fully explored."

"That's where we need to go."

"Yes. But we need to wait until the site clears out a bit. What we're about to do is... not exactly authorized."

They spent the next two hours playing the role of tourists, examining other structures, taking photographs, asking questions of the guides who led groups through the complex. Elena used the time to study the layout of the site, noting the positions of the guards, the patterns of foot traffic, the blind spots where someone might slip away unobserved.

By mid-morning, the main crowds had shifted toward the iconic viewpoints at the far end of the site, leaving the Temple of the Sun relatively quiet. Quispe caught Elena's eye and nodded almost imperceptibly. It was time.

***

The entrance to the Royal Tomb was roped off, a sign in multiple languages warning visitors not to enter. Quispe produced a key from his pocket—obtained, Elena assumed, through the same connections that had gotten them into the site—and unlocked the gate, ushering them through quickly before relocking it behind them.

The cave was cool and dark after the bright morning sun, the air heavy with the smell of damp stone and ancient earth. Elena clicked on her headlamp and swept the beam across the space, revealing walls that had been smoothed and shaped by human hands, niches carved into the rock that might once have held offerings or sacred objects, a ceiling that sloped downward as the cave penetrated deeper into the mountain.

"The passage I found is at the back," Quispe said, leading the way. "It was hidden behind a false wall—stones fitted together to look natural, but actually concealing an opening. We only found it because one of my students noticed that the acoustic properties of that section were different from the rest of the cave."

They moved deeper into the grotto, past formations that gleamed wetly in the lamplight, past carved stones that bore symbols Elena recognized from her studies of Inca iconography. The air grew cooler, damper, and she could hear the drip of water somewhere in the darkness ahead.

Quispe stopped before a section of wall that looked, to Elena's eyes, exactly like all the other sections they had passed. But when he pressed his palm against a particular stone and pushed, the wall shifted—grinding inward to reveal a narrow opening beyond.

"The Ministry ordered this sealed," Quispe said, his voice tight. "I supervised the work myself. But I made sure to leave... an alternative means of access."

"You knew someone would need to come back."

"I suspected. The things we found down here—the carvings, the symbols—they suggested something important had been hidden. Something that was meant to be found, eventually, by the right people." He met her eyes. "I've been waiting twenty years to find out what it was."

They squeezed through the opening one at a time—Elena first, then Ana, then Carlos and Miguel, and finally Quispe. The passage beyond was narrow but passable, carved from the living rock with the same precision that characterized all Inca construction. The floor sloped downward at a gentle angle, leading them deeper into the mountain.

Elena counted her steps as they descended. Fifty. A hundred. Two hundred. The passage twisted and turned, following the natural contours of the rock while maintaining its downward trajectory. The air grew colder, the silence more absolute, until the only sounds were their footsteps and the rasp of their breathing.

And then, without warning, the passage opened into a chamber that made Elena stop in her tracks.

It was vast—far larger than the cave in Colombia, larger than any underground space she had ever seen. The ceiling soared overhead, lost in darkness beyond the reach of her headlamp. The walls were covered with carvings that seemed to stretch into infinity—figures and symbols and scenes that told stories she could barely begin to comprehend. And at the centre of the chamber, illuminated by a shaft of light that filtered down from some unseen opening above, stood a structure that made her heart stop.

An altar. But not like any altar she had ever seen.

It was built from gold.

Not gilded stone or gold-plated metal, but solid gold—thousands of pounds of it, shaped into a platform perhaps three meters square and a meter high. The surface was covered with carvings that matched the symbols on the walls, intricate patterns that seemed to shift and move in the flickering light of their headlamps. And at the centre of the altar, resting in a depression that had been shaped to receive it, was a crystal case.

Inside the case, Elena could see pages of bark paper covered in glyphs.

The fourth fragment of the Codex of Seven Serpents.

"*Dios mío*," Ana breathed from behind her. "It's real. It's all real."

Elena approached the altar slowly, reverently, her footsteps echoing in the vast chamber. The gold gleamed in the light, warm and alive, and she could feel a strange energy emanating from it—a vibration, almost, that seemed to resonate with something deep inside her.

"The Inca called gold the 'sweat of the sun,'" Quispe said, his voice hushed with awe. "They believed it was sacred, a physical manifestation of divine power. They didn't value it for its monetary worth—that was a European obsession. They valued it because it connected them to the gods."

"This much gold..." Elena shook her head, trying to calculate the value. "This would be worth billions on the modern market."

"Which is why it was hidden. The Spanish would have melted it down, turned it into coins and bars, shipped it back to Europe to fund their wars and their churches. The Inca knew that. So, they hid it here, in a place that the conquistadors would never find."

Elena reached the altar and looked down at the crystal case. The fragment inside was similar to the others she had found—bark paper, glyphs in multiple writing systems, the distinctive combination of Maya and Muisca symbols interspersed with the older notation that predated both cultures. But there was something else here too. Something she hadn't seen before.

"These glyphs," she said, leaning closer. "They're different. More complex. This isn't just part of the formula—it's something else."

Ana joined her at the altar, her trained eye scanning the pages visible through the crystal. "You're right. The structure is different. This looks like... instructions. Directions to another location."

"One of the keys?"

"Maybe. Or maybe the location of the final piece of the formula." Ana pulled out her phone and began photographing the fragment through the crystal case. "We need to study this more carefully. But I think this might be the map we've been looking for."

Elena reached for the case, her fingers closing around the cool crystal. It lifted easily from its depression in the gold—no hidden mechanisms, no traps or alarms. The Inca, like the Muisca before them, had relied on secrecy rather than security. Anyone who made it this far was presumed worthy of what they found.

She tucked the case inside her jacket, feeling its weight against her chest alongside the other fragments she carried. Four pieces now. Three more to find.

"We should go," she said. "We've been down here too long. If anyone noticed us entering the tomb—"

A sound from the passage behind them cut her off.

Footsteps. Multiple sets, moving quickly, growing louder.

Carlos and Miguel drew their weapons, positioning themselves between the entrance and the rest of the group. Elena's hand moved to her own gun, her heart pounding as adrenaline flooded her system.

"Is there another way out?" she asked Quispe urgently.

"I don't know. I never explored beyond this chamber." His face was pale in the lamplight. "The passage we came through is the only exit I know of."

The footsteps grew louder. Voices echoed through the stone corridors—commands in German, sharp and professional. Elena felt her blood run cold.

Kroeger's men. They had found them.

"Spread out," she hissed. "Find cover. Maybe we can—"

The first figure emerged from the passage, weapon raised, tactical light cutting through the darkness. Then a second, a third, a fourth. They fanned out across the entrance to the chamber, their weapons trained on Elena and her companions, their movements coordinated with military precision.

And behind them, stepping into the chamber with the calm assurance of a man who had finally found what he had been seeking for sixty years, came Werner Kroeger.

16

The Devil's Bargain

Beneath Machu Picchu — Moments Later

Werner Kroeger looked exactly as Elena had imagined him—and nothing like it at all.

The photographs she had seen showed a younger man, vital and dangerous, his eyes burning with the fanaticism of a true believer. The figure who stood before her now was old—ancient, really, his body withered by the decades, his face a mask of wrinkles and age spots beneath the white stubble of his hair. He walked with the careful deliberation of someone who knew his body might betray him at any moment, and he carried no weapon that Elena could see.

But his eyes. His eyes were exactly as the photographs had shown them. Pale blue, cold as Arctic ice, burning with an intelligence and determination that the years had done nothing to diminish. They swept across the chamber, taking in the golden altar, the crystal case in Elena's hands, the defenders who stood between him and his prize.

"Dr. Vasquez," he said, his voice carrying easily across the vast space. "At last, we meet. I have been looking forward to this moment for quite some time."

Elena kept her hand on her weapon, though she knew it was futile. Kroeger had brought at least eight men—she could see them arrayed across the entrance to the chamber, their weapons steady, their expressions blank. Her group was outnumbered and outgunned. If it came to a firefight, they would lose.

"How did you find us?" she asked, buying time, searching for options.

"You are not as difficult to track as you believe, Dr. Vasquez. Your flight from Bogotá to Lima was noted. Your meeting with Professor Quispe was observed. Your trip to Cusco, your departure for Aguas Calientes—all of it monitored by people who know how to watch without being seen." Kroeger smiled thinly. "I have been hunting for the codex for sixty years. Did you think a few days' head start would be enough to elude me?"

"You killed Martin Thorne. You killed Santiago Ajpop. How many more people have to die for your obsession?"

"As many as necessary." Kroeger's voice was matter of fact, without a trace of remorse. "The knowledge contained in the codex is worth more than any number of individual lives. It is worth more than nations, more than civilizations. It is the key to understanding the true history of humanity—a history that has been suppressed and distorted by those who fear what it reveals."

"And what does it reveal? That some master race taught the indigenous peoples of the Americas everything they knew? That their achievements weren't really their own?" Elena's voice dripped with contempt. "That's not history, Kroeger. It's racist fantasy."

Something flickered in Kroeger's eyes—anger, perhaps, or wounded pride. "You understand nothing. The knowledge encoded in that codex predates all the civilizations of the Americas. It comes from a time before recorded history, before the ancestors of the Maya and the Muisca and the Inca arrived on this continent. The people who discovered the transmutation process were not indigenous to the

Americas—they came from elsewhere, from a civilization so ancient that we have forgotten it ever existed."

"And let me guess—this ancient civilization was Aryan? White? Superior to all the brown-skinned savages who came after?"

"The evidence will speak for itself." Kroeger's voice was calm again, controlled. "When the formula is assembled and tested, when its principles are understood, we will be able to trace its origins. We will know, finally, where the knowledge came from. And that knowledge will reshape our understanding of human history."

"Or it will prove what any competent archaeologist already knows—that ancient peoples were capable of remarkable achievements without any help from mythical white saviours."

Kroeger shrugged. "Perhaps. I am willing to let the evidence decide. Are you?"

The question hung in the air between them. Elena felt the weight of the crystal case against her chest, felt the eyes of everyone in the chamber fixed upon her. She thought about the journal entries she had read, about Fray Tomás's warnings that the formula was too dangerous to be used, that humanity was not ready for it.

She thought about what would happen if Kroeger got his hands on the complete codex.

"What do you want?" she asked finally.

"I want the fragments. All of them—the one you just took from this altar; plus the ones you found in Guatemala and Colombia. I know you have them with you. I also want the journal of Fray Tomás de Ávila and any notes or translations you have made."

"And in exchange?"

"Your lives. And the lives of your companions." Kroeger spread his hands. "I am not a monster, Dr. Vasquez. I take no pleasure in killing. If you give me what I want, you will be free to walk away. You can return to your museum, your academic career, your comfortable life. You can pretend this never happened."

"And you'll use the formula to prove your theories. To justify centuries of colonialism and oppression. To give ammunition to every racist and white supremacist on the planet."

"I will use the formula to reveal the truth. What people do with that truth is their own affair."

Elena looked at Ana, at Quispe, at Carlos and Miguel with their weapons ready but useless against the overwhelming force arrayed against them. She saw the fear in their eyes, the knowledge that they were moments away from death if she made the wrong choice.

And she thought about the Guardians. About Santiago, dying in a burning church to protect the secret he had sworn to keep. About the generations of men and women who had dedicated their lives to ensuring that this knowledge never fell into the wrong hands.

She thought about what they would want her to do.

"No," she said.

Kroeger's expression didn't change. "I beg your pardon?"

"I said no. I won't give you the fragments. I won't help you desecrate the legacy of peoples you consider inferior. I won't—"

"Elena." Diego's voice was urgent, warning. "Think about what you're doing."

"I know exactly what I'm doing." Elena met Kroeger's eyes, her own gaze steady despite the fear that churned in her gut. "You can kill me. You can kill all of us. But you won't get the fragments. They're hidden—not here, not on my person. If I die, the location dies with me."

It was a bluff. The fragments were in her jacket, inches from Kroeger's reach. But she kept her expression neutral, her voice confident, praying that he couldn't see through the deception.

Kroeger studied her for a long moment. Then, slowly, he smiled.

"You're lying," he said. "I can see it in your eyes. The fragments are on you—probably in that jacket you keep touching. My men could take them from your body in seconds."

"Then do it." Elena spread her arms, leaving herself exposed. "Kill me. Take what you want. But know this: the Guardian network is larger than you imagine. There are people watching, people waiting, people who will hunt you down if anything happens to me. You might get the fragments, but you'll never live to use them."

"The Guardian network is a myth. A collection of superstitious peasants playing at secret societies."

"Is it? Then how did I find the fragments in the first place? How did I know where to look, who to contact, what questions to ask?" Elena took a step forward, her voice rising. "The Guardians have been protecting this secret for five hundred years. They survived the conquest, the colonial period, the modern era. They'll survive you too."

For the first time, Elena saw uncertainty flicker across Kroeger's face. He had spent sixty years searching for the codex, following leads, eliminating obstacles. But he had never been this close before. And now, with his prize within reach, he was faced with the possibility that taking it might cost him more than he was willing to pay.

"You're bluffing," he said again, but his voice was less certain now.

"Am I? Are you willing to bet your life on that?"

The silence stretched between them, thick with tension. Kroeger's men stood ready, their weapons trained on Elena and her companions. One word from their leader, and the chamber would erupt in violence.

Then, from somewhere in the darkness behind the altar, a new voice spoke.

"She is not bluffing."

Everyone turned.

A figure emerged from the shadows—an old woman, ancient and frail, her face weathered by countless years of mountain sun. She wore traditional Quechua clothing, brightly coloured weavings that seemed out of place in this underground cathedral. Her eyes were dark and sharp, and they fixed on Kroeger with an intensity that made the old Nazi take an involuntary step backward.

"Who are you?" he demanded.

"I am Mama Qhispi. I am the Keeper of this place." The old woman walked forward slowly, her movements deliberate, unhurried. "I have been watching you, Werner Kroeger. Watching you for many years. You think you understand what you seek, but you understand nothing."

"How did you get in here? My men secured the entrance—"

"There are paths through this mountain that your men will never find. Paths that have been walked for a thousand years, since before your ancestors learned to write." Mama Qhispi stopped beside the golden altar, her hand resting on its gleaming surface. "The Guardian network is real, Kroeger. We are everywhere—in every country, every city, every community where the old knowledge has been preserved. You cannot defeat us. You cannot outlast us. And you will never possess what you seek."

Kroeger's face twisted with fury. "Kill her," he ordered.

One of his men raised his weapon—and then froze, his eyes going wide with shock.

Elena heard it a moment later. Sounds from the passage behind Kroeger's men. Footsteps. Voices. The distinctive click of weapons being readied.

And then, emerging from the darkness like ghosts, came more figures. Men and women, young and old, dressed in the clothing of farmers and labourers and professionals. They carried weapons—some modern, some ancient—and their faces bore the same expression of calm determination that Elena had seen on Santiago's face in the moments before his death.

Guardians. Dozens of them.

"You are outnumbered," Mama Qhispi said quietly. "And you are outmatched. The choice is yours, Kroeger. Leave now, and you may live. Stay, and you will die in this chamber, and your body will never be found."

Kroeger looked at the Guardians who now surrounded his men, at the weapons pointed at him from every direction, at the ancient woman who faced him without fear. Elena could see the calculation in his eyes—the cold assessment of odds, the weighing of risks and rewards.

For a long moment, she thought he might fight anyway. Thought he might order his men to open fire, to take as many Guardians with them as they could, to die rather than surrender his prize.

But Werner Kroeger had not survived eighty-seven years by making foolish decisions.

"This isn't over," he said, his voice tight with suppressed rage. "I will find the remaining fragments. I will complete the codex. And when I do, I will return, and nothing you can do will stop me."

"Perhaps," Mama Qhispi replied. "But not today."

Kroeger turned and walked toward the passage, his men falling in around him. At the entrance, he paused and looked back at Elena.

"We will meet again, Dr. Vasquez. And next time, I will not be so merciful."

Then he was gone, swallowed by the darkness of the passage, his footsteps fading into silence.

***

Elena let out a breath she hadn't realized she'd been holding.

Her legs felt weak, her hands trembling with the aftermath of adrenaline. She wanted to sit down, to process what had just happened, to understand how they had gone from certain death to unexpected salvation in the space of a few minutes.

But Mama Qhispi was approaching her, and Elena forced herself to stand straight, to meet the old woman's eyes.

"You have done well, Elena Vasquez," the Keeper said. "Santiago chose wisely when he passed his burden to you."

"You knew Santiago?"

"I knew of him. The network is large, but the Keepers communicate. We share information, coordinate our efforts, ensure that the secret is protected across generations." Mama Qhispi's eyes were warm now, the fierce intensity of moments ago replaced by something gentler. "He sent word before he died. He told us you were coming. He told us you were worthy."

Elena felt tears prick at her eyes. "He died protecting me. He died so I could escape with the fragment."

"He died fulfilling his purpose. As all Guardians hope to die." The old woman reached out and touched Elena's cheek, her fingers papery and warm. "Do not mourn him. Honor him. Continue the work he began."

"I don't know if I can. Kroeger is still out there. He'll find the remaining fragments—"

"Perhaps. Or perhaps you will find them first." Mama Qhispi smiled. "The codex has been divided for five hundred years. It can remain divided for a while longer. What matters is that it does not fall into the hands of those who would misuse it."

"And the formula itself? If we assemble it, if we learn how to transmute metals—what then?"

The old woman was silent for a long moment. When she spoke again, her voice was heavy with the weight of centuries.

"That is a question each generation must answer for itself. The ancients hid the formula because they believed humanity was not ready for it. Perhaps we are ready now. Perhaps we never will be." She met Elena's eyes. "But that decision is not mine to make. It belongs to you, and to those who will come after you. The Guardians protect the knowledge. We do not dictate how it should be used."

She turned and began walking toward the passage at the back of the chamber—the one she had emerged from, the one that led to paths Kroeger's men would never find.

"Wait," Elena called after her. "The remaining fragments—do you know where they are?"

Mama Qhispi paused at the entrance to the passage. "The Amazon. Mexico. Those are the places you must search next." She looked back over her shoulder. "But be warned, Elena Vasquez. The jungle holds dangers that make Kroeger seem like a minor threat. And the temples of Mexico are guarded by those who do not trust outsiders—even outsiders who carry the serpent's mark."

17

Dark's Heart

Somewhere Over the Amazon Basin — One Week Later

The small aircraft bucked and shuddered as it passed through another pocket of turbulence, and Elena gripped the armrest hard enough to turn her knuckles white.

Below them, the Amazon stretched to every horizon—an endless carpet of green broken only by the brown ribbons of rivers that wound through the jungle like serpents. From this altitude, it looked peaceful, almost inviting. But Elena knew better. The Amazon was one of the most dangerous places on Earth, home to predators both animal and human, diseases that could kill in hours, and terrain so impenetrable that entire expeditions had vanished without a trace.

And somewhere down there—she hoped—lay the fifth component of the formula.

Mama Qhispi had given them nothing.

Elena had asked, of course. After the confrontation with Kroeger, after the old woman's people had escorted them through passages that led out of the mountain to a village on the other side, Elena had pressed for information about the remaining fragments. The Amazon. Mexico. The locations that Fray Tomás had mentioned in his journal.

The Keeper had simply looked at her with those ancient, unreadable eyes.

"You carry what you need," she had said. And then she had turned and walked away, leaving Elena with a contact who could arrange transport out of Peru and nothing else.

No explanations. No helpful exposition about how the Guardian network operated. No convenient hints about where to search next.

Just silence, and the maddening certainty that the old woman knew more than she would ever say.

Elena had spent the journey from Peru in a state of frustrated obsession, poring over the fragments and the journal, searching for patterns she might have missed. Sleep had become a luxury she couldn't afford. Every waking moment was consumed by the puzzle—cross-referencing glyphs, mapping astronomical alignments, trying to decode the layers of meaning that Fray Tomás had buried in his careful, cryptic prose.

The breakthrough had come on the third night, in a safe house outside Bogotá.

She had been studying the Peru fragment, comparing its glyphs to those in the earlier pieces, when she noticed something she had overlooked before. A sequence of symbols in the margin—not part of the main text, almost like a notation or afterthought. The symbols didn't match any Maya or Muisca writing system she knew. But they did match something else.

The older notation. The mathematical language that predated both cultures.

Elena had seen similar sequences in each of the fragments, but she had assumed they were part of the formula itself—technical instructions for the transmutation process. Now, looking at them with fresh eyes, she saw something different. The sequences varied from fragment to fragment, but they shared a common structure. A pattern that repeated with subtle variations.

Coordinates.

Not modern latitude and longitude—the ancients hadn't used that system. But something analogous: a method of encoding location using astronomical references and geographical markers. The Peru fragment contained one set of coordinates. The Guatemala fragment contained another. The Colombia fragment, another still.

And when Elena plotted them on a map, accounting for the differences between ancient and modern astronomical calculations, they formed a pattern.

Three points she had already visited.

And two more she hadn't.

One deep in the Amazon basin, in a region where the borders of Colombia, Brazil, and Peru converged. The other in southern Mexico, in the highlands where Maya and Aztec territories had once overlapped.

It wasn't proof. The calculations involved enormous margins of error, and Elena was working with incomplete data and educated guesses about how the ancient coordinate system functioned. But it was a lead—the first solid lead she had developed on her own, without being handed information by helpful Guardians.

She had felt something shift inside her at that moment. A sense of ownership over the quest that had been missing before. She wasn't just following a trail that others had laid out for her. She was doing what Martin had trained her to do: analysing evidence, forming hypotheses, testing them against the available data.

She was being an archaeologist.

***

The plane began its descent, dropping toward a break in the canopy where a crude airstrip had been carved from the jungle. Elena watched the trees rushing up to meet them, felt the wheels touch down on packed earth, heard the engines reverse as the pilot fought to slow them before they ran out of runway.

They came to a stop at the edge of the strip, where the jungle pressed in on all sides like a living wall. The heat hit Elena the moment she stepped out of the aircraft—thick, humid, oppressive, like walking into a steam bath. Within seconds, her clothes were damp with sweat.

The airstrip served a small community of rubber tappers and Brazil nut gatherers—people who lived at the edge of the modern world, maintaining a precarious existence in one of the most remote regions on Earth. They regarded the newcomers with wary curiosity, and Elena saw how their eyes lingered on the jade pendant she wore openly now, no longer bothering to conceal it beneath her shirt.

No one commented on it. But she noticed an old woman at the edge of the clearing make a subtle gesture—touching her forehead, then her heart—before turning away.

Recognition? Or just coincidence?

Elena filed it away and focused on the immediate challenge: finding a guide who could take them deeper into the forest.

Most of the locals refused outright. The region Elena had identified on her map was known to them, and the knowledge brought fear rather than curiosity.

"Bad place," one man said, shaking his head emphatically. "People go there, they don't come back. The forest swallows them."

"What's in there?" Elena asked.

The man's expression closed like a door slamming shut. "Nothing. Nothing is there. You should go home."

It was Diego who finally found someone willing to talk.

He was an old man, ancient really, his face weathered by decades of jungle sun and his body bent by years of hard labour. He sat alone at the edge of the village, weaving a fishing net with fingers that moved with practiced automaticity. When Diego approached and showed him Elena's map, the old man's hands went still.

He didn't speak for a long moment. Then, without looking up, he said: "Why do you seek the hidden ones?"

Diego glanced at Elena, who had come to stand beside him. She stepped forward and lifted the jade pendant from her chest, letting it catch the dappled sunlight that filtered through the canopy.

The old man's eyes widened. His hands trembled slightly as he set down his work and rose to his feet—slowly, painfully, but with a dignity that transformed his frail frame into something almost regal.

"I have not seen that symbol in sixty years," he said quietly. "Not since my grandmother showed it to me, when I was a boy. She said that someday, someone would come carrying that mark. Someone who needed to find the way."

"Did she tell you where the way leads?"

"No." The old man shook his head. "She said she did not know. She said her own grandmother had not known. The knowledge was lost, long ago—or perhaps it was never ours to begin with." He studied Elena with rheumy eyes that held a sharpness belying his age. "But she taught me the signs to look for. The markers that would show the path, if I ever needed to find it."

"Will you guide us?"

The old man was silent for a long moment. Elena could see the conflict in his face—fear warring with duty, caution battling against a sense of obligation that had been passed down through generations.

"I am too old to walk that far," he said finally. "But my grandson knows the signs. I taught him, as my grandmother taught me." He turned and called out a name in a language Elena didn't recognise.

A young man emerged from one of the huts—perhaps twenty years old, lean and watchful, with the coiled energy of someone accustomed to moving through difficult terrain. He looked at his grandfather, then at Elena, then at the pendant that still hung against her chest.

His expression revealed nothing.

"This is Tomas," the old man said. "He will take you as far as he can. After that..." He shrugged. "After that, you will have to find your own way. Or the way will find you."

***

They travelled by boat for three days, following rivers that grew progressively narrower and more treacherous as they pushed deeper into the jungle.

Tomas spoke little, and what he did say was purely practical — warnings about rapids ahead, instructions for navigating around fallen trees, terse commands to keep hands inside the boat when caimans surfaced nearby. He showed no curiosity about why they were making this journey or what they expected to find at the end of it. Elena suspected his grandfather had told him not to ask.

But he knew the signs.

Elena watched him as they travelled, noting how his eyes constantly scanned the shoreline, pausing occasionally on features that seemed random to her—a particular tree, a rock formation, a pattern in the vegetation. Sometimes he would adjust their course based on these observations, steering toward one bank or another for reasons he didn't explain.

On the second day, Elena began to see the markers herself.

They were subtle—so subtle that she would have missed them entirely if she hadn't been watching for them. A stone placed at the base of a tree; its surface carved with a glyph she recognised from the codex fragments. A pattern of cuts on a branch, too regular to be natural, forming a symbol that matched one in Fray Tomás's journal. A clearing where the trees grew in a configuration that echoed the mathematical proportions she had seen encoded in the ancient notation.

The Guardians—or whoever had created this trail—hadn't left signposts. They had left a language, written in the landscape itself, readable only by those who knew the vocabulary.

"How old are these markers?" she asked Tomas on the evening of the second day, as they made camp on a sandbar in the middle of the river.

He looked at her for a long moment, as if weighing whether to answer. Then he shrugged.

"My grandmother said they were old when her grandmother was young. And her grandmother said the same thing." He turned back to the fire he was building. "The forest remembers things that people forget."

***

On the fourth day, they left the boats behind.

The river had narrowed to the point where navigation was impossible—more stream than waterway, choked with vegetation and debris. Tomas led them into the jungle on foot, following a path that existed only in his mind, marked by signs that Elena was learning to read but couldn't yet interpret with confidence.

The going was brutal. The vegetation pressed in from all sides, vines and branches and roots conspiring to block every step. The heat was suffocating, the humidity so thick that breathing felt like drinking warm water. Insects swarmed around them in clouds, biting every inch of exposed skin despite the repellent they applied liberally.

But Elena barely noticed the discomfort. Her attention was focused on the landscape; on the subtle changes she was beginning to perceive beneath the chaos of the primary forest.

The ground was different here. Harder, more level, as if something solid lay beneath the accumulated leaf litter of centuries. The trees grew in patterns that were too regular to be natural—rows and clusters that suggested orchards or groves, planted by human hands and then abandoned to the jungle's reclamation. And occasionally, jutting from the undergrowth like bones from a shallow grave, she glimpsed stones that were too square, too smooth, to have been shaped by anything but human intention.

"Tomas," she said quietly. "Do you know what this place is?"

The young man had stopped walking. He stood at the edge of a slight rise in the terrain, looking down at something Elena couldn't yet see.

"My grandfather said there was a city here once," he replied, his voice barely above a whisper. "A city that was old when his people first came to this forest, thousands of years ago. They did not build it. They only found it, and they learned to... to respect it. To guard what it contained, even though they did not understand what they were guarding."

He turned to look at her, and for the first time, Elena saw something other than professional detachment in his eyes. Fear. And beneath the fear, a kind of awe.

"This is as far as I go," he said. "The signs end here. What lies beyond..." He shook his head. "My grandmother said that only those who carry the serpent's mark may enter. Anyone else who tries will be... discouraged."

"What does that mean?"

Tomas didn't answer. He simply pointed toward the rise and stepped aside.

Elena climbed the small hill, pushing through the last barrier of vegetation, and stopped at the top.

Below her, hidden in a natural depression in the landscape, lay the ruins of a temple.

It was not Maya or Inca or Muisca—it was something else entirely, something that predated all of those civilisations by centuries or millennia. The architecture followed principles she had never seen, curves where she expected angles, proportions that seemed to shift and flow like water frozen in stone. The structure was covered in vegetation—vines and roots and moss that had been accumulating for ages—but beneath the green shroud, she could see glimpses of worked stone that gleamed with a faint inner luminescence.

And carved above the entrance, barely visible beneath the encroaching jungle, was a symbol she knew.

The serpent swallowing its own tail.

"Stay here," she told the others. "All of you. I need to go in alone."

"Elena—" Diego began.

"Tomas said only those who carry the mark can enter safely. I don't know what that means, but I'm not willing to risk your lives finding out." She touched the jade pendant at her throat. "I have the credentials. You don't."

She didn't wait for further argument. She descended the slope toward the temple entrance, her heart pounding, her senses alert for any sign of the "discouragement" Tomas had mentioned.

The jungle seemed to grow quieter as she approached, the constant background noise of birds and insects fading to an eerie silence. The air grew cooler, carrying a faint metallic scent that reminded her of the chamber beneath Machu Picchu. And the pendant against her chest began to feel warm—not unpleasantly so, but noticeably, as if responding to something in the environment.

She reached the entrance and paused, studying the carved archway above it. The serpent symbol was flanked by other glyphs—some she recognised from the codex fragments, others that were unfamiliar. She traced them with her fingers, feeling the grooves worn smooth by time, and tried to read the message they contained.

The seeker who carries the mark of the seven may enter.

The seeker who comes with false intent will find only darkness.

Not a threat. A warning. A test, possibly.

Elena took a deep breath and stepped through the archway into the temple.

* * *

The interior was dark, but not absolutely so.

A faint luminescence emanated from the walls themselves—the same phenomenon she had observed from outside, stronger here, providing enough light to see by once her eyes adjusted. The chamber she had entered was small, perhaps five metres across, with passages leading off in three directions.

No obvious clues about which way to go.

Elena stood still and let her training take over. She was an archaeologist. She had spent her career learning to read spaces; to understand how ancient peoples had designed their environments and what those designs revealed about their beliefs and intentions.

The three passages were not identical. The one on the left was slightly wider, its floor worn smoother by what might have been frequent foot traffic. The one on the right was narrower, more deliberately constrained, with carvings along its walls that suggested ritual or ceremonial significance. And the one directly ahead was perfectly proportioned, its dimensions following the same mathematical ratios she had observed in the temple's exterior.

Harmony. Balance. The principles that the creators of the codex had embedded in everything they built.

Elena chose the centre passage.

She walked for what felt like hours but was probably only minutes, the luminescent walls providing just enough light to see her next few steps. The passage descended gradually, taking her deeper into the earth, and the air grew cooler and damper as she went.

Finally, the passage opened into a chamber that made her catch her breath.

It was vast—far larger than anything she had expected to find beneath this jungle ruin. The ceiling soared overhead, supported by columns carved in shapes that seemed to represent serpents and jaguars and figures she didn't recognise. The walls were covered with murals that depicted scenes of incredible complexity: people in strange garments performing rituals around structures that might have been furnaces or laboratories, symbols and equations that suggested scientific principles far beyond anything the known ancient cultures had possessed.

And at the centre of the chamber, on a pedestal of polished black stone, sat a crystal case.

Inside it, Elena could see pages of bark paper covered in glyphs.

The fifth fragment.

She approached slowly, reverently, half expecting some trap or test to spring from the shadows. But nothing happened. The chamber remained silent and still, the luminescent walls casting their soft glow over everything, as if the temple had been waiting for this moment and was content to let it unfold.

Elena lifted the case from its pedestal.

The pages inside were similar to the other fragments—the same hybrid notation, the same combination of Maya and Muisca symbols interspersed with the older mathematical language. But there was something else here too: diagrams that looked like chemical processes, instructions that seemed to describe purification procedures, warnings about toxic byproducts that could result from improper execution.

One of the "keys" that Fray Tomás had mentioned. The safeguards without which the formula could not be used safely.

But it was the final page that made Elena's hands tremble.

A diagram. Partial, incomplete—a fragment of a larger map, showing rivers and mountains and a path that led to... something. The lines continued to the edge of the page and stopped, clearly meant to connect with information contained in other fragments.

Directions. Not complete directions, but a piece of the puzzle. A piece that, combined with the information in the other fragments, might reveal the location of the final hiding place.

El Dorado.

Elena tucked the case into her pack and began the long walk back to the surface, her mind already racing through the calculations she would need to perform, the cross-references she would need to check, the patterns she would need to identify.

Two fragments left. And somewhere, encoded in the pieces she had already gathered, was the key to finding them.

She just had to figure out how to read it.

18

Land of the Feathered Serpent

Cancún, Mexico — Two Weeks Later

The heat of the Yucatán was different from the Amazon—drier, more relentless, baking down from a sky that seemed to bleach colour from everything it touched.

Elena stood on the balcony of their hotel room, looking out over the tourist sprawl of Cancún's hotel zone, and felt the familiar frustration that had been her constant companion for the past two weeks.

Five fragments. Five pieces of the puzzle. Yet still, she couldn't find the sixth.

The Amazon fragment had confirmed what she had suspected: each piece of the codex contained partial information about the locations of the others, encoded in the mathematical notation that the ancients had used as a kind of universal language. By comparing the coordinate sequences across all five fragments, Elena had been able to triangulate a region—the Yucatán Peninsula, somewhere in the area where Maya and Aztec cultural spheres had overlapped.

But "a region" was not a location. The Yucatán contained thousands of archaeological sites, ranging from massive complexes like Chichén Itzá to tiny villages that had never been properly excavated. Without more specific information, they could search for years and never find the right place.

The journal of Fray Tomás offered tantalising hints but no clear answers. The friar had written about "the temple of the Feathered Serpent" and "the place where the sun speaks to the earth," but those descriptions could apply to dozens of sites throughout Mesoamerica. He had mentioned "the chamber beneath the chamber," which suggested a hidden space within a known structure, but that too was frustratingly vague.

Elena had spent days analysing the glyphs, mapping astronomical alignments, cross-referencing every piece of information she had gathered. She had called in favours from colleagues at universities across Mexico, requesting access to unpublished survey data and obscure academic papers. She had studied satellite imagery until her eyes burned, looking for anomalies in the landscape that might indicate undiscovered structures.

Nothing.

"You need to sleep," Ana said from inside the room.

"I need to find the fragment."

"You need to do both. You're running on fumes, Elena. You've barely eaten in three days, and I don't think you've slept more than a few hours total. You can't solve this puzzle if you're too exhausted to think."

Elena knew Ana was right. But every hour that passed was an hour that Kroeger could use to catch up. The old Nazi had resources she couldn't match—money, manpower, decades of accumulated research. He might have information she lacked, clues that would lead him to the remaining fragments while she was still stumbling in the dark.

She couldn't afford to rest. She couldn't afford to fail.

"Give me one more hour with the fragments," she said. "Then I'll sleep. I promise."

Ana sighed but didn't argue. She had learned that Elena in this mood was impossible to dissuade.

Elena returned to the table where she had spread out her materials: photographs of the fragments, pages from the journal, maps covered in annotations and calculations. She had been over all of it dozens of times, searching for the pattern she knew must be there, the key that would unlock the final pieces of the puzzle.

She picked up the photograph of the Peru fragment and studied it again, focusing on the partial map it contained. Rivers and mountains, converging on a point that was cut off at the edge of the page. If she overlaid it with the partial map from the Amazon fragment, the lines almost connected—but not quite. There was a gap, a missing piece that prevented her from seeing the complete picture.

Two maps that almost connect, she thought. *What if the other fragments contain the missing pieces?*

She pulled out photographs of the Guatemala and Colombia fragments, searching for similar diagrams. She had assumed the map elements were only present in the later fragments—the "keys" that Fray Tomás had mentioned—but what if she had been wrong? What if the information had been distributed more widely than she realised?

There. In the margin of the Guatemala fragment. A sequence of lines she had initially dismissed as decorative, but which now, viewed in the context of the other maps, looked like they might be part of the same system.

She grabbed a sheet of tracing paper and began copying the elements from each fragment, layering them on top of each other, adjusting for scale and orientation. Her hands were trembling with exhaustion and excitement as the pieces began to come together.

The maps fit.

Not perfectly—there were still gaps, still missing sections that must be contained in the fragments she hadn't yet found. But enough of the picture was visible now to see what the ancients had encoded in their scattered puzzle.

A path. Starting from the temple in the Amazon, winding north through the mountains of Peru, across the isthmus of Central America, and into the Yucatán. Terminating at a point that, when Elena plotted it on a modern map, corresponded to a location she knew.

Not Chichén Itzá. Not Tulum or Cobá or any of the major tourist sites.

A smaller site. Less famous. Often overlooked by visitors who focused on the more spectacular ruins nearby.

Ek' Balam.

***

The drive from Cancún took nearly three hours, winding through countryside that shifted from tourist development to traditional Maya villages to dense scrubland punctuated by ancient stone walls and half-buried structures.

Ek' Balam was smaller than Elena had expected—a compact complex centred on a massive pyramid known as the Acropolis, its facade decorated with elaborate stucco sculptures that had survived remarkably well despite centuries of exposure to the elements. The site was quieter than the more famous ruins, drawing a fraction of the visitors, and as Elena walked through the entrance, she felt a sense of potential that had been missing from their earlier searches.

This could be it. This could be the place.

But where within the complex was the fragment hidden?

The journal offered one more clue: *the chamber beneath the chamber*. A hidden space within a known structure. At Ek' Balam, that almost certainly meant the Acropolis—the largest building on the site, and the one most likely to contain undiscovered rooms or passages.

Elena and her companions spent the rest of the day exploring the pyramid, photographing every surface, looking for signs of the markers she had learned to recognise in the Amazon. The tourists were a complication—it was difficult to examine the structure closely without attracting attention—but by late afternoon, the crowds had thinned, and they had more freedom to investigate.

It was Diego who found it.

"Elena." His voice was carefully controlled, but she could hear the excitement beneath the surface. "Come look at this."

He was standing near the base of the Acropolis, at a point where a stucco sculpture of a winged figure guarded the entrance to a sealed chamber—one of several false doorways that decorated the pyramid's facade. The sculpture was elaborate, depicting a figure with outstretched wings and an elaborate headdress, its face frozen in an expression of serene authority.

But that wasn't what had caught Diego's attention.

On the figure's chest, almost invisible against the weathered stucco, was a symbol.

A serpent swallowing its own tail.

"It's been here the whole time," Elena breathed. "Hidden in plain sight. Thousands of tourists must have photographed this sculpture without ever noticing."

"Because they didn't know what to look for." Diego traced the symbol with his finger. "But we do."

Elena examined the area around the symbol, looking for the mechanism that would open the hidden entrance. The Amazon temple had required the jade pendant; the other sites had used similar keys. There had to be something here—some way to activate whatever ancient technology the builders had installed.

She found it on the figure's hands—a depression in each palm, shaped like a smaller version of the serpent symbol. Two keys, not one. A security measure, perhaps, requiring either two pendants or a single pendant used twice.

"Stand back," she said.

She pressed the jade pendant into the left depression and felt it click into place. Nothing happened. She removed it and tried the right depression—same result. Then, on instinct, she tried something different: pressing the pendant into the left depression while simultaneously pressing her thumb into the right one.

The stone figure shuddered.

A grinding sound emerged from deep within the pyramid—ancient machinery awakening after centuries of dormancy. The false doorway beside the sculpture began to shift, revealing darkness beyond.

Elena retrieved her pendant and clicked on her flashlight.

"Wait here," she told the others. "Same as before."

"Elena, we don't know what's in there—"

"I know. But the rules seem to be consistent. The temples don't hurt people who carry the mark." She touched the pendant. "I'll be fine."

She stepped through the doorway before anyone could argue further.

***

The passage beyond was narrow but passable, descending at a steep angle into the heart of the pyramid. The walls were covered with paintings—not the weathered remnants she had seen on the exterior, but vibrant murals that looked as if they had been completed yesterday. Scenes of ritual and celebration, of astronomical observation and mathematical calculation, of figures in elaborate costumes performing acts that might have been worship or might have been science.

The passage levelled out and opened into a chamber that made Elena's breath catch.

It was smaller than the Amazon temple—perhaps ten metres across—but every surface was covered with the most intricate carvings she had ever seen. Glyphs in a dozen different writing systems, mathematical notation that made her head spin, diagrams that depicted processes she couldn't begin to understand. And above the central pedestal, dominating the chamber, was a carving of the feathered serpent itself—Kukulcán, the Maya called it; Quetzalcoatl to the Aztecs—its coils wrapped around a sphere that might have represented the earth or the sun or something else entirely.

On the pedestal sat two objects.

A crystal case containing the sixth fragment.

And a golden tablet covered in text that Elena recognised immediately.

She approached the pedestal and lifted the crystal case first, examining the pages inside. The glyphs confirmed what she had hoped: this was another "key," containing information about the final stages of the transmutation process—the completion procedures that would allow the formula to be used safely.

But it was the golden tablet that drew her attention.

She lifted it carefully, feeling its weight, studying the symbols etched into its surface. Unlike the bark paper fragments, this was a single coherent document—not part of the formula itself, but something else. Instructions. Explanations. Context.

And at the centre, surrounded by explanatory text, was a complete map.

Not partial, not fragmented. Complete.

Elena traced the lines with her finger, following the path from a starting point she now recognised—the Amazon temple—through intermediate locations that corresponded to the hiding places of the other fragments, and finally to a destination deep in the jungle of the Amazon-Peru border.

She had seen partial versions of this map in the other fragments. But here, at last, was the complete picture.

The location of the seventh fragment.

The location of El Dorado.

Elena photographed the tablet from multiple angles, making sure to capture every detail. Then she tucked both objects into her pack and began the journey back to the surface, her mind racing with the implications of what she had found.

Six fragments. One more to go.

And now, finally, she knew where to look.

***

She emerged from the pyramid to find Diego and Ana waiting anxiously by the entrance. The sun had set while she was underground, and the site was bathed in the blue twilight that preceded full darkness.

"Well?" Diego asked.

Elena pulled out her phone and showed them the photographs of the golden tablet.

"I found it," she said. "The sixth fragment and something else—a complete map to the seventh. To El Dorado."

Ana studied the image, her brow furrowed. "Can you read the location?"

"It's deep in the jungle. The border region between Peru and Brazil—not far from where we found the Amazon fragment, actually. It's going to be difficult to reach, and even more difficult to find once we're there. But we have what we need now." Elena looked at her companions, seeing her own exhaustion reflected in their faces. "We can actually finish this."

"Kroeger is still out there," Diego reminded her.

"I know. But we have something he doesn't—a head start, and the complete map." Elena tucked her phone away. "We need to move fast.

Get out of Mexico, get to Peru, find the seventh fragment before he can catch up with us."

"And then?"

Elena was silent for a moment, thinking about the weight of what she carried. Six fragments of a formula that could transform the world. Keys that protected knowledge that ancient peoples had considered too dangerous to share. Directions to a place that had been hidden for five hundred years.

"Then we make a decision," she said finally. "About what to do with what we find."

They left Ek' Balam as the stars emerged overhead, heading back toward Cancún and the next leg of their journey.

Behind them, the ancient pyramid stood silent and watchful, keeping its secrets as it had for a thousand years.

But one secret, at least, was no longer hidden.

19

River of No Return

Manaus, Brazil — Two Weeks Later

The city rose from the jungle like a fever dream.

Manaus sprawled across the confluence of the Rio Negro and the Solimões, two million people crowded into a metropolis that had no business existing this deep in the Amazon basin. Elena watched it approach from the window of the turboprop that had carried them from Lima—a jumble of high-rises and favelas, industrial ports and colonial architecture, all of it surrounded by an endless sea of green that stretched to every horizon.

This was not the Amazon of documentaries and adventure novels. This was a modern city, with traffic jams and shopping malls and a football stadium that had hosted World Cup matches. It had an international airport, five-star hotels, and a thriving tech sector that had earned it the nickname "the Silicon Valley of the jungle."

It also had, according to Elena's research, one of the highest murder rates in Brazil, a thriving drug trade, and a network of corruption so entrenched that even federal authorities had largely given up trying to untangle it.

Welcome to the gateway of the Amazon.

They cleared customs without incident—Elena traveling on her legitimate Smithsonian credentials, the others on documents that Quispe's contacts had provided before their hasty departure from Peru. The fragments were hidden in specially designed cases that looked like ordinary research equipment, padded and sealed against the humidity. If anyone had opened them, they would have found what appeared to be replicas of pre-Columbian artifacts, the kind of thing academic researchers carried all the time.

No one opened them.

The heat hit Elena the moment she stepped outside the air-conditioned terminal—thick, wet, oppressive, like breathing through a warm towel. Within seconds, her clothes were damp with sweat. The air smelled of exhaust fumes, rotting fruit, and something green and alive that she supposed was the jungle itself, pressing in on the city from all sides.

"Our hotel is in the Centro," Diego said, consulting his phone. "About twenty minutes from here, depending on traffic."

"And our contact?"

"I'm still working on that." Diego's expression was troubled. "The name Quispe gave us—Ribeiro—he's not answering his phone. Could mean anything. Could mean nothing."

Elena nodded, unsurprised. Their network of contacts had been fraying ever since the confrontation in Peru. Kroeger's people were out there somewhere, and they had resources that Elena couldn't match. It was entirely possible that Ribeiro had been bought, threatened, or simply decided that helping them wasn't worth the risk.

They would have to find another way.

***

The hotel was a mid-range establishment near the famous Teatro Amazonas—the opera house that rubber barons had built at the height of the boom, importing Italian marble and French chandeliers to prove that civilisation could flourish even in the heart of the wilderness. Elena barely glanced at the ornate facade as their taxi crawled past. Her mind was already working on the problem of how to reach the coordinates marked on the golden tablet.

The location she had identified was roughly three hundred kilometres northwest of Manaus, in a region where the borders of Brazil, Colombia, and Peru converged. On paper, it should have been accessible—there were rivers that led in that direction, villages that could serve as staging points, guides who made their living taking tourists and researchers into the remote areas of the basin.

In practice, it was considerably more complicated.

The region she needed to reach was technically part of an indigenous reserve—legally protected territory where access required permits that could take months to obtain. It was also, according to the news reports Elena had read on the flight, an active corridor for drug trafficking, with Colombian cartels using the remote waterways to move product toward the Brazilian coast. And it was home to several uncontacted indigenous groups, whose territories were zealously guarded by FUNAI, the Brazilian agency responsible for indigenous affairs.

Going there without proper authorisation would be illegal. Going there with proper authorisation would take time they didn't have. And going there at all would be dangerous in ways that had nothing to do with ancient temples or Guardian networks.

"We need a fixer," Elena said, once they had settled into their rooms. "Someone who knows the region, knows the players, can help us navigate the bureaucracy—or get around it."

"That's going to cost money," Diego pointed out. "Serious money. The kind of people who operate in that space don't work cheap."

"We have money." Méndez-Castellón's accounts had been frozen after his disappearance, but Elena had managed to access emergency funds that the Venezuelan had set aside for exactly this kind of situation. It wasn't unlimited, but it was enough to buy cooperation from people whose cooperation was for sale.

"And if we can't find someone trustworthy?"

"Then we find someone untrustworthy and watch them carefully." Elena opened her laptop and began searching for contacts. "This is Manaus. Everyone has an angle. We just need to find someone whose angle aligns with ours."

***

The fixer's name was Carla Mendes, and she operated out of a cramped office above a boat repair shop in the Educandos district, surrounded by maps, satellite phones, and stacks of paper that might have been permits or might have been something else entirely.

She was not what Elena had expected.

Elena had imagined someone rough, weathered—the kind of person who appeared in movies about the Amazon, all stubble and sweat-stained khaki. Carla was perhaps forty, impeccably dressed in a silk blouse and tailored trousers, her hair pulled back in a sleek ponytail, her nails painted a shade of red that matched her lipstick. She looked like she should be running a PR firm in São Paulo, not arranging illegal expeditions into indigenous territories.

"Dr. Vasquez." Carla's handshake was firm, professional. "I've heard interesting things about you."

"From whom?"

"From people who pay attention to such things." Carla gestured to a pair of chairs facing her desk. "Please, sit. Tell me what you need."

Elena sat, studying the woman's face for any sign of deception. She found nothing—just the polished blankness of someone who had learned to keep her thoughts invisible.

"I need to reach a location approximately three hundred kilometres northwest of here," Elena said. "In the reserve territory, near the Colombian border."

"That's restricted access. You'd need permits from FUNAI, environmental clearances, possibly authorisation from the indigenous communities themselves. The process takes months."

"I don't have months."

"No one ever does." Carla leaned back in her chair, her expression unchanging. "What's at the location?"

"Archaeological site. Pre-Columbian. Possibly significant."

"Significant enough to risk prison time?"

"Significant enough to risk considerably more than that."

Carla was silent for a moment, studying Elena with eyes that gave nothing away. Then she smiled—a thin, professional smile that didn't reach her eyes.

"I can get you into the reserve," she said. "I have contacts at FUNAI who owe me favours, boat captains who know the rivers, guides who won't ask questions. It will cost you fifty thousand US, half up front, half when you reach your destination."

"That's a lot of money."

"It's a lot of risk. If something goes wrong—if you get caught, or if something happens to you out there—I need to be able to disappear for a while. That costs money." Carla shrugged. "You're welcome to find someone cheaper. But cheaper usually means less reliable, and in the reserve, unreliable can get you killed."

Elena thought about the fragments in her pack, about the map that pointed to a location where the seventh piece of the codex had waited for five centuries. She thought about Kroeger, somewhere out there, hunting for the same prize.

"Done," she said. "When can we leave?"

"Three days. I need time to arrange the logistics." Carla stood and extended her hand. "Transfer the first payment by tomorrow evening. I'll be in touch with details."

Elena shook her hand, sealing the bargain.

Three days. Then the final leg of the journey would begin.

***

They spent the waiting time in a state of productive anxiety.

Elena continued her analysis of the fragments, refining her calculations, trying to pinpoint the exact location they were seeking. The coordinates she had derived from the golden tablet pointed to a specific area, but "specific" in the Amazon could still mean hundreds of square kilometres of trackless jungle. She needed more precision.

Diego worked his contacts, trying to gather intelligence about the region they would be entering. What he learned was not encouraging. The area was known to locals as *terra proibida*—forbidden land—not because of any government restriction, but because of the stories that surrounded it. Stories about expeditions that went in and never came out. Stories about compass needles spinning wildly, GPS units losing signal, experienced guides becoming hopelessly lost in terrain they should have known intimately.

Ana focused on practical preparations—supplies, equipment, medical kits, the thousand small necessities that could mean the difference between survival and disaster in the remote jungle. She worked with the quiet efficiency of someone who had done this before, who understood that proper preparation was not glamorous but was absolutely essential.

And Carlos and Miguel maintained security, watching for any sign that Kroeger's people had tracked them to Manaus. They found nothing—which was either reassuring or deeply troubling, depending on how you chose to interpret it.

On the evening of the second day, Elena received a message from Carla.

Change of plans. Meet me at the Porto Flutuante, slip 47, tomorrow at 5 AM. Come alone.

Come alone. Elena stared at the message, weighing the risks. It could be a trap—Carla could have sold them out to Kroeger, or to someone else entirely. It could be a test—the fixer wanting to assess Elena's judgment, her willingness to follow instructions. Or it could be exactly what it appeared to be: a logistical necessity, some complication that required a private conversation.

She forwarded the message to Diego with a brief note: *If I'm not back by noon, assume the worst.*

Then she set her alarm for 4 AM and tried to sleep.

* * *

The Porto Flutuante—the floating port—was a maze of wooden docks and moored vessels that rose and fell with the river's seasonal fluctuations. At five in the morning, it was already bustling with activity—fishermen unloading their night's catch, merchants setting up stalls, boat crews preparing for departure. The air smelled of diesel fuel and fish, and the wooden planks were slick with moisture from the morning mist.

Elena found slip 47 at the far end of the commercial section, where a weathered riverboat was tied up alongside the dock. The vessel was perhaps fifteen metres long, with a covered deck and a small wheelhouse—the kind of craft that carried cargo and passengers to the remote communities scattered along the Amazon's countless tributaries.

Carla was waiting on the deck, dressed considerably more practically than she had been at their first meeting—cargo pants, hiking boots, a light jacket that probably concealed a weapon. She nodded when she saw Elena approach.

"Come aboard. We need to talk."

Elena climbed the gangplank and followed Carla into the wheelhouse, where a man in his sixties sat nursing a cup of coffee. He had the weathered look of someone who had spent his life on the river—skin tanned to leather, hands calloused from years of handling ropes and equipment, eyes that seemed to look through you rather than at you.

"This is Capitão Ferreira," Carla said. "He's been running boats on the upper Amazon for forty years. He knows the rivers better than anyone."

Ferreira grunted acknowledgment but didn't offer his hand.

"I've told him where you want to go," Carla continued. "He has some... concerns."

"What kind of concerns?"

Ferreira set down his coffee cup and spoke for the first time. His voice was rough, gravelly, accented with something Elena couldn't quite place.

"I've taken people into that territory three times," he said. "First time was thirty years ago. Group of Americans looking for some kind of lost city. They had money, equipment, maps. Three weeks later, I picked up one survivor, half-dead from fever, raving about spirits in the forest. The others were never found."

He picked up his cup again, took a long sip.

"Second time was maybe fifteen years ago. Brazilian scientists, government expedition. They had military escort, satellite communications, everything. They lasted two weeks before calling for extraction. Wouldn't talk about what happened. I heard later that two of them ended up in psychiatric care."

"And the third time?"

"Five years ago. A German." Ferreira's eyes met Elena's. "Old man, very determined. Paid very well. Had a team of professionals with him—ex-military, heavily armed."

Elena felt her stomach tighten. "What happened to him?"

"I don't know. I dropped him at a village upriver, same place I'm taking you. He was supposed to radio for pickup in two weeks." Ferreira shrugged. "He never called. I went back to check, but there was no sign of him. The village people said he'd gone into the forest and never returned."

Kroeger. It had to be. Five years ago, the old Nazi had mounted his own expedition to find the seventh fragment—and he had failed.

"But you're willing to take us anyway?" Elena asked.

"I'm willing to take you as far as the village. What you do after that is your business." Ferreira's expression was unreadable. "But I want you to understand what you're getting into. That territory... it's not like other places. The compass doesn't work right. The GPS loses signal. People who go in don't come out. I don't know why, and I don't want to know. I just know that whatever's in there, it doesn't want to be found."

"Maybe it just hasn't found the right person yet," Elena said.

Ferreira studied her for a long moment. Then, slowly, he smiled—a thin, humourless expression that didn't reach his eyes.

"Maybe," he said. "Or maybe you're just another fool who thinks she's special." He stood and moved toward the wheel. "We leave in two hours. Get your people and your gear aboard by then or find another boat."

20

Hidden City

Upper Amazon Basin — Eight Days Later

The river had been narrowing for two days, and now it was barely wide enough for Ferreira's boat to navigate. Vegetation pressed in from both sides, branches scraping against the hull as they pushed upstream. The water was black here—stained dark by tannins from the decaying vegetation, so opaque that Elena couldn't see more than a few centimetres below the surface. The air was thick with humidity and the sounds of the forest: birds calling, insects humming, the occasional splash of something large moving through the water nearby.

They had left the last village three days ago—a small community of perhaps fifty people who made their living fishing and harvesting Brazil nuts. The residents had been friendly enough, happy to sell them supplies and share information about the river conditions ahead. But when Elena had asked about the territory beyond, the conversation had dried up.

Not fear, exactly. More like... discomfort. The look people got when you asked about something they'd rather not think about.

One old woman had been willing to talk, after Elena pressed a hundred-real note into her hand. She'd spoken of stories her grandmother had told her, about a place deep in the forest where the old ones had lived before the river people came. A place that was sacred, forbidden, protected by spirits that didn't like strangers.

"Did anyone ever go there?" Elena had asked.

"Some tried." The old woman's eyes had been distant, remembering. "When I was young, a man from the village decided to find it. He was gone for two weeks. When he came back, his hair had turned white. He wouldn't speak of what he'd seen. A month later, he walked into the forest and never returned."

Stories. Just stories. But stories that were consistent across multiple sources, spanning generations and communities that had little contact with each other. Something was out there. Something that had been protecting itself for a very long time.

"We're getting close," Elena said, studying the GPS unit that had been growing increasingly unreliable over the past day. The signal kept cutting out, then returning, the coordinates jumping erratically before settling down. According to her calculations, they were perhaps twenty kilometres from the target location. "The river should fork soon. We need to take the left branch."

Ferreira grunted acknowledgment from the wheelhouse. He had grown progressively more taciturn as they'd pushed deeper into the territory, his usual gruff demeanour hardening into something closer to grim determination. Whatever he believed about the stories, he clearly didn't like being here.

The fork appeared an hour later—two channels splitting off from the main river, the left one noticeably narrower and more overgrown than the right. Ferreira eased the boat into the smaller passage, cutting their speed to barely more than walking pace.

"This is as far as I go," he said. "Water's too shallow ahead—I'll ground out if I try to push through."

Elena looked at the GPS. They were still fifteen kilometres from the target coordinates—a long distance to cover on foot through trackless jungle.

"Can you wait for us here?"

"For how long?"

"I don't know. A week, maybe longer."

Ferreira was silent for a moment, his weathered face unreadable. Then he nodded slowly. "One week. After that, I'm heading back downriver. If you're not here, I'll assume you're not coming."

"Fair enough."

They unloaded their gear onto the muddy bank—packs loaded with supplies, the fragments secured in waterproof cases, weapons distributed among the group. Elena took one last look at the boat, at Ferreira standing in the wheelhouse watching them with an expression that might have been concern or might have been relief.

Then she turned and led her team into the jungle.

***

The terrain was brutal.

Elena had thought she understood what hiking through the Amazon would be like—she had done research, watched documentaries, read accounts from expeditions that had penetrated the deep jungle. None of it had prepared her for the reality.

The vegetation was a living wall, so dense in places that they had to hack through it with machetes, making progress measured in metres rather than kilometres. The ground was a treacherous mix of mud, roots, and hidden holes that could twist an ankle or swallow a leg up to the knee. The humidity was suffocating, the heat relentless, and the insects attacked in waves that no amount of repellent could fully discourage.

And then there were the other obstacles.

The GPS had stopped working entirely within an hour of leaving the boat—the screen showing nothing but static, the unit unable to acquire a signal despite the clear sky overhead. Their compasses began behaving strangely soon after, the needles drifting and spinning instead of pointing steadily north. Elena had expected this, based on the stories she'd heard, but expecting it and experiencing it were two different things.

They navigated by dead reckoning, using the sun and the terrain features Elena had memorised from the satellite imagery. It was imprecise at best, but it was all they had.

On the second day, they found the first marker.

It was a stone, half-buried in the leaf litter, its surface carved with a glyph Elena recognised from the codex fragments. The serpent swallowing its tail, surrounded by smaller symbols that might have been directional indicators or might have been something else entirely.

"We're on the right track," she said, feeling a surge of relief.

They found more markers over the following days—stones, carvings on trees, patterns in the way the vegetation grew that were too regular to be natural. The ancients had left a trail, just as they had at the other sites. But this trail was different. More subtle. Harder to follow. As if whoever had created it had wanted to make absolutely sure that only the most determined seekers would find their way through.

On the fourth day, they encountered the first test.

* * *

The clearing appeared without warning—one moment they were pushing through dense undergrowth, the next they emerged into a space perhaps fifty metres across, dominated by a structure that made Elena stop in her tracks.

It was a gateway.

Two massive stones, each perhaps five metres tall, supporting a lintel carved with symbols that seemed to writhe in the dappled sunlight. The style was unlike anything Elena had seen before—not Maya, not Inca, not Muisca, but something older, something that predated all of those civilizations by centuries or millennia.

And standing in front of the gateway, blocking the path beyond, were people.

There were perhaps a dozen of them—men and women, ranging from young adults to weathered elders. They were dressed in a mixture of traditional and modern clothing: some wore woven garments decorated with patterns that echoed the symbols on the gateway, others wore t-shirts and cargo pants that could have come from any market in Manaus. Several carried weapons—not spears or bows, but modern rifles and shotguns, well-maintained and clearly functional.

They did not look surprised to see Elena and her team. They looked like they had been waiting.

One of them stepped forward—a woman perhaps Elena's age, with sharp eyes and an expression that gave nothing away. She studied Elena for a long moment, her gaze dropping to the pendant that hung against Elena's chest.

"You've come far," she said in Portuguese. Her accent was strange—not quite Brazilian, not quite anything else Elena could identify. "Further than most."

"I'm looking for—"

"I know what you're looking for." The woman's voice was flat, uninflected. "The question is whether you're worthy of finding it."

"How do I prove that?"

The woman smiled—a thin expression that didn't reach her eyes. "You don't. You've already proven it, or you wouldn't have made it this far. The forest tests everyone who enters. The unworthy turn back, or get lost, or die. You're still here. That tells us something."

She turned and gestured toward the gateway.

"Beyond this point, only the bearer of the mark may pass. Your companions must wait here."

"For how long?"

"For as long as it takes." The woman's eyes met Elena's. "If you return, they'll be free to leave with you. If you don't..." She shrugged. "We'll escort them back to the river. We're not murderers."

Elena looked at Diego, at Ana, at Carlos and Miguel. They had come so far together, risked so much. The idea of leaving them behind, even temporarily, felt like a betrayal.

But she had known this moment would come. The other temples had been the same—each one requiring her to enter alone, to face whatever lay within without the support of her companions. This was how the system worked. This was how the Guardians—or whatever these people called themselves—ensured that the secret remained protected.

"I'll be back," she said.

Diego nodded, his expression troubled but accepting. "We'll be here."

Elena turned and walked toward the gateway, her heart pounding, her hand touching the pendant at her chest. The people parted to let her pass, their faces impassive, their eyes tracking her every movement.

She stepped through the gateway and into the darkness beyond.

***

The path led downward.

Not into a building or a cave, but into the earth itself—a passage carved through rock and soil, reinforced with stone walls that glowed with the same faint luminescence she had seen in the other temples. The light was enough to see by, but barely, casting everything in shades of blue and grey that made the passage feel like something from a dream.

Elena walked for what felt like hours, though it might have been less. The passage twisted and turned, descended and climbed, following a path that seemed designed to disorient. There were no markers here, no glyphs to guide her way. Just the passage, and the light, and the sound of her own breathing echoing off the stone walls.

Finally, the passage opened into a chamber.

It was vast—larger than any of the other temple chambers she had encountered, so large that the far walls were lost in shadow. The ceiling soared overhead, supported by columns carved in shapes that defied easy description: spirals and curves and angles that seemed to shift when she tried to focus on them. The floor was polished smooth, reflecting the luminescent glow like dark water.

And at the center of the chamber, on a pedestal of black stone, sat the seventh fragment.

Elena approached slowly, half-expecting some final test, some ultimate challenge that would determine whether she was truly worthy. But there was nothing—just the fragment, waiting, as it had waited for five hundred years.

She lifted the crystal case from the pedestal and opened it.

The pages inside were similar to the other fragments—bark paper, ancient glyphs, the hybrid notation that combined Maya and Muisca and something older still. But there was something else as well: a folded sheet of different paper, yellowed with age but clearly European in origin.

A letter. Written in Spanish. In a hand she recognized.

Fray Tomás de Ávila.

Elena unfolded the letter and began to read.

To whoever finds this:

If you hold this letter in your hands, you have accomplished what I could not. You have gathered the seven fragments of the Codex of Seven Serpents. You have found your way to this place, which I knew existed only through the testimony of those who had been here before me.

I congratulate you. And I pity you.

For you now face the choice that I spent my life avoiding. The choice of what to do with the knowledge you possess.

The formula works. I have seen the proof with my own eyes—watched as base metal was transformed into gold, as the laws that govern matter were bent by the will of those who understood how to bend them. It is not magic, though it seems like magic. It is science, of a kind that our modern world has forgotten or never discovered.

But the formula is not the true secret. The true secret is what the ancients learned in the process of discovering it.

They learned that matter is not what it appears to be. That the boundaries between substances—between elements, between states of being—are illusions, constructs of perception rather than fundamental truths. They learned that transformation is not just possible but inevitable, that everything in the universe is constantly becoming something else, and that with the right knowledge, this process can be guided, directed, controlled.

They learned, in short, that reality itself is mutable.

This knowledge terrified them.

Not because it was false, but because it was true. Because they understood what would happen if it spread—if every person, every nation, every civilization gained the power to reshape matter according to their will. They saw the wars that would be fought, the destruction that would be wrought, the chaos that would consume the world as everyone struggled to control the ultimate power. So, they hid it.

The formula was divided into seven parts and scattered across the world. They created networks of guardians to protect each piece, passing the responsibility down through generations. They designed the hiding places so that only someone who truly understood what they were seeking would be able to find them.

And they hoped that by the time someone finally assembled all seven pieces, humanity would have evolved enough to handle what they discovered.

I do not know if that hope was justified. I do not know if humanity is ready for this knowledge, or if it ever will be. I only know that the choice is no longer mine to make.

It is yours.

You can use the formula to create gold, to amass wealth beyond imagination. You can use the underlying principles to transform the world in ways I cannot begin to predict. Or you can destroy everything—burn the fragments, scatter the ashes, ensure that this knowledge remains hidden for another five hundred years.

I cannot tell you what to do. I can only tell you what I believe.

Some knowledge is too dangerous to be possessed. Some power is too great to be trusted to any single person, any single na-

tion, any single generation. The ancients understood this. That is why they hid what they discovered.

Perhaps you are wiser than they were. Perhaps you can find a way to use this knowledge for good, to share it with the world without unleashing the chaos they feared.

Or perhaps you will make the same choice they made, and I made. The choice to protect humanity from itself.

Whatever you decide, know that you do not decide alone. The guardians are watching. They have always been watching. And they will continue to watch, long after you and I are dust.

May God guide your hand,

Fray Tomás de Ávila, 1703

Elena read the letter twice, her mind struggling to absorb what it implied.

Then she folded it carefully, placed it back in the case with the fragment, and began the long walk back to the surface.

She had found what she was looking for.

Now she had to decide what to do with it.

21

The Weight of Knowledge

The Hidden City — Later That Day

The passage back to the surface felt longer than the descent. Elena walked in silence, the crystal case heavy in her pack, her mind churning through the implications of what she had read. The formula was real. The ability to transform matter—to reshape reality itself—was not myth or legend but documented fact, waiting to be rediscovered by anyone who assembled the seven fragments.

And she had all seven.

The thought should have felt triumphant. After everything she had endured—the deaths, the betrayals, the desperate flights across continents—she had succeeded where countless others had failed. She had found El Dorado. Not a city of gold, but something far more valuable: knowledge that could change the world.

Instead, she felt only dread.

Fray Tomás's words echoed in her mind: *Some knowledge is too dangerous to be possessed. Some power is too great to be trusted to any single person, any single nation, any single generation.*

The ancients had understood this. They had hidden their discovery not because they feared it would be misused—though surely that was part of it—but because they understood what would happen when everyone had access to it. Wars fought not over territory or resources, but over the power to reshape existence itself. Nations rising and falling as the old constraints of scarcity and material limitation vanished. A world transformed beyond recognition, for better or worse.

Was humanity ready for that?

Was anyone?

The luminescent glow of the passage walls began to brighten, and Elena realised she was nearing the surface. She quickened her pace, suddenly desperate to see sky again, to breathe air that hadn't been filtered through kilometres of stone.

She emerged from the gateway into afternoon sunlight that made her squint after hours in the dim underground. The clearing was as she had left it—the massive stone portal, the jungle pressing in on all sides, the people who had been waiting when she arrived.

But something had changed.

Diego and the others were no longer standing freely. They were on their knees at the edge of the clearing, hands bound behind their backs, surrounded by armed figures who were not the same people Elena had seen before.

And standing in front of them, his aged face creased with satisfaction, was Werner Kroeger.

***

"Dr. Vasquez." Kroeger's voice was calm, almost pleasant, as if they were meeting at an academic conference rather than in the heart of the Amazon jungle. "I must confess, I'm impressed. You've accomplished in weeks what took me decades to merely approach."

Elena's hand moved toward her weapon, but she stopped when she saw the guns trained on her companions. Diego's face was bloody—he'd clearly put up a fight before being subdued. Ana looked terrified but unharmed. Carlos had a wound on his shoulder that was still seeping red through a makeshift bandage.

"How did you find us?"

"The same way I've always found things, Dr. Vasquez. Patience. Resources. And a willingness to do what others won't." Kroeger gestured to the men surrounding him—a dozen at least, hard-faced professionals carrying military-grade weapons. "Your fixer in Manaus. Carla, wasn't it? She was quite willing to share your itinerary once the price was right."

Elena felt a cold fury settle in her chest. "She sold us out."

"Everyone sells out eventually. It's simply a matter of finding the right currency." Kroeger's pale eyes fixed on the pack Elena carried. "But enough about logistics. You have something I want."

"The fragments."

"All seven, if I'm not mistaken. Including the one you just retrieved from that rather impressive underground chamber." He smiled thinly. "Yes, I know about the chamber. I found this place five years ago, but I couldn't get past the guardians. They were... uncooperative. I lost good men trying to force my way through."

Elena glanced around the clearing. The people who had been here before—the ones who had let her pass through the gateway—were gone. Either fled, or killed, or hiding somewhere in the jungle. She had no way of knowing which.

"The guardians let me pass because I carried the mark," she said. "Because I'd earned the right to enter."

"Ah yes. The pendant. The sacred symbol of the serpent cult." Kroeger's voice dripped with contempt. "Superstitious nonsense, of course. The 'guardians' are simply descendants of the people who built this place, maintaining traditions they no longer understand. The tests they impose are nothing but security measures, designed to keep out those who haven't done their homework."

"And yet you couldn't pass them."

Kroeger's expression flickered, anger, then quickly suppressed. "A temporary setback. I would have found another way, given time. But you've saved me the trouble." He extended his hand. "The fragments, Dr. Vasquez. All of them. Now."

"And if I refuse?"

"Then I kill your friends, one by one, until you change your mind." His voice was matter of fact, without heat. "Starting with the woman. She seems to be important to you."

One of his men grabbed Ana by the hair, yanking her head back to expose her throat. A knife appeared in his other hand, its edge glinting in the sunlight.

"Wait." Elena's voice came out steadier than she felt. "Wait. I'll give you what you want."

"A wise decision."

Elena slowly unslung her pack and set it on the ground. Her mind was racing, searching for options, finding none. Kroeger had overwhelming force, he had hostages, and he was clearly willing to kill. There was no clever way out of this. No daring escape. Just the brutal arithmetic of power.

She opened the pack and withdrew the crystal cases one by one, setting them on the ground at her feet. Seven cases. Seven fragments. The accumulated knowledge of a civilisation that had discovered how to reshape reality.

Kroeger's eyes gleamed as he watched the cases emerge. "All of them. Excellent." He gestured to one of his men. "Bring them to me."

The man stepped forward and gathered the cases, carrying them back to Kroeger with the careful reverence of someone handling something precious. Kroeger opened each one in turn, examining the contents, his expression shifting from satisfaction to something approaching rapture.

"Do you understand what this is?" he murmured, almost to himself. "Do you have any idea what I hold in my hands?"

"Knowledge that was hidden for a reason."

"Hidden by cowards. By people too afraid of their own discovery to share it with the world." Kroeger looked up, his pale eyes blazing with an intensity that made Elena's skin crawl. "The formula for transmuting matter. The secret that could have changed history—could have elevated humanity to heights undreamed of—if only it hadn't been buried by superstitious fools who feared their own power."

"They weren't afraid of the power. They were afraid of what people would do with it."

"What people would do with it is *progress.*" Kroeger's voice rose, decades of frustrated ambition pouring out. "Imagine a world where scarcity doesn't exist. Where anyone can create whatever they need from whatever materials are at hand. Where the chains of material limitation that have bound humanity since the beginning of time are finally broken."

"That's not what you want it for."

Kroeger's expression hardened. "What I want is irrelevant. What matters is what will happen when this knowledge is released. The old order will crumble. The structures that have kept humanity divided—nations, economies, hierarchies of wealth and power—will become meaningless. And from that chaos, something new will emerge. Something better."

"Or something worse."

"Perhaps. But that's the price of progress." Kroeger closed the final case and tucked it under his arm. "In any case, the choice is no longer yours to make. Thank you for your assistance, Dr. Vasquez. You've been more helpful than you know."

He turned and began walking toward the edge of the clearing, where Elena could see more of his men waiting with equipment and supplies. A full expedition, properly outfitted. He had planned this carefully.

"What about us?" Elena called after him.

Kroeger paused but didn't turn around. "What about you?"

"You have what you want. Let us go."

"I'm afraid that's not possible." His voice was almost apologetic. "You know too much. You've seen too much. If I let you go, you'll try to stop me—warn people, raise alarms, interfere with my work. I can't allow that."

"So you're going to kill us."

"I'm going to leave you here. What happens after that is up to the jungle." He gestured to his men. "Bind them. All of them. Then we move out."

Elena didn't resist as rough hands grabbed her arms and forced them behind her back. There was no point. She was outnumbered, outgunned, and out of options.

But as the rope tightened around her wrists, she noticed something.

One of the crystal cases—the one containing the seventh fragment—was slightly open. Just a crack, barely visible, but enough that Elena could see the corner of Fray Tomás's letter peeking out.

Kroeger hadn't read it. He had the fragments, but he didn't have the friar's warning. He didn't know about the choice Elena had faced, or the reason the ancients had hidden their discovery.

He thought he had won.

He had no idea what he was walking into.

22

Into the Dark

The Hidden City — Night

They had been left in the clearing, bound hand and foot, as night fell over the jungle.

Kroeger's men had been thorough, checking the knots and confiscating anything that might be used to cut the ropes, even taking their shoes to make escape more difficult. Then they had disappeared into the forest, following their leader toward whatever destination he had planned for his triumphant return to civilisation.

Leaving Elena and her companions to die.

The jungle came alive after dark. Sounds that had been background noise during the day became sharp and immediate—the rustle of predators moving through the undergrowth, the calls of nocturnal birds, the buzzing of insects that seemed to grow louder with each passing hour. The air grew cooler but no less humid, and the darkness was absolute, broken only by the faint glow of stars visible through gaps in the canopy.

"Can anyone move?" Diego's voice came from somewhere to Elena's left, tight with pain but still functional.

"Barely." That was Carlos. "The bastard who tied me knew what he was doing."

"Same here." Ana's voice trembled slightly. "Elena? Are you all right?"

"I'm fine." Elena was working at her bonds, twisting her wrists in the darkness, searching for any give in the rope. There was none. Kroeger's men were professionals. "I'm trying to find something to cut these. There should be rocks nearby—the clearing was full of them."

She began moving, inching across the ground like a worm, using her bound hands to feel for anything with a sharp edge. The leaf litter was damp and slimy beneath her, and more than once she felt something small and many-legged skitter across her fingers. She forced herself not to recoil. There would be time to be disgusted later—if there was a later.

Her fingers found stone. Smooth. Useless. She kept searching.

"Someone's coming." Miguel's voice was barely above a whisper.

Elena froze, straining her ears. At first she heard nothing—just the ordinary sounds of the jungle at night. Then, gradually, she became aware of something else. Footsteps. Quiet, careful, but definitely human.

More than one person.

She felt a spike of fear. Kroeger's men, coming back to finish the job? Predators of the two-legged variety, looking to rob whoever was foolish enough to be caught helpless in the jungle at night?

Or something else entirely.

Figures emerged from the darkness—shadows against shadows, moving with the confidence of people who knew this terrain intimately. Elena counted four, then six, then lost track as more appeared from different directions. They surrounded the clearing, their movements coordinated but unhurried.

One of them approached Elena and crouched down beside her.

"You're still alive." It was the woman from earlier—the one who had spoken to Elena at the gateway. "That's something."

"The man who took the fragments—"

"We know. We watched." The woman's voice was flat, revealing nothing. "We couldn't stop them. They had too many guns, too much willingness to use them. Three of our people are dead."

"I'm sorry."

"Don't be. They knew the risks." The woman produced a knife and began cutting Elena's bonds. "The question now is what we do about it."

"We go after him. Get the fragments back."

"That's not your decision to make." The woman finished with Elena's ropes and moved on to Diego. "You found what you came for. You passed through the gateway, retrieved the seventh fragment. Your part in this is finished."

"My part in this isn't finished until I decide it's finished." Elena rubbed her wrists, trying to restore circulation. "Kroeger has the formula. If he figures out how to use it—"

"He won't."

"You can't know that."

The woman paused in her work, her dark eyes meeting Elena's in the faint starlight. "The formula requires more than knowledge. It requires understanding. The ability to perceive connections that aren't obvious, to manipulate forces that most people don't believe exist. The old man has spent his life studying the fragments from the outside, analysing them as historical artifacts. He doesn't have the..." She struggled for a word. "The *vision* to make it work."

"And if you're wrong?"

"Then the world changes. Maybe for the better, maybe for the worse." She shrugged and resumed cutting. "That's always been the risk."

Elena watched as her companions were freed one by one, each of them stretching and groaning as circulation returned to their limbs.

Her mind was working furiously, trying to process what the woman had said.

The formula required more than knowledge. It required understanding. Vision.

That matched what she had read in Fray Tomás's letter—his description of the ancients' discovery not just of a process, but of a fundamental truth about the nature of reality. The formula worked not because of the specific steps it described, but because of the principles that underlay those steps. Principles that couldn't be grasped through analysis alone.

Kroeger had the fragments. But did he have the understanding to use them?

"You said three of your people died," Elena said slowly. "Does that mean you're going to let him go? Just walk away with the most important discovery in human history?"

The woman finished freeing Miguel and stood, sliding her knife back into its sheath. "I said your part in this is finished. I didn't say anything about ours."

She turned and spoke to her companions in a language Elena didn't recognise. There was a brief discussion—voices low, gestures emphatic—and then the group began to move, melting back into the jungle with the same silent efficiency with which they had arrived.

"Wait." Elena started after them. "Let us help. We know Kroeger—how he thinks, how he operates. We can—"

"You can rest." The woman's voice came from somewhere in the darkness. "Recover your strength. In the morning, you'll be escorted back to the river. Your boat is still there—the captain is waiting."

"I'm not leaving."

Silence. For a moment, Elena thought the woman had simply gone, disappeared into the jungle along with her companions.

Then: "Why?"

"Because I started this. Because people died to get me here—people who trusted me, believed in me, gave their lives so I could find what was hidden. I'm not going to walk away now and leave the ending to someone else."

Another silence. Longer this time.

"The old man has at least twelve armed professionals with him. We have eight people, only three of whom have military experience. Even if we catch him, the odds aren't good."

"Then we improve the odds."

"How?"

Elena's mind raced through possibilities. Kroeger had numbers and firepower, but he also had vulnerabilities. He was in unfamiliar territory. His men were professionals, but they were also mercenaries—fighting for money, not conviction. And he was carrying something he didn't fully understand, something that might prove more dangerous to him than to anyone else.

"We don't attack him head-on," Elena said. "We harass him. Slow him down. Make his people nervous, make them doubt whether the money's worth the risk. And we look for an opportunity—a moment when his guard is down, when we can take back what he stole without a pitched battle."

The woman reappeared at the edge of the clearing, her face barely visible in the starlight. "That would require tracking him through the jungle, staying close without being detected, waiting for days or even weeks for the right moment."

"I'm patient."

"It would also require risking your life for something that may not succeed."

"I've been risking my life for weeks. I'm used to it."

The woman studied her for a long moment. Then, surprisingly, she smiled.

"My name is Yara," she said. "If you're determined to do this, then we do it together. But you follow my lead, and you do exactly what I tell you. Understood?"

"Understood."

Yara nodded once and turned back toward the jungle. "We leave in one hour. Rest while you can."

She disappeared into the darkness, leaving Elena standing in the clearing with her companions, the sounds of the jungle pressing in from all sides.

"Elena." Diego's voice was cautious. "Are you sure about this?"

"No." Elena looked at her friends—battered, exhausted, facing odds that any rational person would call impossible. "But I'm doing it anyway."

***

They moved through the jungle like ghosts.

Yara's people knew this territory in a way that Elena couldn't have matched with years of study. They read the forest—tracks, broken branches, disturbances in the leaf litter—with an ease that made Elena feel like a child learning to walk. They moved silently, communicating through gestures and subtle signals, covering ground at a pace that left Elena breathless while seeming to expend no effort at all.

And they were gaining.

Kroeger's group was larger and better armed, but they were also louder, slower, less attuned to the environment. They left traces everywhere—footprints, discarded wrappers, the faint smell of cigarette smoke that lingered in the humid air. They were following the river, heading back toward the village where they had presumably arranged for extraction.

It would take them three days to reach it. Yara's people could do it in two.

"We get ahead of them," Yara explained during a brief rest on the second day. "Set up at a point where the trail narrows, where they can't spread out. That's when we make our move."

"What kind of move?"

"That depends on how they're arranged. If the fragments are being carried at the front, we hit the rear and draw their fire, then send a small team around to grab them during the confusion. If they're at the rear, we reverse it." She shrugged. "We improvise."

"What about Kroeger himself?"

"What about him?"

Elena hesitated. Part of her wanted Kroeger dead—wanted him to pay for Martin, for Santiago, for all the people who had died because of his obsession. But another part remembered Fray Tomás's letter, his warning about the chaos that would come if the formula was released. Killing Kroeger wouldn't solve that problem. Someone else would find his notes, continue his work, eventually piece together what he had discovered.

The formula couldn't be un-discovered. It could only be hidden, protected, kept out of reach until humanity was ready for it.

If humanity was ever ready.

"If we get the chance to capture him, we take it," she said finally. "But the fragments are the priority. Everything else is secondary."

Yara nodded. "Agreed."

They pressed on.

***

The ambush site was a narrow ravine where the trail descended steeply toward a stream crossing. The walls on either side were too steep to climb quickly, and the vegetation was thick enough to provide cover for Yara's people while limiting the effectiveness of Kroeger's superior firepower.

It was as good a place as they were going to find.

They arrived six hours ahead of Kroeger's group and spent the time preparing. Positions were established, fields of fire were cleared, escape routes were identified in case things went wrong. Elena found herself assigned to a spot on the eastern wall of the ravine, alongside Ana and one of Yara's men—a silent figure named Paulo who communicated primarily through nods and hand signals.

"When the shooting starts, stay down," Paulo said—the most words he had spoken to her in two days. "Don't try to be a hero. Just watch for an opening and be ready to move when I tell you."

Elena nodded, checking her weapon for the tenth time. It was one of the rifles they had recovered from Kroeger's men—the ones who had been left to guard the clearing and had disappeared when Yara's people arrived. Elena didn't ask what had happened to them. She wasn't sure she wanted to know.

The wait was the hardest part.

Hours passed. The sun moved across the sky, filtered through the canopy into shifting patterns of light and shadow. Insects hummed. Birds called. Once, a snake slithered past Elena's position, close enough to touch, its scales gleaming in the dappled sunlight. She forced herself to remain still.

Finally, as the light began to fade toward evening, she heard them coming.

Voices first—low murmurs, the occasional laugh, the casual conversation of men who thought they were safe. Then footsteps, the crack of branches, the distinctive sound of a large group moving through dense vegetation without any attempt at stealth.

They appeared at the top of the ravine. Elena counted them as they began their descent: twelve men, spread out in a loose formation, weapons carried casually rather than at the ready. Kroeger was near the middle, flanked by two of his largest guards, the pack containing the fragments visible on his back.

The fragments. Right there. Within reach.

Elena's finger tightened on her trigger. But she held her fire, waiting for Yara's signal.

The first shot came from the western wall—a single crack that echoed through the ravine, followed by the collapse of one of the lead men. Then everything exploded.

Gunfire erupted from both sides, muzzle flashes strobing in the dim light. Kroeger's men scattered, diving for cover, returning fire in the general direction of the ambush. Screams cut through the noise—wounded men, dying men, professionals whose confidence had evaporated in an instant.

Elena fired twice, aiming at movement rather than specific targets. She saw one of Kroeger's men stagger and fall. Saw another take cover behind a tree, his rifle barking as he searched for targets in the vegetation above.

And she saw Kroeger.

He had dropped to the ground the moment the shooting started, his guards forming a protective barrier around him. But now he was moving—crawling toward the stream, toward the far end of the ravine where the trail continued into the jungle.

Trying to escape.

"Paulo!" Elena pointed. "Kroeger—he's running!"

Paulo looked, assessed, nodded. "Go. I'll cover you."

Elena didn't hesitate. She slid down the ravine wall, half-falling, half-scrambling, hitting the bottom in a spray of leaf litter and mud. The firefight raged around her—bullets whining overhead, shouts and screams filling the air—but she blocked it out, focusing only on the figure struggling toward the stream.

She caught him at the water's edge.

Kroeger turned as she approached, and for a moment, their eyes met. He looked old—older than Elena had ever seen him—his face grey with exhaustion and fear. His guards were gone, either dead or fighting for their lives somewhere in the chaos behind. He was alone.

"Dr. Vasquez." His voice was surprisingly steady. "It seems we find ourselves at an impasse."

"Give me the fragments."

"And if I refuse?"

Elena raised her weapon. "Then I take them."

Kroeger studied her for a long moment. Then, slowly, he shrugged off the pack and set it on the ground between them.

"You won't use them," he said. "I can see it in your eyes. You're afraid of what they represent—afraid of the power they contain. You'll take them, hide them, convince yourself that you're protecting humanity from itself." He smiled bitterly. "Just like all the others. Just like the guardians who have been sitting on this knowledge for five hundred years, too cowardly to let it transform the world."

"Maybe. Or maybe I'll find a way to use them that doesn't end in chaos."

"There is no such way. That's what you don't understand. The formula is absolute—it doesn't distinguish between good intentions and bad ones. Once it's out, once people understand what's possible, there's no controlling what happens next." Kroeger's voice rose. "The only question is who guides that transformation. Someone with vision, with purpose? Or the random chaos of a million individual agendas?"

"And you think you're the one with vision?"

"I know I am. I've spent my entire life preparing for this moment. I understand what the formula means, what it makes possible, how it can be used to reshape human civilisation. You?" He gestured dismissively. "You're a scholar. A researcher. You study the past because you're afraid of the future. You don't have the courage to use what you've found."

The gunfire behind them was dying down—sporadic shots now, rather than the continuous roar of moments ago. The battle was ending. One way or another.

"Maybe you're right," Elena said. "Maybe I don't have the courage to use it. But I have the courage to make sure you don't."

She bent down and picked up the pack, keeping her weapon trained on Kroeger the entire time.

"What will you do?" he asked. "Kill me? Imprison me? It won't matter. The knowledge is out there now—in my notes, my research, the minds of people I've trained. Even if you destroy the fragments, someone will eventually reconstruct what I've discovered. You can't stop progress, Dr. Vasquez. You can only delay it."

"Then I'll delay it. As long as I can. As long as it takes."

She turned and began walking back toward the ravine, where Yara's people were emerging from their positions, the survivors of Kroeger's team lying dead or bound on the jungle floor.

Behind her, she heard Kroeger call out one last time: "You'll regret this! You'll see what you've given up, what you could have been, and you'll regret it for the rest of your life!"

Elena didn't look back.

She had the fragments. She had won.

As she walked through the carnage of the ambush site, though, stepping over bodies and spent shell casings, she couldn't shake the feeling that Kroeger might be right.

She might regret this; forever.

23

Reckoning

The Hidden City — Two Days Later

The rain came on the second day.

Not the gentle showers Elena had experienced in other parts of the Amazon, but a deluge—water falling from the sky in sheets so thick she could barely see three metres ahead. It hammered the jungle canopy with a sound like continuous thunder, found its way through every gap in the leaves, turned the trails to rivers of mud that sucked at their boots and made every step a battle against the earth itself.

Elena's world had shrunk to the few metres of visibility the rain allowed. The person ahead of her—one of Yara's people, a young man named Rafael who moved through the jungle like he'd been born to it—was little more than a dark shape in the grey curtain of water. Behind her, she could hear Diego cursing steadily in Spanish as he fought to keep his footing on the treacherous ground.

They had been moving since before dawn, pushing toward the river where Ferreira's boat waited. The route that had taken them four days to travel inward would take at least three going back, assuming the weather didn't slow them further. Assuming the rivers didn't rise too high to cross. Assuming nothing else went wrong.

Elena had learned to stop assuming.

The pack on her back was heavy—heavier than its physical weight should have accounted for. The seven crystal cases containing the fragments of the Codex of Seven Serpents pressed against her spine with every step, a constant reminder of what she carried. What she was responsible for. What she still hadn't decided to do with.

Ahead, Rafael raised his hand in a signal to halt. Elena stopped, bracing herself against a tree trunk, grateful for even a moment's rest. Her legs were burning, her lungs aching from the humidity, every muscle in her body screaming for relief.

Yara materialised beside her, appearing out of the rain like a ghost. Water streamed down her face, plastering her dark hair to her skull, but her eyes were alert, scanning the jungle around them with the practiced wariness of someone who had spent her life in dangerous territory.

"The river's rising," she said, pitching her voice just loud enough to be heard over the rain. "The crossing ahead—it was ankle-deep this morning. Now it's waist-high and climbing."

"Can we find another way around?"

"Not without adding two days to our journey. And if this rain keeps up, all the crossings will be flooded by then anyway." Yara shook her head, sending droplets flying. "We push through now, or we wait it out and hope the weather breaks."

Elena looked back at the group strung out along the trail behind her. Diego and Ana, both exhausted but determined. Carlos, his wounded shoulder wrapped in bandages that were soaked through and probably useless by now. Miguel, limping from an injury he'd sustained during the ambush but refusing to slow down. And in the middle of the group, surrounded by guards, Werner Kroeger.

The old Nazi walked with his hands bound in front of him, a rope around his waist connecting him to the guards ahead and behind. He had said nothing since the ambush—not during the long hours of walking, not during the brief rest stops, not even when one of Yara's people had offered him water. He simply watched, his pale eyes taking in everything, his face a mask of cold calculation.

Elena didn't trust his silence. Kroeger had spent sixty years pursuing the codex, had killed countless people in his obsession, had built an organisation dedicated to finding what Elena now carried. A man like that didn't simply accept defeat. He was waiting, planning, looking for an opportunity.

She didn't intend to give him one.

"How long until the river becomes impassable?" she asked Yara.

"A few hours. Maybe less if the rain intensifies."

"Then we don't wait. We cross now, while we still can."

Yara studied her for a moment, then nodded. "I'll send Rafael ahead to find the best route. Stay close to him—the current will be strong, and there may be debris in the water."

She moved off to give instructions to her people, leaving Elena alone with her thoughts and the relentless drumming of the rain.

***

The crossing was worse than Elena had imagined.

The stream that had been a gentle trickle four days ago was now a churning torrent, brown water rushing past at terrifying speed, carrying branches and leaves and the occasional larger piece of debris that could knock a person off their feet. The far bank was barely visible through the rain and spray, a dark line of vegetation that seemed impossibly distant.

Rafael went first, a rope tied around his waist, feeling his way across with a long pole that probed for holes and obstacles beneath the surface. The water reached his chest at the deepest point, and Elena saw him stagger more than once as the current tried to sweep him away. But he made it, securing the rope to a tree on the far side and signalling for the next person to cross.

They went one at a time, using the rope as a lifeline, fighting the current with every step. Elena watched as Ana crossed—the smaller woman struggling against the force of the water, her face tight with fear but her movements steady and determined. Then Diego, who was strong enough to make it look almost easy. Then Carlos, whose wounded shoulder made the crossing an exercise in agony that he bore without complaint.

When it was Elena's turn, she tightened the straps on her pack—the fragments couldn't get wet, couldn't be lost, couldn't be allowed to disappear into the brown water—and stepped into the stream.

The cold hit her first. Despite the tropical heat, the water was shockingly cold, fed by rain that had fallen in the mountains and carried down through countless tributaries. Then the current, grabbing at her legs with invisible hands, trying to pull her off balance, to sweep her downstream into the unknown.

She gripped the rope and pushed forward, one step at a time. The water rose to her waist, then her chest, then higher still as she reached the deepest point. Her feet slipped on the rocky bottom. The current tugged at her pack, threatening to spin her around. She heard shouts from the bank—warnings, encouragement, she couldn't tell which over the roar of the water.

Her foot found a rock, then another. The water began to recede—chest, waist, thighs. Rafael's hand grabbed her arm and pulled her up onto the bank, and she collapsed against a tree trunk, gasping for breath, her heart pounding so hard she could feel it in her temples.

"The fragments?" Diego was beside her, his face taut with concern.

Elena shrugged off her pack and checked the cases. Wet on the outside, but the seals had held. The bark paper pages inside were dry, the ancient knowledge preserved.

"They're fine," she said. "Everything's fine."

Behind them, across the churning water, Kroeger was being prepared for the crossing. His guards had untied the rope from his waist—it would be too dangerous to have him tethered to others during the crossing—but they kept a close watch as he approached the water's edge.

Elena saw him pause, looking at the torrent with an expression she couldn't read. Then he turned his head slightly, and their eyes met across the distance.

He smiled.

It was a small expression, barely visible through the rain, but it sent a chill down Elena's spine that had nothing to do with the cold water. That wasn't the smile of a defeated man. That was the smile of someone who saw an opportunity.

"Watch him," she said to Yara, who had crossed just before her. "Something's wrong."

Yara's eyes narrowed. She raised her hand to signal to the guards on the far bank, but before she could complete the gesture, Kroeger moved.

He didn't try to run—that would have been suicide in this terrain, with guards on both sides of the river and nowhere to go. Instead, he simply stepped into the water and let himself fall.

The current took him instantly, sweeping him downstream with terrifying speed. Elena saw his white hair flash above the surface once, twice, then disappear around a bend in the river.

"After him!" Yara shouted.

Two of her people plunged into the water, fighting against the current, trying to follow Kroeger's path. But the river was too fast, too strong. Within seconds, they were forced to grab onto overhanging branches to keep from being swept away themselves.

Kroeger was gone.

***

They searched for three hours.

Yara's people spread out along the riverbank, checking every bend, every pool, every place where a body might have washed up. They found nothing—no sign of Kroeger, no indication of whether he had drowned or somehow made it to shore.

"He's dead," one of the guards said finally, as the rain began to slacken and the grey light of afternoon filtered through the clouds. "No one could survive that current, especially with bound hands. He's at the bottom of the river somewhere, or he's been carried kilometres downstream."

"You don't know that," Elena said. "He could have—"

"Could have what? Swum to safety with his hands tied? Found a branch to grab onto while being swept through rapids?" The guard shook his head. "I've seen what this river can do. He's dead."

Yara's expression was troubled. "We should keep looking. If there's any chance he survived—"

"There isn't." The guard's voice was flat, certain. "We're wasting time. Every hour we spend here is an hour we're not putting distance between us and anyone else who might be looking for those fragments."

Elena looked at the river, at the brown water still churning past, slower now but still powerful. She thought about Kroeger's smile in that final moment—the expression of a man who had seen an opportunity and seized it.

Had it been a calculated escape? Or a final act of defiance, choosing death over captivity?

She would probably never know.

"He's right," she said finally, the words tasting like ash in her mouth. "We need to keep moving. If Kroeger's dead, we can't help him. If he's alive..." She paused. "If he's alive, we need to get as far away from here as possible before he can regroup."

Yara nodded slowly. "We continue to the boat. But we double the watch, and we don't stop again until we reach the river."

They gathered their gear and resumed the march, leaving the unnamed stream behind them. Elena didn't look back, but she couldn't shake the feeling that somewhere out there, pale eyes were watching her go.

***

They reached Ferreira's boat on the evening of the third day.

The captain was sitting on deck when they emerged from the jungle, a cigarette in one hand and a bottle of cachaça in the other. He looked like he had aged ten years in the week since they'd left him—his weathered face more lined, his eyes more hollow, the wariness of a man who had been waiting too long in dangerous territory.

But when he saw them, his face split into a grin of genuine relief.

"*Meu Deus,*" he said, rising to his feet. "You're alive. I was starting to think the jungle had swallowed you after all."

"It tried." Elena climbed aboard, her legs nearly buckling as she stepped onto the solid deck. After days of fighting through mud and water and undergrowth, the simple stability of the boat felt like a luxury beyond measure. "Can we leave immediately?"

"The fuel's topped up, the engine's been running fine. I can have us underway in ten minutes." Ferreira's eyes moved over the group, counting heads, noting the injuries and exhaustion. "Looks like you had some trouble out there."

"Some."

"And the old German? The one you were—"

"He didn't make it."

Ferreira's expression flickered, surprise, then something that might have been satisfaction, quickly hidden. "That's too bad," he said, in a tone that suggested it wasn't too bad at all. "Where do you want to go?"

Elena thought about it. Manaus was the obvious choice—the nearest major city, with airports and communications and all the infrastructure of the modern world. But it was also where Carla Mendes operated, where Kroeger's network had penetrated their plans before.

If Kroeger was alive—and despite her best efforts, she couldn't quite convince herself that he wasn't—Manaus would be the first place he'd look for them.

"Belém," she said. "Take us to Belém."

Ferreira raised an eyebrow. "That's a long trip. Four days, maybe five depending on conditions."

"We're not in a hurry anymore." Elena looked back at the jungle, at the green wall that had concealed secrets for five hundred years. "We have time to think."

***

The journey downriver was a strange interlude—days of travel through a landscape that seemed both alien and oddly peaceful after the intensity of the past weeks. The Amazon opened up around them, the narrow tributaries giving way to broader channels and finally to the main river itself, miles wide in places, its brown waters carrying them steadily toward the Atlantic.

Elena spent most of the trip sitting on the deck, watching the jungle slide past, thinking about what she carried and what she was going to do with it.

The fragments lay in their cases in the cabin below, seven pieces of a puzzle that humanity had been trying to solve for centuries. The formula for transmuting matter. The secret of El Dorado. The knowledge that had been hidden by the ancients because they feared what their descendants would do with it.

She had read Fray Tomás's letter so many times now that she could recite it from memory. His warning about the choice she faced. His admission that he didn't know what the right answer was. His hope that whoever found the fragments would have the wisdom to decide.

But wisdom felt like a foreign concept right now. She was exhausted, traumatised, haunted by the deaths she had witnessed and the lives she had failed to save. How could someone in her condition make a decision that might affect the entire future of humanity?

On the second night, Diego found her on the deck, staring up at stars that were impossibly bright away from the lights of civilisation.

"You should sleep," he said, settling onto the bench beside her. "You've been awake for most of the past three days."

"I can't. Every time I close my eyes, I see..." She shook her head. "It doesn't matter. I'll sleep when we reach Belém."

"You'll collapse before we reach Belém if you keep this up."

"Maybe. But I can't stop thinking about what comes next. About what I'm supposed to do with all of this." She gestured vaguely toward the cabin. "The fragments. The formula. The whole goddamn mess."

Diego was quiet for a moment. Then: "What are the options?"

"Three, as far as I can see. Destroy them—burn the bark paper, scatter the ashes, make sure the formula can never be reconstructed. Hide them—find new locations, new guardians, bury the secret for another five hundred years. Or release them—share the knowledge with the world, let humanity decide what to do with it."

"And which one are you leaning toward?"

"That's the problem. I can see arguments for all three. And arguments against all three." Elena pulled her knees up to her chest, wrapping her arms around them. "The ancients chose to hide the formula because they thought humanity wasn't ready. But what does 'ready' even mean? How do you measure something like that? And who gets to decide?"

"You do. Apparently."

"That's what terrifies me." She looked at Diego, her eyes haunted in the starlight. "I'm not special, Diego. I'm not wiser than the ancients, or more qualified than the Guardians who have been protecting this secret for generations. I'm just an archaeologist who happened to be in the wrong place at the wrong time."

"Or the right place at the right time. Depending on how you look at it."

"It doesn't feel right. It feels like a burden I never asked for and can't put down." She was quiet for a moment. "Martin spent thirty years looking for this. He died for it. Santiago died for it. All those Guardians across all those centuries, passing the responsibility from generation to generation, trusting that someday someone would come who could make the right choice. And now that someone is me, and I have no idea what the right choice is."

Diego didn't respond immediately. He sat beside her in companionable silence, looking up at the stars, giving her space to wrestle with thoughts that had no easy resolution.

Finally, he said: "You know what I remember about Martin? He used to say that the most important skill for an archaeologist wasn't knowing things—it was knowing how to figure things out. How to look at evidence, ask questions, follow the trail wherever it led." He turned to face her. "Maybe that's what you need to do here. Stop trying to know the answer and start trying to figure it out."

"How?"

"I don't know. But you're the smartest person I've ever met when it comes to understanding how civilisations work—how they rise and fall, how they handle change and challenge. If anyone can figure out what to do with something like this, it's you."

Elena wanted to argue, to point out all the reasons why she wasn't qualified for this responsibility. But she was too tired to fight, and somewhere beneath the exhaustion and doubt, a small part of her recognised that Diego might be right.

She had spent her whole life studying how humanity dealt with transformative knowledge. Maybe it was time to put that expertise to use.

"I need to think," she said. "Really think. Not just react to whatever crisis is happening in the moment but actually sit down and work through the problem systematically."

"Then do that. We've got four more days on this boat. Use them."

He stood and moved toward the cabin, pausing at the door. "Get some sleep first, though. You're no good to anyone if you collapse from exhaustion."

He disappeared inside, leaving Elena alone with the stars and the soft sound of the river flowing past.

She stayed on deck for another hour, watching the constellations wheel overhead, letting her mind drift through possibilities. Then, finally, she went below and slept, a deep dreamless sleep that lasted almost twelve hours.

When she woke, she felt something she hadn't felt in weeks.

Clarity.

24

A Choice

Belém, Brazil — Five Days Later

The city sprawled along the southern bank of the Pará River, where the Amazon began its final approach to the Atlantic Ocean. Belém was old by New World standards—founded in 1616 by Portuguese colonists, built on wealth extracted from the jungle that surrounded it. Colonial churches stood alongside modern high-rises. Street vendors sold açaí and tacacá to tourists and locals alike. The air smelled of river water and diesel fumes and the ever-present humidity of the tropics.

Elena barely noticed any of it.

She had spent the final days of the river journey working through the problem systematically, the way Diego had suggested. She had filled an entire notebook with arguments and counterarguments, scenarios and contingencies, trying to map out the implications of each possible choice.

Destruction was the safest option—but it meant giving up on the possibility that humanity might someday be ready for the knowledge. It meant deciding, unilaterally and irrevocably, that the formula should never exist.

Hiding was the traditional option—but it just passed the burden to someone else. It didn't solve the problem; it just delayed it. And as Kroeger had pointed out, the underlying principle would eventually be rediscovered anyway. Modern physics was already probing the edges of what the ancients had discovered. Hiding the fragments might buy decades, even centuries, but it wouldn't buy forever.

Release was the transformative option—but it was also the most dangerous. Once the knowledge was out, there was no controlling what happened next. Nations would compete for advantage. Corporations would seek to monetise it. Criminals would exploit it. The entire structure of human civilisation, built on assumptions of scarcity and material limitation, would come crashing down.

Three options. Three sets of consequences. None of them clearly right. None of them clearly wrong.

And then, somewhere in the middle of the third night, Elena had found a fourth option.

* * *

The hotel room was modest by international standards but luxurious compared to where they'd been sleeping for the past weeks. Elena had gathered everyone—Diego, Ana, Carlos, Miguel, and Yara, who had made the journey with them rather than returning to her people in the jungle.

They sat in a loose circle around the room's small table, where Elena had spread out her notes and diagrams. The fragments themselves were locked in the room's safe, behind a combination that only Elena knew.

"I've made a decision," she said. "But before I explain it, I need you to understand the reasoning."

She walked them through her analysis—the three obvious options, the strengths and weaknesses of each, the implications that rippled out from every possible choice. She laid out the evidence systematically, the way she would present findings at an academic conference, letting the logic speak for itself.

"The fundamental problem," she concluded, "is that any choice I make is a choice made by one person, at one moment in time, based on one set of circumstances. But this isn't a decision that should be made by one person. It's too big for that. Too important."

"So, what are you proposing?" Yara asked.

"A system. A framework for making the decision over time, rather than all at once." Elena pulled out a diagram she had sketched during the river journey. "The fragments stay hidden—but not scattered. The complete formula, kept in one place, under the protection of a network that understands what it represents."

"That sounds like what the Guardians have been doing for five hundred years," Diego pointed out.

"It's similar, but with one crucial difference. The Guardians' mission was to keep the secret forever—or at least until some undefined future when humanity might be 'ready.' But they never established criteria for what 'ready' would look like. They never created a mechanism for reassessing the decision."

Elena leaned forward, her eyes bright with the conviction that had been building over the past days. "What I'm proposing is different. We establish specific conditions—measurable, verifiable conditions—that would have to be met before the formula could be released. Scientific understanding that would need to develop. Social structures that would need to exist. Evidence that humanity has changed in ways that would make the release less catastrophic."

"Such as?" Ana asked.

"I'm still working out the details. But some examples: a global governance structure capable of managing transformative technologies. Scientific understanding of matter and energy that approaches what the ancients knew. Social systems that have successfully managed other disruptive innovations without collapsing into chaos." Elena spread her hands. "The specifics matter less than the principle. The point is to create a path forward—a way for humanity to earn access to this knowledge, rather than having it dumped on them all at once or hidden from them forever."

"And if those conditions are never met?" Yara's voice was neutral, but Elena could hear the scepticism beneath it.

"Then the formula stays hidden. Maybe forever. But at least there's a chance—a real, structured chance—for things to be different." Elena met Yara's eyes. "The ancients made their choice based on the humanity they knew. We can make a different choice, based on the humanity we hope for."

The room was silent for a long moment. Elena watched the faces of her companions, trying to read their reactions. Diego looked thoughtful, his brow furrowed as he worked through the implications. Ana was nodding slowly, as if the pieces were falling into place in her mind. Carlos and Miguel exchanged glances but said nothing.

Yara was the hardest to read. The woman who had led them through the jungle, who had watched three of her people die defending the secret her ancestors had protected for generations, whose entire life had been shaped by the Guardian tradition—she sat motionless, her dark eyes fixed on Elena with an intensity that bordered on unsettling.

Finally, she spoke.

"My grandmother taught me that the secret was sacred. That our duty was to protect it, not to judge when it should be revealed." Her voice was measured, careful. "What you're proposing goes against everything I was raised to believe."

Elena's heart sank. Without Yara's support—without the support of the existing Guardian network—her plan was dead before it started.

But Yara wasn't finished.

"My grandmother also taught me that traditions exist to serve the people who keep them, not the other way around. That blind obedience is not the same as wisdom." A ghost of a smile crossed her face. "She was a complicated woman."

"What are you saying?"

"I'm saying that I've watched you, Elena Vasquez. I've seen how you think, how you approach problems, how you weigh the costs and benefits of every decision. You're not someone who acts rashly or selfishly. You're someone who genuinely wants to do the right thing, even when the right thing isn't clear."

Yara stood and moved to the window, looking out at the city lights below. "The Guardian tradition has preserved the secret for five hundred years. That's an achievement worth honouring. But preservation was never supposed to be an end in itself. It was supposed to be a means to an end—keeping the knowledge safe until the time was right."

She turned back to face Elena. "Maybe the time isn't right yet. Maybe it won't be right for another five hundred years. But your plan—this framework you've described—it gives us a way to know. A way to measure. A way to move forward instead of just standing still."

"Does that mean you'll help?"

"It means I'll bring your proposal to the others. The Guardian network isn't a democracy, but it's not a dictatorship either. Decisions like this require consensus." Yara's expression was serious. "I can't promise they'll agree. Some of them will see this as a betrayal of everything we've stood for. But others..." She paused. "Others have been waiting for something like this. A reason to believe that all the sacrifice, all the secrecy, all the years of watching and waiting—that it's been for a purpose."

"How long will it take? To reach consensus?"

"Weeks. Maybe months. The network is spread across multiple countries, multiple communities. Communication is slow by design—it's one of our security measures." Yara smiled slightly. "But we've been patient for five hundred years. We can be patient a little longer."

***

The next few hours were spent working out logistics.

Yara would return to her people and begin the process of consulting with other Guardian cells across the Americas. The fragments would remain with Elena for now, secured in a location that only she and Yara knew about. They would establish communication protocols, contingency plans, fallback options in case something went wrong.

It was tedious work, the kind of detailed planning that adventure novels usually skipped over. But Elena understood that this was where the real success or failure of her plan would be determined—not in dramatic confrontations or last-minute escapes, but in the careful construction of systems that could endure.

By the time they finished, it was nearly dawn. The others had drifted off to their own rooms, leaving Elena alone with her notes and her thoughts and the weight of what she had set in motion.

She walked to the window and looked out at Belém as the first light of morning touched the colonial spires and modern towers. Somewhere out there—across the jungle, across the ocean, across the world—the consequences of her decision were beginning to unfold.

The fragments would stay hidden. But they wouldn't be forgotten. And someday—maybe decades from now, maybe centuries—humanity would be ready to receive what the ancients had discovered.

Or they wouldn't. And the formula would remain locked away, a secret that had outlasted empires and would outlast more.

Either way, Elena had done what she could. She had taken the burden that had been placed on her shoulders and transformed it into something that could be shared, evaluated, and ultimately resolved by people wiser than herself.

It wasn't a perfect solution. There were no perfect solutions.

But it was a path forward. And sometimes, that was enough.

***

There was one more thing she needed to do.

Elena retrieved the fragments from the safe and spread them out on the table one final time. Seven cases. Seven pieces of bark paper covered in glyphs that held the secrets of matter and transformation. The accumulated wisdom of a civilisation that had discovered how to reshape reality itself.

She photographed each fragment carefully, from multiple angles, capturing every detail of the ancient text. Then she photographed Fray Tomás's letter, and her own notes, and everything else she had assembled during her journey.

The images went into an encrypted file, backed up to multiple secure servers, protected by passwords that would be distributed to Yara and the other Guardian leaders. If something happened to the physical fragments—fire, flood, theft, destruction—the knowledge would survive.

It was a risk, she knew. Every copy was a potential vulnerability, a chance for the secret to leak out before humanity was ready. But it was also an insurance policy against the permanent loss of something that might someday be desperately needed.

The ancients had chosen to divide the formula, scattering it across continents in the hope that it would be harder to find. Elena was choosing to preserve it, consolidating it in protected repositories in the hope that it would be easier to control.

Different strategies for different eras. Different Guardians making different choices, all of them trying to do what they believed was right.

She packed up the fragments and prepared to move them to their new hiding place. The location she had chosen was not in Brazil—it was thousands of kilometres away, in a place that had significance to her personally and would be difficult for outsiders to discover.

But that was a journey for another day. For now, she was content to rest, to recover, to let the enormity of what she had accomplished slowly settle into her bones.

She had found El Dorado. Not a city of gold, but something far more valuable: knowledge that could transform the world, preserved and protected for a future that might be worthy of it.

The adventure was over.

The guardianship was just beginning.

25

Sanctuary

Guatemala City — Three Weeks Later

The aircraft began its descent through clouds that seemed to stretch forever, layers of grey and white that obscured the land below until the final moments before touchdown. Elena watched through the small window as Guatemala City gradually revealed itself—first as scattered lights in the darkness, then as a sprawling mass of buildings and roads and humanity pressed into a valley surrounded by mountains and volcanoes.

She hadn't been back since her mother's funeral, seven years ago.

The memories of that trip surfaced unbidden as the plane banked toward the runway. The endless procession of relatives she barely knew, their faces blurring together into a mass of grief and expectation. The rituals conducted in a mixture of Spanish and K'iche' that she had only partially understood, despite her mother's attempts over the years to teach her the language of her ancestors. The feeling of being simultaneously an insider and an outsider—claimed by a culture that was supposed to be her own, yet unable to fully inhabit it.

Her mother had tried so hard to keep that connection alive. Weekend trips to Guatemalan restaurants in D.C., where Elena had pushed arroz con pollo around her plate while her mother chatted with the owners in rapid Spanish. Summer visits to relatives in Los Angeles and Houston and Miami, where Elena had felt even more out of place among cousins who moved effortlessly between English and Spanish while she stumbled over conjugations. The stories her mother had told about her own childhood in the highlands—stories Elena had half-listened to, more interested in whatever book she was reading or game she was playing.

She had been a terrible daughter in that way. Too wrapped up in her own American life to appreciate what her mother was trying to give her. Too eager to fit in with her peers to embrace the heritage that set her apart.

Now, descending toward the land where her ancestors had lived for millennia, she felt the weight of all those missed opportunities pressing down on her chest like a physical burden.

The plane touched down with a jolt that snapped her out of her reverie. Around her, passengers began gathering their belongings, the mundane rituals of travel reasserting themselves over whatever emotions the journey had stirred. Elena waited until the aisle cleared before standing, retrieving her carry-on from the overhead bin with careful deliberation.

The fragments were distributed among her luggage in ways designed to avoid suspicion. Three of the crystal cases were in her checked bag, wrapped in clothing and toiletries, indistinguishable from the ordinary souvenirs a tourist might bring home. Two more were in her carry-on, nestled among books and research papers. The remaining two she had shipped separately through a secure courier service, addressed to a post office box in Chichicastenango that she had established specifically for this purpose.

Paranoid? Perhaps. But after everything she had been through—the betrayals, the attacks, the discovery that even trusted contacts could be bought or compromised—paranoia seemed like simple common sense.

The airport was modern, efficient, indistinguishable from a hundred other international terminals around the world. Elena moved through customs without incident, her Smithsonian credentials and academic cover story deflecting any curiosity about her luggage. She collected her checked bag, verified that the cases inside were undisturbed, and walked out into the humid night air of Guatemala City.

The taxi stand was crowded even at this hour, a press of travellers and drivers negotiating fares in a mixture of Spanish and indigenous languages. Elena joined the queue, grateful for the anonymity of the crowd. In the days since leaving Belém, she had travelled through São Paulo, Panama City, and Mexico City, deliberately circuitous route designed to make tracking her movements more difficult. If anyone was following her—and she had to assume someone was always following her—they would have their work cut out for them.

Her hotel was in Zona 10, the upscale district of the city where international business travellers and wealthy tourists congregated. It was not the kind of place Elena would normally stay—she had always preferred the character of smaller, locally-owned establishments—but anonymity had its advantages. In a hotel that catered to foreigners, one more American academic attracted no special attention.

She checked in under her own name—maintaining the cover of a legitimate research trip required using real credentials—and took the elevator to the sixth floor. Her room was comfortable, generic, interchangeable with business hotels anywhere in the world. She swept it for listening devices out of habit, found nothing, and finally allowed herself to relax.

The fragments were safe. She was safe. Tomorrow, she would begin the next phase of her plan.

But tonight, she needed rest. Real rest, the kind she hadn't had in weeks. She stripped off her travel clothes, took a shower that was probably longer than necessary, and collapsed into the crisp white sheets of the hotel bed.

Sleep came quickly, and for once, it was dreamless.

***

The drive from Guatemala City to the highlands took nearly four hours, winding through terrain that shifted from urban sprawl to agricultural lowlands to pine-forested mountains that reminded Elena, painfully, of photographs her mother had kept in albums that were probably still stored in a box somewhere in Elena's apartment in Washington.

She had rented a car rather than hiring a driver—another concession to paranoia, though she justified it to herself as a desire for flexibility. The roads were better than she had expected, at least for the first hour, paved highways that carried trucks and buses and private vehicles in a constant stream toward the interior. But as she climbed into the highlands, the pavement gave way to gravel, then to rutted dirt tracks that tested the limits of her rental's suspension.

The landscape was stunning. She had forgotten—or perhaps had never truly appreciated—how beautiful this part of Guatemala was. Mountains rose on all sides, their slopes covered in a patchwork of forest and cultivated fields, the green so vivid it almost hurt to look at. Villages clung to hillsides and nestled in valleys, their red-tiled roofs and whitewashed walls creating splashes of colour against the endless green. Clouds drifted through the passes, occasionally obscuring the road ahead, giving the whole scene a dreamlike quality.

Her mother had grown up here. Had walked these roads, breathed this air, looked out at these mountains every day of her childhood. Elena tried to imagine it—Maria Vasquez as a young girl, barefoot perhaps, helping with chores, learning the traditions that her own mother had learned from her mother before her.

What had her mother dreamed of, back then? Had she known she would someday leave, would marry an American archaeologist and raise a daughter who would barely speak Spanish, let alone K'iche'?

Had she imagined that her own child would someday return to these highlands carrying secrets that connected to the deepest roots of their shared heritage?

Probably not. No one could have imagined that.

Chichicastenango appeared around a bend in the road, its distinctive church spires visible above the surrounding buildings. Elena had been here before—had found the second fragment here, in the chaos and violence that had claimed Santiago's life—but the town looked different in daylight, different without the urgency of pursuit and the shadow of death hanging over everything.

It was market day, and the plaza in front of Santo Tomás church was packed with vendors and customers, a riot of colour and sound that assaulted Elena's senses after the quiet of the mountain roads. She parked near the edge of the plaza and walked into the crowd, letting herself be carried along by the flow of humanity.

The smells hit her first: copal incense burning on the church steps, where *costumbristas* performed rituals that blended Catholic and Maya traditions. Grilled meat from food stalls. Fresh flowers. The earthy scent of vegetables and fruits piled high on blankets spread across the cobblestones. The sharp tang of textiles dyed with natural pigments—reds from cochineal, blues from indigo, yellows from various plants whose names Elena had never learned.

The sounds came next: vendors calling out their wares in Spanish and K'iche' and sometimes a mixture of both. The haggling of customers negotiating prices. Children laughing and crying and demanding attention from parents distracted by commerce. The murmur of prayers from the church steps, the tinkle of bells, the occasional crack of fireworks set off for reasons Elena couldn't determine.

And the colours: everywhere, colours. The traditional clothing worn by many of the women—huipiles embroidered with patterns specific to each village, cortes wrapped in styles that identified the wearer's community of origin. The products for sale—textiles and ceramics and carved wooden masks and painted furniture. The flowers and fruits and vegetables. The painted facades of buildings around the plaza. Everything vivid, everything alive, everything asserting its presence against the muted greens and browns of the surrounding mountains.

Elena had seen markets like this before, in other parts of Guatemala and in Mexico and in Peru. But this one felt different. This one was connected to her—to her blood, her history, her identity. She was not just a tourist here, not just an observer. She was, in some way she was only beginning to understand, a participant. A descendant. A daughter of this land, however long she had been away.

She made her way through the crowd to the church steps, where the smoke of incense rose toward the overcast sky. The *costumbristas* barely glanced at her as she climbed the worn stone stairs, too absorbed in their rituals to pay attention to one more foreigner passing through. Inside, the church was cool and dim, candles flickering in niches along the walls, the smell of flowers mixing with the lingering scent of incense.

Elena walked to the spot where Santiago had been shot. There was no marker, no indication that anything significant had happened here. The stones had been scrubbed clean long ago, the blood washed away, the evidence of violence erased by time and the practical necessities of maintaining a functioning house of worship.

But Elena remembered. She remembered the sound of gunfire echoing off the walls, the chaos of parishioners fleeing, the way Santiago had fought despite his age, his obsidian staff moving with a speed that seemed impossible. She remembered his final words, his command to run, the sound of shots behind her as she fled with Diego down the hidden passage.

This is my purpose, he had said. *This is what I was born for.*

She knelt on the cold stone floor and closed her eyes, trying to summon something—a prayer, a meditation, some appropriate way to honour the man who had died so that she could continue. But the words wouldn't come. She had never been religious, had never found comfort in ritual or faith. All she had was memory, and gratitude, and the weight of responsibility that Santiago had passed to her in those final moments.

I'll try to be worthy of it, she thought. *I don't know if I can be, but I'll try.*

She stayed for a few more minutes, letting the peace of the church settle over her. Then she rose, crossed herself in a gesture that was more habit than belief, and walked back out into the noise and colour of the market.

She had a long drive ahead. And at the end of it, someone was waiting.

***

The village of San Andrés Xecul was smaller than Chichicastenango, tucked into a fold of the mountains about an hour's drive away. Elena had called ahead—the village had cell coverage now, a development that would have seemed miraculous to her mother's generation—and arrangements had been made for her arrival.

The woman who had made those arrangements was named Ixchel Batz, and Elena had never met her.

But Ixchel had known Elena's mother. Had known Elena's grandmother, and great-grandmother, and the generations before that who had lived in these highlands and kept the traditions that connected them to an ancient past. Ixchel was ninety-three years old, one of the last living links to a time when the old ways were still practiced openly, before the violence of the civil war had driven so much underground.

She was also, according to the information Elena had painstakingly gathered over the past months, a Guardian.

The drive to San Andrés Xecul wound through countryside that grew progressively more rural, the paved roads giving way to gravel and then to dirt tracks that challenged even the sturdy rental car. Elena passed through villages where children stopped their play to stare at the unfamiliar vehicle, where old women in traditional dress watched from doorways with expressions that mixed curiosity and suspicion.

She thought about what she was doing—bringing the fragments here, to a remote village in a region she barely knew, trusting them to a woman she had never met. It went against every instinct of self-preservation she had developed over the past months. But it also felt right, in a way she couldn't entirely articulate. This was where the second fragment had been hidden. This was where the Guardian tradition had survived despite everything the modern world had thrown at it. If anywhere could keep the secret safe for another generation, it was a place like this.

The village appeared around a final bend in the road, its houses clustered around a central plaza dominated by a church whose yellow facade was painted with an explosion of colours and figures that blended Catholic iconography with older, deeper imagery. Saints stood alongside jaguars and serpents; angels shared space with figures that might have been Maya deities or might have been something else entirely.

Elena parked near the plaza and climbed out of the car, stretching muscles that had grown stiff from hours of driving. The air was cool and thin at this altitude, scented with woodsmoke and something floral she couldn't identify. A dog barked somewhere in the distance. A rooster crowed, confused by the overcast sky into thinking it was dawn rather than midafternoon.

She gathered her bags—the cases containing the fragments distributed among them, heavy but manageable—and began walking toward the edge of the village, where she had been told Ixchel's house was located.

The villagers watched her pass. Not hostile but not welcoming either—the wariness of people who had learned through hard experience to be careful around strangers. Elena met their eyes when she could, nodding politely, trying to project an aura of harmlessness. Just a visitor. Just a foreigner with business in the village. Nothing to be concerned about.

Ixchel's house was set slightly apart from the others, a small structure of adobe and thatch that looked like it had been standing for generations. The old woman herself was sitting on the porch, weaving on a backstrap loom, her fingers moving with a speed and precision that belied her age. She looked up as Elena approached, and for a long moment, neither of them spoke.

Elena had rehearsed this meeting a dozen times in her head, had planned exactly what she would say, how she would introduce herself and explain her purpose. But standing here, under the weight of Ixchel's steady gaze, all of that preparation evaporated.

"You look like your mother," Ixchel said finally. Her Spanish was accented with K'iche', the rhythms of an older language shaping the words. "The same eyes. The same way of holding yourself, like you're ready to run."

"You knew her?"

"I knew her grandmother. Maria I only met once, when she was a girl about to leave for the United States. She was frightened and excited and trying very hard to be brave." A ghost of a smile crossed Ixchel's weathered face. "You have the same look now."

Elena felt something loosen in her chest—a tension she hadn't realised she was carrying. "I came to ask for your help. I have something that needs to be protected. Something important."

"I know what you have." Ixchel's hands never stopped moving, the shuttle flying through the warp threads with hypnotic regularity. "Santiago told me before he died. He said you would come eventually, and that I should be ready."

"Santiago told you. I thought the Guardian cells were isolated from each other—"

"Isolated, yes. But not entirely alone. We have ways of communicating, when the need is great." The old woman finally set aside her loom and rose to her feet, her movements slow but steady. "You carry the fragments of the Codex of Seven Serpents. You have assembled what was scattered, found what was hidden, survived what should have killed you. And now you have come here, to the land of your ancestors, looking for a place to keep what you have found."

"Yes."

"Then come inside. We have much to discuss."

26

Networking

Six Months Later — Various Locations

The secure phone buzzed against Elena's hip, pulling her out of a discussion about Maya astronomical notation systems that had been going well until that moment.

She excused herself from the conference room, where a group of researchers from the *Universidad Nacional Autónoma de México* were assembled around a table covered with papers and photographs, and stepped into the hallway to check the message.

A string of coordinates. A date and time two days from now. And a single word: *Come.*

Elena felt her pulse quicken. She had been expecting this message—or hoping for it, at least—for weeks. The Guardian network's deliberations about her proposed framework had been ongoing since the meeting in Peru, a slow process of consultation and debate that involved cells scattered across multiple countries and communication channels that were deliberately difficult to use.

Yara had warned her that it would take time. The network had survived for five centuries by being careful, by never rushing decisions that could have consequences stretching generations into the future. But the waiting had been excruciating, especially as Elena had continued her work—travelling, researching, building connections—without knowing whether any of it would ultimately matter.

Now, apparently, the waiting was over.

She returned to the conference room and apologised to the researchers, explaining that an urgent matter required her immediate attention. They were understanding—academics were accustomed to the sudden disruptions that fieldwork and grant deadlines could cause—and promised to send her their notes from the session.

Back at her hotel, Elena began making arrangements. The coordinates pointed to a location in Peru, in the Sacred Valley near Cusco—the same region where she had found the fourth fragment, where the Guardians had revealed themselves during the confrontation with Kroeger. It would take at least a day to get there from Mexico City, allowing for connections and the unpredictability of travel in South America.

She booked flights, notified Diego and Ana of her destination, and began packing the materials she would need for what she suspected would be a consequential meeting. The fragments themselves were distributed among secure locations across the Americas now—part of the security protocol she had implemented during the months of waiting—but she carried copies of her research, her translations, the framework she had developed for evaluating humanity's readiness for the knowledge the codex contained.

The flight to Lima was uneventful, the kind of anonymous hours in the air that had become routine over the past months of constant travel. Elena used the time to review her notes, to rehearse the arguments she would make, to anticipate the objections she would face.

The framework she had developed drew heavily on the document Ixchel had given her—the supplementary text that contained the ancients' own reasoning for hiding their discovery. That document had been invaluable, providing a philosophical foundation that Elena had adapted to modern conditions while trying to preserve the essential logic of the original approach.

The core concept was straightforward: rather than hiding the formula indefinitely or destroying it entirely, establish specific criteria that would need to be met before it could be considered for release. Scientific criteria—advances in the understanding of matter and energy that would make the formula's principles comprehensible rather than magical. Social criteria—governance structures capable of managing transformative technologies without collapsing into chaos. Ethical criteria—evidence that humanity had developed the moral frameworks necessary to use such power responsibly.

Each criterion would be periodically reassessed by a council of Guardians, who would determine whether the world was moving toward or away from readiness. If and when all criteria were satisfied, the council would then face a separate decision about whether to actually release the knowledge—the criteria were necessary conditions, not sufficient ones.

It was a compromise, Elena knew. It satisfied no one completely. Those who believed the formula should remain hidden forever saw it as a dangerous step toward eventual release. Those who believed it should be shared immediately saw it as an unnecessary delay, a perpetuation of the paternalism that had kept the knowledge from humanity for five centuries.

But Elena had come to believe that the best solutions were often the ones that made everyone a little unhappy. Perfect was the enemy of good, as the saying went, and in this case, good might be the best anyone could hope for.

The connection in Lima was tight, barely an hour between gates, but Elena made it with minutes to spare. The flight to Cusco was shorter, just over an hour, and she spent it watching the Andes roll past below—snow-capped peaks and green valleys, a landscape that had been home to civilisations that rose and fell while Europe was still struggling out of the Dark Ages.

A driver was waiting for her at the airport, holding a sign with a name that wasn't hers—a security precaution, one of many that the network employed. He drove her through Cusco without speaking, navigating the narrow colonial streets with the practised ease of someone who had made this trip many times before.

The Sacred Valley opened up around them as they descended from the city, a broad expanse of agricultural land flanked by mountains that seemed to touch the sky. Elena had been here before, during the search for the fragments, but she still found herself catching her breath at the beauty of it. The Inca had chosen well when they made this region the heart of their empire.

The meeting place was a hacienda outside the small town of Urubamba, a colonial-era building that had been converted into a conference centre while retaining much of its original character. Thick adobe walls, wooden beams blackened by centuries of cooking fires, a courtyard filled with flowers that seemed to glow in the late afternoon light.

Yara was waiting in the courtyard, sitting on a stone bench beneath an ancient tree whose species Elena didn't recognise. She looked tired—there were lines around her eyes that Elena didn't remember seeing before—but her posture was alert, her expression carefully neutral.

"You came quickly," she said as Elena approached.

"Your message suggested it was urgent."

"It is. The network has reached a decision." Yara paused, her dark eyes studying Elena's face. "Or as close to a decision as we're likely to get."

Elena felt her heart rate accelerate despite her efforts to remain calm. This was the moment she had been working toward for months—the verdict on whether her vision for the fragments' future would be accepted or rejected.

"Tell me," she said.

"There are three factions." Yara's voice was measured, clinical, the tone of someone delivering a report rather than news that would shape the rest of Elena's life. "The largest faction supports your proposal—the framework, the criteria, the path toward eventual release. They see it as a way forward that honours our tradition while acknowledging the reality of the modern world."

Elena let out a breath she hadn't realised she was holding. "That's good."

"Yes. But there are complications." Yara gestured for Elena to sit beside her on the bench. "The second faction opposes your proposal. They want to continue as we have always continued—hiding the fragments, protecting the secret, waiting for a future that may never come. They are fewer in number than the first faction, but they are passionate, and some of them have been Guardians for generations. Their opposition carries weight."

"I expected that. What about the third faction?"

Yara was silent for a moment, her expression troubled. "The third faction does not trust any of us to make this decision. Not you, not me, not the network as a whole. They believe the fragments should be destroyed—permanently eliminated, so that the knowledge can never fall into the wrong hands."

Elena felt a chill despite the warm afternoon sun. She had known there would be opposition, had prepared arguments against the position of continued hiding. But destruction was something else entirely—an irreversible act that would erase a piece of human heritage forever.

"How many support that position?"

"Fewer than either of the other factions. But enough to matter. And some of them are... emphatic in their views." Yara's voice dropped slightly. "There have been threats. Implications that if the network does not choose destruction, some might take matters into their own hands."

"You mean they might try to destroy the fragments themselves?"

"Or the people who control access to them." Yara's eyes met Elena's. "Including you."

The implications settled over Elena like a cold weight. She had survived Kroeger's attacks, had navigated the dangers of the search for the fragments, had built a network of allies across the Americas. But she had assumed that the Guardians themselves were on her side—or at least that their disagreements would be resolved through deliberation rather than violence.

Apparently, she had been naive.

"What happens now?" she asked.

"Now we meet. All three factions, face to face, in a formal council that will determine the network's path forward. Representatives from every cell have been summoned. They've been arriving over the past few days." Yara stood and began walking toward the hacienda. "You will present your proposal tomorrow morning. You will answer questions, address concerns, defend your reasoning against whatever challenges are raised. And then we will vote."

"And if the vote goes against me?"

Yara paused at the door, looking back over her shoulder. "Then we will do what the majority decides. That is how the network has always functioned." Her expression softened slightly. "But Elena... I don't think the vote will go against you. The majority supports your vision. What concerns me is what happens after—how the minority responds when they lose."

"What do you think they'll do?"

"I don't know. That's what concerns me."

She disappeared into the hacienda, leaving Elena alone in the courtyard with the flowers and the ancient tree and the weight of everything that was about to happen.

***

The council chamber had been prepared with careful attention to symbolism.

It was a large room on the ground floor of the hacienda; its walls lined with tapestries that depicted scenes from indigenous mythology—jaguars and serpents and feathered figures that might have been gods or heroes or something in between. Chairs had been arranged in a circle, emphasising equality among the participants rather than the hierarchy that a more traditional arrangement would have implied.

Elena counted thirty-four people as she entered the room the next morning, representing Guardian cells from across the Americas. She recognised some of them—Mama Qhispi from Peru, Fernando Quispe who had helped her find the passages beneath Machu Picchu, Ixchel Batz who had made the long journey from Guatemala despite her age. Others were strangers, faces she had seen in photographs during her research but never met in person.

They all turned to look at her as she entered, their expressions ranging from curious to hostile to carefully neutral. Elena felt the weight of their attention like a physical pressure, the accumulated scrutiny of people who had devoted their lives to protecting a secret that she was now proposing to change.

She took her assigned seat—near the centre of the circle, where she would be visible to everyone—and waited for the proceedings to begin.

Yara opened with a statement of purpose, explaining the reason for the council and the procedures that would govern their deliberations. Her voice was formal, ritualistic, drawing on language that had probably been used in Guardian councils for generations. Elena listened with only half her attention, using the rest to study the faces around her, trying to identify allies and opponents.

The presentations began with a spokesperson for the traditionalist faction—a man from Colombia named Rodrigo whose family had been Guardians for eleven generations. He spoke eloquently about the importance of maintaining the network's historical mission, about the dangers of changing course after five centuries of successful protection. His arguments were familiar to Elena—she had anticipated them in her own preparations—but he delivered them with a passion that clearly resonated with many in the room.

The spokesperson for the destruction faction was a woman from Brazil named Teresa, younger than Elena had expected, her intensity barely contained behind a veneer of calm. She argued that the world had changed in ways that made continued protection impossible. Digital technology, satellite imaging, advances in materials science—all of these were making secrets harder to keep, making the network's task more difficult with each passing year. Better to destroy the fragments now, she argued, while they were still within the Guardians' control, than to risk losing them to forces that might use them for terrible purposes.

Elena listened to both presentations with careful attention, taking notes, formulating responses. Then it was her turn.

She rose and moved to the centre of the circle, acutely aware of the eyes following her every movement. This was the moment everything had been building toward—the culmination of months of research and travel and alliance-building. If she failed to convince this council, all of that work would be for nothing.

She began with history. Not the history of her own search for the fragments, but the history of the network itself—the choices the founders had made, the reasoning behind the division and scattering of the codex. She drew on the document Ixchel had given her, quoting passages that showed the ancients had never intended for the formula to remain hidden forever. They had hidden it because they judged their own time to be unprepared. They had built in the possibility of reassessment because they recognized that times could change.

She moved on to her framework—the specific criteria she proposed, the process for evaluating them, the safeguards against premature release. She acknowledged the concerns of both opposing factions, showing how her proposal addressed them. For the traditionalists, she emphasised continuity—her framework preserved the core mission of protection while adding a mechanism for eventual evolution. For the destruction faction, she emphasized security—her proposal included enhanced protocols for guarding the fragments, reducing the risk that they would fall into the wrong hands.

She spoke for nearly an hour, answering questions as they arose, defending her positions against challenges from all sides. Some questioners were genuinely curious, seeking clarification on technical points. Others were openly hostile, their questions designed to expose weaknesses in her reasoning rather than to understand it.

Through it all, Elena maintained her composure. She had prepared for this. She had anticipated these objections. She knew her arguments were sound—not perfect, but sound—and she trusted that the majority of the Guardians would recognise that.

When she finished, there was a long silence. Then Yara stood to announce that the council would recess for deliberation. The representatives would discuss among themselves, and a vote would be taken that evening.

Elena was escorted to a small room where she was to wait. Food was brought, water, everything she might need. But she had no appetite, no thirst. She sat by the window and watched the shadows lengthen across the valley, her mind running through every word she had spoken, wondering if it had been enough.

Hours passed. The sun set. Stars emerged, brilliant in the clear mountain air.

Finally, near midnight, Yara came to bring her back to the council chamber.

The vote had been taken.

27

The Shadow

Guatemala Highlands — Eight Months Later

The rainy season had transformed the highlands into something from a dream.

Water fell from the sky in endless curtains, cascading down mountainsides that had turned impossibly green, feeding streams that became rivers that carved their way through valleys shaped by millions of years of similar transformations. The air smelled of wet earth and growing things, and the clouds that settled over the peaks gave the villages a sense of isolation that persisted even in the age of cell phones and satellite television.

Elena had returned to San Andrés Xecul for what she expected would be a routine visit. One of the regular check-ins she had established with Guardian cells across the Americas, part of the network maintenance that had become her primary responsibility since the council had accepted her framework eight months ago.

The vote had been close—closer than Elena would have liked—but the majority had ultimately supported her proposal. The framework was now official policy, the criteria for eventual release established and codified, the process for periodic reassessment set in motion. The fragments remained hidden, but they were no longer simply being preserved indefinitely. They were being held in trust, waiting for a future that might or might not arrive.

It was a compromise, and like all compromises, it satisfied no one completely. The traditionalists had accepted it grudgingly, their opposition noted in the official record but their compliance secured. The destruction faction had been less gracious—several of their members had withdrawn from the network entirely, their future intentions unknown.

Yara had warned Elena to be careful. The dissenters might accept the council's decision, or they might take matters into their own hands. There was no way to know until something happened.

For eight months, nothing had happened. Elena had travelled constantly, visiting cells, building relationships, strengthening the network that would implement her framework across generations. She had found the work satisfying in a way that surprised her—the quiet accomplishment of creating something that would outlast her own lifetime, that would continue long after she was gone.

But she had never stopped looking over her shoulder. Never stopped wondering when the other shoe would drop.

She was thinking about this as she drove up the winding road toward San Andrés Xecul, her rental car struggling against the mud that the rains had churned into the unpaved surface. The windshield wipers beat a steady rhythm, barely keeping pace with the water that sheeted down from the darkened sky.

Ixchel had become a friend over these past months. More than a friend—a mentor, a connection to a past that Elena was only beginning to understand. The old woman's sharp mind and encyclopaedic knowledge of Guardian traditions had proven invaluable in refining the protocols that would govern the network's operations for generations to come. And her perspective—grounded in decades of waiting and faith, of maintaining traditions that the world had forgotten—had helped Elena understand what it truly meant to be a Guardian.

Not a hero. Not a saviour. Just a link in a chain that stretched back centuries and would stretch forward into an unknowable future.

The village came into view around a final bend, its painted church visible even through the rain. Elena pulled into the small plaza and parked, gathering her bag and the umbrella that would be completely inadequate against the deluge but was better than nothing.

She noticed the silence first. Even in the rain, villages like this were never completely quiet—there were always children playing, dogs barking, radios blaring, the sounds of daily life persisting regardless of weather. But San Andrés Xecul was still, the plaza empty, the windows of the surrounding houses shuttered.

Then she noticed the smoke.

It rose from the direction of Ixchel's house, a darker column against the grey sky, barely visible through the rain but unmistakable once she saw it.

Elena broke into a run.

The path to Ixchel's house was slick with mud, treacherous underfoot, but Elena barely noticed. Her heart was pounding, her mind racing through possibilities—an accident, a cooking fire gone wrong, a lightning strike—even as a deeper part of her knew that none of those explanations were likely.

She rounded the final corner and stopped dead.

The house was engulfed in flames.

Despite the rain, despite the water pouring from the sky in sheets, the fire burned with an intensity that could only be deliberate. Accelerant of some kind, Elena's mind supplied automatically—gasoline or kerosene, something that would overcome the dampening effect of the weather.

And lying in the doorway, visible in the flickering light of the flames, was a figure she recognised.

Ixchel.

Elena ran to her, sliding the last few metres through the mud, dropping to her knees beside the old woman's body. Ixchel's eyes were closed, her face peaceful despite what had obviously been a violent end. There were wounds on her chest—gunshots, Elena realised, two of them, close together over the heart.

Professional. Efficient. The work of someone who knew exactly what they were doing.

Elena searched for a pulse, knowing she wouldn't find one, needing to try anyway. The skin beneath her fingers was already cooling, the life that had animated this body for ninety-three years already gone.

She was too late. She had been too late from the moment she saw the smoke.

"She fought them."

The voice came from behind her, thin and trembling. Elena spun around, her hand going instinctively to the weapon she carried—one of the many changes she had made to her habits since the council meeting, one of the many concessions to the reality that not everyone accepted the network's decision.

A young girl stood at the edge of the clearing, perhaps ten years old, her face streaked with tears and ash. Elena recognised her from previous visits—Ixchel's great-granddaughter, one of the few family members who had remained in the village after the civil war scattered so many others.

"What happened?" Elena asked, forcing her voice to remain calm despite the grief and rage churning in her chest. "Who did this?"

"Men came. Foreigners." The girl's voice was barely audible over the rain. "They wanted to know about the old papers. The things the grandmother kept hidden. She wouldn't tell them. They hurt her, but she wouldn't say."

"How many men?"

"Three. Maybe four. They had guns." The girl's face crumpled. "The grandmother told me to hide. She made me hide in the corn shed behind the house. I heard..." Her voice broke. "I heard everything. The questions. The screaming. Then the shots."

Elena closed her eyes, fighting to maintain control. Ixchel had been tortured before she was killed. Tortured for information about the fragments—information that Elena had trusted her with, that Elena had brought into her life.

This was her fault. Whatever her intentions, whatever the network had decided, this death was on her hands.

"Where did they go?" she asked, opening her eyes. "The men who did this. Which way?"

"Down the mountain. Toward the road. They had a car—a big black one."

Elena did the calculation automatically. The attack had probably happened within the last hour—the fire was still burning intensely despite the rain, which meant it had been set recently. An hour's head start, on roads that the rain would have made treacherous. They could be anywhere by now, but the most likely route was toward Chichicastenango and from there to the main highway.

She could try to follow. Could try to catch them, identify them, learn who had sent them and why.

Or she could stay here, grieve, help the village deal with the aftermath.

"Listen to me," Elena said, kneeling to meet the girl's eyes. "I need you to do something important. Can you be brave for me?"

The girl nodded, her lower lip trembling.

"Go to the neighbours. Tell them what happened. They need to put out the fire before it spreads to other houses. Can you do that?"

"What about the grandmother?"

Elena looked back at Ixchel's body, at the flames consuming the house where generations of Guardians had kept their sacred trust. "I'll take care of her. I promise. But right now, I need to find the men who did this. I need to make sure they don't hurt anyone else."

The girl hesitated, then nodded again. She turned and ran toward the nearest house, her small figure quickly disappearing into the rain.

Elena allowed herself one more moment—one more look at Ixchel's face, peaceful in death despite the violence of her final moments—then rose to her feet and began walking back toward her car.

The men who had done this were still out there. They had information about the fragments, about the network, about things that Ixchel had protected for nearly a century. Whatever they had learned, whatever they planned to do with that knowledge, Elena needed to find out.

She reached the plaza and climbed into her car, her clothes soaked, her hands shaking with a combination of grief and adrenaline. The engine started on the first try—a small blessing—and she pulled out onto the muddy road, heading down the mountain toward Chichicastenango.

The rain showed no sign of letting up. The visibility was terrible, the road conditions worse. Any sensible person would pull over and wait for the storm to pass.

Elena pressed the accelerator harder.

She had driven perhaps ten kilometres when her phone buzzed with an incoming call. The screen showed a number she didn't recognise—no name, no location identifier. She answered anyway, putting it on speaker.

"Dr. Vasquez." The voice was male, cultured, accented in a way she couldn't quite place. "I wondered how long it would take you to respond to our message."

"Who is this?"

"Someone who shares your interest in the Codex of Seven Serpents. Someone who has been watching your activities with great interest over the past months." A pause. "Someone who was very disappointed by the outcome of the Guardian council's deliberations."

Elena felt ice form in her stomach. The destruction faction. The dissenters who had withdrawn from the network after the vote. They hadn't simply accepted their loss and moved on—they had been planning, waiting, preparing for this moment.

"What do you want?"

"What we have always wanted. To ensure that the formula never falls into the wrong hands." The voice remained calm, reasonable, as if discussing business arrangements rather than murder. "The old woman refused to tell us where the fragments are hidden now. A pity—her suffering could have been avoided if she had simply cooperated."

"You killed her for nothing. I moved the fragments months ago. She didn't know where they are."

"We suspected as much. The old networks are compartmentalised—each cell knows only its own piece of the puzzle." A slight sigh. "But the Guardian traditions include methods of communication between cells. Records, protocols, information that might help us locate others who do know where the fragments are hidden."

"And you think those records were in Ixchel's house?"

"We think that if such records exist, someone in the network knows where they are. The old woman was simply our starting point." Another pause. "You could end this quickly, Dr. Vasquez. Tell us where the fragments are. Help us destroy them, as they should have been destroyed centuries ago. No more innocent people need to die."

Elena's grip tightened on the steering wheel. The rain hammered against the windshield, and for a moment she allowed herself to imagine it—giving in, surrendering the fragments, watching them burn. It would end the danger, end the running, end the weight of responsibility she had carried since Santiago pressed the jade pendant into her hands.

But it would also end any chance that humanity might someday be ready for what the ancients had discovered. It would be giving up on the future, surrendering to fear, choosing the easiest path rather than the right one.

"No," she said.

"That's unfortunate. I had hoped you would be reasonable." The voice hardened slightly. "Very well. We will continue our work. The old woman was only the first. We know the locations of other Guardian cells—the vote at the council required them to identify themselves. We will visit each one in turn, until someone tells us what we need to know."

"You're talking about mass murder."

"We're talking about protecting humanity from itself. The same thing the Guardians have always claimed to do." A bitter laugh. "The difference is that we're willing to do what's necessary, rather than hiding behind frameworks and criteria and the fantasy that some future generation will be more responsible than this one."

The line went dead.

Elena pulled the car to the side of the road, her hands shaking too badly to drive safely. The rain continued to fall, drumming on the roof, streaming down the windows, surrounding her in a cocoon of grey noise.

Ixchel was dead. The network was under attack. And somewhere out there, fanatics who believed they were saving the world were preparing to kill again.

She had to warn the others. Had to organise defences, move the fragments to new locations, find the traitors within the network who were providing information to the attackers. Had to do everything at once, with resources that were already stretched thin and allies she wasn't sure she could trust.

But first, she had to make a call.

She dialled the secure number that connected to the Guardian network's emergency protocols, the line that was monitored around the clock by people who would know what to do.

The phone rang once. Twice. Then clicked.

"This is Elena Vasquez," she said. "We have a situation."

28

The Hunt Begins

Chichicastenango, Guatemala — That Same Night

The rain had not let up by the time Elena reached Chichicastenango, and the streets of the town were rivers of mud and debris that made navigation treacherous even at the slow speeds she was forced to maintain. Market day was tomorrow, and vendors had already begun setting up their stalls under tarps and awnings that snapped and billowed in the wind, their goods covered in plastic sheeting that did little to keep out the relentless water.

She parked near the plaza and sat for a moment, trying to gather her thoughts. The phone call with the Guardian emergency line had lasted nearly twenty minutes, and by the end of it, protocols had been activated that would alert cells across the Americas to the threat. But protocols were abstract things, words on paper, procedures that might or might not translate into actual safety for the people whose lives depended on them.

Ixchel was dead. That was not abstract. That was real, concrete, irreversible.

Elena pressed her palms against her eyes, fighting the grief that threatened to overwhelm her. She could not afford to break down now. There would be time for mourning later, if she survived, if she managed to stop whatever was happening before more people died. Right now, she needed to think clearly, to act decisively, to be the leader that the network apparently believed she was.

Her phone buzzed with an incoming message. She checked the screen and saw coordinates—a location about three kilometres outside of town, in the hills overlooking the valley. The message was from Yara, sent through the secure channel they had established months ago.

Safe house. Come now. Bring no one.

Elena started the car and pulled out of the plaza, following the GPS toward the coordinates. The roads outside of town were even worse than the ones she had already travelled—unpaved tracks that wound through agricultural land and forest, barely wide enough for a single vehicle, treacherous with mud and standing water.

She almost missed the turnoff. A narrow path branched off from the main track, marked only by a stone that might have been natural or might have been deliberately placed. Elena turned onto it and found herself climbing through dense vegetation that closed in on both sides, branches scraping against the car's roof and windows.

The safe house appeared suddenly—a small structure of adobe and corrugated metal, nestled into a fold in the hillside that made it invisible from the main road. Smoke rose from a chimney, the only sign of habitation in the surrounding wilderness.

Elena parked and climbed out, her hand resting on the weapon at her hip. The rain had finally begun to ease, reduced to a steady drizzle that was almost pleasant compared to the deluge of the past hours. She approached the door and knocked in the pattern that had been established during the council meeting—three quick raps, a pause, two more.

The door opened, and Yara's face appeared in the gap.

"You're alone?"

"Yes."

"Good. Come in."

The interior of the safe house was spartan but functional—a single room with a cot, a table, a small stove, and little else. Yara had clearly been here for some time; there were papers spread across the table, a laptop open to a screen filled with what looked like a map, and the remains of a meal pushed to one side.

"You heard about Ixchel," Elena said. It was not a question.

"I heard. The emergency protocols worked as designed—the alert reached me within minutes of your call." Yara's expression was grim. "I've been trying to reach other cells, warn them of what's happening. Most have responded. A few..." She shook her head. "A few have gone silent."

"What do you mean, silent?"

"I mean they're not answering. Not through the secure channels, not through the backup methods, not at all." Yara moved to the laptop and turned it so Elena could see the screen. "This is a map of all the Guardian cells in Central America. The green dots are the ones that have confirmed receipt of the alert. The red dots are the ones that haven't responded."

Elena studied the map, feeling her stomach clench. There were five red dots—five cells scattered across Guatemala, Honduras, and El Salvador that had not acknowledged the warning. Five potential targets, five groups of people who might already be dead or captured or on the run.

"How long since you sent the alert?"

"Three hours. Long enough that anyone monitoring their channels should have responded by now." Yara's voice was flat, controlled, but Elena could hear the tension beneath it. "Either their communications have been compromised, or they've already been hit."

"The man who called me said they knew the locations of other cells. That the council vote required the factions to identify themselves." Elena felt cold despite the warmth of the small room. "He was right, wasn't he? The destruction faction knows where everyone is because we told them."

"We told them because we thought we were all on the same side. Because the Guardian tradition has always been built on trust between cells, even when we disagree." Yara's jaw tightened. "We were fools."

"We were hopeful. There's a difference."

"Is there? Because right now, it feels like the same thing." Yara sat down heavily on the cot, her usual composure cracking slightly. "I've been a Guardian my whole life, Elena. My mother was a Guardian, and her mother before that, going back generations. We were taught that the network was sacred, that the bonds between cells were unbreakable. And now..."

"And now some of those cells are hunting the others." Elena pulled out a chair and sat across from her. "How many people are we talking about? The destruction faction—how big is it?"

"At the council, maybe eight or nine representatives spoke in favour of destruction. But that doesn't mean much. Each representative speaks for a cell, and cells can have anywhere from a handful of members to dozens. Some of them might have changed their minds since the vote. Others..." She shrugged. "Others might have been planning this from the beginning."

"Planning mass murder? Planning to kill people they've worked alongside for years?"

"Planning to do whatever it takes to achieve their goal. In their minds, they're the true Guardians—the only ones willing to do what needs to be done." Yara's voice was bitter. "They see the rest of us as cowards, collaborators with the forces that want to release the formula. They believe that anyone who supports your framework is a traitor to the Guardian mission."

Elena thought about the voice on the phone—cultured, reasonable, explaining the logic of murder as if it were a business proposition. The man had genuinely believed he was protecting humanity. That was what made him dangerous.

"We need to find them," she said. "Before they can hit any more cells."

"How? We don't know who they are, not really. We know which representatives spoke in favour of destruction at the council, but we don't know who's actually involved in these attacks. It could be some of them, all of them, or people we haven't even considered."

"The attackers in San Andrés Xecul were professionals. Three or four men, the girl said, with guns and a vehicle. That's not a group of idealistic Guardians acting on their own—that's a team with training, resources, and a plan." Elena leaned forward. "Where would they get that kind of capability?"

Yara was silent for a moment, her brow furrowed in thought. "Some of the cells have connections to... let's call them unofficial sources. People who can provide services that legitimate channels can't. It's how the network has survived in regions where governments are hostile or corrupt."

"You're talking about criminals. Drug traffickers, mercenaries, that kind of thing."

"I'm talking about people who know how to operate in the shadows. Some of them are criminals, yes. Others are former military, or private security, or intelligence operatives who've gone freelance." Yara met Elena's eyes. "The Guardian network has always existed on the margins of society. We've made alliances with whoever could help us achieve our mission. It's not pretty, but it's kept the secret safe for five centuries."

"And now those same alliances might be what's killing us."

"Yes." Yara stood and moved to the window, looking out at the rain-soaked hillside. "There's something else you should know. Before the attack on Ixchel, there were rumours. Whispers through the network about someone trying to recruit specialists for an operation in Central America. Big money, complete secrecy, no questions asked."

"Who was doing the recruiting?"

"We don't know. The rumours were third or fourth-hand, the kind of information that's impossible to verify. At the time, I thought it was probably nothing. Criminal organisations are always recruiting in this region. But now..."

"Now it looks like the destruction faction was building a private army."

"Or hiring one." Yara turned back to face her. "Either way, we're not just dealing with a few rogue Guardians. We're dealing with a coordinated operation that has resources, planning, and professional killers willing to do the dirty work."

Elena absorbed this information, feeling the situation grow more complex with each new revelation. When she had proposed her framework to the Guardian council, she had known there would be opposition. She had expected arguments, debates, perhaps even some cells withdrawing from the network in protest. She had not expected warfare.

"We need help," she said. "More than the network can provide on its own."

"What kind of help?"

"The kind that can track down professional killers and stop them before they hit anyone else. The kind that has resources, intelligence capabilities, the ability to operate across borders." Elena hesitated, knowing that what she was about to suggest would be controversial. "I'm thinking about reaching out to external contacts. People I worked with during the search for the fragments."

Yara's expression hardened. "You mean outsiders. People who don't know about the network, who might compromise our security if they learned what we're protecting."

"I mean people who have skills we desperately need right now. And yes, it's a risk. But the alternative is sitting here while the destruction faction picks us off one by one."

"The network has survived for five centuries by keeping our existence secret. By trusting no one outside the cells. By maintaining absolute compartmentalisation between ourselves and the rest of the world." Yara's voice rose slightly. "You want to throw all of that away because you're scared?"

"I'm not scared, Yara. I'm realistic. We're facing an enemy that has professional resources, inside knowledge of our operations, and a willingness to kill without hesitation. The traditional approach isn't going to work this time."

"So you want to compromise everything the Guardians have built—"

"I want to save as many lives as I can!" Elena was on her feet now, her own voice raised. "Ixchel is dead. Five cells have gone silent. How many more people have to die before we admit that we need help?"

The two women faced each other across the small room, the tension crackling between them like electricity. For a long moment, neither spoke.

Then Yara let out a breath and looked away.

"You may be right," she said quietly. "I don't like it—everything in my training rebels against it—but you may be right. The situation is unprecedented. The old rules may not apply."

"I'm not saying we throw open the doors to everyone. I'm saying we bring in a few trusted individuals, people who've already proven their loyalty, and use their skills to help us track down the attackers." Elena sat back down, forcing herself to calm. "Diego and Ana have military contacts from their time with Méndez-Castellón's organisation. Carlos and Miguel may be wounded, but they still have connections in the security world. And I have academic colleagues who might be able to help with the intelligence side—tracking movements, identifying patterns, that kind of thing."

"You're talking about building a counter-operation. Turning the network from a preservation society into some kind of... paramilitary force."

"I'm talking about survival. Ours and everyone else's in the network." Elena leaned forward. "The destruction faction has already escalated to violence. We can either respond in kind, or we can die on our principles."

Yara was silent for another long moment. Then she moved to the table and began gathering her papers.

"I need to consult with the other Keepers," she said. "This decision is too big for me to make alone. But in the meantime," she looked up at Elena. "In the meantime, I won't stop you from reaching out to your contacts. Just be careful. Very careful. The wrong person learning about the network could be as dangerous as the destruction faction itself."

"I understand."

"Do you?" Yara's eyes were searching. "Because once you invite outsiders in, you can never truly uninvite them. They'll know things they're not supposed to know, have access they're not supposed to have. And even if they're trustworthy now, people change. Circumstances change. The information could end up anywhere."

"I know the risks. But right now, the greater risk is doing nothing."

Yara nodded slowly. "Then do what you need to do. I'll be in touch when the Keepers have reached a decision."

She gathered the last of her papers and moved toward the door. Then she paused, her hand on the handle.

"Ixchel was a good woman," she said quietly. "A faithful Guardian. She deserved better than what she got."

"Yes. She did."

"Then make sure her death means something. Stop these people, Elena. Whatever it takes."

She opened the door and disappeared into the night, leaving Elena alone in the safe house with the rain drumming on the roof and the weight of impossible choices pressing down on her shoulders.

***

The next several hours were a blur of phone calls, encrypted messages, and difficult conversations.

Elena reached Diego first. He was in Colombia, following up on a lead related to the network's operations in that region, and the connection was poor—his voice cutting in and out, fragments of words lost in static. But he understood the situation quickly, and his response was immediate.

"I'm on my way. I can be in Guatemala by tomorrow afternoon."

"Bring whoever you can. People you trust absolutely."

"That narrows the list considerably, but I'll see what I can do."

Ana was harder to reach—she was in transit somewhere, her phone going straight to voicemail. Elena left a coded message and moved on, knowing that Ana would understand its meaning and respond as soon as she could.

Carlos and Miguel were together in Peru, recovering from wounds that had healed physically but still affected their mobility. They were less enthusiastic about getting involved—their experiences during the search for the fragments had left scars that went beyond the physical—but they agreed to help in whatever way they could, even if that meant working from a distance.

By the time Elena had finished her calls, the sky was beginning to lighten outside the safe house window. She had been awake for over twenty-four hours, and her body was screaming for rest. But every time she closed her eyes, she saw Ixchel's face—peaceful in death, despite the violence that had ended her life.

She forced herself to eat something from the meagre supplies in the safe house—canned beans, stale bread, water from a jug that tasted of plastic. The food sat heavy in her stomach, but she knew she needed fuel for whatever was coming next.

Her phone buzzed with an incoming message. She checked the screen and felt her heart skip.

It was from a number she didn't recognise, but the content was unmistakable.

Two more cells visited tonight. Honduras and El Salvador. Same method as Guatemala. No survivors.

Elena stared at the screen, the words blurring as exhaustion and grief pressed in from all sides. Two more cells. Dozens more people, probably. Families and communities that had been part of the Guardian network for generations, wiped out in a single night.

The destruction faction was accelerating. They knew that the emergency protocols would alert the remaining cells, that their window of opportunity was closing. So they were moving fast, hitting as many targets as they could before the network could regroup.

How many more would die before this was over?

Elena set down her phone and stared at the wall, trying to think. The attackers had resources, yes, but they also had limitations. They couldn't hit every cell simultaneously—they had to move from location to location, which took time. And each attack generated information: witness descriptions, vehicle sightings, traces that could be followed.

If she could get ahead of them—figure out which cell they would target next, set up an ambush, capture one of the attackers for interrogation—she might be able to unravel the entire operation.

It was a long shot. A desperate gamble that could easily go wrong. But it was better than sitting here, waiting for the next notification that another cell had been destroyed.

She pulled out her map of the region and began to study it, looking for patterns in the attacks. Guatemala, Honduras, El Salvador—the targets so far had been in a rough line, moving southeast from the highlands toward the Pacific coast. If the attackers continued in that direction, the next logical target would be...

Elena's finger stopped on a small village in western Nicaragua. A cell that had been part of the network for nearly two hundred years, protecting knowledge that traced back to pre-Columbian trading routes.

She checked her phone. No alert from that cell yet, which meant either they hadn't been hit, or they had been hit and there was no one left to send an alert.

Either way, Nicaragua was where she needed to go.

She gathered her things, memorised the route she would need to take, and headed for the door. The rain had stopped, and the first rays of sunlight were breaking through the clouds, painting the hills in shades of gold and green.

It was going to be a beautiful day and Elena just wished she could appreciate it.

29

Trail of Blood

Western Nicaragua — Three Days Later

The village of San Marcos de Colón sat in a valley that might have been beautiful under other circumstances—green hills rising on all sides, a river winding through the centre, fields of coffee and corn stretching toward the horizon. But Elena saw none of the beauty as she drove toward it on the third morning after leaving Guatemala. She saw only the smoke rising from the centre of the village, and the vehicles gathered around what looked like the main plaza.

She was too late. Again.

She pulled off the road about a kilometre from the village, parking in a copse of trees that would hide the car from casual observation. Then she grabbed her pack—weapon, first aid kit, the emergency supplies she had learned to carry everywhere—and began making her way toward the village on foot, staying low, using whatever cover the terrain provided.

The smoke was thicker now, and she could smell it—the acrid scent of burning plastic and wood, mixed with something else underneath. Something that made her stomach clench with recognition.

Burning flesh.

She had smelled it before, in the aftermath of other attacks, other atrocities. It was not something you ever forgot.

The village came into view as she crested a small rise, and Elena dropped to her stomach, pressing herself into the grass, making herself as small as possible. Through the scope of the small binoculars she carried, she could see the plaza clearly—the smoking ruins of what had been a church, the bodies lying in the open, the armed men moving among them.

Not local police. Not military. Private contractors, from the look of their equipment—tactical vests, assault rifles, the kind of professional gear that cost serious money. Half a dozen of them, moving with the coordinated efficiency of people who had done this before.

The destruction faction's hired killers.

Elena forced herself to breathe slowly, steadily, fighting the urge to rush down there and start shooting. She was one person with a handgun against six professionals with automatic weapons. If she attacked head-on, she would die, and her death would accomplish nothing.

But if she could follow them—find out where they went next, learn something about their operation—she might be able to stop them before they hit another cell.

She waited, watching through the binoculars as the men completed their work. They were methodical, thorough—checking bodies, collecting documents, making sure that nothing and no one had survived. After about twenty minutes, they began loading their equipment back into the two black SUVs that were parked at the edge of the plaza.

Elena memorised the license plates, the makes and models, every detail she could see. Then she watched as the vehicles pulled out, heading south on the main road that led toward Managua.

She waited another ten minutes, making sure they weren't coming back. Then she rose from her hiding spot and walked down into the village.

The scene was worse up close. The bodies were mostly old people—Guardians who had been protecting this cell for decades, their knowledge and traditions now lost forever. A few younger people as well, probably children or grandchildren who had been in the wrong place at the wrong time. And in the centre of the plaza, tied to a post that had probably once held a religious statue, was a woman whose face had been beaten beyond recognition.

Elena knelt beside her, checking for a pulse she knew she wouldn't find. The woman was cold, her body stiffening with rigor mortis. She had been dead for hours.

But there were marks on her that Elena recognised. Burns. Cuts. The kind of wounds that came from systematic torture, from someone trying to extract information.

The destruction faction wasn't just killing. They were interrogating. Trying to learn the locations of fragments, the identities of other cells, anything that would help them achieve their goal.

Which meant they didn't have all the information they needed. They were still searching, still gathering intelligence. Still vulnerable.

Elena photographed everything, forcing herself to be thorough despite the horror of what she was documenting. Every detail might be important. Every piece of evidence might help track down the killers.

She was photographing the church ruins when she heard the sound—a faint moan, coming from beneath a pile of debris near the altar.

Elena froze, then moved toward the sound, her weapon drawn. It could be a trap. It could be an attacker who had been left behind. It could be—

A hand, reaching out from beneath the rubble. Small, delicate, covered in blood and ash.

Elena holstered her weapon and began pulling away the debris, working as quickly as she could without causing further collapse. Beneath the broken timbers and fallen plaster, she found a young woman—late teens or early twenties, her face pale with blood loss, her breathing shallow but steady.

"Can you hear me?" Elena asked, clearing the last of the debris and checking for injuries. "Can you tell me your name?"

The young woman's eyes fluttered open. They were dark, glazed with pain and shock, but there was awareness in them.

"They're gone?" she whispered.

"They're gone. You're safe now."

"Safe." The word came out as something between a laugh and a sob. "No one is safe. Not anymore."

Elena found the source of the bleeding—a wound in the woman's side, probably from a bullet that had grazed her rather than hitting directly. Painful, but not immediately life-threatening if she could stop the bleeding and get medical attention.

"I need to move you," Elena said, pulling out her first aid kit. "I have a car about a kilometre away. Can you walk if I help you?"

"I... I think so." The woman tried to sit up, then gasped and fell back. "Maybe not."

"Then I'll carry you. But first, let me bandage this wound." Elena worked quickly, pressing a dressing against the injury and wrapping it tight with gauze. "What's your name?"

"Lucia. Lucia Ortega." The woman's voice was stronger now, the shock beginning to recede as her survival instincts kicked in. "I'm... I was... one of the junior Guardians. My grandmother was the Keeper here."

"Was?"

Lucia's face crumpled. "They killed her. They killed everyone. I only survived because..." She gestured at the debris around them. "I was hiding in the storage cellar when the shooting started. The church collapsed on top of the entrance. They thought I was dead."

"Did you see them? The attackers?"

"Some of them. When they first arrived. Before..." Lucia's voice trailed off, and Elena saw the thousand-yard stare that came with trauma, with having witnessed things that the human mind wasn't designed to process.

"It's okay. You don't have to talk about it now. Let's get you out of here first."

Elena helped Lucia to her feet, supporting most of her weight as they made their slow way out of the ruins and toward the edge of the village. The young woman was stronger than she looked—she managed to stay conscious, managed to keep moving despite the pain that must have been screaming through her body with every step.

The kilometre to the car felt like ten. By the time they reached it, both women were exhausted, and Lucia was on the verge of collapse. Elena got her into the back seat, made sure she was as comfortable as possible, and then climbed behind the wheel.

"There's a hospital in Managua," she said. "About two hours from here. I'm going to get you there as fast as I can."

"No." Lucia's voice was weak but firm. "No hospitals. They'll ask questions. Report it to the police. The network—"

"The network will understand. You need medical attention."

"I need to stay hidden." Lucia's eyes met Elena's in the rearview mirror. "The attackers—they knew things. Things they shouldn't have known. Names, locations, security protocols. Someone is feeding them information from inside the network."

Elena felt a chill despite the tropical heat. She had suspected as much, but hearing it confirmed made it real in a way that suspicion couldn't.

"Are you sure?"

"They knew about the cellar. Knew exactly where to look for people who might be hiding. They just didn't know about the old entrance, the one that collapsed." Lucia's voice was fading, her energy depleted. "Whoever's helping them knows the old secrets. The ones that only senior Guardians are supposed to know."

Elena processed this information as she started the car and pulled onto the road. A traitor inside the network. Someone with access to the most closely guarded information. That narrowed the list considerably—only the Keepers and their immediate deputies would have the kind of knowledge Lucia was describing.

But it also meant that no one could be fully trusted. Not the cells that had responded to the emergency alert. Not the Keepers who were supposedly coordinating the network's response. Not even Yara, who had been Elena's closest ally in the Guardian hierarchy.

Anyone could be the traitor. Anyone could be leading the destruction faction to their targets.

"I know a place," Elena said, making a decision. "A safe house that's not in the network's records. No one knows about it except me and a few people I trust absolutely. Can you hold on for about four hours?"

"I'll try."

"Good. Because I need you to stay alive, Lucia. You're a witness. Maybe the only witness. And when this is over, your testimony is going to help us find the people who did this."

She pressed the accelerator and headed south, toward the border and the relative safety that lay beyond.

Behind her, Nicaragua's green hills fell away, and ahead lay a road she had never expected to travel.

***

The safe house was in Costa Rica, in the cloud forests of Monteverde—a small cabin that Elena had purchased under a false name three months ago, part of her preparation for exactly this kind of emergency. It had no connection to the Guardian network, no paper trail that could be traced, no communication systems that could be compromised.

It was also, she realised as she helped Lucia inside, completely inadequate for treating a gunshot wound.

She did what she could—cleaned the wound properly, applied fresh bandages, gave Lucia antibiotics from her emergency kit and painkillers that would take the edge off without knocking her out completely. But the young woman needed real medical care, the kind that only a hospital or a trained doctor could provide.

"I know someone," Elena said, once Lucia was settled on the cabin's single bed. "A doctor who's treated Guardian members before, off the books. He's in San José, about three hours from here. I can have him here by morning."

"Can you trust him?"

"I've trusted him before. He patched up a friend of mine after an... incident... last year. Never asked questions, never reported anything." Elena pulled out her phone. "It's a risk, but the alternative is you getting worse until I have no choice but to take you to a hospital anyway."

Lucia nodded weakly. "Do it."

Elena made the call, using coded language that the doctor would recognise. He agreed to come, as she had expected—he was well paid for his discretion, and he understood the value of keeping relationships with people who might need his services in the future.

While she waited, Elena checked her other messages. Diego had arrived in Guatemala and was coordinating with the cells that had responded to the emergency alert. Ana had finally made contact and was enroute from Peru. Yara had sent a brief message saying that the Keepers were still deliberating, which Elena interpreted as meaning that they were deadlocked on whether to authorise outside help.

She also had a message from an unknown number. Just three words: *We're still watching.*

The destruction faction. Letting her know that they knew she was involved, that they were tracking her movements, that she was a target as much as any of the cells she was trying to protect.

Elena stared at the message for a long moment, then deleted it. Fear was a luxury she couldn't afford right now.

She turned back to Lucia, who was watching her with eyes that were clearer than they had been hours ago. The rest and the painkillers were doing their work.

"Tell me about them," Elena said, pulling up a chair beside the bed. "The attackers. Anything you can remember."

Lucia was silent for a moment, gathering her thoughts. Then she began to speak, her voice low and steady, recounting the morning that had destroyed everything she knew.

The attackers had arrived at dawn, while most of the village was still sleeping. Four vehicles, at least a dozen men, all of them armed and moving with military precision. They had gone straight to the church, where the Guardian elders met to conduct their business, and they had been inside for less than five minutes before the shooting started.

Lucia had been in the storage cellar, retrieving supplies for her grandmother's morning tea. She had heard the gunfire, had frozen in terror, had stayed hidden as boots pounded overhead and screams echoed through the village. Then there had been an explosion—a grenade, she thought—and the church had collapsed, sealing her in the cellar and saving her life.

She had stayed there for hours, listening as the attackers searched the village, as they interrogated the survivors, as they executed anyone who wouldn't or couldn't tell them what they wanted to know. She had heard her grandmother's voice, defiant to the end, refusing to reveal the location of the documents that the attackers were seeking.

And then she had heard nothing, and the silence had been worse than the screams.

"What documents were they looking for?" Elena asked.

"The protocols. The communication codes. The list of all the cells in Central and South America, with their locations and the identities of their Keepers." Lucia's voice was bitter. "My grandmother burned them before they could take them. It's why they killed her—because she destroyed what they wanted instead of handing it over."

"She was brave."

"She was stubborn. Said she'd rather die than betray the network." Lucia's eyes filled with tears. "And she did. She died protecting secrets that someone had already sold."

Elena processed this information. The destruction faction had been looking for the master list of cells—which meant they didn't have complete information about the network's structure. They knew some locations, enough to launch attacks, but not all of them. That was why they were interrogating prisoners, why they were hitting multiple targets in rapid succession. They were trying to build a complete picture before the network could reorganise.

Which meant that there was still time. Some cells remained hidden, unknown to the attackers. If Elena could reach them, warn them, help them disappear before the destruction faction found them...

"I need to make some calls," she said, standing. "Rest. The doctor will be here in a few hours."

She stepped outside onto the cabin's small porch, looking out at the cloud forest that surrounded them. The mist was thick tonight, obscuring everything beyond a few metres, creating a world that was soft and grey and strangely peaceful.

Somewhere out there, killers were hunting for her. Hunting for the fragments she protected. Hunting for the knowledge that could transform the world or destroy it, depending on who controlled it.

And somewhere out there, a traitor was feeding them information. Helping them find their targets. Enabling the slaughter that had already claimed dozens of lives.

Elena needed to find that traitor. Needed to stop the attacks. Needed to protect what remained of the Guardian network while somehow still preserving the framework she had fought so hard to establish.

It seemed impossible. Too many threats, too few resources, too little time.

But she had faced impossible odds before. Had survived when survival seemed unlikely. Had found the seven fragments of the Codex of Seven Serpents when everyone said they were lost forever.

She could do this. She had to do this.

There was no one else.

30

The Traitor

San José, Costa Rica — Five Days Later

The meeting took place in a warehouse on the outskirts of the city, far from the tourist districts and business centres where strangers might attract attention. Elena had chosen the location specifically for its isolation—multiple exits, good sightlines, easy to secure against surveillance or attack.

She had also chosen it because it was a trap.

Diego arrived first, slipping through a side door with the quiet competence of someone who had spent years operating in dangerous environments. He looked tired—dark circles under his eyes, several days of stubble on his jaw—but his movements were sharp, his attention focused.

"The perimeter's clear," he reported. "No surveillance that I can see, no unusual activity in the surrounding area. If anyone's watching this place, they're very good at hiding."

"They might be." Elena checked her weapon for the third time, a nervous habit she had developed over the past weeks. "The people we're dealing with are professionals. We can't assume anything."

"Agreed. Which is why I still think this is a bad idea."

"You've made that clear. Several times."

"And yet here we are." Diego moved to a window, peering out through a gap in the boards that covered it. "Who else is coming?"

"Ana should be here in about twenty minutes. She's bringing Carlos and Miguel—they insisted on being part of this, despite their injuries." Elena paused. "And I've invited one other person. Someone who might be able to help us identify the traitor."

Diego turned, his expression sharpening. "Who?"

Before Elena could answer, there was a knock at the warehouse door—three quick raps, a pause, two more. The Guardian signal.

Elena nodded at Diego, who moved to a covering position while she approached the door. She opened it carefully, her hand on her weapon, ready for anything.

Yara stood in the doorway, her face unreadable.

"You came," Elena said.

"You asked me to. Despite everything, I still believe we're on the same side." Yara stepped inside, her eyes sweeping the warehouse, taking in the layout, the exits, Diego's position by the window. "Though I admit I was surprised by your message. You said you had information about the traitor."

"I do."

"Then share it. The Keepers are waiting for any intelligence that might help us stop the attacks."

Elena closed the door and turned to face Yara, studying the woman who had been her closest ally in the Guardian hierarchy. They had been through so much together—the council debates, the implementation of the framework, the desperate scramble to respond to the destruction faction's offensive. Elena had trusted Yara with her life, had confided in her about strategies and fears and hopes for the future.

But trust was a luxury she could no longer afford.

"Before I share anything," Elena said carefully, "I need to ask you some questions."

"Questions? Elena, we don't have time for—"

"Make time." Elena's voice was harder than she had intended. "People are dying, Yara. Dozens of Guardians, killed by attackers who knew exactly where to find them, exactly how to bypass their security, exactly who to interrogate for information. Someone is feeding them intelligence. Someone who knows the network's secrets."

"You think it's me?" Yara's expression shifted, surprise, then anger, then something that might have been hurt. "After everything we've been through, you suspect me?"

"I suspect everyone. I have to." Elena gestured to a pair of chairs that had been set up in the centre of the warehouse. "Sit. Please. Let me explain what I've learned, and then you can tell me whether my suspicions are justified."

Yara hesitated, her eyes flicking to Diego by the window, to the exits, to Elena's hand resting near her weapon. For a moment, Elena thought she might refuse—might turn and walk out, ending whatever remained of their alliance.

Then she sat.

Elena took the other chair, positioning herself so she could watch both Yara and the door.

"The attackers in Nicaragua were looking for the master list of cells," she began. "The protocols, the communication codes, all of it. The Keeper there—Lucia's grandmother—burned the documents rather than let them fall into enemy hands."

"Yes. I heard about that. A heroic act."

"But here's what doesn't make sense. If the destruction faction already had complete information about the network—if their inside source had given them everything—why would they need to interrogate prisoners? Why would they care about documents that their source could have provided directly?"

Yara was silent, her brow furrowed in thought.

"There are only two explanations," Elena continued. "It would mean the traitor doesn't have access to the complete network records—which would mean they're someone relatively junior, without full access to Guardian secrets. Or..."

"They're deliberately withholding information," Yara finished. "Giving the destruction faction enough to launch attacks, but not enough to destroy the entire network at once."

"Exactly. And why would they do that? Why hold back?"

"To maintain leverage. To ensure they remain valuable to the destruction faction." Yara's eyes narrowed. "Or because they have their own agenda. They're not just helping the destruction faction—they're trying to manipulate them."

"That's what I think too. The traitor isn't a true believer in the destruction faction's cause. They're using the situation for their own purposes." Elena leaned forward. "Which raises the question: what purposes? What would someone gain by helping attackers destroy parts of the network while keeping other parts intact?"

"Control," Diego said from his position by the window. "If you destroy your rivals but preserve your allies, you end up controlling whatever's left."

"Yes. Exactly." Elena kept her eyes on Yara. "Someone is trying to reshape the Guardian network to serve their own ends. They're using the destruction faction as a weapon, pointing them at cells that oppose their vision while protecting cells that support them."

Yara's face had gone very still. "You think I'm doing this. You think I'm the one manipulating the destruction faction."

"I think you're one of the very few people who could be doing it. You're a Keeper. You have access to the network's most sensitive information. You know which cells supported my framework and which ones opposed it. You could easily have identified targets for the attackers while protecting cells that align with your own interests."

"My interests?" Yara's voice rose. "My interests are the same as they've always been—protecting the secret, preserving the network, ensuring that the formula doesn't fall into the wrong hands. How dare you suggest—"

"Then explain this." Elena pulled out her phone and displayed a message she had received the day before. "This was sent to me from an anonymous source. It contains a list of cells that have been attacked or are being targeted for attack. Every single one of them voted against my framework at the council. Every single one of them was part of the destruction faction or the traditionalist faction."

Yara stared at the screen, her face pale.

"Not a single cell that supported my framework has been hit," Elena continued. "Not one. Out of more than thirty cells in the Central and South American region, the attackers have exclusively targeted those who opposed the path forward I proposed. That's not coincidence, Yara. That's selection."

"It could be..." Yara's voice trailed off. She seemed genuinely shaken, her composure cracking in a way Elena had never seen before. "It could be that the destruction faction is targeting its own. Eliminating the more moderate voices to ensure that only the extremists remain."

"That's possible. But it doesn't explain how they know which cells to target. The council vote was supposed to be confidential. The positions of individual cells weren't shared outside the Keepers' circle." Elena paused, letting that sink in. "Someone with access to that information is directing the attacks. Someone who knows exactly how each cell voted and is using that knowledge to reshape the network."

"And you think that someone is me."

"I think it could be. I also think it could be any of the other Keepers, or their deputies, or anyone else who might have gained access to the council records." Elena set down her phone. "That's why I asked you here, Yara. Not to accuse you, but to ask for your help. If you're not the traitor—and I genuinely hope you're not—then I need your assistance to find out who is."

The warehouse was silent except for the distant sounds of the city. Diego remained at his post by the window; his attention divided between the conversation and the outside world. Yara sat motionless, her dark eyes fixed on Elena's face.

"You've thought this through," she said finally. "The logic, the evidence, the implications. You've built a case."

"I've tried."

"And you've concluded that the traitor must be someone in the Keepers' circle. Someone with access to the council records and the ability to communicate with the destruction faction without being detected."

"Yes."

Yara nodded slowly. "Then I'll tell you something that I probably shouldn't. Something that may help you narrow down your list of suspects."

Elena waited.

"The council records aren't stored in a single location. Each Keeper receives only the portions relevant to their region, along with a summary of the overall vote. The complete records—including how each cell voted—are held by only one person." Yara's voice dropped. "The Keeper of Keepers. The one who convenes the councils and maintains the network's most sensitive archives."

"Who is that?"

"A man named Hernández. Joaquín Hernández. He's based in Medellín, has been Keeper of Keepers for nearly twenty years." Yara's expression was troubled. "He was the one who proposed the destruction faction's position at the council. He argued passionately for eliminating the fragments, even though he knew the majority would never agree. At the time, I thought he was simply stating his principles. Now..."

"Now you think he might have had another agenda."

"I think it's worth investigating. If anyone has the access and the motivation to direct the attacks, it's him."

Elena absorbed this information, feeling pieces fall into place. Hernández. The Keeper of Keepers. A man who had argued for destruction and then, when that argument failed, might have decided to take matters into his own hands.

"I need to get to Medellín," she said.

"That's suicide. If Hernández is the traitor, he'll know you're coming. He has resources, connections, the kind of power that comes from two decades at the top of the Guardian hierarchy."

"Then I'll need help. More than just Diego and the others." Elena met Yara's eyes. "I'll need the Keepers who still support me. Who still believe in the framework. Who are willing to confront one of their own if it means saving the network."

Yara was silent for a long moment. Then she stood, her expression resolute.

"I'll make the calls. There are three other Keepers I trust absolutely—people who I know didn't support the destruction faction, people who have as much to lose as any of us if Hernández succeeds." She moved toward the door. "But Elena—you need to understand what you're asking. If we move against Hernández and we're wrong, we'll tear the network apart. The trust that holds us together will be destroyed. We'll have done the destruction faction's work for them."

"And if we're right and we do nothing, the destruction faction will tear the network apart anyway. At least this way, we have a chance of stopping them."

Yara nodded. "Then we do it. God help us, we do it."

She opened the door and stepped out into the night, leaving Elena alone with Diego and the weight of what was coming.

The hunt for the traitor had begun.

31

Gathering Storm

San José to Medellín — One Week Later

The preparations took longer than Elena had hoped. Moving against the Keeper of Keepers was not something that could be done hastily or without careful planning. Hernández had spent two decades building his position within the Guardian network, cultivating alliances, accumulating information, and establishing himself as the indispensable centre around which the entire organisation revolved. If Elena's suspicions were correct—if he was indeed the traitor directing the destruction faction's attacks—then he would have anticipated the possibility of discovery and prepared accordingly.

They needed allies. They needed intelligence. They needed a plan that accounted for every possible contingency.

And they needed to move before Hernández realised they were coming.

The week following Elena's meeting with Yara was a blur of encrypted communications, clandestine meetings, and sleepless nights spent poring over whatever information they could gather about

Hernández and his operations. Diego proved invaluable during this phase, his experience in covert operations translating seamlessly to the task of building an intelligence picture of their target. Ana arrived from Peru with Carlos and Miguel in tow, all three of them ready to contribute despite the lingering effects of wounds that had never fully healed.

And Lucia—the young survivor from Nicaragua—surprised everyone by insisting on being part of the operation.

"They killed my grandmother," she said when Elena tried to convince her to stay behind. "They killed everyone I knew. I'm not going to hide in a safe house while you go after the people responsible."

"You're still recovering. The doctor said—"

"The doctor said I'll have a scar and some reduced mobility in my left arm. He didn't say I couldn't function." Lucia's dark eyes were hard, determined. "I know things about the network that might be useful. I grew up in it, learned its traditions, understand how it operates. And I want to see this through."

Elena recognised the look in the young woman's eyes—the same combination of grief and fury that had driven her own actions since Ixchel's death. There was no point in arguing with that kind of determination. It would only waste time and create resentment.

"Fine," she said. "But you follow orders. No improvisation, no heroics. We can't afford to lose anyone else."

Lucia nodded, accepting the terms.

The team that assembled in the San José safe house over the following days was an unlikely collection of people bound together by circumstance and shared purpose. Diego, the former security professional whose quiet competence masked depths of capability that Elena was still discovering. Ana, whose medical training and steady nerves had saved lives more than once during their previous adventures. Carlos and Miguel, wounded veterans of a shadow war that had claimed their employer and nearly claimed them. Lucia, the youngest among them, carrying a burden of loss that no one her age should have to bear.

And Elena herself, who still wasn't entirely sure she was qualified to lead any of this but had somehow ended up in charge anyway.

Yara made contact on the fourth day with news that was both encouraging and troubling. She had reached out to three other Keepers—women named Esperanza, Dolores, and Carmen, who led cells in Ecuador, Bolivia, and Argentina respectively—and all three had agreed to support the operation against Hernández. They shared Elena's suspicions about the pattern of attacks, and they were willing to risk everything to protect what remained of the network.

But Yara had also learned something disturbing.

"Hernández knows something is happening," she reported during a secure video call. "He's been reaching out to cells across the network, asking questions about communications, about loyalty, about whether anyone has been in contact with 'disruptive elements.' He's using language that sounds like concern for network security, but the subtext is clear—he's trying to identify who might be moving against him."

"Has he mentioned me specifically?"

"Not by name. But he's asked about 'the American woman' and her 'unauthorised activities.' He's framing it as concern about operational security, suggesting that your involvement with outside contacts may have compromised the network." Yara's expression was grim. "He's good, Elena. He's been doing this for twenty years. He knows how to manipulate perception, how to turn allies against each other, how to make himself look like the reasonable one while painting his opponents as threats."

"Then we need to move before he can consolidate support. Before he can turn the network against us."

"Agreed. Esperanza is already in position in Colombia—she arrived yesterday under cover of visiting family. Dolores and Carmen are coordinating with cells in their regions, making sure that Hernández's messages are being viewed with appropriate scepticism." Yara paused. "But we still don't have a solid plan for actually confronting him. His compound in Medellín is well-protected—private security, surveillance systems, multiple layers of access control. We can't just walk up and knock on the door."

"We don't need to get inside his compound. We need to get him to come to us."

"How?"

Elena had been thinking about this for days, turning the problem over in her mind, looking for angles that might give them an advantage. Hernández was cautious by nature—he had to be, given the sensitive position he occupied—but he was also arrogant. Twenty years at the top of the Guardian hierarchy had convinced him that he was smarter, better informed, and more capable than anyone who might challenge him.

That arrogance was his weakness.

"We give him something he can't resist," Elena said. "We make him think he has an opportunity to eliminate multiple threats at once—me, you, the other Keepers who oppose him. We set up a meeting, ostensibly to discuss network security concerns, and we make it look like we're walking into a trap."

"You want to use ourselves as bait."

"I want to make him overconfident. Make him think he's in control of the situation when actually we're the ones controlling it." Elena leaned forward, her eyes intense. "Hernández has been operating from a position of strength because he has information we don't have. He knows who's loyal to him, who's vulnerable, where the bodies are buried. But if we can get him out of his compound, away from his security apparatus, into a situation where we control the environment..."

"Then we can turn the tables."

"Exactly. We let him think he's springing a trap on us. And then we spring our own trap on him."

Yara was silent for a moment, considering the plan. "It's risky. If he suspects anything, if he brings more force than we anticipate, if any of a dozen things go wrong..."

"I know. But what's the alternative? Siege his compound? Try to infiltrate his security? Wait for him to pick off the remaining cells one by one?" Elena shook her head. "We don't have the resources for a prolonged campaign, and we don't have time to wait. Every day we delay is another day the destruction faction uses to hunt down Guardians."

"You're right. I just..." Yara sighed. "I've known Joaquín for fifteen years, Elena. I respected him. Trusted him. The idea that he could be behind all of this—that he could have ordered the deaths of people who considered him a friend and mentor—it's difficult to accept."

"I understand. But we have to deal with the situation as it is, not as we wish it were."

"Yes. We do." Yara straightened, her expression hardening with resolve. "I'll start making arrangements. We'll need a location for the meeting—somewhere that seems neutral but where we can control access. And we'll need a cover story that makes our gathering seem legitimate, something that Hernández will believe."

"I have some ideas about that. Let me work on the details and I'll send you a proposal by tomorrow."

"Good. And Elena?" Yara's voice softened slightly. "Be careful. Hernández isn't just smart—he's ruthless. If he realises what we're planning, he won't hesitate to eliminate the threat. All of us."

"I know. That's why we need to be smarter and more ruthless than he is."

The call ended, leaving Elena alone in the safe house with the weight of everything that was about to happen pressing down on her shoulders. Outside, the Costa Rican night was alive with the sounds of insects and birds, the ordinary rhythms of a world that had no idea what was being planned in this small cabin in the cloud forest.

She thought about Ixchel, tortured and murdered for secrets she had protected her entire life. She thought about Lucia's grandmother, defiant to the end, choosing death over betrayal. She thought about all the nameless Guardians across the centuries who had sacrificed everything to protect knowledge that most of humanity didn't even know existed.

Their legacy was in her hands now. Their trust, their faith, their hope that someday the burden they carried would prove to have meaning.

She would not let them down.

***

The flight to Colombia left San José early on a Tuesday morning, the aircraft climbing through clouds that seemed to stretch forever before finally breaking into clear blue sky above. Elena sat by the window, watching the landscape fall away below—green mountains giving way to the glittering expanse of the Pacific, then the isthmus of Panama narrowing to a thread before widening again into the vast reaches of South America.

Diego sat beside her, pretending to read a magazine but actually scanning the cabin for any sign of surveillance or threat. It was a habit born of years in security work, and Elena found it oddly comforting—someone was watching out for danger so she could focus on the task ahead.

The rest of the team was scattered throughout the aircraft and across multiple flights, a precaution against the possibility that their travel plans had been compromised. Ana and Carlos were on a different airline, arriving in Bogotá via Miami. Miguel and Lucia were taking a more circuitous route through Ecuador. They would all converge on Medellín over the next two days, assembling the pieces of their operation with the care and precision of a complex puzzle.

"You've been quiet," Diego said, setting aside his magazine. "More than usual."

"I've been thinking."

"About the operation?"

"About what happens after." Elena turned from the window to face him. "Assuming we succeed—assuming we expose Hernández and stop the destruction faction—what then? The network will be in ruins. Dozens of cells destroyed, decades of accumulated knowledge lost, trust shattered beyond repair. How do we rebuild from that?"

"One step at a time. Same as always."

"That's not an answer."

"It's the only answer that makes sense right now." Diego's voice was calm, practical. "We can't plan for a future we might not live to see. All we can do is deal with the present, handle what's in front of us, and trust that if we survive, we'll figure out the rest."

"Is that how you've always approached things? One crisis at a time?"

"Pretty much. When you spend your life in security work, you learn that long-term planning is mostly an illusion. The world changes too fast, too unpredictably. The best you can do is stay flexible, adapt to circumstances, and keep moving forward even when you can't see where you're going."

Elena considered this. It was a philosophy born of experience, of years spent dealing with threats that couldn't be anticipated and challenges that defied planning. In some ways, it was the opposite of her academic training, which emphasised careful research, systematic analysis, and the construction of frameworks that could explain and predict patterns over time.

But maybe Diego was right. Maybe the Guardian network's greatest mistake had been its insistence on long-term thinking—on frameworks and criteria and protocols that were supposed to guide decisions across centuries. That kind of planning created rigidity, making the organisation vulnerable to people like Hernández who could manipulate the structures for their own ends.

Maybe what the network needed was not a new framework, but the flexibility to operate without one.

"I've been so focused on building systems," she said slowly. "On creating rules and processes that would outlast any individual. But systems can be corrupted. Rules can be twisted. Maybe the ancients had it right when they scattered the fragments and trusted individuals to protect them, rather than trying to create an organisation that would function automatically."

"Maybe. Or maybe the problem isn't systems versus individuals, but how you combine them." Diego turned to face her more fully. "You need structure to coordinate action, to preserve knowledge, to transmit purpose across generations. But you also need people who can think independently, who can recognise when the structure is failing and take action even if it means breaking the rules."

"People like us."

"People like us." He smiled slightly. "For better or worse, we're the ones who ended up in this situation. We didn't ask for it, didn't plan for it, but here we are. And the only thing we can do is our best."

"What if our best isn't good enough?"

"Then at least we'll know we tried." Diego's expression grew serious. "I've seen a lot of people fail over the years, Elena. Some of them failed because they weren't capable enough, or didn't have the resources, or just got unlucky. But the worst failures—the ones that really haunt me—were the people who didn't even try. Who saw a problem, knew they could do something about it, and chose to walk away because they were afraid of failing."

"You're saying I shouldn't worry about whether I'm good enough. I should just act."

"I'm saying that action is the only thing that matters in the end. Everything else—the doubts, the fears, the what-ifs—that's just noise. It's what you actually do that defines you."

Elena nodded slowly, feeling something shift inside her. The doubt was still there—it probably always would be—but it was no longer paralysing. It was just another factor to be managed, another obstacle to be overcome on the way to doing what needed to be done.

The aircraft began its descent toward Bogotá, the engines changing pitch as the pilots adjusted for the approach. Below, the sprawl of Colombia's capital spread across a high plateau, millions of people going about their lives with no idea that a war for the future of humanity was being waged in the shadows around them.

Elena watched the city grow larger, the buildings and roads resolving from abstract patterns into recognisable structures, and she felt a strange sense of calm settle over her.

She was ready.

Whatever came next, she was ready.

***

Medellín was not what Elena had expected.

The city of her imagination—shaped by decades of news coverage about drug cartels and violence—bore little resemblance to the vibrant, modern metropolis she found when she arrived. The city had transformed itself over the past twenty years, investing in public transportation, urban renewal, and social programs that had turned former no-go zones into thriving neighbourhoods. The hills that surrounded the valley were covered in a mixture of sleek high-rises and colourful working-class communities, connected by cable cars that glided silently above streets alive with commerce and culture.

It was, Elena thought, a testament to what was possible when people decided to change their circumstances rather than accept them. A city that had been written off as hopeless had become a symbol of urban renewal, proof that even the most entrenched problems could be overcome with sufficient will and resources.

She wondered if the same could be true for the Guardian network. If the destruction and betrayal they were experiencing now could somehow be transformed into an opportunity for renewal, for building something better on the ashes of what had been lost.

But that was a question for another day. Right now, she had a traitor to catch.

The team assembled at a rented apartment in the Laureles neighbourhood, a middle-class area far from both the tourist districts and the more dangerous outlying zones. The apartment was unremarkable—three bedrooms, a small living area, a kitchen that had seen better days—but it had the essential virtue of anonymity. One more group of visitors in a city that hosted thousands of them, invisible among the crowds.

Yara was waiting when Elena arrived, along with Esperanza, a small woman in her sixties whose gentle appearance belied a reputation for ruthless efficiency in protecting her Ecuadorian cell. They had arrived separately, through different airports, using credentials that would not attract attention from either Colombian authorities or Hernández's surveillance network.

"The others are in position," Yara reported as Elena set down her bag. "Dolores is monitoring communications from La Paz, watching for any indication that Hernández suspects what we're planning. Carmen is coordinating with cells in the southern cone, making sure they're prepared to act if things go badly here."

"And the meeting?"

"Scheduled for tomorrow evening. Hernández accepted the invitation without hesitation—he thinks we're gathering to discuss emergency security protocols in response to the attacks. I implied that there was division among the Keepers about how to respond, and that we needed his leadership to resolve it."

"He believed that?"

"He wanted to believe it. That's almost the same thing." Yara's expression was grim. "Men like Hernández always assume they're the smartest person in the room. It never occurs to them that someone might be manipulating them."

Elena moved to the window, looking out at the city lights spread across the valley below. Somewhere out there, Hernández was in his compound, confident in his power and position, probably planning how to use tomorrow's meeting to consolidate his control over the network. He had no idea that his carefully constructed world was about to collapse.

Or maybe he did. Maybe he suspected something and was even now preparing his own countermeasures, his own traps, his own plans for eliminating the threats to his position.

That was the problem with facing an intelligent, experienced opponent. You could never be entirely sure what they knew or what they were planning. All you could do was prepare for as many contingencies as possible and trust that your own intelligence and preparation would be enough.

"Walk me through the location," Elena said, turning back to face Yara and Esperanza. "Every detail."

Yara pulled out a tablet and called up a map of the meeting site—a private restaurant in the El Poblado district, the kind of upscale establishment where wealthy Colombians and international businesspeople met to discuss deals they didn't want anyone to overhear. The restaurant had private dining rooms that could be reserved for confidential meetings, along with security protocols designed to ensure discretion.

"Hernández chose the location," Yara explained. "He owns a minority stake in the restaurant—one of many investments he's made over the years to create safe spaces for Guardian business. He feels comfortable there, which is both an advantage and a disadvantage for us."

"Advantage because he won't be expecting trouble in a place he controls. Disadvantage because he'll have people there who are loyal to him."

"Exactly. The restaurant staff includes at least two people who report directly to Hernández—a manager and one of the waiters. They'll be watching for anything unusual, and they'll alert him immediately if they notice anything suspicious."

"Can we neutralise them?"

"We can't remove them without raising alarms, but we can distract them. Esperanza has arranged for a minor incident in the kitchen—nothing dangerous, just enough chaos to keep the staff occupied during the critical moments of the meeting."

Elena studied the map, noting the layout of the restaurant, the positions of exits, the locations of the private dining rooms. The plan was taking shape in her mind—a complex choreography of movements and actions that would need to be executed with precision.

"What about Hernández's personal security?"

"He travels with two bodyguards—former Colombian military, very capable. They'll be in the restaurant during the meeting, probably positioned near the entrance to the private room. We won't be able to get past them without a confrontation."

"Then we don't try to get past them. We let Hernández come to us." Elena traced a route on the map with her finger. "After the meeting, when Hernández thinks he's in control, we reveal what we know. We confront him with the evidence of his betrayal, in front of witnesses—you, Esperanza, whoever else is in the room. We force him to respond, to defend himself, to make mistakes."

"And if he doesn't make mistakes? If he simply denies everything and walks away?"

"Then we follow him. We document his movements, his contacts, his communications. We build a case that's impossible to deny, and we take that case to the rest of the network." Elena's voice hardened. "One way or another, we expose him. The only question is whether he gives us the evidence we need voluntarily, or whether we have to extract it."

Esperanza spoke for the first time, her voice soft but carrying an edge of steel. "And if he decides to fight? If he orders his bodyguards to eliminate the threat—meaning us?"

"Then we fight back." Elena met the older woman's eyes steadily. "I'm not planning to die tomorrow, Esperanza. But I'm also not planning to let Hernández walk away just because confronting him is dangerous. Too many people have already died because of his betrayal. It ends here, one way or another."

Esperanza studied her for a long moment, then nodded slowly. "I believe you. And I think Hernández will believe you too, when he sees that we're not afraid of him." She smiled grimly. "Men like him expect their opponents to be cautious, to hedge their bets, to look for ways out. When they encounter someone who's willing to risk everything, it throws them off balance. That may be our greatest advantage."

"Let's hope so." Elena turned back to the window, watching the lights of Medellín twinkle in the gathering darkness. "Because tomorrow, we find out if all of this—the planning, the preparation, the risk—has been worth it."

Behind her, she heard Yara and Esperanza begin discussing the final details of the operation, their voices low and intent. Outside, the city continued its nightly rituals, oblivious to the drama that was about to unfold in its midst.

Elena allowed herself a moment of quiet contemplation, marshalling her thoughts for what was to come. Tomorrow would bring answers—answers to questions that had haunted her since the attacks began. Who was really behind the destruction faction? What was Hernández's ultimate goal? And could the Guardian network survive the revelations that were about to tear it apart?

She didn't know. But she was determined to find out.

32

The Confrontation

El Poblado District, Medellín, Colombia — The Following Evening

The restaurant occupied the top floor of a building that offered panoramic views of Medellín's skyline, its floor-to-ceiling windows showcasing the city's transformation from troubled past to hopeful present. Elena arrived early, wanting to observe the space before the other participants gathered, to get a feel for the environment where everything would come to a head.

The maître d' greeted her with professional warmth, recognising her name from the reservation list and escorting her to the private dining room that had been reserved for the evening. It was an elegant space—dark wood panelling, soft lighting, a table large enough to seat a dozen people arranged around a central floral arrangement that probably cost more than most Colombians earned in a week.

Through the windows, Elena could see the lights of the city spreading across the valley, a sea of illumination that made it easy to forget the poverty and violence that still existed in the shadows of those gleaming towers. Medellín had reinvented itself, but the reinvention was incomplete—a work in progress that could still be derailed by the forces of corruption and greed that had nearly destroyed it once before.

Not unlike the Guardian network itself.

Elena took a seat that gave her a clear view of both the entrance and the windows, a habit she had developed over months of operating in dangerous environments. She ordered a glass of wine she didn't intend to drink—she needed her mind clear for what was coming—and settled in to wait.

Esperanza arrived next, dressed in conservative business attire that made her look like exactly what she was supposed to be: a senior executive attending a confidential meeting. She exchanged a glance with Elena as she entered, a brief acknowledgment that everything was in position, then took a seat on the opposite side of the table and began reviewing documents that she had brought as props for her cover story.

Yara came shortly after, accompanied by two men Elena didn't recognise—representatives from other cells, she assumed, brought along to give the meeting the appearance of a legitimate gathering. They nodded politely to Elena and Esperanza, taking seats around the table, making small talk about the view and the restaurant's reputation.

And then Hernández arrived.

Elena had seen photographs of the Keeper of Keepers during her research, but they hadn't prepared her for the man's physical presence. He was tall, well-built for someone in his sixties, with silver hair swept back from a face that combined distinguished features with an air of absolute authority. He moved like someone accustomed to being the most important person in any room, his bodyguards flanking him with the casual alertness of professionals who had long since learned to read threats before they materialised.

His eyes swept the room as he entered, taking in each face, assessing and categorising with the practiced efficiency of someone who had spent decades navigating the treacherous waters of Guardian politics. When his gaze reached Elena, he smiled—a warm, avuncular expression that didn't quite reach his eyes.

"Dr. Vasquez. I've heard so much about you." His English was accented but fluent, the product of extensive international dealings. "The woman who found the seven fragments. A remarkable achievement."

"Thank you." Elena rose to shake his hand, noting the firm grip, the way he held contact a moment longer than necessary—a dominance display, subtle but unmistakable. "I'm grateful you could join us on such short notice."

"When the network faces a crisis, we must all do our part." Hernández released her hand and moved to take the seat at the head of the table, his bodyguards positioning themselves near the door. "I understand there are concerns about how we should respond to the recent... unpleasantness."

"That's one way to describe it." Yara's voice was carefully neutral. "Dozens of Guardians murdered, multiple cells destroyed, centuries of accumulated knowledge lost. 'Unpleasantness' seems inadequate."

"Of course. I meant no disrespect to those we've lost." Hernández's expression shifted to one of appropriate gravity. "But we must be careful not to let grief cloud our judgment. Whoever is behind these attacks—and I have my suspicions—they want us to panic, to make rash decisions, to tear ourselves apart. We must not give them that satisfaction."

"And what would you suggest instead?" Elena asked.

"Patience. Caution. A careful investigation to identify the perpetrators before we take any action that might make the situation worse." Hernández spread his hands in a gesture of reasonableness. "I know it's frustrating, especially for those of you who lost people you cared about. But rushing into a confrontation without proper preparation would be exactly what our enemies want."

Elena studied him as he spoke, looking for any sign of the duplicity she suspected. But Hernández was good—very good. His concern seemed genuine, his reasoning sound, his manner that of a wise leader trying to guide his organisation through a difficult time.

If she hadn't spent weeks piecing together the evidence of his betrayal, she might have believed him.

"There's another possibility," she said carefully. "One that we should at least consider."

"Oh? And what's that?"

"That the attacks aren't coming from outside the network. That whoever is directing them has access to information that only someone in a position of authority could possess." Elena held Hernández's gaze steadily. "That the traitor is one of us."

The temperature in the room seemed to drop several degrees. The other Keepers shifted uncomfortably, exchanging glances that conveyed uncertainty and concern. Hernández's expression didn't change, but something flickered in his eyes—a quick calculation, a reassessment of the situation.

"That's a serious accusation," he said quietly. "I hope you have evidence to support it."

"I have a pattern." Elena pulled out her phone and displayed the data she had compiled—the list of attacked cells, their positions on the network, their votes at the council meeting. "Every cell that's been hit was part of either the destruction faction or the traditionalist faction. Not a single cell that supported my framework has been targeted. The probability of that happening by chance is essentially zero."

"That could mean many things. Perhaps the destruction faction is eliminating its own moderates. Perhaps the attackers are working from a list that was compromised years ago—"

"A list that only the Keepers had access to?" Elena shook her head. "The pattern is too precise, Joaquín. Whoever is directing these attacks knows exactly how each cell voted at the council. And the only people with that information are the people in this room—and you."

Hernández's mask of concern slipped slightly, revealing something harder underneath. "You're suggesting that I—the Keeper of Keepers, who has devoted my entire life to protecting the network—am somehow responsible for these attacks?"

"I'm suggesting that we need to consider all possibilities. Including uncomfortable ones."

"This is absurd." Hernández's voice rose, taking on a note of indignation. "I have given everything to the Guardian cause. My wealth, my time, my family's safety—all sacrificed for the mission we share. And now you accuse me of betraying everything I've worked for?"

"I'm not accusing you of anything. I'm asking questions that need to be answered."

"Questions designed to undermine my authority, to sow division among the Keepers, to advance your own agenda." Hernández turned to the others at the table. "You all know me. You know my record, my commitment, my sacrifices. Are you really going to let this outsider—this American who's been part of the network for less than a year—convince you that I'm a traitor?"

The silence that followed was heavy, charged with tension and uncertainty. Elena watched the faces of the other Keepers, seeing the conflict playing out behind their eyes. They wanted to believe Hernández—he was their leader, their mentor, a man they had trusted for decades. But they also couldn't ignore the evidence she had presented, the logical pattern that pointed toward betrayal at the highest level.

Esperanza spoke first.

"Joaquín, no one wants to believe that you're involved in this. But Elena raises valid concerns. The pattern of attacks is too precise to be coincidence, and the information required to execute them could only have come from someone with access to our most sensitive records." She spread her hands in a gesture of reluctant inquiry. "If there's an explanation that exonerates you, we need to hear it. For your sake as much as ours."

"The explanation is that I'm innocent," Hernández said flatly. "I don't need to prove a negative. The burden is on Dr. Vasquez to demonstrate that I've done something wrong—not to speculate about possibilities and patterns."

"Then you won't object to an investigation." Yara's voice was quiet but firm. "Open your records to independent review. Let us examine your communications, your finances, your contacts. If you have nothing to hide, an investigation will clear your name and allow us to focus on finding the real traitor."

For a moment—just a moment—Elena saw something flash across Hernández's face. Fear? Calculation? Whatever it was, it was gone almost before she registered it, replaced by an expression of wounded dignity.

"You want to investigate me. The man who has led this network for twenty years. The man who has protected its secrets, guided its decisions, defended it against threats that most of you don't even know existed." He shook his head slowly. "I never thought I would see this day. The Guardians turning on each other, eating their own, destroying what we've spent centuries building."

"We're not turning on anyone," Elena said. "We're trying to find the truth. If you're innocent, you should want that too."

"What I want is irrelevant. What matters is what's best for the network." Hernández stood, his bodyguards immediately coming alert. "I will not submit to an investigation that presumes my guilt. I will not dignify these baseless accusations with a response. And I will not allow Dr. Vasquez or anyone else to destroy the Guardian network in the name of 'finding the truth.'"

He began walking toward the door, his bodyguards falling into formation around him. For a moment, Elena thought he was simply going to leave—to walk away from the confrontation and fight another day, from a position of greater strength.

But then she played her final card.

"We have a witness," she said. "Someone who survived one of your attacks. Someone who can testify about what the attackers were looking for, what questions they asked, what they knew about the network's internal operations."

Hernández stopped. He didn't turn around, but his shoulders tensed visibly beneath his expensive jacket.

"A witness who knows things that only you could have told them, Joaquín. A witness who's willing to testify before the entire network about what she saw and heard." Elena rose from her chair, her voice hard. "You can walk away from this meeting, but you can't walk away from the truth. It's going to come out, one way or another. The only question is whether you face it now, with some possibility of explaining yourself, or whether you wait for it to destroy you completely."

For a long moment, no one moved. The tension in the room was almost unbearable, a pressure that seemed to push against Elena's chest and make it difficult to breathe. She could see Hernández's bodyguards exchanging glances, their hands moving subtly toward their weapons, uncertain whether the situation was about to escalate into violence.

Then Hernández turned.

His face had changed. The mask of the dignified leader was gone, replaced by something colder, harder, more honest. For the first time, Elena felt she was seeing the real man behind the carefully constructed persona—the man who had decided that the Guardian network's mission was more important than the people who served it, and who had been willing to sacrifice anyone who stood in the way of his vision.

"You think you understand what you've stumbled into," he said softly. "You think this is about power, or control, or personal ambition. But you don't understand anything."

"Then explain it to me."

"The network is dying, Dr. Vasquez. It has been dying for decades—rotting from within, paralysed by tradition, incapable of adapting to a world that has changed beyond anything the founders imagined." Hernández's voice was calm, almost gentle, as if he were explaining something obvious to a slow student. "The attacks were not betrayal. They were surgery. Removing the diseased tissue so that what remains might have a chance to survive."

"You're admitting it." Yara's voice was barely a whisper. "You actually orchestrated the murders of our own people."

"I orchestrated the elimination of cells that would never agree to the changes that need to be made. Cells led by people so wedded to tradition that they would rather see the network destroyed than allow it to evolve." Hernández's gaze swept the room. "You all know the truth, even if you won't admit it. The Guardian model is obsolete. The framework that Dr. Vasquez proposed—criteria for release, periodic reassessment—it's not enough. The formula needs to be either destroyed completely or released immediately. There is no middle ground that can survive the next fifty years."

"So, you chose destruction," Elena said. "You aligned yourself with the faction that wanted to eliminate the fragments entirely."

"I chose clarity. The destruction faction understood what the traditionalists refused to accept—that half-measures would only prolong the inevitable collapse. Better to end it cleanly, to destroy the formula and eliminate the burden that has weighed on our families for five hundred years."

"And the people who disagreed? The Guardians who supported my framework, who believed in the possibility of eventual release? What about them?"

Hernández smiled—a cold expression that held no warmth or humour. "They were always going to resist. They would have fought the destruction, worked to preserve what needed to be eliminated, prolonged the agony for another generation. I couldn't allow that. The surgery had to be complete."

"You're insane." The words came from Esperanza, her soft voice cracking with emotion. "You murdered our brothers and sisters, people who trusted you, followed you, believed in you, because you decided their opinions were inconvenient?"

"I saved them from themselves. Saved them from decades more of carrying a burden that was destroying them. The Guardians who died went quickly; their suffering ended in moments rather than drawn out over their lifetimes." Hernández shook his head. "You call me insane, but I'm the only one who sees clearly. The only one willing to do what needed to be done."

Elena felt a wave of nausea wash over her. She had suspected Hernández's involvement, had built a case against him based on logic and evidence. But hearing him admit it—hearing him justify the murder of dozens of people as an act of mercy—was something else entirely.

"It's over, Joaquín," she said quietly. "Whatever you thought you were accomplishing, it ends here. The other Keepers know the truth now. The network will know soon. You can't—"

She never finished the sentence.

Hernández's hand moved in a sharp gesture, and his bodyguards drew their weapons with the smooth efficiency of trained professionals. Before anyone could react, two pistols were pointed at the Keepers around the table, their black muzzles steady and unwaveringly targeted on vital organs.

"Actually," Hernández said calmly, "I think I can. The question is whether any of you will be alive to disagree."

33

The Traitor's Hand

El Poblado District, Medellín — Moments Later

The situation had gone from tense to deadly in the space of a heartbeat.

Elena assessed the tactical situation with the part of her mind that had learned to function under pressure, cataloguing threats and possibilities with cold precision. Two armed bodyguards, weapons drawn, positioned to cover the entire table. Hernández himself, unarmed but clearly in control. Six potential targets—herself, Yara, Esperanza, and the three other Keepers who had been brought along as witnesses.

No good options. Any attempt to resist would result in immediate casualties.

"This doesn't have to end badly," Hernández said, his voice still carrying that unsettling calm. "I have no desire to kill any of you. You're not my enemies—you're simply people who made the wrong choice, aligned yourselves with a path that was always going to fail."

"Then what do you want?" Elena asked, keeping her voice steady despite the fear clawing at her chest.

"I want what I've always wanted. To complete the mission that the destruction faction began—to eliminate the fragments once and for all, to free humanity from the burden of knowledge it was never meant to possess." Hernández began moving around the table, his bodyguards adjusting their positions to maintain their fields of fire. "You're going to help me do that."

"Help you? After everything you've done?"

"After everything I've done, you don't have a choice. The fragments are scattered across multiple locations—locations that only you and your closest allies know. I need that information, Dr. Vasquez. I need to know where you've hidden the pieces of the codex so that I can destroy them."

"And if I refuse?"

"Then I start killing people you care about until you change your mind." Hernández stopped beside Esperanza, resting a hand on her shoulder in a gesture that was almost paternal. "Starting with the Keepers who followed you into this trap. One by one, until you give me what I want."

Elena felt the trap closing around her. Hernández had turned the confrontation to his advantage, used their own strategy against them. They had planned to surprise him with evidence of his betrayal; instead, he had used the meeting as an opportunity to gather his enemies in one place and neutralise them.

She thought about the fragments, hidden in locations across the Americas. Thought about the centuries of effort that had gone into preserving that knowledge, the lives that had been sacrificed to protect it. Was she willing to let more people die for a secret that might never be revealed anyway?

But she also thought about what the fragments represented. Not just the formula for transmutation, but the possibility that humanity might someday be ready for it. The framework she had built, the criteria for eventual release, the hope that the burden wouldn't have to be carried forever.

If she surrendered that hope, if she allowed Hernández to destroy the fragments, then everything the Guardians had worked for—everything Elena had fought for—would be lost. Not just for now, but forever.

"I can't give you what you want," she said quietly. "Even if I wanted to, I don't have all the information. The fragments are protected by protocols that require multiple keys, multiple people working together. Killing me wouldn't get you any closer to your goal."

"Perhaps not. But killing your friends might motivate you to find a way around those protocols." Hernández nodded to one of his bodyguards. "Start with the old woman. She's been a Guardian longer than any of us—let's see if her death helps Dr. Vasquez focus."

The bodyguard moved toward Esperanza, his weapon rising.

Elena had a split second to decide. She could maintain her defiance, let the situation play out, hope for some opportunity to turn the tables. Or she could do something desperate, something that might get her killed but might also create enough chaos to give the others a chance.

She chose chaos.

Her hand moved to the glass of wine on the table—the wine she hadn't touched—and flung its contents into the face of the nearest bodyguard. In the same motion, she dove toward him, using the momentary distraction to close the distance before he could bring his weapon to bear.

Everything after that was instinct and training—the hours Diego had spent teaching her close-quarters combat, the drills she had practiced until the movements were automatic. She grabbed the bodyguard's gun arm, twisted, felt the weapon discharge harmlessly into the ceiling as she brought her elbow up into his throat.

The room exploded into chaos.

Yara moved at almost the same moment, tackling the second bodyguard before he could fire. Esperanza dropped to the floor, pulling the other Keepers down with her, getting them out of the line of fire.

Someone was screaming—maybe the bodyguard Elena had throat-punched, maybe someone else entirely.

And then another sound cut through the chaos: breaking glass, followed by voices shouting in Spanish.

Elena looked up from where she was struggling with the disoriented bodyguard to see figures pouring through the windows—men in tactical gear, rappelling from the roof, weapons drawn. For one terrible moment, she thought Hernández had called in reinforcements, that the situation had gone from bad to catastrophic.

Then she heard Diego's voice: "Federal police! Everyone on the ground!"

The cavalry had arrived.

***

It took nearly an hour to sort out the aftermath.

The "federal police" turned out to be Diego and his contacts from the Colombian security services—professionals who had agreed to assist on the condition that they could claim credit for breaking up a criminal conspiracy if the operation succeeded. They had been positioned around the restaurant since before the meeting began, monitoring the situation through hidden cameras and microphones, ready to intervene if things went wrong.

Things had definitely gone wrong. But the intervention had come in time.

Hernández was taken into custody, along with his bodyguards and several other members of his security team who had been waiting outside the restaurant. He went quietly, his face a mask of cold resignation, offering no resistance as handcuffs were placed on his wrists. Whatever defiance he still felt, he knew better than to express it in front of armed professionals who had no stake in Guardian politics.

The Keepers were shaken but uninjured. Esperanza had a few bruises from hitting the floor, and one of the other representatives had cut his hand on broken glass, but no one had been seriously hurt.

It was, as Diego observed later, a minor miracle given how badly the situation could have gone.

Elena found a quiet corner of the restaurant and sat down, letting the adrenaline drain out of her system as she watched the Colombian authorities do their work. She felt hollow, exhausted, uncertain whether what they had accomplished represented victory or merely a temporary respite.

Hernández's capture solved one problem—the immediate threat of a traitor directing attacks against the network. But it created others. The Keeper of Keepers was in custody, facing charges that would require careful handling to avoid exposing the Guardian network's existence. The destruction faction was still out there, its foot soldiers scattered across multiple countries, leaderless now but potentially more dangerous than ever.

And the fundamental questions that had divided the network remained unanswered. What should happen to the fragments? When, if ever, should they be released? How could an organisation that had been torn apart by betrayal rebuild itself into something capable of fulfilling its ancient mission?

Yara sat down beside her, looking almost as exhausted as Elena felt. "It's over," she said. "At least this part of it."

"Is it? Hernández was just one man. He had allies, supporters, people who believed in what he was doing. They're still out there."

"Yes. But without his leadership, without his resources and connections, they're much less dangerous. We can deal with them one at a time, dismantle what's left of the destruction faction piece by piece." Yara paused. "It won't be quick or easy, but it can be done."

"And the network itself? How do we rebuild after something like this?"

"I don't know. That's a problem for tomorrow, and the day after, and probably the rest of our lives." Yara turned to look at Elena, her dark eyes reflecting the restaurant's soft lighting. "But we have time now. Time to think, to plan, to figure out a way forward. That's more than we had a few hours ago."

Elena nodded slowly, acknowledging the truth of Yara's words. They had survived. They had exposed the traitor. They had bought themselves a chance to rebuild.

It wasn't victory. Not yet. But it was a beginning.

Through the window, she could see the lights of Medellín spread across the valley—a city that had transformed itself from a symbol of violence into a beacon of hope. It had taken decades, countless setbacks, the efforts of thousands of people who refused to give up even when giving up seemed like the only rational choice.

Maybe the Guardian network could do the same. Maybe the destruction and betrayal of the past months could be transformed into an opportunity for renewal, for building something better on the ashes of what had been lost.

It would take time. It would take effort. It would take faith in possibilities that seemed impossibly distant.

But Elena had come this far by refusing to accept that impossible meant impossible. She wasn't about to stop now.

She stood, straightening her clothes, composing her face into an expression of calm determination.

"Let's go," she said to Yara. "We have work to do."

They walked out of the restaurant together, into the Medellín night, into a future that was uncertain but no longer hopeless.

The Guardian network had survived. Whatever came next, that was the foundation they would build on.

And Elena intended to make sure they built something worthy of the five centuries of sacrifice that had brought them to this moment.

34

Aftermath

Bogotá, Colombia — Two Weeks Later

The safe house in the Chapinero district had become the de facto headquarters for what remained of the Guardian network's leadership structure.

It was not an impressive space—a three-bedroom apartment in a nondescript building, chosen specifically for its anonymity and its multiple exits.

The furniture was functional rather than comfortable, the walls bare of decoration, the windows covered with blinds that remained permanently closed, but it was secure, or as secure as anything could be in the current circumstances, and it provided a place where the surviving Keepers could gather to begin the long process of rebuilding what had been destroyed.

Elena stood at the window, peering through a gap in the blinds at the street below. The neighbourhood was coming alive with the rhythms of early morning—vendors setting up their stalls, commuters heading to work, children in uniforms walking toward schools that would swallow them up for the day. Normal life, continuing as it always did, oblivious to the shadow war that had been fought in its midst.

Two weeks had passed since Hernández's capture. Two weeks of interrogations, investigations, and the painstaking work of tracing the connections between the former Keeper of Keepers and the destruction faction he had enabled. The Colombian authorities had been surprisingly cooperative, once Diego's contacts had explained the situation in terms they could understand—a criminal conspiracy involving international actors, money laundering, and murder for hire. The Guardian network's true nature remained hidden behind a cover story of competing archaeological preservation societies, a fiction that was close enough to the truth to be believable.

Hernández himself had proven less cooperative. He had retreated into a shell of dignified silence, refusing to answer questions about his contacts in the destruction faction, the locations of their cells, or the identities of the mercenaries who had carried out the attacks. His lawyers—expensive, well-connected, clearly paid for by resources that predated his arrest—had filed motion after motion to delay proceedings and limit the scope of interrogations.

It was frustrating, but Elena had expected nothing less. Hernández was playing a long game, banking on the possibility that the case against him would collapse under the weight of its own contradictions, that the Guardian network would prove unwilling to expose its secrets in open court, that time and legal manoeuvring would eventually set him free.

She couldn't allow that to happen. But preventing it would require resources and strategies that she was still struggling to assemble.

A knock at the door interrupted her thoughts. She turned to see Diego entering, carrying two cups of coffee and wearing an expression that suggested he had news—whether good or bad, she couldn't yet tell.

"The Keepers are assembling," he said, handing her one of the cups. "Yara just arrived from Peru. Esperanza is on her way from the airport. The others are already in the main room."

"How many?"

"Seven, including you. That's everyone who's confirmed their support. The rest are either dead, missing, or refusing to commit until they see how things develop."

Seven Keepers out of the twenty-three who had attended the council meeting less than a year ago. The destruction faction's attacks and Hernández's betrayal had reduced the network's leadership by more than two-thirds. Entire regions were now without representation—Central America, the Caribbean, large portions of Brazil and Argentina where cells had been systematically eliminated or driven underground.

"It's a start," Elena said, though the words felt hollow even as she spoke them. "We work with what we have."

"That's what I keep telling myself." Diego took a sip of his coffee, then set it down, his voice shifting register slightly — the tone he used when a report was bad. "Kroeger."

Elena turned from the window. "They found him?"

"The opposite. He's gone. Méndez-Castellón's people had been tracking the last known position of his network since the ambush. Three of his men were recovered from the site — two dead, one wounded and useless for interrogation. But Kroeger himself left no trace. No body, no blood trail, no signal." Diego paused. "His accounts — the ones we'd flagged — were liquidated within forty-eight hours of the Amazon. Professional-grade disappearance. He'd clearly prepared for the possibility of needing to vanish."

"And Méndez-Castellón?"

"Surfaced three weeks ago. He was wounded in the cave — took a bullet getting his security team out. He's been recovering at a private facility in Cartagena. Alive, but out of the field for now."

"Brecker and Holtz?"

"Gone. Same pattern as Kroeger — accounts cleared, passports burned, no trace. Holtz was overheard in Cartagena the night before they vanished." Diego paused. "He told Brecker that Weller had always been too curious for his own good. That a man who goes down a tunnel he wasn't ordered to check deserves what he finds."

Elena said nothing. She filed it away.

"Venezuela?" she asked.

"Or Paraguay. Or anywhere. He's done it before."

Diego held her gaze. "An eighty-seven-year-old man who has been doing this for sixty years does not just stop because he lost a round. He retreats. He waits. He finds new resources."

Elena said nothing for a moment. She thought of those pale eyes in the chamber beneath Machu Picchu, burning with the absolute certainty of a man who had given his entire life to a single purpose.

"He'll come back," she said. It wasn't a question.

"That would be my assumption. Yes."

She turned back to the window. The street below was ordinary, indifferent, full of people who had no idea what had been fought over in the jungles and chambers of the last several months. She scanned it without meaning to — doorways, sight lines, vehicles that had been parked too long.

Old habits, she realised. She was already learning new ones.

"Keep watching for him," she said. "Whatever resources it takes."

"Already underway." He paused. "The Colombian investigators also found something in Hernández's financial records. A series of payments to an account in Panama, made over the past eighteen months. Large sums, irregular intervals, no obvious legitimate purpose."

A series of payments to an account in Panama, made over the past eighteen months. Large sums, irregular intervals, no obvious legitimate purpose."

"The mercenaries?"

"That's what they think. The account is held by a shell company that traces back to a private security firm based in Miami. The firm has connections to former military personnel from several countries—Colombia, the US, Israel, South Africa. Exactly the kind of people who would have the skills and the willingness to carry out the attacks we've seen."

Elena felt a spark of hope beneath her exhaustion. This was the first concrete lead they had found to the actual perpetrators of the violence—the men who had pulled triggers and set fires and tortured elderly Guardians for information. If they could identify those men, trace their movements, perhaps even apprehend some of them...

"Can we pursue it?"

"The Colombians are willing to share what they find, but they're limited in what they can do outside their jurisdiction. Panama isn't going to cooperate with an investigation that might embarrass their banking sector, and the US firm is protected by lawyers who know exactly how to stonewall foreign inquiries."

"So, we need to pursue it ourselves."

"That's what I was thinking." Diego set down his coffee and leaned against the wall, his posture casual but his eyes intense. "I have contacts who might be able to dig deeper—people who aren't constrained by the niceties of international law. But it would require resources we don't currently have, and it would mean taking risks that might expose the network further."

Elena considered this, weighing the potential benefits against the potential costs. Every action they took carried risks—risks of exposure, risks of retaliation, risks of making mistakes that would compound the damage already done. But inaction carried risks too. The mercenaries were still out there, still potentially working for whatever remained of the destruction faction. If they struck again while the network was vulnerable...

"Do it," she said. "Find out who these people are and where they're operating."

"There's one more thing the trail showed." Diego's voice was careful now, the way it got when he was delivering something he knew she wouldn't like. "The Panama account wasn't the origin. It was a relay. The payments passed through two other structures before reaching it — one in the Cayman Islands, one in Luxembourg. Our forensic contact traced them as far back as she could before the trail went cold behind a private wealth management firm that doesn't appear in any public registry."

Elena was very still. "How large?"

"The total payments to Hernández's mercenaries? Significant. But the firm itself —" Diego paused. "The capitalisation our contact estimated, based on what little she could see, was in the billions."

The word settled in the room.

"Kroeger had a patron," Elena said quietly. "Someone who funded him and probably gave the order to kill Martin."

"Yes."

"And we don't know who."

"Not yet." Diego held her gaze. "But whoever it is, they're still out there. Still wealthy. Still anonymous. And they now know that Kroeger failed, that the fragments are secured, and that we exist." He paused. "They haven't made another move. That could mean they've walked away. Or it could mean they're waiting to see what we build before they decide how to come at it."

Elena said nothing for a long moment. She thought of Martin Thorne, dead across his manuscript in the Newberry Library. Sixty years of someone's money behind that rosary.

"Add it to the list," she said finally. "Find out who these people are and where they're operating. We can decide what to do with the information once we have it."

Diego nodded and turned to leave, then paused at the door. "The Keepers are waiting. They're going to have questions about the future—questions about leadership, about structure, about what happens next. Do you have answers for them?"

"Some. Not enough." Elena drained the last of her coffee and set the cup aside. "But I suppose that's why we're meeting. To figure out the answers together."

"Good luck."

"Thanks. I'll need it."

***

The main room of the safe house had been transformed into something resembling a conference space, with chairs arranged in a circle and a table in the centre holding water, notebooks, and the secure communication equipment that allowed them to connect with allies who couldn't attend in person.

Seven Keepers, representing what remained of the Guardian network's central authority. Elena knew them all by now—had fought alongside some of them, negotiated with others, spent countless hours in conversation about the future of the organisation they all served.

Yara Quispe-Vidal, whose Peruvian cell had been the first to openly support Elena's framework and whose personal loyalty had been tested repeatedly over the past months. Esperanza, the Ecuadorian grandmother whose gentle appearance concealed a core of steel. Carmen, from Argentina, whose network of contacts in the southern cone had proven invaluable for coordinating the response to the attacks. Dolores, from Bolivia, quiet and observant, who rarely spoke but whose judgements carried weight when she did. Two others—a man named Sebastián from Chile and a woman named Graciela from Uruguay—who had joined Elena's coalition more recently, their commitment still being tested by the realities of the situation.

And Lucia, who was not technically a Keeper but who had earned a place at the table through her survival and her willingness to testify against Hernández. The young Nicaraguan woman sat slightly apart from the others, her injured arm still in a sling, her dark eyes watchful and wary.

Elena took her seat and looked around the circle, meeting each person's gaze in turn. These were the people who would determine the Guardian network's future—if it had a future at all.

"Thank you for coming," she began. "I know the journey was difficult for some of you, and I know the risks you're taking by being here. But we need to have this conversation face to face, without the delays and uncertainties of electronic communication. Too much is at stake to trust to messages that might be intercepted or misunderstood."

"We all understand the necessity," Yara said. "What we need to understand is the path forward. The network is shattered, Elena. Cells destroyed, Keepers dead or missing, trust broken at every level. How do we rebuild from this?"

"We start by acknowledging what we've lost." Elena paused, gathering her thoughts. "The attacks eliminated nearly a third of our cells in Central and South America. We've lost archives, records, accumulated knowledge that took generations to compile. We've lost people—friends, mentors, family members who dedicated their lives to the Guardian mission. That loss is real, and it can't be minimised or glossed over."

"But we've also gained something," Esperanza said quietly. "We've gained clarity. The traitor has been exposed. The destruction faction has been decapitated. For the first time in months, we know who our enemies are and what they're trying to accomplish."

"Do we?" Sebastián's voice was sceptical. "Hernández is in custody, yes. But his allies are still out there. The mercenaries who carried out the attacks are still at large. And we have no idea how many cells might still be sympathetic to the destruction faction's goals, even if they weren't directly involved in the violence."

"That's why we need to move carefully," Elena said. "Not just rebuilding but in a way that makes the network more resilient against future threats. The old structure—with the Keeper of Keepers at the centre, controlling information and coordination—that structure failed us. It concentrated too much power in one person, created single points of failure that could be exploited."

"What are you proposing instead?"

"A distributed model. No single leader, no central repository of information. Each region operates with greater autonomy, coordinating with others when necessary but maintaining the ability to function independently if coordination breaks down." Elena looked around the circle. "The framework I proposed before—the criteria for eventually releasing the formula—that doesn't change. But the organisational structure that protects the fragments and evaluates those criteria needs to be fundamentally different from what we had before."

"You're describing something that would be much harder to control," Carmen observed. "Much harder to ensure consistency, to prevent individual cells from going rogue, to maintain the unified purpose that has held the network together for five centuries."

"Yes. But also, much harder to corrupt, to infiltrate, to destroy from within." Elena leaned forward, her voice intense. "Hernández was able to do what he did because the network trusted him implicitly. Because the structure gave him access to information and authority that no one person should have had. If we rebuild the same structure with different people at the top, we're just setting ourselves up for the same failure again."

The room was quiet as the Keepers absorbed her words. Elena could see the conflict in their faces—the desire for the security of familiar structures warring with the recognition that those structures had failed catastrophically.

Dolores spoke for the first time, her voice soft but clear. "The fragments themselves. Where are they now?"

"Distributed. Each piece is held by a different cell, in locations known only to the Keepers of those cells and to me. No single person—including me—can assemble the complete codex without the cooperation of multiple others."

"That seems wise." Dolores nodded slowly. "But it also means that if enough cells are destroyed or compromised, the fragments could be lost forever. We nearly lost pieces during the attacks—it was only luck that prevented the destruction faction from capturing what they were looking for."

"I know. That's a vulnerability we need to address." Elena had been thinking about this problem for weeks, turning it over in her mind, looking for solutions that balanced security against preservation. "I'm proposing that we create redundant copies of the information contained in each fragment—not the physical artifacts themselves, but detailed documentation that would allow the fragments to be reconstructed if the originals were lost."

"Copies that could themselves be stolen or compromised," Sebastián pointed out.

"Yes. But copies that would be distributed across multiple locations, encrypted with keys held by different Keepers, accessible only through a process that requires consensus from the network's leadership." Elena spread her hands. "There's no perfect solution. Every approach has vulnerabilities. The question is which vulnerabilities we're willing to accept."

The discussion continued for hours, moving through topics that ranged from immediate security concerns to long-term strategic planning. How to verify the loyalty of cells that had survived the attacks. How to communicate securely in an environment where traditional Guardian protocols had been compromised. How to rebuild the trust that Hernández's betrayal had shattered.

By the time they broke for lunch, Elena was exhausted but cautiously optimistic. The Keepers were engaged, thoughtful, willing to challenge her proposals while also taking them seriously. They weren't simply deferring to her judgment—they were participating in a genuine deliberation about the network's future.

That, more than anything else, gave her hope that they might actually succeed.

***

The afternoon session focused on more immediate concerns: the ongoing legal proceedings against Hernández, the hunt for the mercenaries who had carried out the attacks, and the question of what to do about cells that had been sympathetic to the destruction faction but hadn't directly participated in the violence.

This last issue proved the most contentious. Some Keepers argued for a clean break—cutting ties with anyone who had expressed support for destruction, regardless of their level of involvement. Others advocated for reconciliation, arguing that the network couldn't afford to lose more members and that many destruction sympathisers had been manipulated by Hernández rather than acting from genuine conviction.

Elena found herself caught between the two positions, seeing merit in both arguments but unable to fully commit to either. The network needed unity to survive, but unity built on ignoring genuine disagreements was fragile and ultimately self-defeating. Yet driving out everyone who had questioned the framework she had proposed would leave them dangerously weakened, potentially unable to protect the fragments they were sworn to guard.

"Perhaps we're approaching this the wrong way," Lucia said during a pause in the debate. All eyes turned to the young woman, who had been silent throughout most of the day's discussions. "We keep talking about who to include and who to exclude, as if the network's boundaries are the most important thing. But maybe the more important question is what we're asking people to commit to."

"Explain," Yara said.

"The destruction faction didn't arise because people were evil or because they wanted to betray the network. It arose because people genuinely believed that destroying the fragments was the right thing to do. They had reasons—reasons that seemed compelling to them, even if we disagree." Lucia shifted in her chair, wincing slightly as the movement pulled at her injured arm. "If we just drive those people out without addressing their concerns, we're not solving the problem. We're just postponing it until the same disagreements emerge again."

"What would you suggest?"

"A process for ongoing debate. Not just the periodic reassessment that Elena's framework calls for, but a genuine, continuing conversation about whether the network's mission still makes sense. Let people argue for destruction if they believe in it. Let them make their case, present their evidence, try to convince others." Lucia's dark eyes moved around the circle. "If we're right—if preserving the fragments for eventual release really is the best path—then we should be able to defend that position in open debate. And if we can't... maybe we need to listen to what the other side is saying."

The room was quiet as the Keepers considered this. Elena felt a mixture of admiration and concern—admiration for Lucia's willingness to engage with the destruction faction's arguments rather than simply dismissing them, concern about the practical implications of what she was proposing.

"That's a significant shift from how the network has operated historically," Esperanza observed. "The founders established clear principles—protect the fragments, preserve the knowledge, wait for the right moment to release it. They didn't envision ongoing debate about whether those principles were correct."

"The founders also didn't envision a Keeper of Keepers using the network's resources to murder his own people," Lucia replied. "The old ways failed. We need new ways—or at least, we need to be open to the possibility that the old ways need to change."

Elena made a decision. "Lucia is right. We can't rebuild the network on a foundation of enforced orthodoxy. The destruction faction emerged because people felt their concerns weren't being heard, their arguments weren't being engaged. If we want to prevent that from happening again, we need to create space for genuine disagreement."

"Within limits," Carmen added. "Debate is one thing. Violence is another. Anyone who advocates for or participates in violence against other Guardians should be expelled, regardless of their ideological position."

"Agreed. That's a bright line we don't cross." Elena looked around the circle. "But short of violence, we should be willing to engage with uncomfortable questions. Why are we preserving the fragments? What would actually happen if they were released? What would happen if they were destroyed? These aren't questions we should be afraid of. They're questions we should be able to answer—and if we can't answer them convincingly, maybe that tells us something we need to hear."

The discussion continued, gradually coalescing around a framework that combined Elena's structural proposals with Lucia's call for ongoing deliberation. The new network would be distributed, resilient, designed to survive attacks and betrayals that would have crippled the old structure. But it would also be more democratic, more open to debate, more willing to engage with fundamental questions about its own purpose.

It was a compromise, like everything else they had built since the crisis began. Not perfect, not entirely satisfying to anyone, but workable. Sustainable. A foundation they could build on.

By the time the session ended, as the sun was setting over Bogotá and the city lights were beginning to flicker on, Elena felt something she hadn't felt in weeks.

Hope.

35

The Hunt

Miami, Florida — Three Weeks Later

The private security firm occupied a nondescript office building in the Doral district, surrounded by similar buildings housing import-export companies, logistics firms, and the various other businesses that thrived in Miami's role as a gateway between North and South America.

Elena watched the building from a rented car parked across the street, cataloguing the security measures she could see, cameras at the entrances, a guard station in the lobby, what looked like reinforced glass on the ground-floor windows. Professional, thorough, but not exceptional. The kind of security you'd expect from a firm that dealt in sensitive matters but wasn't actively expecting an assault.

Diego sat beside her; his own attention focused on a tablet that displayed the results of weeks of investigation. Financial records, personnel files, movement patterns—the accumulated intelligence that his contacts had gathered on Meridian Security Solutions and its connections to the attacks on the Guardian network.

"Fourteen employees, not counting administrative staff," he said. "Eight of them have backgrounds in special operations—Colombian military, US Army Rangers, Israeli Defence Forces. The rest are support personnel: logistics, communications, transportation."

"And we're sure they're the ones?"

"As sure as we can be without a confession. The payments from Hernández's accounts match the timing of the attacks. Three of the operatives were photographed in Guatemala City the week before the Chichicastenango cell was hit. Communications intercepts show contact between the firm's leadership and known destruction faction sympathisers." Diego set down the tablet. "It's them. The only question is what we do about it."

That was indeed the question. For weeks, Elena had been wrestling with it, turning over the options in her mind, trying to find a path that achieved justice without creating new problems.

The legal route was effectively closed. The evidence they had gathered would never survive in a courtroom—it was obtained through methods that no judge would sanction, from sources that could never be revealed. Even if they could somehow get the case before a sympathetic prosecutor, the firm's lawyers would shred it within days.

The violent route was tempting but dangerous. They had the capability to strike at Meridian—Diego's contacts included people who could execute an assault on the building, neutralise the operatives, extract whatever information they held. But that kind of action would attract attention, raise questions, potentially expose the Guardian network to scrutiny it couldn't survive.

Which left the complicated middle ground: applying pressure indirectly, using the information they had gathered to create leverage without revealing their hand.

"The founder," Elena said. "Marcus Webb. What do we know about him?"

"Former CIA, left the agency about fifteen years ago under circumstances that were never fully explained. Built Meridian from the ground up, specialising in operations that required deniability—the kind of work that governments want done but don't want to be connected to." Diego scrolled through his tablet. "He's careful, professional, and by all accounts, amoral. He'll work for anyone who pays, as long as the money's good and the exposure risk is manageable."

"So, he's a businessman. He weighs costs and benefits, makes decisions based on rational self-interest."

"That's the profile, yes."

"Then we need to change his calculation." Elena turned to face Diego fully. "Right now, working for the destruction faction—or whatever's left of it—seems like a good deal to him. Reliable payments, minimal risk, no consequences. We need to make it look like a bad deal. Make him decide that continuing to target Guardians isn't worth the trouble."

"How?"

"By showing him that we know who he is and what he's done. That we have evidence that could destroy his business, land him in prison, ruin everything he's built. And by making it clear that we're willing to use that evidence if he doesn't stand down."

Diego considered this, his expression thoughtful. "You're talking about blackmail."

"I'm talking about deterrence. Making the cost of continued aggression higher than the benefit." Elena shook her head. "I know it's not clean. I know it's not the kind of solution I would have chosen a year ago. But the people in that building killed dozens of Guardians—people who had dedicated their lives to protecting something important. I can't let that go unanswered, but I also can't afford a war that would expose everything we're trying to protect."

"And if Webb doesn't respond to pressure? If he decides to call our bluff?"

"Then we escalate. Share what we know with his other clients, let them decide if they want to continue doing business with someone who's been compromised. Target his finances, his reputation, his ability to operate." Elena's voice hardened. "One way or another, we make it clear that attacking Guardians has consequences. That we're not just victims waiting to be picked off."

Diego was quiet for a long moment, studying her face as if seeing something new there. Finally, he nodded.

"I'll set up a meeting. Somewhere neutral, somewhere Webb will feel safe enough to talk. It'll take a few days to arrange."

"Do it."

Elena turned back to the window, watching the Meridian building as the afternoon sun reflected off its ordinary glass facades. Inside, people were going about their work—planning operations, managing logistics, doing whatever it was that private security firms did between assignments. Some of them had participated in the attacks that had killed Ixchel, killed Lucia's grandmother, killed dozens of other Guardians whose names Elena would never know.

She wanted justice for those deaths. Wanted the people responsible to face consequences for what they had done. But justice, she was learning, was a luxury that the Guardian network couldn't always afford. Sometimes you had to settle for deterrence. For making sure that the people who had hurt you wouldn't hurt you again.

It wasn't satisfying. But it was survival. And right now, survival was enough.

***

The meeting took place five days later, in a private room at a restaurant in Key Biscayne that catered to the kind of clientele who valued discretion above all else. Elena arrived early, positioning herself at the table with a clear view of both entrances, her back to the wall.

Diego was somewhere nearby—she didn't know exactly where, and that was intentional. If things went wrong, she needed him in a position to respond, not trapped in the same room with her.

Marcus Webb arrived precisely on time, which told Elena something about his character. He was a man who valued control, who didn't like variables he couldn't manage. Punctuality was a way of demonstrating that control, of showing that he operated on his own schedule rather than anyone else's.

He was older than Elena had expected from his photographs—mid-sixties, with close-cropped grey hair and a face that had been weathered by years of operating in harsh environments. He moved with the careful economy of someone who had learned to conserve energy for when it mattered, and his eyes swept the room with the automatic alertness of a professional assessing threats.

"Dr. Vasquez." He sat down across from her, his manner polite but wary. "I have to admit, your invitation intrigued me. We don't usually receive requests for meetings from our subjects' associates."

"I'm not here to discuss semantics, Mr. Webb. I'm here to discuss your future."

"My future?" A slight smile crossed his face. "That sounds almost like a threat."

"It's an observation. Your firm has been involved in operations targeting a specific group of people—operations that have resulted in multiple deaths across several countries. I have evidence of those operations, including financial records, communications intercepts, and eyewitness testimony. That evidence could be very damaging if it found its way to the wrong people."

Webb's expression didn't change, but Elena saw something shift behind his eyes—a recalculation, an adjustment to new information. "I'm not sure what you're referring to. Meridian is a legitimate security consulting firm. We provide services to clients who have lawful needs."

"I'm sure your lawyers would make that argument very effectively. They might even win, given the difficulties of prosecuting cross-border operations with unconventional evidence." Elena leaned forward slightly. "But that's not really the point, is it? The point is what happens to your business while the argument is being made. The clients who decide they can't afford to be associated with a firm under investigation. The contracts that get cancelled, the references that dry up, the insurance that becomes impossible to obtain."

"You're describing a scenario that assumes a great deal."

"I'm describing a scenario that I can make happen. Today, if I choose to." Elena held Webb's gaze steadily. "I have contacts in law enforcement agencies across the hemisphere. I have connections to journalists who specialise in exposing private military contractors. I have access to channels that could make your life very difficult very quickly. The question is whether I need to use them."

Webb was silent for a moment, his face unreadable. Then he leaned back in his chair, his posture shifting from wary to something more like professional respect.

"What do you want?"

"I want you to stop. No more operations targeting people connected to the organisation I represent. No more working with the clients who hired you to carry out those operations. You walk away, you stay away, and this evidence stays in a drawer where no one ever sees it."

"And if I can't simply walk away? If there are contractual obligations, expectations, relationships that can't be easily severed?"

"Then sever them anyway. Whatever inconvenience that causes you is considerably less than the inconvenience of what happens if you don't."

Webb studied her for a long moment, his expression thoughtful. Elena could almost see the calculations happening behind his eyes—the weighing of risks and benefits, the assessment of whether she was bluffing, the consideration of what it would cost to comply versus what it would cost to resist.

"You're not what I expected," he said finally. "When I took this contract, I was told I'd be dealing with academics, archivists, people who preserve old documents and argue about historical interpretations. Not someone who talks like she's been in the field."

"I've learned to adapt."

"Clearly." Webb was quiet for another moment. "The people who hired me—they're not going to be happy if I walk away. They have resources, connections, the ability to make my life difficult in their own ways."

"That's your problem, not mine. I'm offering you a way out of a situation that's become untenable. What you do with that offer is up to you."

"And if I need time to consider? To consult with my partners, review our obligations?"

"You have forty-eight hours. After that, I start making calls." Elena stood, signalling that the meeting was over. "I hope you make the right choice, Mr. Webb. For both our sakes."

She walked out of the restaurant without looking back, her heart pounding despite the calm she had projected throughout the conversation. Diego fell into step beside her as she reached the parking lot, his presence reassuring in a way she hadn't expected.

"Well?" he asked.

"He's thinking about it. That's something."

"You think he'll comply?"

"I think he'll do whatever serves his interests. Right now, I've made it clear that his interests are better served by walking away than by continuing." Elena unlocked the car and climbed in. "But people like Webb don't stay bought. Even if he agrees now, he might change his mind later if the calculation shifts. We'll need to stay vigilant."

"We always need to stay vigilant. That's the job."

Elena started the engine and pulled out of the parking lot, leaving Key Biscayne behind as she headed back toward the city. The meeting had gone as well as she could have hoped, but she felt no sense of victory. Just the grim satisfaction of having done something necessary, something that might protect the people she was responsible for.

It was a small win in a much larger war. But small wins accumulated. And right now, accumulation was all she had.

36

The Revelation

Cusco, Peru — One Year After Hernández's Capture

The laboratory was hidden beneath a colonial-era building in the San Blas district, accessible only through a series of passages that had been carved into the hillside centuries ago by people whose purposes were lost to history. Elena had discovered it during her search for the Peru fragment, and she had kept its existence secret even from most of the Guardian network—a private space where she could work without interruption, where she could pursue questions that she wasn't yet ready to share with others.

For the past three months, she had been coming here whenever her duties allowed, spending long hours with the fragments and the supplementary documents that Ixchel had entrusted to her. The framework she had built for the Guardian network was functioning well enough, the distributed structure proving resilient against the kinds of threats that had nearly destroyed them. But Elena had begun to feel that preservation alone was not enough—that the Guardians needed a purpose beyond simply protecting knowledge for some hypothetical future.

The formula worked.

She had not believed it, not truly, not in the part of her mind that had spent twenty years in academic institutions where extraordinary claims were more often than not debunked, until the moment it happened.

The lead ingot had been small, no larger than her thumb, sourced from a plumbing supplier in Bogotá under a pretext so mundane the man behind the counter hadn't looked up from his phone. She had followed the procedures encoded in the fragments with painstaking precision, cross-referencing every step against the supplementary documents Ixchel had entrusted to her, checking and rechecking until she was certain she had misunderstood nothing.

And then she had done it.

The change had not been dramatic. No flash of light, no thunder, no sensation of reality bending beneath her hands. Just a shift in the quality of the surface — the dull grey of lead giving way to something warmer, deeper and unmistakable. She had picked it up with fingers that were not entirely steady and turned it in the light, and her heart had done something she had no clinical term for, not racing exactly but hammering with a kind of disbelief that her body apparently needed to express physically because her mind had simply stopped.

Gold. Pure, warm, undeniable.

She had sat there for a very long time, just staring at it.

Everything she had believed about the nature of reality had shifted in that moment and everything she had believed about the Guardian mission with it.

The formula wasn't just dangerous knowledge to be protected. It was a tool — a tool that could be used for good or ill, depending on who wielded it and how. The ancients had hidden it because they feared what humanity would do with unlimited access to material wealth. But what if access wasn't unlimited? What if the knowledge remained in the hands of people committed to using it responsibly, for purposes that served the common good rather than individual greed?

The formula wasn't just dangerous knowledge to be protected. It was a tool—a tool that could be used for good or ill, depending on who wielded it and how. The ancients had hidden it because they feared what humanity would do with unlimited access to material wealth. But what if access wasn't unlimited? What if the knowledge remained in the hands of people committed to using it responsibly, for purposes that served the common good rather than individual greed?

These were the questions that had consumed Elena for months, driving her to experiment further, to refine her understanding of the formula's capabilities and limitations. She had learned that the process was demanding—it required specific conditions, rare materials, and a level of concentration that was exhausting to maintain. Mass production was impossible with a single practitioner. But with a network of trained individuals, working in coordination...

The possibilities were staggering.

Tonight, she had called a meeting of the inner circle—the handful of Keepers she trusted absolutely, the ones who had stood with her through the worst of the crisis and earned her confidence through months of shared struggle. Yara was there, along with Esperanza, Carmen, and Lucia, who had grown from a traumatised survivor into one of Elena's most capable lieutenants. Diego attended as well, though he was not technically a Guardian—his loyalty and his skills had made him indispensable.

They gathered in the underground chamber, surrounded by equipment that would have looked primitive to a modern scientist but that represented the accumulated wisdom of civilisations that had achieved things modern science couldn't explain. Elena had prepared a demonstration, wanting them to see with their own eyes what she had discovered.

"What I'm about to show you changes everything," she began. "Everything we thought we knew about our mission, about the formula, about what's possible. I need you to watch with open minds and think carefully about the implications."

She turned to the workbench where she had arranged the materials—a small ingot of lead, the compounds and catalysts specified by the codex, the implements required for the procedure. The others watched in silence as she began the process, her movements precise and deliberate, following steps she had practiced until they became automatic.

The transmutation took nearly an hour. By the time it was complete, Elena was drenched in sweat, her hands trembling with exhaustion. But on the workbench, where the lead ingot had been, sat a piece of gold the size of her thumb—pure, gleaming, unmistakably real.

The silence in the chamber was absolute.

"How?" Yara's voice was barely a whisper.

"The formula. Exactly as the codex describes." Elena sat down heavily, letting the exhaustion wash over her. "I've been experimenting for months, refining the technique, learning what works and what doesn't. It's real, Yara. Everything the ancients claimed, everything the Guardians have protected for five centuries—it's all real."

"But this changes..." Esperanza trailed off, seemingly unable to complete the thought.

"Everything. Yes." Elena looked around the circle of stunned faces. "The question is what we do with it. Do we continue to hide the knowledge, protect it for some future that may never come? Or do we use it—carefully, responsibly, in ways that serve the people we've been claiming to protect?"

"Use it how?" Carmen asked. "If this becomes known, if people learn that transmutation is possible, the chaos the ancients feared—"

"It doesn't have to become known. Not the formula itself, not the details of how it works. But the results..." Elena gestured at the gold on the workbench. "The results could be used without revealing their source. Imagine what we could do with unlimited resources. The schools we could build, the hospitals, the infrastructure that South America so desperately needs. We've spent five centuries protecting knowledge. Maybe it's time we started using it."

The discussion that followed lasted until dawn, voices rising and falling as the implications were debated from every angle. There were objections—serious, thoughtful objections about the risks of discovery, the dangers of corruption, the possibility that using the formula would inevitably lead to its exposure. But there was also excitement, a growing sense that Elena had identified something transformative, a way forward that broke the stalemate between preservation and destruction.

By the time the sun rose over Cusco, painting the colonial rooftops in shades of gold and rose, they had reached a tentative consensus. The formula would be used—but carefully, secretly, in ways designed to minimise the risk of exposure. The resources it generated would flow to purposes that served the common good, creating tangible benefits for the communities that the Guardians had always claimed to protect.

It was the beginning of something new. Something that would require all of Elena's skill and determination to build, something that would transform the Guardian network from a preservation society into an active force for change.

She was ready. After everything she had been through—the searches and the betrayals, the losses and the victories—she was finally ready to stop protecting the future and start building it.

***

The weeks that followed were consumed by planning.

Elena worked with her inner circle to design a structure that would allow them to use the formula's products without revealing their source. The key insight came from Lucia, who had been thinking about the problem of legitimacy—how to introduce large quantities of gold into the financial system without attracting the kind of scrutiny that would lead to uncomfortable questions.

"Mining," she said during one of their planning sessions. "South America is full of gold mines, legal and illegal. If we establish operations that appear to be legitimate mining ventures, we can explain the gold as coming from the earth rather than from transmutation."

"That would require actually controlling land," Diego pointed out. "Permits, employees, all the infrastructure of a real mining operation."

"The infrastructure, yes. But not actual mining." Lucia spread a map across the table, pointing to various locations in Colombia, Peru, and Ecuador. "These are areas with known gold deposits that have never been commercially exploited—too remote, too difficult to access, not worth the investment for a traditional mining company. We buy the rights, establish a presence, and then produce gold through transmutation while maintaining the appearance of conventional extraction."

"The workers would know something was wrong," Carmen objected. "You can't run a fake mine without people noticing that there's no actual mining happening."

"The workers would be Guardians. Or descendants of Guardians, people we can trust absolutely." Elena had been thinking along similar lines, and Lucia's proposal crystallised the approach she had been groping toward. "We staff the operations with our own people, train them in the transmutation process, and create a closed system where the true source of the gold never leaves the network."

"That's ambitious," Yara said slowly. "We're talking about building an entire industry from scratch, staffing it with hundreds of people, maintaining secrecy across multiple countries and years of operation."

"We have hundreds of people. The Guardian network spans the entire hemisphere—families who have been keeping secrets for generations, who understand the importance of discretion." Elena felt the plan taking shape in her mind, the pieces fitting together with a logic that felt almost inevitable. "This is what we were built for. Not just protecting knowledge but using it. The founders hid the formula because they didn't trust humanity. We can prove that their caution was justified—that the knowledge can be used responsibly, for purposes that benefit everyone."

The planning continued, growing more detailed and more complex as they worked through the implications of what they were proposing. They would need legal structures to hold the mining rights and manage the finances. They would need facilities where the transmutation could take place, secure enough to prevent discovery but accessible enough to allow regular operation. They would need systems for moving the gold from production to storage to eventual deployment, creating paper trails that would satisfy regulators while concealing the true nature of the operations.

It was, Elena realised, the most ambitious undertaking the Guardian network had ever attempted—more challenging than protecting fragments scattered across a continent, more demanding than rebuilding after Hernández's betrayal. They were proposing to create an entire shadow economy, one that would generate resources on a scale that could transform nations.

And at the centre of it all would be her.

She hadn't sought this role, hadn't asked to become the person responsible for decisions that would affect millions of lives. But the path of events had brought her here, and she couldn't turn away from the opportunity it represented. The formula existed. The knowledge was real. The only question was whether it would be used—and if so, by whom, and for what purposes.

Better that it be used by people committed to the common good than that it remain hidden forever, its potential unrealised, its benefits denied to those who needed them most.

Elena made her decision. She would build what needed to be built, create what needed to be created, and trust that the Guardians who came after her would continue the work she had begun.

The future was no longer something to be protected.

It was something to be made.

37

Foundations

Bogotá, Colombia — Six Months Later

The law offices of Mendoza & Associates occupied three floors of a modern tower in the financial district, their glass and steel facades reflecting the energy of a city that had transformed itself from a symbol of violence into one of Latin America's most dynamic economies. Elena had chosen this firm specifically for its expertise in corporate structuring and its reputation for discretion—qualities that would be essential for what she was about to undertake.

The meeting room where she sat overlooked the Andes, their peaks visible on clear days like this one, a reminder of the ancient forces that had shaped this land long before humans arrived to complicate it with their ambitions and their conflicts. Elena found the view calming, a perspective that helped her maintain focus during negotiations that would determine the shape of everything that followed.

Across the table sat Roberto Mendoza himself, the firm's founding partner, a man whose silver hair and measured manner concealed a sharp intelligence and a willingness to work with clients whose needs extended beyond the conventional. He had been recommended by contacts in the Guardian network—people who had used his services before for matters that required both legal expertise and absolute confidentiality.

"Let me make sure I understand what you're proposing," Mendoza said, reviewing the documents Elena had prepared. "You want to establish three interconnected corporate entities. The first—" he consulted his notes "—El Fondo de Elección del Pueblo, will be a foundation focused on charitable activities throughout South America. The second, Golden Codex Bank, will be a private banking institution. And the third, Colombian Vaults, will provide secure storage services."

"That's correct."

"The structure you've outlined would have Colombian Vaults owning Golden Codex Bank, which in turn would manage the financial assets of El Fondo de Elección del Pueblo. The foundation's charitable activities would be funded by revenues from mining operations that you intend to establish separately." Mendoza set down the papers and looked at Elena directly. "It's an unusual arrangement. Most clients who want to engage in philanthropy simply establish a foundation and fund it from their existing wealth. They don't create an entire financial infrastructure to support it."

"Most clients don't have my particular circumstances."

"No, I imagine they don't." Mendoza's tone was carefully neutral, revealing nothing of his thoughts about what those circumstances might be. "The structure you're proposing would provide significant insulation between the mining operations and the charitable activities. Multiple layers of corporate separation, each domiciled in different jurisdictions with different regulatory requirements. If someone wanted to trace the flow of funds from the mines to the hospitals and schools, they would have considerable difficulty doing so."

"That's the intention."

"May I ask why such elaborate precautions are necessary? The activities you've described—schools, hospitals, healthcare facilities—are entirely legitimate. Admirable, even. Why go to such lengths to obscure their funding source?"

Elena had prepared for this question. "The people I work with have learned through hard experience that visibility attracts attention, and attention attracts complications. We've had... encounters with individuals who would prefer that our work not continue. The structure I'm proposing isn't designed to facilitate anything illegal. It's designed to protect legitimate activities from interference by people who don't share our goals."

Mendoza nodded slowly, apparently satisfied with the explanation. "The Colombian banking regulations will require certain disclosures, but there are ways to structure the ownership that minimise what must be made public. The vault operations are more straightforward—secure storage is a well-established business, and the regulatory requirements are manageable. The foundation will need to comply with charitable organisation rules, but those are designed to ensure accountability rather than transparency about funding sources."

"Then it can be done?"

"It can be done. It will require several months to establish all the necessary entities, obtain the required licenses, and implement the operational infrastructure. The costs will be significant—legal fees, registration costs, initial capitalisation requirements." Mendoza named a figure that would have been staggering to Elena a year ago but that now seemed almost modest given the resources she would soon have access to.

"That won't be a problem."

"I didn't imagine it would be." Mendoza gathered the papers and stood, extending his hand. "Dr. Vasquez, I've been practicing law for thirty-five years. In that time, I've worked with many clients who had complex needs and unconventional approaches. I've learned not to ask too many questions about the details that don't concern me. What I can tell you is that the structure you're proposing is legally sound, practically achievable, and—if implemented correctly—highly effective for the purposes you've described."

"Thank you."

"One piece of advice, if I may." Mendoza paused at the door. "The elaborate precautions you're taking will protect you from casual scrutiny. But if someone with real resources and real determination decides to investigate, no corporate structure will hide everything. The best protection isn't legal complexity—it's ensuring that your activities, if discovered, can withstand examination. Do good things, do them honestly, and the rest becomes much less important."

Elena nodded, accepting the wisdom in his words. "That's the plan."

"Then I look forward to working with you."

He left, and Elena turned back to the window, watching the clouds drift past the mountain peaks in the distance. The legal framework was beginning to take shape—the skeleton on which everything else would be built. But there were still many pieces to put in place before the vision she had conceived could become reality.

She had work to do.

* * *

The first mining concession was acquired three months later, a tract of land in the remote highlands of Antioquia that had shown promise in geological surveys but had never been commercially developed due to its inaccessibility. Elena paid well above market value, ensuring that the sellers had no reason to ask questions about the buyer's intentions, and immediately began the process of establishing infrastructure.

The site was perfect for their purposes. Located hours from the nearest major road, accessible only by helicopter or by a tortuous journey along mountain tracks that turned to impassable mud during the rainy season, it offered the isolation that the operation required. Any visitors would be noticed long before they arrived, giving ample time to ensure that what they found matched what they expected to see—a small-scale mining operation staffed by workers who lived on-site and processed their extraction in facilities that ran day and night.

The reality, of course, was different.

The buildings that rose on the mountainside over the following months housed not conventional mining equipment but laboratories for transmutation, designed according to specifications that Elena had developed through her months of experimentation. The "ore processing" facility was actually a gold production center, where teams of trained Guardians worked in shifts to generate the precious metal that would fund everything else. The "accommodation blocks" housed the workers, yes—but workers whose loyalty was to the network rather than to any paycheck, who understood the true nature of what they were doing and the purposes it served.

Elena visited the site regularly during the construction phase, overseeing the details, ensuring that the operation would function as intended. The logistics were complex, materials had to be brought in without attracting attention, waste products had to be disposed of in ways that wouldn't reveal the true nature of the work, the gold itself had to be transported to the vaults in Bogotá through channels that would withstand scrutiny if questions were ever asked.

But the Guardian network had been managing complex logistics for centuries. Moving sacred objects across borders, maintaining communication between far-flung cells, preserving knowledge through wars and revolutions and the rise and fall of empires—compared to all that, running a fake mining operation was almost straightforward.

The first gold reached Golden Codex Bank's vaults six months after the concession was acquired. Elena was present when it arrived—bars of pure gold, each one stamped with the serial numbers and certifications that made them indistinguishable from conventionally mined metal, each one representing hours of painstaking transmutation by workers who understood that they were participating in something historic.

She held one of the bars in her hands, feeling its weight, marvelling at the journey that had brought her to this moment. A year ago, she had been a museum curator whose greatest ambition was publishing papers about pre-Columbian metallurgy. Now she was holding gold that she had helped create, gold that would fund schools and hospitals across a continent, gold that represented the first tangible fruits of knowledge that had been hidden for five hundred years.

"It's beautiful, isn't it?" Yara had come to stand beside her, her own eyes fixed on the gleaming metal. "I've spent my whole life protecting the idea of this. The possibility that it existed. And now..."

"Now it's real."

"Real enough to change the world. If we're careful. If we're wise." Yara turned to look at Elena directly. "Are we being wise, Elena? Using the formula like this—is it what the founders would have wanted?"

"I don't know. I don't know if anyone can know that." Elena set down the gold bar, placing it carefully with the others in the vault. "But I know that hiding the knowledge forever wasn't working. People died protecting secrets that might never have been revealed. The destruction faction nearly tore the network apart because they saw no purpose in endless preservation. This gives us a purpose. A reason to continue. A way to make all the sacrifice mean something."

"And if we're discovered? If someone figures out where the gold is really coming from?"

"Then we deal with it. The same way we've dealt with every other threat the network has faced." Elena smiled slightly. "We've survived for five centuries, Yara. We've survived conquest and colonisation, wars and revolutions, betrayal from within and attacks from without. We'll survive this too. And maybe—just maybe—we'll do some good along the way."

Yara was quiet for a moment, her expression thoughtful. Then she nodded slowly.

"My grandmother would have approved, I think. She always said that protection without purpose was just fear dressed up in noble clothes. That someday, the Guardians would have to choose whether to act or to fade away."

"We're choosing to act."

"Yes. We are." Yara reached out and touched one of the gold bars, her fingers tracing its smooth surface. "Then let's make sure we act well. Let's make sure that what we build is worthy of what we've protected."

"That's the plan," Elena said. "That's always been the plan."

38

Growth

Across South America — Two Years Later

The school in Cartagena opened on a bright Monday morning in March, its corridors filled with children whose families had never imagined they would have access to education of this quality.

Elena stood at the back of the assembly hall, watching as the principal welcomed the first students to a facility that had been designed to meet international standards—modern classrooms, a library stocked with books in Spanish and English and indigenous languages, computer laboratories with equipment that would have been the envy of many schools in Europe or North America. The building itself was beautiful, its architecture drawing on traditional Colombian forms while incorporating sustainable technologies that would serve as a teaching tool in themselves.

This was the seventeenth school that El Fondo de Elección del Pueblo had built in the past two years, part of a network that now stretched across Colombia, Ecuador, Peru, and Bolivia. Each one represented months of planning, construction, and negotiation with local authorities who were sometimes suspicious of a foundation that seemed to have unlimited resources and ambitious goals.

But the results spoke for themselves. Thousands of children now had access to education that would have been impossible without the foundation's intervention. Teachers received salaries that attracted talented professionals rather than whoever was willing to work for pittance wages. Curricula incorporated the latest research on effective pedagogy while respecting local cultures and traditions.

And no one suspected that the funding came from anything other than a particularly successful mining operation run by foreign investors who preferred to remain anonymous.

The mining operations themselves had expanded significantly since the first site in Antioquia. There were now three "mines" in Colombia, two in Peru, and one each in Ecuador and Bolivia—each one a carefully constructed fiction that produced enough gold to justify its existence while the real production happened in laboratories hidden beneath the surface. The Guardian network had grown to accommodate the expanded operations, recruiting from families with long traditions of discretion and training new practitioners in the arts of transmutation.

Elena had become something she never expected to be. A businesswoman, philanthropist, a leader of an organisation that employed hundreds of people and controlled assets measured in the hundreds of millions of dollars. The persona of Dr. Elena Vasquez, archaeological consultant, had been largely set aside in favour of something more complex—a figure who moved between the worlds of high finance and grassroots development, who met with government ministers and village elders with equal facility, who was known throughout the region as someone who got things done.

She had also become, though she didn't think of herself in these terms, a target.

The attention had been inevitable, she supposed. Any organisation that accumulated significant resources and used them to influence social conditions would attract scrutiny—from governments, from competitors, from people who simply wanted to understand where all the money was coming from. Elena had prepared for this, building layers of legitimate business activity around the core operations, creating paper trails that led investigators to dead ends or to explanations that, while not entirely true, were plausible enough to satisfy most inquiries.

But some inquiries were more persistent than others.

The journalist's name was Alejandra Reyes, and she worked for one of Colombia's most respected investigative outlets. She had been looking into El Fondo de Elección del Pueblo for nearly six months, filing freedom of information requests with government agencies, interviewing former employees, analysing financial records that were technically public but practically opaque.

Elena learned about the investigation through contacts in the media world—people who owed favours to the foundation and were willing to provide early warning when someone started asking uncomfortable questions. She had monitored Reyes's progress with growing concern, watching as the journalist peeled back layer after layer of corporate structure, getting closer with each article to questions that couldn't be answered without revealing the truth.

The meeting she had arranged for this afternoon was an attempt to manage the threat—to understand what Reyes knew, what she suspected, and whether some accommodation could be reached that would satisfy her journalistic curiosity without exposing the network's operations.

They met at a café in Bogotá's Zona G, a neighbourhood known for upscale restaurants and the kind of discretion that wealthy clients expected. Elena arrived first, choosing a table in the back where their conversation would not be overheard, and ordered coffee while she waited.

Reyes arrived precisely on time—a woman in her forties, sharp-featured and professionally dressed, with the alert manner of someone who spent her life asking questions that people didn't want to answer. She sat down across from Elena without preamble, her recorder already in her hand.

"Dr. Vasquez. Thank you for agreeing to meet."

"Thank you for your patience. I know you've been trying to reach me for some time."

"I've been trying to reach anyone who can explain where El Fondo de Elección del Pueblo gets its money." Reyes set the recorder on the table between them, her finger hovering over the button. "May I?"

"Of course."

The interview that followed was one of the most challenging conversations Elena had ever navigated. Reyes was smart, well-prepared, and relentless in her questioning. She had traced the foundation's funding to Golden Codex Bank, the bank's ownership to Colombian Vaults, the vault's investments to the mining operations scattered across the Andes. She had noted discrepancies between the reported output of those mines and their apparent profitability. She had interviewed geologists who expressed scepticism that the deposits being worked could possibly yield the amounts of gold that the company claimed.

Elena answered each question carefully, sticking to the prepared explanations where they sufficed, deflecting where they didn't, buying time while she assessed how much the journalist actually knew versus how much she suspected.

"Let me be direct," Reyes said finally, after nearly two hours of fencing. "I don't believe your mining operations are what they appear to be. The numbers don't add up. The logistics don't make sense. And I've found too many connections between your organisation and a network of people who seem to be involved in something much more complicated than gold extraction."

"What do you think we're involved in?"

"I don't know. That's what I'm trying to find out." Reyes leaned forward, her eyes intense. "But I'll tell you what I do know. Whatever you're doing, it's producing real results. I've visited your schools, your hospitals, your clinics. I've talked to teachers and doctors and patients who say their lives have been transformed by what El Fondo has built. The money is going to good purposes, whatever its source."

"Then why pursue the investigation?"

"Because the truth matters. Because transparency is the foundation of democratic society. Because whatever good you're doing doesn't give you the right to operate outside the law." Reyes paused. "And because I'm curious. Whatever the explanation for what you're doing, it's a story. Maybe the biggest story I'll ever tell."

Elena considered her options. She could continue to stonewall, to deflect, to hope that Reyes would eventually run out of leads and move on to other projects. But looking at the determination in the journalist's eyes, she didn't think that was likely. Reyes had caught the scent of something significant, and she wouldn't let go until she understood what it was.

Which left two choices: eliminate the threat or co-opt it.

Elena had no interest in the first option. The network had killed when necessary during the crisis with Hernández, but she had no desire to start silencing journalists who were simply doing their jobs. That path led to becoming the very thing they had fought against.

The second option was riskier, but potentially more valuable.

"What if I told you that the truth, if you found it, would be something you couldn't publish?" Elena asked. "Something that would be more dangerous to reveal than to keep secret?"

Reyes's eyes narrowed. "I'd say that's a convenient excuse for avoiding accountability."

"And normally, you'd be right. But this isn't a normal situation." Elena took a deep breath, making a decision that would either save the foundation or destroy it. "What if I offered you something better than a story? What if I offered you the truth—the full truth, including things I've never told anyone outside my innermost circle—on the condition that you help us rather than expose us?"

"Help you do what?"

"Change the world. In ways that go far beyond what you've seen in our schools and hospitals. In ways that require the kind of secrecy you've been trying to penetrate." Elena held Reyes's gaze steadily. "I'm offering you a choice, Ms. Reyes. You can keep investigating, keep pushing, keep trying to piece together a story that you'll never be able to tell completely. Or you can come inside, learn everything, and become part of something that matters more than any article you'll ever write."

The silence stretched between them, heavy with possibility. Elena watched as Reyes processed what she had said, the journalist's mind clearly racing through implications and considerations that her training couldn't have prepared her for.

"That's a hell of an offer," Reyes said finally.

"It's a hell of a secret."

"And if I say no? If I keep investigating, keep trying to expose whatever you're hiding?"

"Then you keep investigating. I won't try to stop you, won't threaten you, won't do anything except continue to answer your questions as honestly as I can without revealing things that could endanger people I'm responsible for." Elena shrugged. "You might eventually find enough to publish something. But I don't think it would be the story you're hoping for. And I don't think it would do anyone any good."

Reyes was quiet for a long moment, her gaze turned inward as she weighed the choices before her. Then, slowly, she reached out and turned off the recorder.

"Tell me," she said. "Tell me everything."

Elena smiled.

"It begins with a codex," she said. "A very old codex, hidden for five hundred years by people who understood that some knowledge is too powerful to be shared carelessly. Let me tell you about the

Guardians, and what we've spent centuries protecting, and why I decided it was finally time to use what we'd been hiding..."

39

Rebuilding

Six Months Later — Across the Americas

The network was healing.

It was a slow process, measured in small victories rather than dramatic transformations. Cells that had gone silent during the attacks gradually re-established contact, their members emerging from hiding once they were convinced the immediate danger had passed. New recruits were carefully vetted and brought into the fold, their commitment tested through months of observation before they were trusted with sensitive information. The distributed structure that Elena had proposed was taking shape, each region developing its own protocols while maintaining the connections that bound them into a coherent whole.

Elena spent those months in constant motion, travelling from cell to cell, meeting with Keepers and junior Guardians, listening to their concerns and sharing what she had learned. She visited Guatemala, where Lucia was working to rebuild the Central American presence from a base in her grandmother's former territory. She travelled to Peru, where Yara was coordinating efforts to document the knowledge held by surviving cells before any more of it could be lost. She went to Argentina, Chile, Brazil—wherever her presence might help, wherever her expertise might be useful.

It was exhausting work, but it was also deeply satisfying. For the first time since the crisis began, Elena felt that she was building something rather than just fighting to survive. The network that was emerging from the ashes of Hernández's betrayal was different from what had come before—more resilient, more democratic, more capable of adapting to challenges that the founders could never have anticipated.

The fragments remained safe, distributed across locations that only a handful of people knew. The framework Elena had proposed—the criteria for evaluating humanity's readiness for the knowledge the codex contained—was being implemented by cells across the hemisphere, each one contributing to a collective assessment that would continue for generations. It wasn't perfect. Nothing was perfect. But it was working.

Marcus Webb had kept his word, as far as Elena could tell. Meridian Security Solutions had quietly withdrawn from any operations connected to the destruction faction, and the mercenaries who had carried out the attacks had scattered to other employment. There had been no new assaults on Guardian cells, no indication that the destruction faction was regrouping for another offensive.

That didn't mean the threat had disappeared. Elena knew better than to assume that enemies defeated today wouldn't return tomorrow. The ideological division that had fuelled the crisis—the fundamental disagreement about whether the fragments should be preserved or destroyed—hadn't been resolved. It had only been suppressed, driven underground by the failure of Hernández's campaign.

Someday, those disagreements would resurface. Someday, someone would decide that the network's mission was misguided, that the formula should be eliminated or released immediately rather than preserved for an uncertain future. When that day came, the network would need to be ready—not just to defend itself, but to engage with the arguments and address the concerns that drove the opposition.

That was the lesson Elena had taken from the crisis: that disagreement couldn't be suppressed indefinitely, that the only way to maintain unity was to create space for genuine debate. The new structure she had built included formal channels for dissent, regular forums where Guardians could argue for changes to the network's mission or methods. It was messy, contentious, often frustrating. But it was better than the alternative.

In October, eight months after Hernández's capture, Elena called a gathering of the Keepers to review the progress they had made and plan for the next phase of the network's development. The meeting took place in a rented villa outside Cusco, chosen for its isolation and its symbolic significance—this was the region where Elena had first encountered the Guardian network, where she had begun to understand the magnitude of what she had stumbled into.

Fourteen Keepers attended, representing cells from across the Americas. Some had been part of Elena's coalition from the beginning; others had joined more recently, their loyalty earned through months of cooperation and shared purpose. Together, they represented the largest gathering of Guardian leadership since the council meeting where Hernández had first been confronted—a sign of how far the network had come in rebuilding itself.

Elena opened the gathering with a review of the past months' activities: cells re-established, security protocols updated, communication channels secured. She presented statistics on membership, on resources, on the geographic distribution of the network's presence. It was dry material, but necessary—the foundation on which everything else would be built.

Then she turned to the harder questions.

"We've survived," she said, looking around the circle of faces. "That's more than many of us expected six months ago. But survival isn't the same as success. We need to ask ourselves whether we're actually accomplishing what we set out to accomplish—whether the framework we've built is working, whether the sacrifices we've made have been worth it."

"That seems premature," Sebastián observed. "The framework is designed to operate over generations, not months. We can't expect to see results this quickly."

"We can't expect final results. But we can look for signs that we're moving in the right direction." Elena pulled out a folder of documents she had prepared for the meeting. "I've been tracking indicators—scientific developments, social changes, anything that might be relevant to the criteria we've established. The picture is... mixed."

She walked them through the data: advances in materials science and quantum physics that brought human understanding closer to the principles underlying the codex, but also political upheavals and social conflicts that suggested humanity was far from ready to handle transformative knowledge responsibly. Progress in some areas, regression in others, the complex and contradictory patterns of a world that refused to move in simple directions.

"The point isn't that we have answers," she concluded. "The point is that we're asking the questions, tracking the information, maintaining the kind of ongoing assessment that the original Guardians never managed. We're not just sitting on the fragments and hoping that someday things will change. We're actively monitoring for change, preparing to recognise it if it comes."

"And if it never comes?" The question came from Graciela, the Uruguayan Keeper whose scepticism had been a constant presence in the network's deliberations. "What if we monitor for generations, for centuries, and the criteria are never met? Do we just keep waiting forever?"

"That's a decision future Guardians will have to make. Our job is to give them the tools and the information they need to make it wisely." Elena met Graciela's eyes directly. "I don't have all the answers. None of us do. But we're building something that can outlast our individual limitations, that can accumulate wisdom over time, that can eventually reach conclusions none of us could reach alone. That's the best we can offer."

The discussion continued through the afternoon and into the evening, covering topics that ranged from tactical security concerns to philosophical questions about the nature of human progress. By the time they broke for dinner, Elena was exhausted but satisfied. The network was functioning—not perfectly, not without friction, but functioning. That was more than she had dared hope for in the dark days after Hernández's betrayal.

After dinner, she walked alone in the gardens of the villa, letting the cool mountain air clear her head. The stars were brilliant overhead, undimmed by the light pollution of distant cities, and she found herself thinking about the ancients who had discovered the formula—the people who had looked at these same stars thousands of years ago and wondered about the nature of matter and reality.

They had made their choice: to hide what they had learned, to protect humanity from knowledge it wasn't ready to possess. Elena had made a different choice: to preserve that knowledge while creating conditions for its eventual release. Neither choice was obviously right or wrong. Both were gambles, bets on a future that no one could predict.

But at least Elena's choice left the possibility open. Left the door unlocked, even if it remained closed for now. That, she had come to believe, was the essence of guardianship: not controlling knowledge, but stewarding it. Holding it in trust until the time was right.

If the time ever came.

And if it didn't... well, future generations would make their own choices. That was as it should be. The dead shouldn't rule the living, not forever. Someday, the Guardians of that distant future would have to decide for themselves what to do with the burden they had inherited.

Elena hoped they would choose wisely. But that wasn't something she could control. All she could do was her best, in the time she had, with the resources available to her.

For now, that would have to be enough.

40

The Convert

Bogotá, Colombia — Three Months Later

Alejandra Reyes had always believed that journalism was a calling, not a career.

She had grown up in a Colombia that was tearing itself apart—cartels and paramilitaries and government forces locked in a cycle of violence that seemed to have no end. Her father had been a reporter for El Tiempo, back when reporting on the wrong people could get you killed, and she had watched him navigate that dangerous world with a combination of courage and cunning that she had spent her own career trying to emulate.

He had taught her that the truth mattered. That transparency was the disinfectant that societies needed to heal themselves. That holding power accountable was the most important work a person could do.

And now she was sitting in a laboratory hidden beneath the streets of Cusco, watching a woman she had spent months investigating transform lead into gold, and everything she had ever believed about truth and transparency was being tested in ways she had never imagined.

Elena finished the transmutation and stepped back from the workbench, her face pale with exhaustion but her eyes bright with the satisfaction of successful demonstration. On the bench, where a dull grey ingot had rested an hour before, sat a gleaming bar of gold that Alejandra had watched emerge through a process that should have been impossible.

"You can have it tested," Elena said. "Take it to any assayer you trust. It's pure gold, indistinguishable from metal that came out of the earth."

"I believe you." Alejandra's voice sounded strange to her own ears—hoarse, uncertain, the voice of someone whose worldview had just been fundamentally upended. "I've seen enough. I believe all of it."

The past three months had been an education unlike anything her career had prepared her for. Elena had been true to her word, opening the doors of the Guardian network to Alejandra's scrutiny, answering questions with a candour that went far beyond what the journalist had expected. She had met the Keepers, visited the "mines," reviewed the financial records that she had spent so long trying to penetrate. She had learned about the codex and its history, about the centuries of protection and the recent crisis that had nearly destroyed everything.

And she had seen the results—the schools and hospitals and clinics that were transforming communities across South America, funded by gold that had been created rather than extracted, deployed for purposes that served the common good rather than individual enrichment.

It was, objectively, the biggest story of her career. Perhaps the biggest story in the history of journalism. The discovery that transmutation was real, that an ancient formula had been preserved by a secret society for five hundred years, that the laws of chemistry as the world understood them were incomplete—any of those revelations would have earned her every award the profession could offer.

And she couldn't publish a word of it.

Not because Elena was threatening her, not because she feared retaliation. But because she had come to understand that some truths were more dangerous than lies, that some secrets deserved to be kept, that transparency wasn't always the highest value.

It had been the hardest realisation of her life.

"What happens now?" she asked, turning away from the gold to face Elena directly. "You've shown me everything. You've trusted me with secrets that could destroy everything you've built. Why? What do you want from me?"

"I want your help." Elena sat down on a bench against the wall, the exhaustion of the transmutation still evident in her posture. "We've accomplished a great deal in the past two years, but we've also created vulnerabilities. The mining operations are becoming harder to sustain—too many questions about production levels, too much scrutiny from geologists who know the deposits can't possibly yield what we're claiming. Sooner or later, someone is going to look closely enough to see what you almost saw."

"So, you need to change the story."

"We need to diversify. To build legitimate operations that can stand up to any level of investigation, while maintaining the core activities that fund everything else." Elena met Alejandra's eyes. "You've spent your career understanding how power works, how institutions function, how to see through the stories that people tell to hide the truth. I need someone with those skills helping us rather than investigating us."

Alejandra laughed—a short, sharp sound that echoed off the stone walls of the underground chamber. "You want me to become a propagandist. A flack for your secret society."

"I want you to become an advisor. Someone who can help us anticipate threats, identify vulnerabilities, develop strategies that will keep the network safe while we do the work that matters." Elena's voice was earnest, intense. "You've seen what we're building, Alejandra. Schools that are changing children's lives. Hospitals that are saving people who would have died without access to care. Infrastructure that's transforming communities that have been neglected for generations. Is that really something you want to tear down?"

"I don't want to tear it down. But I don't know if I can be part of it either." Alejandra walked to the window—a small opening that looked out onto a courtyard where the afternoon light was fading toward evening. "I've spent my whole life believing in certain principles. Transparency. Accountability. The public's right to know. What you're asking me to do violates all of those principles."

"Does it? Or does it just require you to think about them differently?" Elena rose and joined her at the window. "The principles you're describing exist to serve a purpose—to prevent the abuse of power, to ensure that those who wield authority are answerable to those they affect. But the Guardian network isn't a government. It's not elected, not accountable to voters, not subject to the constraints that public institutions face. We operate in the shadows because we have to—because the knowledge we protect would be abused if it fell into the wrong hands."

"That's what every secret power structure says to justify itself."

"Yes. And sometimes they're lying, using secrecy to hide corruption and self-dealing. But sometimes they're telling the truth. Sometimes secrets really do need to be kept, not because those keeping them are afraid of accountability, but because the consequences of revelation would be worse than the costs of concealment." Elena gestured toward the gold bar still sitting on the workbench. "Imagine what would happen if this became public. If everyone knew that transmutation was possible, that unlimited gold could be created by anyone who learned the technique. The economic chaos alone would be catastrophic. And that's before you consider the political implications—the wars that would be fought to control the knowledge, the governments that would fall, the human suffering that would result."

"So, you get to decide? You and your network of Guardians? You get to choose what humanity is ready for, when they're ready for it?"

"Someone has to. That's been true for five centuries, and it's still true today. The only difference is that now we're using the knowledge rather than just hiding it—using it to help people, to make the world better, to justify all the sacrifice that's gone into keeping it safe." Elena's voice dropped, becoming more personal. "I didn't ask for this responsibility, Alejandra. I was a museum curator who stumbled into something I didn't understand. But here I am, making decisions that affect millions of lives, trying to do right by people who trusted me with their most sacred secrets. All I'm asking is for you to help me do that job better."

Alejandra was quiet for a long moment, staring out at the courtyard as the last light faded and the first stars began to appear in the darkening sky. She thought about her father, about the principles he had taught her, about the life she had built on those foundations.

And she thought about the children she had seen in the foundation's schools, the patients in its hospitals, the communities that had been transformed by resources that came from something impossible made real.

"If I do this," she said finally, "I need to know that I'm not just providing cover for something corrupt. I need to see everything—not just what you choose to show me, but everything. The finances, the operations, the decision-making processes. I need to be able to challenge you when I think you're wrong, to push back when I see problems."

"That's exactly what I want."

"And I need to be able to leave. If I ever decide that what you're doing is harmful, that the secrecy is serving your interests rather than the public good, I need to be free to walk away. Not to publish what I know—I understand why that would be dangerous—but to remove myself from something I can't in good conscience support."

"Agreed."

Alejandra turned to face Elena, searching her expression for any sign of deception or manipulation. She found only sincerity—the earnest determination of someone who genuinely believed in what she was doing and wanted others to believe in it too.

"Then I'm in," Alejandra said. "God help me, but I'm in."

Elena smiled—a warm expression that transformed her tired face into something almost beautiful. "Welcome to the Guardian network, Ms. Reyes. Now let me tell you what I've been thinking about the mining operations..."

***

The strategy that Alejandra helped develop over the following months was elegant in its simplicity.

The fake mining operations—the elaborate fictions that had concealed the true source of the foundation's gold—would be gradually wound down. Not abruptly, which would raise questions, but systematically, over a period of years. Production would decline, explanations would be offered about exhausted deposits and changing market conditions, and eventually the operations would be closed and the land sold or donated to conservation groups.

In their place would rise something more sustainable: real mining operations, purchased from existing owners or developed on legitimately promising sites. These would produce actual gold and other precious metals—not at the fantastic rates that transmutation allowed, but at levels consistent with what the geology could support. The reduced revenue would be supplemented by transmutation conducted elsewhere, in facilities that weren't connected to any mining claims and couldn't be discovered by geologists puzzled about production figures.

"The key is diversification," Alejandra explained during one of the planning sessions that had become a regular feature of Elena's schedule. "Right now, too much of the foundation's credibility depends on the mining story. If that story collapses, everything collapses with it. We need multiple revenue streams, multiple explanations for the wealth that funds your activities."

"What do you suggest?"

"Emeralds, for one. Colombia is one of the world's largest producers, and the market is less scrutinised than gold. There are legitimate operations for sale throughout Boyacá and other producing regions. If the foundation acquires some of those operations, it provides another explanation for wealth that doesn't depend on transmutation."

"What else?"

"Forestry. But not the destructive kind—sustainable forestry, combined with aggressive replantation programs. The Amazon is being destroyed at a horrifying rate, and there are legitimate businesses trying to fight that destruction. If the foundation invests in those businesses, develops its own replantation operations, it accomplishes multiple goals at once. Good publicity, legitimate revenue from sustainable timber sales, and actual environmental benefit."

Elena nodded slowly, seeing the pieces come together. "And it creates opportunities for other activities. People working in remote forest areas, moving through regions that aren't under constant scrutiny..."

"Exactly. The same infrastructure that supports reforestation could support other things—facilities hidden in the forest, movement of materials and personnel, activities that would be difficult to conduct in more developed areas."

"Biopharmaceuticals," Elena said, the idea crystallising as she spoke. "The Amazon contains thousands of species with potential medical applications, most of them barely studied. If the foundation established a research program focused on discovering and developing those applications..."

"It would provide another revenue stream, another explanation for activity in remote areas, and another public benefit that reinforces the foundation's reputation." Alejandra smiled. "I was going to suggest that eventually. You're getting good at this."

"I've had good teachers."

The planning continued through the spring and into the summer, the strategy growing more sophisticated as more minds contributed to its development. Yara and the other Keepers provided operational expertise, identifying how the network's existing resources could be redirected to support the new activities. Diego and his security contacts assessed the risks and vulnerabilities, developing protocols to protect the expanded operations from the threats that had nearly destroyed them before.

And Alejandra—journalist turned advisor, sceptic turned believer—served as the voice of the outside world, constantly challenging assumptions, identifying weaknesses, asking the questions that people who weren't immersed in the Guardian culture might ask.

It was, Elena came to realise, exactly what the network had been missing. For five centuries, the Guardians had operated in isolation, making decisions based on their own understanding of the world without input from people who saw things differently. That isolation had made them vulnerable—to Hernández's manipulation, to the destruction faction's arguments, to the gradual drift toward irrelevance that came from protecting knowledge without using it.

Alejandra's presence changed that. She brought perspective, challenge, the healthy scepticism of someone who had spent her life questioning power rather than wielding it. Her willingness to push back, to disagree, to force Elena to defend her decisions—it made the network stronger, more adaptable, more capable of navigating a world that had changed beyond anything the founders had imagined.

By the end of the summer, the diversification strategy was ready for implementation. The first real mining acquisitions had been completed, the forestry investments were underway, and the groundwork had been laid for what would eventually become Guardian Bioceuticals—a research and development company focused on discovering medical applications for the Amazon's vast botanical resources.

The Guardian network was evolving. Transforming from a society of protectors into something more ambitious—an organisation that didn't just preserve knowledge but deployed it, that didn't just hide from the world but engaged with it, that used its unique capabilities to address problems that conventional approaches couldn't solve.

And at the centre of it all was Elena, the museum curator who had become something she never expected to be: a leader, a visionary, a guardian not just of ancient secrets but of a future that was being built one decision at a time.

41

The Empire

Five Years Later — Across South America

The headquarters of El Fondo de Elección del Pueblo occupied the top three floors of a tower in Bogotá's financial district, its glass facades reflecting the Andes in the morning light and the city's glittering sprawl at night. From her office on the highest floor, Elena could see the neighbourhood where she had first met with Roberto Mendoza to establish the corporate structures that now controlled assets measured in the billions of dollars.

Five years. It seemed impossible that so much had changed in so short a time.

The foundation had grown beyond anything she had imagined during those early days of planning and experimentation. The school network now included over two hundred institutions across seven countries, educating more than fifty thousand children who would otherwise have had access to nothing better than inadequate public facilities or expensive private schools their families couldn't afford. The hospital system was smaller but equally impactful—thirty-seven facilities ranging from rural clinics to full-service medical centres, providing care to communities that had been neglected by governments focused on urban populations and profitable markets.

But education and healthcare were just the most visible parts of what the foundation had built.

Colombian Vaults had expanded from a single facility in Bogotá to a network of secure storage operations across the continent, serving clients who ranged from wealthy individuals to central banks to corporations that needed secure storage for valuable assets. Golden Codex Bank had grown into a significant regional financial institution, its services tailored to clients who valued discretion and its investment policies shaped by the foundation's commitment to sustainable development.

The mining operations had been successfully transitioned according to Alejandra's strategy. The fake mines had been closed, their land donated to conservation organisations or returned to indigenous communities who had ancestral claims. In their place stood legitimate operations—gold mines in Colombia and Peru, emerald mines in Boyacá, copper and lithium operations in Chile that positioned the foundation to benefit from the coming transition to renewable energy.

And Guardian Bioceuticals had exceeded every expectation.

What had begun as a cover story—a plausible explanation for activity in remote forest regions—had evolved into something genuinely transformative. The research teams the foundation had assembled had made discoveries that traditional pharmaceutical companies had missed, identifying compounds in Amazonian plants that showed promise for treating everything from cancer to Alzheimer's disease. Three products had already reached the market, generating revenues that rivalled the foundation's other operations while advancing the mission of healing that had always been central to Elena's vision.

The Amazon reforestation program had grown alongside the bioceuticals business, the two operations intertwined in ways that reinforced each other. Teams working on replantation documented species they encountered, collecting samples for the research laboratories. Researchers identified plants with particular potential and flagged them for protection in areas being restored. The result was a virtuous cycle—conservation supporting discovery, discovery generating resources that funded more conservation.

At the centre of it all, hidden from public view, the transmutation operations continued. The gold they produced still flowed through channels that Alejandra had helped design—laundered through the legitimate mining operations, deposited in the vaults, deployed through the bank to fund activities that no conventional philanthropy could have sustained. The scale had grown as the network had grown, more practitioners trained, more facilities constructed, more of the ancient knowledge put to practical use.

Elena sometimes wondered what the founders would think if they could see what their secret had become. They had hidden the formula because they feared humanity wasn't ready for it—feared the chaos that would result if unlimited wealth could be created by anyone who learned the technique. But she had found a middle path, using the knowledge for collective benefit while keeping it out of hands that might abuse it.

Had she proven them wrong? Or had she simply delayed the reckoning they had foreseen?

She didn't know. Perhaps no one could know, until enough time had passed to see how things developed. But for now, the path she had chosen seemed to be working. The foundation was doing good in the world, the network was stronger than it had ever been, and the secret remained safe.

That was enough. It had to be enough.

***

The board meeting that afternoon brought together the key figures who had helped build everything the foundation represented.

Alejandra was there, of course—no longer a journalist, not really, though she still maintained the cover of independent researcher for public purposes. She had become Elena's most trusted advisor, the person who challenged assumptions and identified risks that others missed. Her transformation from investigator to advocate had been complete; she believed in the mission now as deeply as any Guardian who had grown up with the tradition.

Yara represented the Guardian network's traditional leadership, her Peruvian cell having grown into the operational hub for activities across the southern part of the continent. She had aged gracefully in the years since Hernández's betrayal, her dark hair now streaked with grey, her fierce determination tempered by the wisdom that came from watching impetuous plans mature into sustainable institutions.

Diego had taken charge of security, not just protecting the foundation's physical assets, but managing the intelligence operations that kept them informed about potential threats. His network of contacts had expanded significantly, providing early warning about everything from government investigations to criminal organisations that might see the foundation as a target.

Lucia had grown into one of the network's most capable leaders, her trauma transformed into drive, her grandmother's murder into a commitment to ensuring that such losses would never happen again. She oversaw the Central American operations now, coordinating cells in Guatemala, Honduras, El Salvador, and Nicaragua that had been rebuilt from the ashes of the destruction faction's attacks.

And there were others—Keepers and advisors who had joined the inner circle as the foundation's scope had expanded, each bringing skills and perspectives that strengthened the whole. Carmen from Argentina, whose financial expertise had shaped the banking operations. Esperanza from Ecuador, whose diplomatic talents smoothed relationships with governments that might otherwise have asked uncomfortable questions. A dozen more whose contributions were essential even if their names would never be known outside the network.

They gathered around the conference table in Elena's office, reviewing reports and discussing the decisions that would shape the foundation's next phase of growth. The formal agenda covered the usual topics—financial performance, operational updates, risk assessments—but the real conversation happened in the spaces between agenda items, in the informal discussions that shaped strategy and built consensus.

"The bioceuticals division is ready for significant expansion," Alejandra reported, pulling up projections on the room's display screen. "The Phase III trials for the anti-inflammatory compound are showing exceptional results. If approval comes through as expected, we'll have our first genuine blockbuster drug—something that could generate revenues in the billions over the next decade."

"What are the implications for the cover operations?" Elena asked. "If Guardian Bioceuticals becomes too visible, too successful, won't that attract the kind of scrutiny we've been trying to avoid?"

"Potentially. But it also creates opportunities." Alejandra switched to a different slide, showing a complex organisational chart. "A publicly successful pharmaceutical company can acquire other companies, enter new markets, build relationships with governments and regulators that would be difficult for a mysterious foundation to develop. The visibility is a double-edged sword, but on balance, I think the benefits outweigh the risks."

"What about the research programs?" Yara asked. "The deeper we go into the Amazon, the more we're going to encounter communities and territories that have their own claims on the resources we're documenting. How do we handle that?"

"By making them partners rather than subjects." This came from Lucia, who had been thinking about the issue for some time. "The traditional approach to bioprospecting treats indigenous knowledge as raw material to be extracted and monetised by outside corporations.

We can do better. We can share the benefits of what we discover, invest in communities that help us find promising compounds, create relationships that are genuinely mutual rather than extractive."

"That's expensive," Diego observed. "And complicated. The more people we involve, the more potential points of failure in our security."

"It's also the right thing to do," Elena said firmly. "We didn't build all of this just to replicate the extraction patterns that have exploited this continent for five centuries. If we can't find a way to share the benefits of what we're doing, then we're not really different from the systems we're trying to replace."

The discussion continued, moving through topics that ranged from the practical to the philosophical. They debated investment strategies and expansion plans, discussed threats that might be emerging and opportunities that might be developing. By the time the meeting ended, as the sun was setting over the Andes and the city lights were beginning to flicker on below, they had made decisions that would shape the foundation's activities for years to come.

Elena remained in her office after the others had left, looking out at the city that had become her home. She thought about the journey that had brought her here—from a museum in Washington to a dying man's confession to a quest across continents that had changed everything she thought she knew about the world.

She thought about the people who had died along the way. Martin Thorne, murdered before he could share what he had learned. Santiago Ajpop, sacrificing himself so that she could escape. Ixchel Batz, tortured and killed for secrets she had protected her entire life. Dozens of Guardians whose names she would never know, lost in the violence that had nearly destroyed the network.

Their sacrifice had made all of this possible. The schools, the hospitals, the research facilities, the reforestation programs—all of it built on a foundation of courage and commitment that stretched back five centuries to the moment when the founders had decided to hide what they had discovered.

Elena hoped she was doing justice to that legacy. Hoped that the choices she was making would prove worthy of the trust that had been placed in her. Hoped that when her time came to pass the burden to the next generation, she would be able to do so knowing that she had used the knowledge wisely.

It was a heavy responsibility. But she had learned to carry it.

And tomorrow, she would wake up and do it all again.

42

The Godmother

Ten Years Later — Across South America and Mexico

The village school in Oaxaca opened on a morning that reminded Elena of other openings, other beginnings, other moments when the foundation's work became tangible in bricks and mortar and the faces of children who would have access to opportunities their parents had never known.

This was the five hundredth school that El Fondo de Elección del Pueblo had built. The number seemed almost mythical—half a thousand institutions of learning, scattered across a dozen countries, educating more than two hundred thousand students at any given time. When Elena had first proposed the foundation's educational mission, she had imagined perhaps a dozen schools, maybe two dozen if things went well. She had never imagined this.

The ceremony was modest by choice—the foundation had learned that ostentatious displays attracted attention and resentment, that quiet effectiveness was more powerful than loud self-promotion. Local officials spoke, teachers were introduced, children performed songs they had learned for the occasion. Elena sat in the audience rather than on the stage, one more visitor among many, her role in making all of this possible known only to a handful of people in attendance.

But she watched with the satisfaction of someone who understood exactly what was being created. Not just a building, not just a curriculum, but a pathway—a chance for children born into poverty to acquire skills that could transform their lives, to become doctors and engineers and teachers and leaders who would lift their communities in ways that no external intervention could accomplish.

Education was the foundation's most visible work, but it was not its most important. The hospitals and clinics had saved hundreds of thousands of lives over the past decade, providing care that would otherwise have been inaccessible to people living far from major cities. The reforestation programs had restored millions of hectares of Amazon rainforest, creating carbon sinks that helped address climate change while preserving biodiversity that might otherwise have been lost forever. Guardian Bioceuticals had brought four major drugs to market, treatments that were improving lives around the world while generating revenues that funded ever more ambitious programs.

And underneath all of it, invisible to everyone except the network's innermost circle, the transmutation continued. More practitioners than ever, more facilities, more gold flowing through channels that had been refined over years of experience until they were virtually undetectable. The wealth that funded the foundation's activities had no natural limit—the only constraints were practical ones, the need to maintain secrecy, the challenge of deploying resources faster than they could be generated.

It was, Elena sometimes reflected, exactly what the ancients had feared: unlimited wealth in the hands of a small group of people, deployed according to their own judgment of what was good and necessary. The nightmare scenario that had motivated them to hide the formula in the first place.

But somehow, it was working. The wealth was being used for purposes that genuinely served the common good. The secrecy was being maintained without corrupting the people who kept it. The network had not become a tyranny, had not used its power to dominate or exploit, had not descended into the darkness that seemed to inevitably claim those who operated beyond accountability.

Why? Elena had asked herself that question many times. Why had they succeeded where so many others had failed?

She thought the answer lay in the network's structure—the distributed authority, the tradition of service, the culture of mutual accountability that had been preserved even as the organisation transformed itself. No single person controlled the resources or made the decisions unilaterally. Elena was influential, respected, often deferred to—but she was not a dictator. Her proposals could be challenged, her judgments questioned, her authority checked by Keepers who her equals in the network's governance were.

And she was mortal. In a few decades, perhaps less, she would be gone, and the network would continue without her. The institutions she had built would outlast her individual leadership, guided by people who would bring their own perspectives and make their own choices about how to use the resources they controlled.

That was the key, she had come to believe. Not finding the perfect leader but building structures that didn't depend on perfect leadership. Creating systems that could function even when the people running them made mistakes, which could correct course when they drifted off track, that embedded values and principles in processes rather than relying on individual virtue.

The ancients had understood that, in their way. They had scattered the fragments and created the Guardian network precisely because they didn't trust any individual or group to wield unlimited power responsibly. They had built in checks and balances, distributed authority across cells that watched each other as much as they watched the outside world.

Elena had inherited that structure and transformed it, but she hadn't abandoned its essential wisdom. The network she led was more active than the one the ancients had created, more willing to use the knowledge it protected—but it was still distributed, still accountable to itself, still grounded in the recognition that power unchecked would inevitably be abused.

It was working. For now, it was working.

* * *

The flight back to Bogotá gave Elena time to review the reports that had accumulated during her absence—updates from operations across the continent, financial summaries, intelligence assessments, the endless stream of information that flowed into the foundation's headquarters from its far-flung activities.

Alejandra had sent a summary of media coverage from the past week, flagging stories that mentioned the foundation or its various subsidiaries. The coverage was almost universally positive, profiles of successful graduates from the schools, testimonials from patients whose lives had been saved by the hospitals, features on the reforestation programs that highlighted the environmental benefits while carefully avoiding any hint of the foundation's true funding sources.

The journalist had done her work well over the past decade. She had helped shape the foundation's public image, managing relationships with media outlets across the region, ensuring that the stories told about El Fondo de Elección del Pueblo reinforced its reputation as a force for good rather than raising questions about its origins or methods. She had become, as she sometimes joked, the world's most effective propagandist for a cause she had once tried to expose.

But she had also remained true to the principles that had motivated her investigation in the first place. She challenged Elena regularly, pushed back against decisions she thought were unwise, insisted on transparency within the network even as she helped maintain secrecy from the outside world. Her presence was a constant reminder that the foundation's activities, however beneficial, operated outside the normal structures of accountability that democratic societies relied upon.

"We're doing good," she had said once, during a late-night conversation after a particularly difficult board meeting. "But we're also deciding what good means, without input from the people we're supposedly serving. That's a kind of arrogance, even when it produces positive results."

"What's the alternative?" Elena had asked. "Submit to governments that are often corrupt, incompetent, or hostile to the communities we're trying to help? Let democratic processes that have failed these populations for centuries continue to fail them?"

"I don't know. Maybe there isn't an alternative. Maybe this is the best we can do in an imperfect world." Alejandra had paused, her expression troubled. "But we should never forget that we're making choices for other people. That we're exercising power without being accountable to those we affect. Even when we're doing it well, that's a dangerous thing."

Elena remembered that conversation as she reviewed the latest reports. Alejandra was right, of course. The foundation's activities were fundamentally paternalistic, decisions made by a small group of people about what was best for populations that had no voice in the process. It was benevolent paternalism, intended to serve rather than exploit, but it was paternalism, nonetheless.

The only justification was results. If the schools were actually educating children, if the hospitals were actually saving lives, if the reforestation was actually restoring ecosystems—then maybe, just maybe, the ends justified the means. Not forever, not without limit, but for now, in these circumstances, with these constraints.

It wasn't a perfect answer. But Elena had learned to live with imperfect answers. The world didn't offer perfect options, only choices between various forms of inadequacy. All she could do was choose the least inadequate path and work to make it better.

***

The Guardian council met twice a year now, in locations that rotated across the network's territories.

This year's autumn gathering took place in a resort outside Medellín that the foundation had acquired for precisely this purpose—a secure facility where the network's leadership could assemble without attracting attention, where conversations that could never be held over electronic channels could take place face to face.

Nearly forty Keepers attended, representing cells from Mexico to Argentina, from the Caribbean islands to the remote reaches of the Amazon. They came to review the network's activities, debate its policies, elect new members to the coordinating council that handled day-to-day governance, and—most importantly—to renew the bonds of trust and shared purpose that held the organisation together.

Elena presided over the opening session, delivering a state-of-the-network address that had become traditional over the years. She spoke about accomplishments and challenges, about goals achieved and obstacles still to be overcome. She spoke about the network's history—the five centuries of protection that had brought them to this moment—and about its future, the generations of Guardians who would inherit what the current leadership was building.

But the most important part of her speech came at the end.

"Twenty-two years ago, I was a museum curator in Washington, D.C., whose greatest ambition was publishing papers about pre-Columbian metallurgy. I had never heard of the Guardian network, never imagined that the secrets I studied in dusty archives might have practical implications for the modern world. When Martin Thorne died in my arms, passing along a burden I didn't understand and didn't want, I had no idea what I was being asked to carry."

She paused, looking around the room at faces that had become familiar over years of collaboration—some of them lined with age now, others still young, all of them united by their commitment to a mission that transcended individual lifetimes.

"Now I look at what we've built together, and I can barely comprehend it. The schools, the hospitals, the research facilities, the conservation programs. The hundreds of thousands of lives we've touched, the communities we've transformed, the future we're creating for children who would otherwise have had no future at all. We've done something remarkable—something that the founders never imagined, something that previous generations of Guardians might have thought impossible."

"But we're not finished. We'll never be finished, because the work we've undertaken is larger than any generation, larger than any individual, larger than anything that can be completed in a single lifetime. We are guardians—not just of ancient knowledge, but of the future that knowledge makes possible. We protect not by hiding, but by building. We preserve not by hoarding, but by using. We serve not by standing apart, but by engaging with the world in all its complexity and contradiction."

"The people of South America and Mexico have been neglected, exploited, abandoned by systems that were supposed to serve them. For five hundred years, since the first conquistadors arrived with their hunger for gold, the resources of this continent have been extracted and exported, enriching distant powers while leaving local populations in poverty. We are changing that. Not through politics or revolution, but through patient work—building institutions that serve communities rather than exploiting them, creating opportunities that empower people rather than making them dependent."

"Some call this charity. I call it justice. The wealth we're deploying comes from knowledge that originated on this continent, developed by civilisations that flourished here long before Europeans arrived. We're returning that wealth to the people whose ancestors created it, using it for purposes that honour their legacy rather than betraying it."

"This is what it means to be a Guardian in the twenty-first century. Not hiding in the shadows, protecting secrets for some hypothetical future. But stepping into the light—carefully, strategically, with full awareness of the risks—and using what we know to make the world better. Our ancestors hid the formula because they didn't trust humanity. We are proving that their caution, while understandable, was not the final word. Humanity can be trusted—not all of it, not all the time, but enough. Enough to justify taking the risk of action rather than accepting the certainty of inaction."

She fell silent, letting the words settle over the assembly. Then she smiled—the warm expression that her closest allies had come to know well.

"The work continues. The mission endures. And as long as there are Guardians willing to carry the burden, the future remains bright."

The applause that followed was sustained, genuine, the sound of people who believed in what they were doing and trusted the leader who had brought them to this point. Elena accepted it graciously, then ceded the floor to the next speaker, content to take her place among the council as one voice among many rather than the sole authority.

That was, she had learned, the secret to sustainable leadership. Not accumulating power but distributing it. Not making yourself indispensable but building systems that would function without you. Not seeking glory but finding satisfaction in work that would outlast your individual contribution.

The Guardian network would continue long after she was gone. The schools would keep educating children, the hospitals would keep healing patients, the laboratories would keep discovering new medicines. The transmutation would continue, the gold would keep flowing, the foundation's deep pockets would keep funding the transformation of a continent.

And somewhere, in archives that would be passed down through generations, her story would be preserved, the American archaeologist who had stumbled into a secret five centuries old and decided to use it for good. The woman who had transformed the Guardian network from a preservation society into an engine of change. The Godmother of South America, who had used impossible wealth to make possible things that should never have been denied.

It was, Elena thought as the council session continued around her, not a bad legacy. Not a bad way to have spent a life, though the work was far from over.

THE END

About the Author

Christian was born and raised in Melbourne, Australia. He spent most of his younger year immersed nightly in the fantasy worlds of Margaret Weis & Tracy Hickman, David Gemmell, Robert Jordan, Frank Herbert, Raymond E. Feist, Janny Wurts, R.A. Salvatore and many others, all whispering dreams in his ear each night of becoming a fantasy writer.

Following several personal tragedies, including the loss of his step-daughter, first partner of twenty years and father, Christian decided to travel extensively throughout Asia seeking inspiration and met his now-wife, Ginky, whilst writing and travelling between their respective home countries of Australia and the Philippines.

He continues to write extensively in many different genres, enjoying the challenge of tackling different projects and lines of thought, and he also self-publishes given his experience in the I.T. industry.

Christian writes in the quiet of his own home and has created literally hundreds of "pieces" that he works on to put together to become what you're reading today.

When people are dying for ancient secrets, who can you trust?

Dr. Elena Vasquez's world shatters when her mentor is found strangled in a library, a rosary wound tight around his throat. Only hours earlier, he'd sent photographs of a discovery that shouldn't exist—hidden text in a Maya manuscript revealing a map connecting civilizations separated by thousands of miles and five centuries of lies.

The map points to fragments of a legendary Codex of Seven Serpents. It is apparently the truth behind El Dorado; knowledge so dangerous that Maya priests, Spanish friars and the indigenous ancestors conspired across generations to keep it hidden.

Now Elena must race from Chicago to the highlands of Guatemala and beyond, pursued by a former Nazi researcher who has hunted this secret for sixty years. Her only ally, a Venezuelan billionaire whose obsession with El Dorado rivals the Nazis and whose ruthlessness may be just as deadly.

Some secrets were meant to stay forgotten, but in a world where satellite imaging penetrates jungle canopies and infrared scanners reveal what was hidden for centuries, nothing stays buried forever.

The race for El Dorado is on and only the ruthless will survive.

www.ingramcontent.com/pod-product-compliance
Lightning Source LLC
Chambersburg PA
CBHW011548190726
48287CB00010B/2795

9781764513036